A WEDDING AT THE JANE AUSTEN DATING AGENCY

FIONA WOODIFIELD

BLOODHOUND
— BOOKS —

www.bloodhoundbooks.com

Print ISBN 978-1-914614-26-2

ALSO BY FIONA WOODIFIELD

The Jane Austen Dating Agency

For all those who love Jane Austen and happy ever afters...
And for my mother who wanted to know what happened next...

CHAPTER 1

'Stop right where you are!'

I keep walking, because a) I'm not quite sure who this person is talking to, it's probably not me and b) even if it is me, I figure that maybe if I ignore them, there's always the hope they might go away.

'Stop right there, madam!' I feel a hand on my arm. Okay, so he obviously means me, this man who turns out to be ominously dressed in black security uniform with a body vest. To be honest I'm a bit scared now.

'Yes?' I ask as innocently as I can.

'You're not allowed to walk down this road without a security pass,' the man states sternly. He's sort of scrawny looking, not what you'd expect for a security guard, but I notice a gun in his holster. Maybe I won't make a run for it then.

'Oh? I'm awfully sorry, I didn't realise that.' This is awkward.

'Well I s'pose there's no harm done.' The man peers at me as though he's not too sure. Rude, I mean do I really look like a robber? 'I'll just escort you to the end of the street, madam.'

'But...' I stutter as he starts propelling me towards the junction of the handsome tree-lined avenue.

'No being difficult now.'

'But I'm here on business to visit the Baroness Mayer.' I pause a moment, expecting him to be extremely impressed and to offer to personally escort me to her door.

He is however totally unmoved. 'And I'm the Queen's first cousin.' This guy is the limit. I thought he might be okay, but he just isn't.

'No, I really am visiting the Baroness,' I blurt as I'm being marched along the road.

'I was hoping you was going to come along quietly, but I'll have to call in backup if you won't!' He gestures ominously towards his walkie-talkie.

'I can prove it,' I squeak, as I definitely don't want to be arrested, it wouldn't be a good thing at all.

The man stops, he's still holding my arm and sighs heavily. 'If you want to be making any private visits in this road, you need a security pass, love, it's as simple as that. It's part of the Kensington Palace Estate.'

'But I have an email.' I grab my phone and frantically scroll down the page. Darn, I can't find it. It's always the way when you're trying to point something out whilst someone is staring at you – it vanishes, as though it has never existed. I was already feeling hot and flustered and I'm sure I look as guilty as anything.

I always had the terrible misfortune at school of being the child who had a guilty expression. If the teacher asked who had done something, I would look embarrassed and culpable even if I had nothing to do with the alleged offence. It's a terrible misfortune to have a guilty face and I kind of hoped I had grown out of it, but obviously not. I'm sure possible terrorist or supposed thief is written all over my face and I am bound to be flushed red as a beetroot, which will be clashing horribly with my pink Miu Miu top.

'It won't be on an email, it's a pass.' The man is annoyingly persistent. 'Now move along, love. It's nearly time for my tea and biscuits break.'

'The Baroness is going to be extremely angry if I don't arrive,' I say, with a reasonable attempt at bravado.

'Let her be angry.' Having done his job and reached the barrier at the end of the road, he relinquishes my arm and walks off without a by-your-leave. How rude.

I stand and stare after his retreating back. How was I to know you needed a security pass to get into this road? No one had said anything. Aha, there it is, I've found the email I had been searching for from the Baroness – but on looking up, the security guard has disappeared down the other end of the street. Disgruntled, I dial Emma's number.

She answers promptly. 'The Jane Austen Dating Agency, Emma Woodtree speaking, how may I help?'

'Emma,' I pant down the phone. 'It's a disaster!'

'What's a disaster? What's going on? I thought you were visiting the Baroness this morning.'

'I was but the security guard removed me.'

'For goodness' sake, Sophie. I thought I told you not to mention anything controversial.'

'I didn't. I didn't mention anything about politics or High Society Magazine. I don't understand half of the political stuff anyway.'

'Yes, but you do have an unfortunate habit of putting your foot in it.' Emma sounds distracted, there's a rustling in the background, I think she must be sorting out papers.

'Anyway,' this is totally out of hand, we need to return to the point as I'm already late for my meeting, 'I didn't even get to the Baroness's house; apparently you need a security pass to access Kensington Palace Road.'

'Oh,' Emma says brightly, 'I thought I told you that.'

'Er, no.' Quite honestly it was hardly helpful sending me into the lion's den to be manhandled by a weedy security guard. He could at least have been young and beefy.

'The Baroness sent a whole load of stuff, I think it was in that.' There are more sounds of rustling and riffling. 'Oh, here it is!'

'Just great, thanks a lot, it's not much good to me there.'

'Sorry, Soph. Do you think it will help if I speak to the security guard?'

'Unlikely. He's a right jobsworth.'

'Okay, I'll have to phone the Baroness and explain. Hang on a tick.' The phone line goes dead. This isn't a good start at all. It's only the first week of my new job and I was going to do so well, everything was going to be totally organised and here I am, shut out of the house, in fact not even able to get to the front door of our wealthiest ever potential client! Whilst I wait, a long dark-screened Bentley roars past, the driver flashes his pass at the recently returned security guard, who nods amicably and waves him through. I catch a glimpse of the dark-skinned man in the back, black hair, snappy suit and wonder randomly if he is looking for a partner, not for me of course, because I am already going out with every woman's dream man – Darcy Drummond. But he might like to join the agency.

As Jane Austen herself said, 'It is a truth universally acknowledged that a man in possession of a fortune must be in want of a wife.' He simply doesn't know it yet. And it's my job to help him do just that. Because I, Sophie Johnson, am the new Managing Director of The Jane Austen Dating Agency. I know, I can't quite believe it myself, but it's true. It's so much fun and I love it. It's every Jane Austen fan's dream job and it's mine.

I have to pinch myself every day just to make sure I'm not dreaming. Although actually that's not strictly true. Because the reality is pretty much always different from the dream. But on the whole it's fab and after all, there are always ups and downs when starting a new job. Like today – being thrown out of the client's road by a security guard wasn't really part of the plan. But I'm sure it'll sort itself out in the end, it usually does.

My phone blasts out and makes me jump even though I was kind of expecting it. 'Sophie? It's okay, I've sorted it. Baroness Mayer was most upset, she said she had told security you were coming.'

'Oh, so she's not cross?' I still have nightmares about my previous wrangles with Lady Constance, a scarily stern ex-client.

'Not at all, she's charming as always. She's sending someone down for you.'

'Oh, there's a man coming towards me now. Got to go. Bye, bye...'

'Do not mention tax evasion or money generally or...' Emma adds, but I ignore her. How stupid does she think I am?

'Miss Johnson?' The man is dressed all in black, shoes immaculately polished, swarthy, designer stubble; you know the kind of thing.

'Yes, I am.' I'm unsure what else to say – after the debacle so far nothing in this street would surprise me and this guy does look rather worryingly like someone from the Mafia.

'I am here to greet you.' He smiles suddenly, showing a flash of very white teeth, at least if he's from the Mafia he's friendly, on the surface at any rate. I can't quite place his accent, but then I'm not very good at recognising them.

'Thank you very much,' I say meekly and trot along at his heels, aware that mine are ridiculously noisy. I don't know why, I adore them, they're from Office, quite chunky with funky bows but they do seem to ring out like gunshots every time I put my foot down. No wonder I didn't get very far without attracting the notice of the security guard. Then again I wasn't exactly planning to be sneaking around. I wonder vaguely if I should try and make polite conversation as we go but decide against it. I, Sophie Johnson, am a reformed woman, no more blithering, trying to be polite, no more chronic people-pleaser extraordinaire.

I've stopped the whole romance novel thing too. Not that I don't still love happy romantic stories, but I've decided to try a bit more reality, not that romance isn't reality – I mean, of course it is, I'm going out with Darcy Drummond, for goodness' sake.

Anyway, I am now totally into psychological thrillers, they are so gripping and I love the way you never know what is going to happen next. In fact, *Rebecca* is probably one of the best books I have ever read, that plot twist was amazing – I can remember exactly where I was when I first read it. I won't tell you what it is because it would totally spoil it for those of you who haven't read it yet, but for those who have, you know where I am coming from.

I've read *Girl on a Train* and couldn't put it down so I had to finish it in a couple of sittings, shivers scuttling down my neck the whole time. It put me off taking the train late at night though, sort of creepy. Of course that doesn't mean I've replaced Jane Austen and to be fair, Mr Darcy still does it for me when it comes to romantic heroes and my new man, Darcy Drummond, is proving to be pretty downright gorgeous. We've only been together for a few months, but when he looks at me with those dark eyes, he is ridiculously handsome and I still can't quite believe he's going out with me. I kind of worry that it's a dream and one day I'll wake up and he will be dating someone else. We had our fair share of ups and downs over the past year and at first I had hated him. But then I realised he's actually very sweet when you get to know him and the way he helped sort out my sister's ex-husband and his criminal activities a while ago, was an act of true love...

'This way please.' I am jolted out of my musings on Darcy by

Mafia guy; shouldn't really call him that, he's probably perfectly nice, has two small children and lives in a quaint little cottage with a dog. Although looking at him, I don't think so. He's got the cool black headset, earpiece and everything like someone on *The Bodyguard*.

We have stopped in front of an enormous building; so vast I can't believe it's a private property. It's quite beautiful, rather like Osborne House, Queen Victoria's holiday home, with a multitude of windows and turrets at the corners, in fact such a quantity of windows that Mr Collins would be quite squashed at how it outshines Lady Catherine de Bourgh's residence, and I think even Lizzie would be impressed.

Huge electric gates slide open noiselessly and we enter the front terrace and lawns, striding all the way up to a wide central staircase adorned with large coach lanterns, leading to the front door.

As if by magic this opens at our approach and a uniformed butler appears. 'It's okay, Gustav, Miss Johnson is expected,' my mafia friend remarks and we waft past into an entrance hall with a vast staircase rising up ahead of us into a large central step which splits into two. High above us is a magnificent diamond chandelier dropping down from a dizzying height.

'Through here, madam.' I follow Mafia guy through the vast hall into another courtyard room, which is dazzlingly white and at first sight looks as though it is made from ivory but I think it must be porcelain. I fervently hope it is.

In the middle is a fountain, which appears to be made from ice, with elegant weaving fish all spouting water in tiny jets. The floor is marble and the walls and ceiling are all carved intricate networks of miniature white tiles and sculpture. Up above is a vast dome, through which the light reflects and hits the water, casting clouds of tiny diamond lights all across the floor and surrounding surfaces. I have a job not to stop and stare with my mouth open.

In the midst of all this beauty, without warning, my phone goes off and echoes up and out into the vast space, polluting it with Shawn Mendes crooning 'Señorita' and causing my mafia friend to turn abruptly. 'No phones,' he hisses. Okay so perhaps he's not my friend after all.

'S-sorry,' I stutter, grasping the phone and desperately trying to stop the blasting lyrics – I do love this song but in the tranquil beauty of this room it sounds totally incongruous. Unfortunately, however, whilst trying to turn it off, I seem to have managed to hit the answer button. 'Sophie?'

'Mum,' I gasp, 'sorry but I can't talk right now.'

'Sorry, Sophie, I can't hear you. Dad and I are having trouble with the phones, they keep getting stuck on speaker. I'll just get him to sort it. Phillip!'

I am deafened by the phone whistling and blasting with interference and hit the red button quickly. Never mind, Mum will understand.

'Wait in here please,' Mafia Man says. I still don't know his name but then it doesn't seem appropriate when he's so stern and remote, it wouldn't feel quite right to be on first-name terms.

Thank goodness he vanishes and I pause to take a look at my surroundings. I am in yet another huge space, with an ornate painted ceiling and I'm sure what must be priceless paintings suspended on great gold chains, notably one in the centre with richly plumaged birds. In the middle of the room stands a large round table, highly polished with elegant chairs placed around ready for a meeting. I wonder what happens at these gatherings in here, whoever owns such an incredible house must be very important and would make Lady Constance look like a bit of a try hard.

I'm unable to think much further about any of it before I am

8

startled out of my wits by the sudden loud rendition of 'Señorita' once more; darn, I thought I had turned the phone off. It's Mum again, perhaps I should just press the red button – I glance surreptitiously at the door. I guess no one is coming. I'll quickly tell her I'll phone back later.

'Hi, Mum,' I whisper.

'Phillip!' my mum shouts. 'It's no good, I still can't hear her...'

'That's because I'm whispering,' I say a little louder.

'Can you speak up a bit,' Mum blasts, oblivious. 'It's these wretched phones, your dad changed them because Ben said they give out dangerous signals but these new ones don't seem to work.'

I wonder why – they probably don't have any signal. Honestly, I'm getting deafened again by the echo... 'Can't Ben sort them out?' You'd think my brother, Ben, could try to help Mum and Dad learn to use these phones, if it was his idea to get them in the first place, it might give him something to do other than chase his latest female conquest.

'It's all right, I've managed to turn it off,' my dad comes on the line sounding exasperated, 'your mother keeps getting it stuck on speakerphone. Here she is.'

For goodness' sake, I only wanted to say I'd phone her back later. Dad always does that; before I can stop him he passes the phone over to Mum. Sometimes he phones me and says, 'Your mother wants to talk to you,' as though he's Carson the butler on *Downton Abbey* or something. It's very bizarre but kind of sweet I suppose.

'Hi again, Mum,' I say patiently. 'Look, I'm in a bit of a hurry.'

'Oh that's better. I can hear you now, won't take a minute.'

'Can't it wait until later?' I say desperately. 'I'm at a client's house for an interview.'

'Oh sorry, love. Of course we can speak later, I wanted to ask you about Ben joining the agency?'

'Ben joining the agency?' I shriek. Just at that moment, a slight and terribly upright woman of indeterminate age, but must be over sixty at least, enters the room with the air of one who demands respect, in spite of her diminutive size and apparent fragility. I shove my mobile back in my bag, I don't think I've even remembered to turn it off.

Mustering any sangfroid I can gather, I step forward to greet her. 'Good morning, Baroness.' I shake the proffered hand and bob a slight curtsey, bowing my head at the same time. Oh my goodness, how embarrassing – she's not royalty, what was I thinking? I feel like Julie Andrews meeting the Baroness in *The Sound of Music* for the first time, although I guess at least I'm not soaking wet, having just fallen out of a boat, or wearing a dress made from flowery curtain material.

The Baroness appears gratified however. 'Miss Johnson? It is a pleasure to meet you.' Her handshake is firm, almost crushingly so. 'If you come through to the drawing room? I can't think why Rodrigo put you in here, it's for business meetings, not private discussions.'

'Oh absolutely,' I say blithely, 'although it's very impressive.'

The Baroness ignores my pleasantries and I follow her back through the tranquil courtyard and out under another archway to a vast sitting room with chaise longues. Each window is adorned with huge drapes, probably velvet and encrusted with gold leaf. In the fireplace a log fire roars and crackles, the portraits on the wall are of English hunting scenes but there are a couple of icons either side of the fire which catch my eye, the gold around the Virgin Mary's head vibrant in the firelight.

'Those are simply beautiful,' I say as I sit in the chair suggested by the Baroness. She has a quiet air of authority, which makes it imperative to do exactly as she asks. I can imagine her whole empire within this house working seamlessly, a well-oiled machine with no raised voices or anything else on the surface at least. I shiver involuntarily – for goodness' sake, I've obviously been reading too many psychological thrillers. The Baroness seems perfectly pleasant.

'Would you like some coffee?' She rings a little silver bell beside her without waiting for my answer.

'If it's not too much trouble, that would be lovely, thank you.' I fidget awkwardly in my chair, it is rather sinky and the Baroness is so upright. I feel that if I sit back I will look as though I am slouching.

'So,' the Baroness fixes me with a stare, 'you are from The Jane Austen Dating Agency?'

'Yes – I'm Sophie, the managing director, and I am very much looking forward to discussing your requirements.' No more questionnaires and form responses for our exclusive guests. Emma and I both feel the more personal approach is best.

'And was that your mother on the phone?' Oh no, how embarrassing, I thought I had managed to get away without her noticing.

'I'm so sorry, yes it was. I should not have been on the phone in your house, especially on speaker. I answered it by mistake.' For goodness' sake – why do I always come out with the wrong thing? I'm never going to be any good at this.

'My dear, never apologise for speaking to your mother, it shows you have a sense of responsibility. And honesty, I think.' She smiles for a fleeting moment and I feel as though the ice has broken a little.

'Definitely that.' I blush furiously. 'Perhaps a little too honest at times.'

'That's a good thing where I come from, and in this world, there is precious little of it to be found.'

She sighs and gazes at a photo on the mantelpiece of a man in a suit with a rather severe face. She's totally lost in thought and I wait politely for her to continue. She appears to give herself a little shake. 'So is your mother the CEO of the agency?'

'Gosh no.' I want to roar inwardly at the thought of my mother running a dating agency, it would be hilarious. 'No, she was just phoning about my brother.'

'Ah, she wants him to join?' she asks, smoothing her straight skirt with her long bony hands.

This is all going wrong, I do not want to even think about my brother, Ben, joining the agency, let alone tell one of our most prestigious potential clients about him. How am I going to explain this total disaster to Emma?

'Well, yes.'

'And does Ben struggle to find a partner?'

'Yes. No, not really, he finds women, just not the right ones.' My whole pre-rehearsed speech has totally gone out of the window.

The Baroness laughs suddenly, making me jump, as the sound is so unexpected. I'm desperately thinking how to respond when the door opens noiselessly and in walks an immaculately uniformed young woman, hair scraped back in a bun with not a tiny bump or strand out of place. She is carrying a silver tray containing a weird-looking silver type of coffee pot thing, from which she empties a very strong smelling coffee.

She places a cup and saucer next to me on a small table, which has such delicate legs, I'm not sure how it is able to stand up and for a moment I have a terrible feeling of déjà vu – what if I knock it all over the floor? I am one of the most klutzy people. I'm afraid I was born with the gene. I'll never forget the time I was invited round to this child's house, not one of my closest friends, in fact looking back, I don't know why she invited me especially when they had just had a beautiful new cream carpet fitted. For some reason we were sitting on the floor, I think I was only aged about nine, and why we were given cups of tea I don't know.

But anyway, the mother, who was an extremely stern, scary sort of person put my teacup on this low coffee table (why are they called that when you can drink tea from them as well – doesn't make any sense, does it?) and I delicately took the bone china flowery cup with the hand-painted periwinkles – just like those owned by Mrs Bucket (pronounced Bouquet) and I had just breathed a sigh of relief at putting the cup down safely when I accidentally brought my hand away with the teacup still attached by its silly little handle to my finger.

You would have thought I had committed a serious crime by the crisis level response of those around me. Everyone leapt about calling for cloths, dabbing frantically at the awful seeping brown stain, with my friend's mother tersely brushing off my stammered apologies. 'No, no it's fine, it's only a new carpet – I'm sure the stain will come out *eventually*.'

To this day, cream carpets and bone china handles make me nervous. Not that there's a cream carpet in this case, it's dark blue, but even so. The last time I went to one of my disastrous ex-boyfriend's parents' house, they had a new cream carpet throughout and I didn't dare to eat or drink a thing, I was still so traumatised.

Gingerly, I stretch out my hand and take the exquisite cup and sip what appears to be coffee. I've never tasted anything like it. This is not your average cup of instant.

'What lovely coffee,' I say inanely.

'It's Kopi Luwak. I will drink nothing else.'

'Oh.' I smile. There's not a lot else to say. I suspect it's incredibly exclusive. 'So where were we, would you like to look at the brochures?' I brandish them in the air.

'We were discussing your brother and his dating requirements.'

'I think we should move on to yours, don't you? I mean Ben isn't really that interesting,' I say desperately.

'Believe me, neither am I, I would far rather discuss Ben – tell me a bit about him?'

This is too bizarre for words. Why would someone who lives this amazing lifestyle want to know all about my brother? I peer at her uncertainly. I guess I have to humour such a wealthy client, but I find myself almost wishing for a script in similar vein to those at the dreaded Modiste, in my days of being a sales executive.

'Ben? There's not a lot to say really. He's a few years older than me, he was married and his ex-wife left him after a short while. She ran off with another man. He was heartbroken and ever since he seems to choose the worst women to go out with – some of them already have partners or are married. It's as though he's on a one-way self-destruct.'

'Oh dear, the poor man, no wonder your mother wants him to join.'

'I'm not sure, honestly, it's a good–'

'Do you think it will work for him?' She fixes me with a steely glare.

I laugh nervously. 'My brother barely knows who Jane Austen is; he's hardly a candidate for the dating agency!'

'Yes but that's not the point, do you think he might find his true love with your agency?' she persists.

I pause a moment. 'Yes, I think he might – if anyone can do it, we can.'

'Then sign me up,' she says simply.

'But...? I haven't even shown you the brochures yet.'

'No need. I am a very busy woman.'

'But don't you need to hear more about it?' I wave a glossy brochure at her. 'The strawberry picnics in the gardens at Kew, the ball at Pemberley?'

'Not at all. That all sounds very nice and I shall look forward to them greatly, but if it's good enough for your own brother it's good enough for me.'

And that it seems is the end of the conversation, I am shown out through the vast entrance halls and the tranquil courtyard, all the while pondering what just happened. I suppose the meeting wasn't quite as I had planned but I guess at least, I have won my first client for the dating agency and the Baroness is probably the most prestigious customer we have ever had. Even if the only reason she has signed up is because my brother, Ben, is joining – my brother, Ben, who thinks Jane Austen is a character in a book.

CHAPTER 2

The next day my euphoria has died down a little. Of course it's wonderful that we have such an amazing client on our books and I can't wait to tell Darcy, but there's one almighty downside to this. Who are we going to match the Baroness with on a first date, or any other date for that matter?

I ponder this conundrum whilst getting ready for my date with Darcy. I'm pretty darned excited because we're going out on his boat and I know it's a bit sad but I have only ever been in a dinghy. Of course, as always, it's caused a complete dilemma about what I'm going to wear because, well, what do you wear on an expensive boat floating in the lap of luxury when you have a rather limited budget, to put it mildly? I've taken everything out of my wardrobe, which isn't difficult because I always kind of throw everything in when I'm tidying my room.

The downside to this system is that when I open the door it's like playing Russian roulette because sometimes it all falls on me from a great height. Incidentally, what is that shelf for at the top of the wardrobe? You know, the bit above the hanging section, I'm sure it must have a purpose. I tend to shove bottles, sewing stuff (yes, I can sew on a button) and clothes up there, and quite honestly it is a safety hazard. Whoever designed it should be ashamed of themselves – I mean, think of all the accidents it could cause.

I am disturbed from my reverie by my phone blasting out 'Señorita' once again. I must change that ringtone; it's getting kind of annoying. I grab it, pressing the green button – it's Mel, my best friend and flatmate. She's moved down to Chawton with me – although it is quite a commute for her to her design studio in London, but the apartment's pretty much rent-free so it is not to be sniffed at.

'Hi?' I reply, hefting through clothes and trying to remove a pair of tights I have half on half off.

'What are you doing, Sophie?' Mel asks. I can hardly hear her as she sounds as though she is in a noisy street somewhere.

'I'm running around panicking. It's my date with Darcy and I don't know what to wear.'

'I'm not surprised, I made the mistake of looking for my shoes in your room the other day, you know the flat green pumps with the scroll on the front, and was completely crushed by the entire contents of the wardrobe falling on my head.'

'You shouldn't be in there,' I say unsympathetically. 'It's a very sophisticated alarm system which defends against intruders.' Maybe the shelf does have a purpose after all. 'Anyway, I didn't take those pumps, the colour doesn't suit me.'

'I saw you wearing them the other day,' Mel insists.

Okay so maybe I was, but that's only because I couldn't find anything else to put on my feet and I was in a hurry.

'What do you think I should wear anyway?' I persist. 'Something romantic and floaty or simple, suave and boaty? Ha, I'm a poet and I know it!'

'You're so sad.' Mel sighs heavily. 'I'd go in whatever you're comfortable in. How about those skinny jeans you got from H&M and a pair of pumps?'

'Okay, if I can find them.' I rummage about some more in the bottom of the cupboard; I know I left my shoes in here somewhere. 'Aha – that's where those gold sparkly heels went, well one of them anyway, I couldn't find them anywhere when I needed them the other day.'

'I'm amazed you can find anything in there, quite honestly,' Mel says wryly.

It is always the case, though it doesn't matter how many times you look for something when you need it desperately, it disappears – probably to the place all the odd socks go to. Then just when you've given up and don't need it anymore and you're looking for something completely different, it turns up mockingly right where you have looked in the first place.

'Your room isn't much better,' I retort, although actually Mel is fairly tidy these days. It's one of the things left over from her thankfully brief, but nonetheless for me, totally traumatic relationship with Rob Bright, geek of the year. Ever since, she spends loads of time at IKEA and has invested in all those cool little plastic pots that stick on a grid along the wall so she can put all her bits and bobs and arty things in. It's quite unnerving actually because she was always really messy like me and now she's had some weird conversion.

Worse than that she has also recently become a vegan, which is a bit stressful. It's not that I don't like vegans – they are usually really nice and relaxed and yoga-loving and I enjoy vegan food. But not Mel – oh no, she's not one of your chilled-out, tofu-eating, peace-seeking ambassadors for the movement, she is more your hardcore angry, violent vegan who believes in animals before people and follows all these strange individuals preaching vengeance on farmers and the 'end of the world is nigh' stuff.

I don't mind it really because she's still Mel who I know and love, and to be fair I agree with a lot of what she says, but she's suddenly become so serious about it all and apart from anything else, I'm really worried that one of these days she's going to get arrested.

Mind you, the whole vegan thing has become a major part of her fashion design business and she's doing incredibly well – her brand is totally cruelty-free, she won't use wool or any animal product in her creations and people seem to love it. She has so many pre-orders on her new collection due out next year, she's had to hire a personal assistant. It makes me laugh every time, for goodness' sake, Mel with a personal assistant! Fleur is lovely, totally grunge, with dreadlocks and vegan Doc Martens.

'What are you doing a few Wednesday's from now, by the way?' Mel asks.

'Working,' I say shortly, I really don't want to get caught up in one of Mel's crazy schemes.

'All day and evening?' Mel asks.

'Most of it,' I retort in a businesslike manner. 'We're going through an extremely busy time of growth at the agency and I'm just in the process of signing up a very rich client.'

'Huh.' Mel snorts. 'I bet she has a cupboard full of animal fur, most rich people do. Show off their wealth at the expense of the poor creatures round them. You should refuse to let her join.'

'There wasn't a trace of fur anywhere, she was quite nice actually,' I protest. Besides if everyone who joined the agency had to be vegan and cruelty-free, it would be the vegan dating agency.

'I bet if you looked in her wardrobe you'd find loads of it: Ugg boots, mink...' Mel persists.

'Everyone wears Ugg boots – they're extremely popular.'

'They shouldn't. I showed you the video from Peta on how they're made.'

'Don't remind me,' I grumble. I'm still jolly well traumatised by it. I wanted a pair of Ugg boots for years, having tried them on in various shops, even the retail outlet at Bicester, where they were supposed to be reduced but were of course still annoyingly expensive. When I earned a bit of extra with my freelance writing, I treated myself to a pair and walked into our apartment feeling on top of the world, only to be shown this hideous video by Mel about what happens to make them. It was totally disgusting and I can't believe it was genuine to be honest. The trouble is, now I can't wear the boots without feeling guilty about it.

Mel continues, 'Anyway, I only need you for a bit to come and film my involvement in the Vegan Action/Climate Change protest on Wednesday.'

'I'd love to but I do have to work,' I say as firmly as possible.

'Come on, Soph. I can't do it myself, Fleur is off that day and I want to get some of the girls down there in my designs – it's a great opportunity to manage both things at the same time. You honestly won't have to do much.'

'Maybe, then,' I just need to get Mel off the phone at this point, 'but I've got to go – I still haven't found the other shoe!'

'Okay, Soph – thanks, you're the best, I'll pay you back!'

'I might just hold you to that.'

An hour later, I am sort of ready for my date with Darcy, but have a few minutes to dash carefully across the cobbled courtyard into the office for a quick catch-up with Emma. It's actually really handy being able to live right next door to work, no more commuting or tube closures, it's wonderful. The only thing is, it is a bit cold, Chawton House is so big and draughty. I know it's Elizabethan but these days, we could do with some more heating. I can only assume that Jane Austen's brother,

Edward, and his family who lived there, as well as the childless Knight family who adopted him, were used to the chill or had thicker clothes. Emma and I always end up wearing loads of layers even when it's sunny.

'Ooh, you look nice,' Emma says, looking up from her papers.

'Thanks, I do my best,' I say nonchalantly. 'Any luck with finding a match for the Baroness?'

'No.' Emma sighs. 'I'm not sure who we've got on our books who will be suitable for her?'

'William Morris?'

'Which one's that?' Emma riffles through her papers.

'That solicitor chap, you know, quite formal but nice enough.'

'Oh him, yes but I think he's too young.'

'I suppose so, though I never think age matters and he must be at least fifty,' I say.

'I can't help thinking of Sir Henry Greaves.'

'You've got to be joking,' I splutter. 'I wouldn't inflict him on anyone!' I suppose my experience with him is somewhat jaded. He is, I kid you not, a true-to-life Sir Walter Elliot, vain, arrogant and miserly. His daughter, Maria, however, is one of my best friends, we met through the dating agency last summer and she is engaged to one of our other clients, Charles. Their Regency wedding is planned for this December and Mel is designing and creating the wedding and bridesmaids' dresses. I haven't seen what she's planning yet, but I reckon it'll be amazing.

'Besides I still think he is a perfect match for Lady Constance,' I say.

Lady Constance is a tyrant of the first order, bossy, overbearing and totally insufferable.

'Trouble is, Lady Constance doesn't think so. Anyway, she's

technically no longer a client after the whole kerfuffle with Mel snooping in her cupboard.'

'Yes, I suppose that was a hindrance to friendship.' I smile at the recollection. 'She and Sir Henry do make a perfect match however.'

'The trouble is we need more men. We can't have a Jane Austen Dating Agency without men who are in possession of a fortune.'

'Or even those without.'

A couple of hours later and I am swooshing my way with Darcy to London Bridge for our date in his stylish silver Aston Martin. I peek at him. He is looking incredibly good, his Pierce Brosnan hair swept back and I love his blue shirt; it really suits him. He puts his hand on my knee which sends shivers up my spine and he smiles. 'So are you excited for your first cruise?' he jokes, his brown eyes crinkling at the corners.

'Yes totally,' I say quietly because I am still a bit shy around Darcy. Girls like me don't usually go out with men like him, his last few dates were all supermodels so I feel a bit as though they are a hard act to follow.

I have tried talking to my sister, Chloe, about it, but she just laughed. 'Stop comparing yourself with other people, Soph, and enjoy the moment. He chose to go out with you because you're different from the other airheads he dated before, he told you that himself.'

Chloe is lucky though, she tends to obsess less over these things than me. Right now she's over the other side of the world in New York with Nick Palmer Wright, her new guy who is the loveliest man ever and also happens to be Darcy's best friend. I'm so glad she got away from her awful ex-husband and is finally happy. 'Are you going to marry again?' I asked her the other day when she facetimed me, looking sickeningly tanned and loved-up.

'What's the point?' she asked, and I suppose she's probably right. Marriage isn't everything really. I take another peek at Darcy's handsome side profile. Hmm, then again I *would* like to marry him. We could have a huge ceremony in Westminster Abbey, I'd be like Princess Kate and have trees in the aisle and everything and Mel and Chloe could be bridesmaids.

For a moment I'm lost in happy thoughts but am rudely awakened by the thought of Darcy's mother at the wedding. The very idea of it makes me feel sick. She is so intimidating and, in any case, she'd probably contest the whole thing. Or she'd boycott the ceremony like Lady Catherine in *P and P*. Perhaps we'll just take one day at a time, I think I might be jumping ahead of myself again.

Darcy pulls into a driveway, outside a tall Victorian House opposite the river. 'There she is.'

I follow his gaze to a mooring in front of Tower Bridge where there is a huge white boat with a smart blue stripe down one side, several floors high, moored by a comparatively tiny pontoon.

'Oh.' What else is there to say? That isn't a boat; it's a cruise liner for about twenty people.

'Nice, isn't she?' Darcy smiles.

'I should say so, but how do you drive that thing?'

'Drive it?' He laughs. 'We have a crew.'

We leave the car and walk towards the ship and I begin to have serious misgivings. The boat is teaming with people; glisteningly white-uniformed staff crawling everywhere like tiny sparkly beetles.

I tentatively totter over the gangplank, which is quite wide and sturdy actually but a la Princess Kate I had decided on the wedge heels with my tight jeans. I never did find the other shoe in my wardrobe; I must clear it out when I've got nothing better to do. There is an immaculate-suited steward waiting. 'Welcome aboard, madam, sir.'

Darcy nods at the man and puts his arm behind my back gently to escort me round to the front of the magnificent vessel. I think I'd feel better if he held my hand but guess I'm being a bit childish so take a deep breath and walk ahead towards a smart throng of people, hopefully looking more confident than I feel. Oh God, this is not what I was expecting at all. I feel majorly underdressed.

'Oh, there you are, darling.' A glamorous raven-haired tall woman, aka Darcy's mother, Veronica, dressed in flowing Catherine Walker and an excessive amount of eye make-up, approaches Darcy and squeezes his hand. I peer at him, amazed he isn't embarrassed but it doesn't faze him in the least.

'Hello, Mummy!' He kisses her on both cheeks. 'You remember Sophie.' I step forward to greet her but am rebuffed as she is already turning towards a group of plastic looking women of a similar age at her side. They all coo and fawn over Darcy as though he's the handsomest man in the world, which obviously he is, but it's a bit annoying and I feel rather superfluous.

'You haven't met Sophie Johnson, have you?' Darcy asks, interrupting the adulation.

The women pause momentarily to nod or smile vaguely in my direction, then continue to question Darcy about his latest assets. I follow the group as they swarm up a magnificent glass staircase onto a massive sundeck. The view is amazing, right up close to Tower Bridge and across the River Thames.

'Glass of champagne, madam?' asks a smartly dressed waiter. I gratefully take a glass and a large slurp. I so don't want to be here. This was not what I was expecting at all.

When Darcy had asked me out on the new yacht, I thought we were going, just the two of us, for a trip up the River Thames, maybe stopping at a little fashionable pub in Henley, then popping back home for a romantic takeaway in front of a roaring log fire at Darcy's Kensington flat. If I had known it was going to be a social trip with all these people, especially Darcy's horrible mother, I would have certainly at least dressed differently, if not made an excuse that I was washing my hair or going on a vegan protest or something. Where is Mel when you need her?

Darcy appears to be still embroiled in conversation with the plastic squad, so I wander to the edge of the balcony, hoping I look soulful and romantic, rather than sad and lonely all on my own. The last thing I want to be is a needy girlfriend. The crew is busy winding up the mooring ropes and as I watch, fascinated, we glide effortlessly away from the pontoon.

I squash down a flicker of panic as I suddenly realise I'm more than a little trapped with all these people. At least if we were on shore I could get off at any time, pretending there's an emergency at work or my parents have broken down somewhere or something. But I guess I'm being ridiculous, I've had to put up with worse people, Lady Constance for example. I hold my head up high, I've got this, I am the MD of The Jane Austen Dating Agency. I am going to mingle.

More confidently than I feel, I walk towards a group of people and at the last minute want to run away as they are so deep in conversation, I'm not quite sure how to start. As I approach, to my great relief, I notice a girl on her own to one side looking as though, like me, she would rather be anywhere else other than here.

'Hello,' I say. 'This is a beautiful boat, isn't it?' Oh great, not the most original conversation starter, but never mind, it's better than nothing.

'Yes it is, although it's rather large, I'm worried I'm going to get lost.'

'I agree,' I say, surprised. 'I'm Sophie, by the way.'

'Freya. Freya Nelson.'

'Nice to meet you. Are you with this crowd?'

'Yes I am,' she says, looking as though she wishes she weren't whilst being too polite to say so. 'The crowd are my step-cousins, I can introduce you if you like?'

'Perhaps in a minute.' I'm happy to be on the periphery of conversation for the moment, although this could be a great opportunity to recruit some new clients. 'I'm with Darcy but he's been kidnapped by a group of women!'

'Oh.' Freya is rather attractive in a pale interesting way, with long dark hair and delicate skin. 'He is very handsome, isn't he?'

'Yes he is,' I say dreamily, 'but I must admit I was rather thinking this was going to be a small gathering.'

'Me too, but then I don't like large groups of people, makes me feel a bit overwhelmed.'

'I know what you mean.' We stand and watch the bridge gates open slowly and the boat glides smoothly through the gap. The group next to us laughs loudly at something and one of the men joins us. He's quite good looking, thickset, with a square jaw and a mop of hair that is determined to stand on end.

'Hiding in the corner as always, Freya?' he asks with a grin.

'Yes I am.' She visibly perks up. 'You know I hate these occasions, although I've met an ally here – Sophie, this is my step-cousin, Edward.'

'Hi,' I say politely, and we shake hands.

'Nice to meet you,' he says. 'How do you know the Drummonds?'

'I'm here with Darcy, I run The Jane Austen Dating Agency.'

'Wow.' Freya's face lights up. 'A Jane Austen Dating Agency, how does that work? I love Jane Austen.'

'It's a dating agency for anyone who loves Jane Austen's world, women who are looking for real gentlemen to wine and dine them as well as Regency Balls, strawberry picnics, and meet and greets with the actors from recent productions,' I say enthusiastically.

'Sounds amazing. How do you join?'

'I'd be more than happy to tell you all about it, I've made some wonderful friends through the agency, they're such a nice group of people.'

'I'm not sure about Austen.' Edward looks doubtful, he is obviously a rather serious man. 'I would like to meet some fellow readers however, is it a sort of literary dating agency?'

'Yes it is. Actually, to be perfectly honest with you, we haven't managed to get as many men to join since the Regency Gambling Nights were discontinued.'

That was actually a right old drama as a result of the scandalous behaviour of the infamous Jessica Palmer Wright (Nick Palmer Wright's particularly nasty sister) who had been Head of Membership of the dating agency, and Daniel Becks (a plausibly charming and good-looking ex-client of the agency who I went out with earlier this year) who, along with my sister's horrible ex, Kian, were running a gambling scam and Jessica and Daniel had disappeared together with the profits. It nearly finished the agency, although the one good thing to come out of it all was that my sister, Chloe, ended up dating Jessica's gorgeous brother, Nick Palmer Wright, and is very happily living with him in New York. Thank goodness he has a completely different personality from his sister.

We definitely have a problem here with recruiting men for the agency. I make a mental note to discuss the issue with Emma at our next team meeting, aka catch up over a cappuccino and cake at Costa in Winchester.

'You get to meet with like-minded people who enjoy

literature and visits to places of interest and picnics.' I continue, 'There are quite a few men who join because they find it difficult to meet the right person and we do put a lot of effort in matching personalities. No computers, it's the traditional values, sending cards, building friendships and of course romance. This year we are celebrating our very first Regency wedding.'

'How lovely.' Freya is obviously totally convinced.

'Sounds an interesting idea,' Edward says, 'and I wouldn't have liked the gambling anyway, I'm not into that kind of thing. My sisters are a disaster when it comes to choosing the wrong people. They just think of money without giving a hoot for personality at all. Well, Caitlin does anyway.'

'Oh,' I say doubtfully, we don't particularly want money-grabbing clients, it's not really the idea of the agency. Although we do have Sir Henry Greaves who is exactly that – it's not what you are but who you are in his mind. He's still giving me daily grief about finding a woman who not only has loads of money but the right pedigree as well as being, in his words, 'a potential brood mare'. At his age, it seems a tall order. But we do need new clients and I've taken a liking to Freya and Edward.

'Have my card and if you would like to give me your info, I'll send you some details. I don't have any brochures with me as I'm not really supposed to be working.'

Just at that moment Darcy approaches. 'Are you networking already?' he asks, amused.

'Oh yes, Freya and Edward may be potential new clients,' I say, pleased he's back.

'Fast work,' he says with a smile.

'It sounds lovely,' Freya says shyly. I notice she stepped back when Darcy approached.

'Darcy!' For goodness' sake, it's Veronica. 'I wondered where you had gone,' she snaps, glancing at me from under her heavily made-up lashes. 'Isn't it wonderful; Tara is here.'

'Tara, lovely to see you.' Darcy politely kisses the willowy woman next to Veronica on both cheeks.

Tara is tall and slim with striking vibrant auburn hair. Her skin is creamy white with a tiny delicate smattering of freckles. She is quite beautiful. I would say she is a little older than me, but obviously oh-so confident.

'Darcy.' Her voice is low and breathy – so much so, I peer at her uncertainly. Does she really speak like that? I wonder what happens if she ever gets angry. Does she still talk at that volume? 'I haven't seen you since that party at Cannes. It was such a giggle – those canapés!' She laughs as though it had been the best thing ever. 'And who is this?' She peers at me either short-sightedly or critically, I'm not sure which but I think I have a pretty good idea.

'This is Sophie,' he says. I would have preferred *my girlfriend, Sophie.*

'Hello, Sophie.' She eyes me up and down appraisingly but I gaze back as confidently as I can. I can cope with this; the new Sophie is more than adequate to deal with women like her, and anyway I'm with Darcy now.

'Hello.' I smile coolly, returning her cold bony handshake.

She snaps her attention back to Darcy. 'Not drinking champagne? You always did prefer a vermouth. *Such* a *discerning* palate.'

'Trust you to know Darcy so well.' Veronica smiles at her. Oh great, Tara is obviously top of Mrs Drummond's list of eligible females.

My smile remains plastered on my face, it's probably becoming rather fixed. Okay so I might as well just go home. Who is this woman and what's her history with Darcy?

'So what do you do, Sophie?' Tara asks.

'I run the agency for Darcy.'

'Oh how sweet,' she simpers. 'I didn't realise you worked for him, I hope you aren't too hard on her, Darcy, I know how you can be.' She pushes him playfully in the chest. 'But we obviously disturbed your conversation with these two charming people.' She gestures towards Freya and Edward who both appear transfixed. 'Don't let us stop you. Darcy and I will have a little chat about old times. I'm sure Veronica won't mind me stealing him away.'

Veronica is only too keen, I'm surprised she hasn't packaged him in gift wrap. 'Of course, Tara darling. You must have so much to catch up on,' she coos, before stalking off to be with her other guests, satisfied she has done her duty. Tara takes Darcy's arm and he gives me a small apologetic smile and a shrug of his shoulders as the pair disappear in the direction of the upper deck. I'm left standing there with Freya and Edward, feeling horribly out of my depth.

'Well, that's one sorted woman.' Edward stares after her thoughtfully. 'I wonder who she is?'

Who indeed? All I know is she's just snatched Darcy from right under my nose. I may be the MD of The Jane Austen Dating Agency and have discovered two potential new clients, but it's going to require the brilliant writing skills of Jane herself to write me a script to wrangle my way out of this ridiculous situation. Darcy is laughing at something Tara has said, she's draped her arm over his shoulder and quite honestly, he doesn't look as though he minds at all.

CHAPTER 3

'*And* the evening just got worse,' I say dramatically, leaning back on one of the chairs in the kitchen of our tiny flat. 'I managed to spill Moet Chandon down my favourite top and I got to see Darcy for about five minutes throughout the whole thing.'

'Nightmare,' Mel sympathises, 'but then I don't agree with private yachts, not good for the environment.'

'No, but the point is, I barely got to spend any time with Darcy and he seemed totally oblivious – he even asked me in a serious tone on the way home if I had enjoyed myself.'

'You know what men are like; they don't always pick up on the sophisticated nuances of us women. Did you ask him who Tara was?'

'I did, but only in a subtle way because I didn't want to appear like some kind of neurotic stalker girlfriend. We've only been going out a few weeks, I don't want to be too full-on.'

'Huh, I thought you'd practically got the whole wedding planned.' Mel sniffs, turning out patterns from a piece of newspaper.

'No, we hardly know each other,' I say innocently.

'I'm sure I saw a copy of *Brides Magazine* on your bed the other day.'

'That was an old one from Modiste days.' I pour some wine. 'Do you want some?'

'Only if it's vegan. What about that new Pinterest page you have on designer wedding dresses?'

'Research for the agency,' I say shortly. 'Of course the wine's vegan, it's not got meat in or milk, has it?'

'You never know.' Mel takes the bottle from my hand and studies it. 'Nope it's fine. I'll have some, thanks.'

Actually I was kind of having a look at wedding dresses because they are rather lovely, aren't they, and a girl can dream. Also I do like Darcy a lot and I know it's early days, but I really do think he might be *the one*. I just got this funny feeling about it when I first met him, well when I'd got over not liking him anyway. I think it might have been when I walked with him around the extensive grounds at Chatsworth House. In any case, that's when I initially noticed he has a sense of humour after all.

'Besides,' I continue, 'I like Darcy very much but...'

'But?' Mel slurps her wine.

'He's still a bit distant, if you know what I mean.'

'Distant?'

'Yes, it's kind of hard to get to know him, to get close to him.'

'You have got quite close to him, haven't you?' Mel giggles, peering at me.

'Yes, quite close,' I smile and blush, 'but it's not that; he never really talks about his emotions or feelings.'

'Typical man then, stiff upper lip, that sort of thing. He's probably repressed. I told you to go out with a vegan activist, they get all the stress out of their system through their campaigning. You get a more sensitive new-age type of guy.'

'I know, no man is perfect, but I was kind of hoping we'd go on some romantic picnics, or loved up weekends abroad or something amazing,' I say wistfully.

'Maybe you will, but the reality is, life isn't like that and at some time you need to come back down to earth.'

'I guess.' I switch on the oven, as it's my turn to cook. 'I just hoped it would be different, that's all. I guess I want my fairy-tale ending.'

'You have, but this is real life not a Jane Austen novel. And remember you did say you always had a shrewd suspicion that Mr Darcy was a bit arsey and full of himself in the book. Maybe he really is.'

'No he isn't,' I say defensively, 'he's very passionate and romantic underneath I'm sure, he's just a bit serious on the surface. I'm merely going to have to dig a bit deeper and I reckon in time I'll really get to know him. Look how hard Lizzie had to work to get Darcy to come out of his shell in *P and P* and make him laugh at himself.'

Mel looks doubtful but I ignore her amused expression and start chopping carrots. I bet Cinderella never had to do this once she found her handsome Prince. It isn't just Jane Austen who has an awful lot to answer for; it's the writers of every romantic fairy tale in the world. And they all lived happily ever after. Huh.

Things are looking up tomorrow however, as I am going on a research trip to a masked Regency Ball in Bath. I told you this job is the best thing ever. The only problem is, Emma is unable to come at the last minute as her aunt in Gloucestershire has become unwell and she has to go and visit her. I really don't want to go on my own; it's times like this I miss Chloe.

'Mel,' I say whilst throwing all the chopped veg in a pan. 'You know you owe me a favour?'

'I know that tone and I am beginning to worry.' Mel pops a piece of chopped carrot in her mouth.

'I really need you to come with me on a research trip tomorrow night to a ball,' I say casually.

'Not Regency dress, Soph. I told you never again after what happened with Rob Bright.'

'I know and it was very kind of you to make an exception to your rule,' Mel does not like wearing dresses of any kind at the best of times, 'but I don't think you can blame your outfit for attracting Rob Bright! And it was your decision to go out with him when the rest of us were tripping over each other trying to escape his boring conversation and hideous lack of manners.' I turn up the heat under the pan.

'I suppose I was using him but he gives me the heebie-jeebies now. I wonder what he's doing these days, have you seen him since?' Mel shudders at the memory.

'No, but Emma says Lady Constance mentioned him the other day. Apparently he still plays chess and dances attendance on her at all hours of day and night!' We both laugh. 'Look, I understand why you did it. Desperate situations call for desperate measures. But please, Mel, I'm coming to this hideous march thing of yours and I don't particularly want to go to a ball on my own.'

'Where's the gallant Darcy?'

'Business trip, but I am so excited because he's promised when he returns he will take me to Paris.'

'Sounds good, but I'd like him a lot more if he were taking you to this ball. I haven't even got anything to wear.'

'That's a laugh.' I snort. 'You're a dress designer, for goodness' sake!'

'Yes but Regency dress, it's so last year.'

I give her my best pleading face.

'I have still got my green gown from the ball you dragged me to, I suppose,' she says reluctantly.

'It would be perfect. Mel, you're a star!' I give her a massive hug.

'Yeah well you'd better be an active part of the rabble rousing at the vegan climate protest.'

'Yeah right.' I laugh and throw a piece of carrot at her.

The next night, we arrive at the ball in the most annoying of conditions. It's been raining steadily all day, as it has been for several days, it's damp, rain lashing, windswept and dismal, i.e., typical October weather in this country. That's all well and good as long as you are wearing wellies and leggings but somehow I don't think Regency dance slippers and floor-length gowns are very suited to it. The Bath streets today, instead of being mysterious and romantic, are merely wet and soggy and so are we, as soon as we are dropped off outside the Pump Rooms.

'Where are goloshes when you need them?' I ask Mel, laughing as she tries to jump a puddle and ends up splashing half of it over her shoe.

'It's not funny,' she snaps. 'I hate dresses at the best of times.'

We manage to squeeze our way inside the Pump Rooms where it is hard to even find a space to stand. The rain has forced everyone inside and there are people everywhere right through the hallway and into the ballroom.

'This is hideous,' mutters Mel, squashing past a rather large woman who is wrestling with her chemise.

'I know!' I shout back. I seem to be crushed up against a beautiful fountain with fish pouring water from their mouths. 'I hate it when you can't move anywhere at all.'

After some time and effort we have barely managed to get more than a couple of feet into the room.

'Someone just tore my dress,' I say angrily, pulling up my

skirt, but am unable to see properly because I can't even bend down to look; I'm hemmed in by the sheer volume of people.

'Sorry, I think I may have trodden on it,' a deep voice from behind me announces, but not very apologetically.

'Oh, how annoying.' I try not to be rude enough to say what I really feel about the matter.

The man is dark haired, tallish with dancing eyes which belie his apology. 'If you will wear dresses with ridiculously long trains, they're going to trip people up. In fact, I could sue you for causing a hazard.'

'I haven't got a train on this dress,' I say crossly, having managed to get myself to a corner where I have enough space to examine the bottom of my skirt. Thank goodness it seems to be okay.

'Looks fine to me.' He appears to have traipsed along too.

'What a relief. This sort of net won't repair if you tear it.'

'No, I know it doesn't, it's so delicate.'

I peer at him surprised. 'Are you a fashion designer or something?'

'No, but I have a sister who also likes to wear long dresses, especially romantically flowing gowns with absurdly long skirts and impractical amounts of net.'

'It kind of goes with the territory, doesn't it?'

'It does,' he says with a grin. 'Nice to have met you. Now I know your dress remains unblemished, I must go and find my party.'

I peer around looking for Mel, who I seem to have lost somewhere but after some time manage to push my way through to the drinks.

'Sophie,' Mel gasps, having finally reached me with a glass of alcohol-free vegan beer. 'You made it!'

We manoeuvre through the scrum into the ballroom where there is room enough for people to dance and a string quartet is playing behind some round tables. They all seem to be occupied, however.

'This is a nightmare,' Mel grumbles. 'There's nowhere to sit and I just want to go home.'

'It does feel rather like one of those evenings which are going to drag on and on.' I peer desperately around the room; it would be nice if we knew someone.

'Sophie, oh my gosh, Sophie!'

There's a scuffle a small distance away and out bursts Izzy Fenchurch from within a group of people, several of whom tut and glare after her as she gives me a huge hug.

'Izzy! What on earth are you doing here?'

She looks amazingly well; she's filled out a little since I last saw her and it suits her. Izzy Fenchurch became one of my best friends when I joined the dating agency earlier this year, she had a tough time over a complete loser – Josh, who went off with some rich bitch but she's been going out with the nicest guy ever since.

'Where's Matthew?' I ask.

'He's over there somewhere.' Izzy smiles. 'He was very gallant and offered to get us some drinks.'

Matthew appears through the crowd and passes Izzy a glass of bubbly. He gives Mel then me a kiss hello. 'Right old scrum this, isn't it? Might be less stressful playing rugby.'

'That would be much more my thing.' Mel is really unamused by now.

❧

After a while, the seemingly never-ending regimented dance with a lot of bowing and scraping ends and the violinist strikes up a jaunty tune. 'Let's join in,' Izzy suggests, 'I haven't been to a Regency Ball and actually danced with you yet.' Matthew ever obliging leads Izzy off to where the dancers are assembling.

I must admit I have itchy feet myself; I love to dance and not for the first time wish Darcy were here. It's hard to watch everyone whirling and twirling from the side of the room, their colourful gowns shining in the candlelight. I'm beginning to realise how difficult it must have been for Lizzie at the beginning of *P and P* when she had to stand like a wallflower and Mr Darcy refused to dance with her.

'Excuse me.' The Master of Ceremonies appears with, to my great surprise, the man from earlier at his side.

'Miss Melanie Threepwood and Miss Sophie Johnson, may I present Mr Henry Baxter and his sister, Miss Ellie Baxter?' the Master booms.

We all smile and bow and make the right sort of noises and I look at Ellie who is tall and blonde with a kind smile and is wearing a lovely sheer white dress that is practically translucent – I think it must have cost a lot of money.

'I hear my clumsy-as-ever brother managed to tread on your dress, I hope it's okay?' she says with a grin.

'It's fine, thank you,' I reply. I like the look of Ellie.

'I didn't mean to, it just got under my foot.' Henry's face is serious, but I can somehow trace the merest hint of amusement at the corner of his mouth. 'But I could prove that I'm not totally spatially unaware by asking you to dance?'

I glance at Mel, but she seems happy enough to chat with Ellie and I would really like to join in, I mean if Darcy isn't available then Henry Baxter, or should I say Henry Tilney, will do very nicely indeed.

CHAPTER 4

*H*enry Baxter and I stand opposite each other in the line-up and I hope desperately I can remember the moves. I needn't have worried however, there is a caller who reminds us when to stand forward and move to the side and the rest seems to be mostly a little polka step which isn't too difficult.

'See, I haven't trodden on your dress once yet, have I?' Henry asks when we meet in the centre, hold hands, turn and move back to the side together along with the other couples on our half of the room.

'We're only part way through the dance, give it time,' I say sarkily. But actually he moves surprisingly well.

'I have been practising.'

We are parted momentarily by the movement of the dance but soon meet again in the middle.

'I was going to ask if you come to many Regency dances?' I say.

'No, this is my first but Ellie dragged me to a couple of hops with the Jane Austen Dancers in Alton, so I learnt my steps well.'

'But how come you're into Jane Austen?' He doesn't seem very likely to be the type.

'Because of Ellie – she's having a rather difficult time and I wanted to cheer her up so I offered to come along, although I have read *Pride and Prejudice*, it was really good,' he says, sounding surprised that it might be.

'A very kind, brotherly thing to do.' I laugh. 'My brother, Ben, would never be so thoughtful! And is it as bad as you thought it would be?'

'Well to be honest with you, things are looking up!' Henry says glancing at me with amusement, his eyes crinkling at the corners.

He's nice and I smile back because there's no harm in being polite, of course I'll tell him about Darcy but why shouldn't we be friends? At the end of the dance, we meander back to Ellie and Mel who are chatting and seem to be getting on incredibly well. I can always tell if Mel likes someone or not.

'So you are crazy about all things Austen?' I ask Ellie.

'Absolutely, I love the whole Regency thing, where else do you get to dress up in gorgeous clothes and dance in beautiful surroundings like this?'

'At The Jane Austen Dating Agency,' I sound rather like a commercial break, but am unable to stop myself, 'we have so many balls and outings and all sorts of events where you can escape reality as much as you like.'

Ellie's face clouds. 'As for escaping reality, that would be amazing, but a dating agency wouldn't be for me, even a Jane Austen one.'

Her phone bings and she pulls from her reticule a bright pink iPhone. Henry looks at her face, concerned. 'It's my father,' she says. 'We need to go now, Henry, it's getting late.'

We murmur our goodbyes and the couple meander off through the scrum.

'That was a bit odd,' I say to Mel. 'Was it something I said?'

'Probably. You're not always very subtle, are you?'

I am about to make a snidey retort because actually I try to be sensitive but I do sometimes put my foot in it. I can't seem to help it; I think I was born that way.

'Another glass of punch,' I say trying not to feel too crushed, as at that moment Izzy and Matthew appear.

'Ooh, yes please. Just a small one, it's thirsty work all that dancing.'

'I'll get them.' I meander my way through the melee to the drinks area.

'Sophie.' I feel a hand on my shoulder, it's Henry.

'I thought you'd gone.'

'We had. My father has prehistoric ideas of what time Ellie should be back home.'

'That must be a nightmare. She's not a child.'

'Try telling that to him. Anyway, he'll be chafing at the bit if I don't get her back soon, but I wanted to grab a card for The Jane Austen Dating Agency if you have one, of course.'

'Absolutely.' I rummage indecorously inside my bag and manage to pull out a card, which is in fairly good condition. 'Here you go.'

Henry takes it with a small bow and a smile. 'I think The Jane Austen Dating Agency is just what she needs right now.'

'Great,' I say, surprised. 'We'll look forward to hearing from you then.'

The rest of the evening passes in a blur and I must admit I wish I hadn't taken Mel because she has become far too serious for dancing and was pretty grumpy about the whole thing. Izzy and I joined in a couple of circle dances and I managed to hand out cards and speak to people but all in all it felt a little flat after Henry and Ellie had left, almost as though something was missing.

Back in the office the next morning, Emma asks for a rundown of events.

'I gave some cards out, but a lot of people there were in couples already. Quite a few girls took some info though,' I say in a hopeful tone.

'That's something.' Emma sips her raspberry tea. It smells disgusting actually. It's a weird thing but I hate fruit teas, they are so revolting, yet I love fruit. It's a bit like chocolate with fruit in it – all wrong. Now fruit on its own is delicious and chocolate, well I don't need to say any more, but mix the two together and it's all over as far as I'm concerned. Chocolate is sacred, it should not be tainted with the presence of fruit. 'But not much good if we haven't any fit Regency men to fulfil the demand,' she continues.

I take a gulp of my nicely caffeinated coffee. 'Yes, it's a real problem. It will just end up being a group of sad women dancing round their Regency handbags if we're not careful!'

'Hmm.' Emma looks worried. 'Have you spoken to Darcy about it, surely he must know some eligible young bachelors?'

'I could ask him, but I didn't want to admit we're struggling at this stage, he's trusted us to run this agency and I want to prove we can do a good job.'

'I know what you mean. Maybe we won't tell him yet.'

'No, we'll think of something,' I say brightly. 'Also I'm hoping a few of the guys I've met recently might come along with their sisters or cousins. There must be a way to spread the word.'

At that moment, my phone sings out and I grab it hopefully.

'Sophie?'

'OMG, Miffy, long time no speak,' I shriek. Miffy Pemberton-Smythe is tall and sloaney and works in the Editorial Department at Modiste, the top fashion magazine where I used to work in sales. It had sounded terribly glamorous at the time, but had turned out to be a cold-calling position, with me frequently being told to get lost and not very politely either. I originally wanted to work in Editorial, but there hadn't been any opportunities to graduate from different departments. Miffy was incredibly kind to me earlier this year and tried to include me in some of her social outings with the Editorial Team. She's also an old school friend of Emma's and I'm very fond of her. She even gave me a little freelance editorial work when I left Modiste.

'I know, darling. Been simply crazy, you know how this place works, it's such a relentless machine – currently all systems go for India Fashion Week next month.'

'Of course,' I say more knowledgeably than I feel because, since leaving Modiste, I've lost touch with what's on when. I still read the magazine and everything but that whole world seems a long way away now.

'How's the agency going?'

'Pretty well. Of course it's a steep learning curve, but business is brisk.' Emma raises her eyebrows at me and I grimace back at her, we need to keep up appearances here.

'So I guess you're super busy then.' Miffy sounds disappointed.

'Fairly. How's it all going in Editorial? Did you ever find out what happened to Nina and Bunty?'

Nina and Bunty were Miffy's colleagues in the Editorial Department at Modiste. They had both randomly disappeared earlier this year and were then arrested, when it transpired that they had been involved in the illegal gambling scam, along with Jessica Palmer Wright and Daniel Becks, two of the key players in The Jane Austen Dating Agency. It had all been a total disaster.

'Yes they're still vaguely in touch, they've been let off. Not enough evidence or something.'

'I can't believe they got away with that.'

'When Daddy's an oil tycoon and Mummy's a top model you can get away with pretty much anything. It's called paying people off, darling.'

'Good grief. Modiste has got a whole load more exciting than when I was there. So haven't you got anyone else in the team?'

'Not yet. There's huge restructuring further up the ladder, so we're having to make do one staff member down. That's what I wanted to talk to you about.'

'I am all ears.' That's a strange expression and I feel weird saying it, but Miffy continues regardless as she obviously knows what I mean.

'How would you feel about doing a little more freelance writing for us on a more formal basis? I know you are super busy with the dating agency but we do need more help than we're getting.'

I take a moment to punch the air, do a little twirl and silent scream 'woo hoo', much to the consternation of Emma, before I reply casually, 'I can maybe check my diary and see what I can fit in. What were you thinking?'

'We could perhaps have a chat this week and discuss ideas?'

I peer at my empty diary for the next few days. 'Erm, I can change a few things around I guess.'

Emma has started to giggle now at my studied role-play.

'Fabulous, darling. Look forward to catching up with you. How about Gunpowder, we could have a quick bite to eat.'

'Gunpowder? Is that a place or a thing?'

'It's the new Indian restaurant near Tower Bridge, sweetie. Jolly good nosh. See you then. Byeee.'

Before I can say another thing, she's gone and I peer at Emma. 'Bizarre name for a restaurant – I hope the food isn't ridiculously hot, I'm not that good with spice.'

'Is that with Darcy?'

'No, Miffy – you know from the Editorial Team at Modiste. Sounds as though she wants me to do some writing. It's tailed off a bit lately although I've been busy, to be fair.'

'Ask her if she knows any eligible men who would like to join the agency.' Emma swings her elegant legs out from under the desk. 'And don't forget the meeting with Charles and Maria to discuss wedding plans next week.'

'It's in my diary with a big heart next to it. I can't wait, I'm so excited. I am determined Maria's wedding is going to be absolutely perfect. She deserves it.'

'Agreed! I think we should be fairly up to date with the caterers and the vicar. We just need to discuss decorations and any other extras or entertainment they might like. Some fruit tea?'

'Please not,' I say.

§.

I'm on my way to the restaurant a few days later when my mother rings. I've been avoiding her a little since the whole Ben joining the agency thing; it's too terrible to contemplate. I only pick the phone up now because if I don't she will soon start to send out search parties to see where I am and what I'm doing to not respond to her calls for the last day or so.

'Hi, Mum,' I say casually, as though I'm not avoiding her at all.

'Oh, Sophie, I've been trying you for days.' She puffs as though she was sprinting at the same time in an attempt to search for me or power the phone; I'm not sure which.

'Sorry, Mum, I've been a bit busy.'

'That's okay, I know you're hard at work, it's just I do need to speak to you about a couple of things.'

'Okay, but I'm on my way out to dinner.'

'It'll only take a minute.'

I very much doubt this but my mum is still talking anyway, '...and the long and short of it is that your father and I think it's about time we meet this Darcy because you've been going out for a while and I know you think we never entertain.'

'I don't think that,' I protest. 'You do, though mostly family.'

'Yes I know and although that's lovely, we'd like to meet Darcy and–'

'That would be great,' I say, dashing onto the bottom of the escalator.

'I can't quite hear you!' shouts Mum. 'It's not these phones messing about, is it? Phillip!'

Here we go again. 'Mum!' I'm shouting now and tripping up the escalator, something has gone very wrong with my multitasking skills.

'Are you okay?' asks a man, looking concerned, which makes a change. Usually on the underground I get trampled underfoot at this time of day, not that I've commuted much at all since moving to Chawton, but in any case, from my experience, no one would even notice if you trip, they just keep right on walking all over you.

'Fine thanks. Look, Mum, I'm at the tube station. It'll be quieter when I get outside.'

'That's better. There was a terrible buzzing noise in the background. What's Darcy's favourite food?'

'Erm, I don't know,' I say, confused. I've come out of London Bridge Station and have momentarily lost my bearings. 'Mum, I'll phone you back about dinner.'

'Of course, don't need to know now,' my mum replies cheerfully, 'any time will do.'

'Okay, speak to you later.'

'I need to talk to you about Ben too,' Mum says as a parting shot.

For goodness' sake.

Thinking about it, Ben is the only man interested in joining The Jane Austen Dating Agency right now and he's the only one I really don't want to join. As Alanis Morissette once so perfectly put, life is just so ironic.

CHAPTER 5

*I*t is a universally acknowledged fact, in our family at any rate, that once my mother gets a bee in her bonnet about something, she will not rest until it becomes reality. This is certainly the case with regards to my brother joining the dating agency.

'I have Ben's application form,' I say disconsolately to Emma one dingy afternoon. The light is already getting dim outside our office window and it's only half past three. I have to admit I don't really enjoy winter; the dark mornings and evenings are enough to depress anyone.

'That's great.' She peers at my disgruntled face. 'Isn't it?'

'Yeah right, you haven't met Ben.'

'Oh come on, he can't be that bad.' Emma laughs.

'No he's not, it's just he's a nightmare with the opposite sex, has no idea how to behave, has never read a Jane Austen book in his life and is a bit of a male chauvinist.'

'Apart from that.' Emma smiles. 'Come on, he can't be as bad as some of our past clients, look at Rob Bright.'

'Okay, so he's not as bad as that.' No one's that bad to be fair. 'But he's trouble all the same.'

'He's one more male client than we had before.' She shuts her book with a bang. 'Although two actually if I count Edward.'

'Edward.' I'm confused as I'm not really listening. I'm still stressing about Ben and trying to figure out how I'm going to stop him causing complete and utter chaos in the agency.

'Edward. You met him the other day?'

'I thought his name was Henry,' I say vaguely.

'No. Who's Henry? Anyway, a lovely chap called Edward phoned, he was quite serious, but very polite and is interested in joining the agency with his cousin, Freya. He said he met you last week, on a boat?'

'Oh, of course, when I was on Darcy's yacht.'

'Hark at you!' Emma laughs. 'Casually mentioning your rich, gorgeous boyfriend's yacht.'

'It wasn't great actually.' I colour at the memory. 'Meeting Edward and Freya was a highlight. He seemed a nice guy though, although I thought he was too shy to do anything about it.'

'No, he's quite keen and even said he's going to try to persuade his sisters to come along to some events.'

'That's fab. At least something positive came out of the evening.'

'It's two more men anyway, but we're going to have to get busy pronto thinking of another scheme to somehow bring a whole horde of chaps along ASAP.'

'I don't know about getting more guys, I'm worried I'm going to lose the one I've got,' I say quietly.

Emma looks up from her paperwork. 'I thought you and Darcy were getting along really well.'

'We are, but he hasn't met my parents yet.'

'That's no big deal, is it?'

'Yes, it's huge. They're a complete nightmare; my mother will chatter away in the style of Mrs Bennet and my father is bound to do something embarrassing. I love them dearly but our house isn't anything like what Darcy's used to.'

'Does that have to matter? I'm sure he won't mind.'

'I hope not, and it's not that I'm embarrassed of my parents as they are wonderful, but...'

'But...'

'Darcy and his family are G and T and my family is more cup of tea.'

'Great analogy.' Emma smiles. 'But I'm sure he will overlook that; he seems besotted with you. Look how he saved the dating agency and relocated it here, all for you.'

'Yes, I guess he did.' I blush at how happy this has made me, yet I still somehow have imposter syndrome as though it's all going to disappear. 'But also he did it for his gran's memory as well.'

'You have some serious self-esteem issues.' Emma starts to gather her stuff. 'Right, I'm off early this evening as I have a couple of things I need to do before tomorrow.'

'Okay bye, I'll lock up then.' I peer back at my brother's application form.

Honestly, under hobbies, he's put golf and running. I haven't seen my brother run for years, more like running after every woman he can find. Under ideal traits in a woman he's written, 'attractive, blonde and up for a good time'. I mean, really? Could he be any more obvious? I carefully copy his details into our registration form and put it with new members. Shame I can't refuse him entry but my mother would be furious. She would definitely want to know why. Lost in thought, I pack my things in my bag.

I know Darcy obviously does like me but I would be a lot happier if I could dismiss the image of the hideously over familiar Tara. It's no good, I'm going to try putting her out of my mind, after all, my date with Darcy last week at La Rouge had been so romantic. The time had flown by, with no shortage of things to talk about. We had talked and laughed. He's not only gorgeous but also a great listener. That is, of course, when he's not fidgeting. I mean, I don't expect a man to gaze into my eyes the whole time throughout dinner but I was a little surprised that he was so easily distracted. He obviously likes people watching and I guess it is difficult for him when he knows so many important individuals, so maybe he likes to scout the room for familiar faces when he is out to dinner, to check out the lie of the land so to speak.

Yet somehow I wish he had gazed into my eyes just a little, or at least focused on me some of the time, in an intense and meaningful manner, brooding even. I know, I know, perhaps I'm comparing him with his fictional namesake and that's a really bad idea. Of course we don't know what happened to Elizabeth Bennet and Darcy after they married. I'm sure they lived happily ever after, but along the way there were bound to be teething problems. I can't imagine Miss Bingley suddenly underwent a major personality transplant and became a nice person or that Lady Catherine de Bourgh stopped writing rude letters. I'm sure Darcy put up with Mrs Bennet as much as he could for Elizabeth's sake, but it would have been difficult and there must have been loads of times they argued about it.

I feel better, thinking of these issues – as I don't even like to mention this to anyone, even Mel or Emma, as they would probably laugh at me. I suppose it could be that Darcy doesn't like sitting at tables for long periods of time, although he goes to enough dinner parties to be used to it. Or perhaps I make him nervous, but the thought of that makes me laugh. I don't think I could make anyone nervous! Maybe I need to just give it some time, my expectations are running away with me again.

I pick up my papers to check over later and switch off the lights. It's no good, I'm going to have to be strong and invite

Darcy to my parents' house and surely if he really likes me and I think he does, it will all be okay. I get a sudden image of our last lingering kiss the other night after our date at The Ivy. Yes I need to believe in myself, he obviously likes me, Darcy is not the kind of guy to pretend. It will be fine, I'm sure.

I'm about to turn off the light in the entrance hall and lock the large oak front door, when there's a noise from upstairs. It sounds as though someone has dropped a book or something. I hesitate. What was that? I could lock the door and leg it back to our apartment. I peer over my shoulder and the empty courtyard looks blankly back at me. But my treacherously doubting mind suggests that it is my duty as protector of this beautiful house, to check it's secure and everything is okay. Or, I could ask Mel to come back with me, but she'll think I'm a right wimp and be grumpy about being disturbed in the middle of her work.

It's no good, I'm going to have to be brave and go and find out what the noise was. It was probably just a book falling off a shelf. I hesitate momentarily. It's so silent I wonder if I have imagined the whole thing. An owl hoots loudly from a nearby tree, making me start violently.

Come on, Sophie, you're not a child, you can do this.

Resolutely I shut the great oak door behind me and creep back into the entrance hall, my feet barely making a noise on the flagstone floor. I reach the bottom of the stairs, switching the lights on as I go, as though their reassuring brightness will keep away any ghoulies or ghosties from my fevered imagination. I'm wondering whether to brave upstairs or, as it is so quiet and it is obviously nothing, I can just go home, but then I hear the noise again. I feel a shiver down my back and I don't know if it is my imagination but I feel cold all over. I think I'm going to have to go and get Mel. Of course, that's it, I'll phone her. I whip out my mobile and select her number. Just having the phone in my hand is familiar, reassuring.

'Sophie, are you nearly back? I've got some veggie curry on the go.' I can hear sizzling noises in the background. They're strangely comforting.

'Yeah I'm on my way, just locking up,' I say casually, not wanting to sound like an idiot.

'Are you all right?' Mel asks. 'Did you want something?'

'No, that is... yes, I thought I heard a noise, but it was nothing so I'm on my way now.'

'Okay, great, see you in a mo.' Mel has gone.

For goodness' sake, I'm going to have to get over this. Grabbing every last ounce of courage I have and having turned the light on, I creep carefully up the creaky stairs.

When I get to the top, I hasten my steps, as all the people in the portraits seem to follow me with their eyes. I'm sure someone told me once that all paintings do this – it's something to do with the way the painter paints them, but it's jolly creepy either way.

As I stalk along the corridor to the front room, the window in the small alcove swings open to the end of its hinges with a clang, and at the same time, the thick heavy curtain billows out towards me like a giant flying carpet. It makes me jump so violently, I almost knock a vase off a nearby table and have to take a moment to calm down. Honestly, how silly.

I walk determinedly forward to lean out to grab it as quickly as I can, shutting out a sudden fear of some unknown assassin coming up behind me and shoving me out of the window whilst leaning in this precarious position. I manage with an effort to reach the latch and shut the window with a firm bang, securing it in place. Odd it was open, I presume Emma must have been trying to air the room; it certainly smells musty. There isn't even much wind today. Most odd.

On the floor is a very old, incredibly precious first edition of *Northanger Abbey* and *Persuasion*. Even odder. I guess maybe it was knocked on the floor by the curtain, but I wouldn't have thought it would be strong enough. Besides it should have been down in the library, in the women's collection. It's an extremely valuable book, they're always kept in a locked cabinet. I presume Emma must have taken it out, but I can't imagine she'd have left it here.

Carefully, almost reverently, I pick up the precious book and, holding it delicately, I draw the curtain with a resounding swish, survey the room briefly and leave with as much dignity as I can muster considering I'm in a real hurry to get out of it. This reminds me of when I was a child and would leg it up the stairs like a mad thing, panicking that someone could be coming up after me.

I hasten back down the staircase with relief, methodically turning the lights off. I love that little alcove with the writing bureau in the room above. It was reputedly where Jane Austen would sit when she was visiting her brother Edward Knight's house. How silly of me to let my imagination get the better of me, I'm sure Jane would be looking out for me against any strange things that go bump in the night.

I am quite proud of myself really, I am now acting like a proper grown up, though to be honest I still don't like removing those spiders with long hairy legs, I have to get Mel to do it. You know the ones I mean, they're fine when they stand still but it's their horrible habit of suddenly running at you that freaks me out. It's the sudden unexpectedness of it that's the problem. My dad always says they're scared of people but why do they run towards us then? It really doesn't make any sense.

Carefully, I place the precious book back in the cabinet in the library, turn the key which for some reason has been left in the lock – I'll have to ask Emma about that tomorrow, and switch off the light. As I am opening the heavy oak front door once more, the noise upstairs comes again. Just the same thump as though a book has been dropped on that old oak floor. That's it, I've had enough of this. Mel can come back with me later or better still, we could simply ignore the whole thing and hope it was nothing at all.

❧

Back in the warm and cosy apartment infused with the delicious smell of cooking, I feel a little foolish.

'Are you all right?' Mel asks, looking up from the pan at my flushed face with amusement. I guess I've come in the door rather quickly.

'Yes, fine thanks.' I breeze in casually, dropping my files on the table with an effort at careless abandon.

She isn't fooled one bit. 'You were scared over there on your own, weren't you?'

'Not at all, just checking what time dinner was.'

'Yeah right. Come on, Soph, I've known you too long to believe you on that one!'

'Okay.' I pour myself a glass of wine with a sigh, Mel as usual already has one. 'Maybe I was a bit.'

'I knew it.' Mel guffaws.

'Yeah well, there was a noise and the window was open and it was dark up there. And all the portraits were freaking me out, all those eyes following me.'

'That's hilarious, I thought you liked historical houses.'

'Maybe in the daytime or even at night when there's people around but not on a dark lonely evening on my own.'

'Perhaps you should stop reading those psychological thrillers you have such a thing for,' Mel remarks drily.

'Not at all, they're brilliant. It's that moment when you find out the twist which you didn't see coming and you think, wow.'

'All very well until you think you can see intruders in the shadows and serial killers in the cupboard.'

'I don't.'

'You've been locking the door, even in the daytime.'

'That seems sensible.'

'We're in the middle of nowhere. This is Chawton, where Jane Austen grew up. It's very English and genteel. Nothing more exciting than someone's dog getting out and chasing the local farmer's chickens has ever happened here.'

'You obviously haven't read *Death Comes to Pemberley* or *Pride and Prejudice and Zombies*.'

'No I haven't. Funnily enough, I prefer real life problems such as what are we going to do without a planet and how to get politicians to take the climate crisis seriously.'

'I know that's important too but what about a bit of escapism?' I ask.

'We'll all be trying to escape if we continue killing the planet. Are you ready to eat?' Mel dishes up the dinner, which looks absolutely delicious. She shoves my copy of *Gone Girl* out of the way with distaste. 'Sometimes I wish you'd go back to reading Regency romance. It was a whole lot less trouble.'

CHAPTER 6

'The avocados are all brown,' my mum laments, slamming the knife down with a bang.

'There must be some that aren't,' Dad comments, examining them carefully and gingerly as though they are something that might bite. Mind you, he isn't wearing his glasses, which is not a good start. In his hand he has a depressingly brown avocado with a slight bit of green hinting at its desired colour in a tantalising manner.

'It's no good, Phillip. You're going to have to go back to Waitrose and buy some more.'

'You've got to be joking, these cost an absolute fortune, I bought ripe and ready,' Dad protests.

'We have no time to argue about this. Darcy is going to be here in three quarters of an hour and the avocados are brown. I've been slaving away for hours to get this right whilst you've been sitting watching the cricket. Get in the car and drive to Waitrose, for goodness' sake, dear.'

'I'm taking the other ones back, they can swap them over, you have to take out a second mortgage to shop in there.'

'No you're not.' My mum physically wrenches the offending

avocados from my dad who is desperately trying to wrestle them back into their non-environmentally friendly plastic wrapping. She has the sort of look not to be messed with, her face is bright red, the mottled tone of which is already spreading like a raging river down her neck. We all know this is not a good sign and Dad just needs to get on with it. We wait for the blast. 'This is why I never have anyone round, you do absolutely nothing to help.'

Dad has already gone; I see the back of his jacket disappearing out of the door. This is how he has survived all these years of marriage; he knows when to beat a hasty retreat.

'I'll put the glasses ready, Mum,' I offer. 'Do you want me to do anything else to help?' I feel a rush of warmth towards my kind-hearted mother, it is really sweet of her to do all this for our first family dinner with Darcy, especially as she's been flat out all week with mid-term assessments at work.

'If you could do the avocados when they return. I should have cooked a roast instead of trying to be all modern and doing smashed avocado.'

'It'll be lovely when it's done. I'll prepare it when Dad comes back. Everything looks amazing. I just wish Dad hadn't had all that manure delivered yesterday, it might have been better next week.'

'Don't even mention it.'

Oh no, I've got Mum really stressed again, although I can totally see her point. It is a tiny bit embarrassing that my dad has had an entire load of extremely smelly pig manure delivered in our driveway right before Darcy is coming for dinner.

'I told your father that Darcy was coming today and that he should have it delivered next Saturday,' she says tersely. 'He insists I didn't tell him and it's my fault. But I said quite clearly.'

'Selective deafness,' I say philosophically. 'I wouldn't mind normally, it's only I don't think Darcy is very used to manure being kept next to a house and it smells terrible.'

I should mention that my mum and dad are both very keen gardeners but because my dad is extremely frugal, he is always looking out for a good deal on manure, or compost, or building materials, or anything really. It's just his sense of timing is rather out. He wasn't even concerned when I mentioned it to him. 'Darcy won't mind. Show him a bit of real life, make a change from yachts and conferences, stocks and shares. Make a man of him.'

This, rather unsurprisingly, had been small comfort; I don't think Darcy is very keen on the countryside except for walking in it and I suspect his gardeners keep their manure well away from the house.

My phone bings in the arrival of a text.

'Oh good, I hope that's Darcy saying he's going to be late,' Mum says optimistically.

I pick up my phone and read the message.

Sorry Soph, running half an hour late or so, Mum had a couple of business emails she had to action. Won't be long x

Yeah right, on a Sunday morning? I suspect Veronica has been hard at work making sure Darcy is delayed. My mum, however, is extremely grateful for the slight reprieve. 'Thank goodness for that, it buys us a little more time. Can you cut some bread for the avocado toast, Sophie?'

Just over an hour later and we're all sitting round my mum's dining room table, munching beautifully green avocado on perfectly crisp toast, finished with a succulent poached egg and

a small mound of spinach picked fresh from my parents' garden. Darcy would never suspect the chaotic running around his visit had necessitated. It's delicious and I'm gratified by his evident enjoyment of the starter. 'This is quite amazing,' he remarks, munching happily.

'All grown in the garden... apart from the avocado,' my dad says. 'Not sure about this pear business, doesn't taste of much.'

'Phillip.' My mum glares at him reproachfully. I think she was trying to give the impression that we dine on such fare all the time.

'I'd rather have calamares, all this veggie stuff is a bit healthy.' Ben has joined us for lunch along with his latest friend's dog who currently seems to be staying with Mum and Dad. In fact, he is whining away in the kitchen, where my mum has had to shut him in.

I like dogs very much. Although I've never owned one, I desperately wanted a dog as a child, but due to the fact both my parents were always working, I never got very far. I'd have loved a little spaniel, or a Golden Retriever, something soft and cuddly with gorgeous brown eyes. But this dog is nothing like that. It's large and wiry with a horrible long, wet, slimy beard.

He means awfully well and gallumps towards visitors with an air of joie de vivre anyone would be proud of, but he somehow at the same time manages to barge into your legs and wipe his disgusting wet beard all over you and whatever smart clothes you are wearing, leaving a smear of slime mark over the fabric. To be frank, he's a close contender in the revoltingly annoying stakes as Rob Bright. I wonder what happened to Rob? I consider this whilst chomping on my spinach, can he still be trying to find a wife, or maybe Lady Constance has set him up with a suitable young lady?

The dog, Roland I believe, gives a mournful whine, reminiscent of *The Hound of the Baskervilles* and makes us all jump. Darcy starts and nearly drops his knife on the floor; Ben typically carries on eating, totally unfazed.

'Do you like gardening, Mr Darcy?' Mum asks, trying to distract us all from the recalcitrant Roland who we can now hear hacking at the back door with his great heavy paws, with all the delicacy of a stampeding elephant. I frown at her in the hope she won't repeat her error, but Darcy of course, ever the gentleman, ignores her accidental reference to his literary namesake.

'No, not really,' he replies politely. 'But I do like walking in them and admiring the view. Sophie and I often wander round the grounds at Chawton.'

'Yes, it's so beautiful. I was thinking it would be lovely to recreate the old rose gardens there from Jane Austen's time.' I look at Darcy hopefully.

'Did they have roses in Austen's time?' Ben is picking out pieces of avocado and casting them unceremoniously to one side of his plate whilst tucking vociferously into his egg.

'Yes they did.' I glare at him.

'Oh I wasn't sure,' he grins back, 'and was she a real person or a character in a book?'

Darcy looks up from his dinner with amusement at my horrified face.

'If you're not careful, Ben, I'll buy you "Jane Austen for Dummies" for your birthday!' I retort.

'That's a good idea,' Mum says, 'especially as Ben is going to join the agency.'

'I had no idea. Are you a secret fan?' Darcy asks Ben with a smirk.

'Yeah, something like that,' Ben mumbles, attacking his toast with vigour.

'Ben is in need of some decent female company,' Dad remarks cheerfully, wiping his mouth with a napkin, 'preferably someone who isn't already attached.' He continues stabbing at his avocado with his fork as though to emphasise his point, thus totally missing Mum's stony stare, which would frighten most sensitive people at twenty paces.

'I have perfectly good taste in women,' Ben says nonchalantly. 'I can't help it they keep throwing themselves at me.'

'That's what you think,' I retort. 'More like they see you coming.'

Darcy is so polite his mouth only smirks slightly at the corner.

'Has everyone finished?' Mum gamely changes the subject and clears the plates.

'That was very nice,' Darcy says politely, but I think he means it. That's the only thing with Darcy, he's still rather formal and you can never quite read him.

The chicken for the main course is delicious too, my mum is a brilliant cook and we manage to spend most of the meal on safe and polite topics such as the weather, Darcy's business – which I don't think my parents really understand, and rather bizarrely, golf.

'Hope everyone likes Eton mess?' Mum asks and I go to the kitchen to help her serve the pudding. 'So far so good,' she hisses at me as though we are entertaining the Queen herself.

'It's fine. Relax, Mum. This isn't a test,' I say, but actually it does feel a bit like one. It's not Darcy's fault, he's pleasant and polite, but I keep wondering if he's comparing things with his immaculate bachelor flat in the most expensive part of Knightsbridge. To be honest, Darcy's flat is rather a sore point. Veronica constantly refers to it as a *bachelor* flat with an uncannily ridiculous amount of emphasis on the 'bachelor' part mainly to warn me off, but also to highlight the fact he is single and nothing to do with me.

Her other lovely habit is to introduce me to people, if she bothers at all, as Darcy's 'friend', which is totally insulting. It would be nice if I could at least be promoted to girlfriend, obviously I don't expect wife or fiancé or anything majorly serious like that. But to be acknowledged at least would be something. Although maybe not being recognised by Veronica Drummond is a good thing.

Mum comes in with the Eton mess and dishes it out into the best flowery china bowls.

'Do you grow all your own produce?' Darcy is asking politely when suddenly there's an almighty bang which makes us all jump, and the rampant dog, now even more enthused than ever, as he has been so cooped up, barges into the room at a hundred miles an hour and with one great bound leaps with the full force of his heavy hairy paws onto Darcy's immaculate suit.

Darcy tries to grab at his dessert bowl in vain as it follows its inevitable downward trajectory, to fall upside down on his lap. I'm stuck between complete and utter horror and an overwhelming desire to laugh hysterically.

Ben and my dad have no such self-control and are lost in helpless laughter, so only my mum is left to grab the bowl from Darcy's lap, in total embarrassment, apologising profusely as she has to gingerly scrape the contents of cream, squashed in bits of meringue and strawberries, from his previously pristine trousers.

Darcy takes it all in his stride but I can tell he is not used to having dessert poured over his clothes, by his slightly harassed expression, and stilted murmured assurance to my mum that it's all fine really.

'Ben, get that hairy creature out of here.' Mum shoots him a glare that requires instant obedience. You can tell she's only holding in any last remnants of self-control due to Darcy's presence.

Ben gets up with a sigh, as though the party is over. 'Roland, come here, come on, old boy.'

Roland however has really got the wind up him now and has absolutely no intention of being incarcerated back in the utility room, so promptly proceeds to run round the dining room table, neatly managing to pilfer a spare meringue nest which was hovering delicately on the edge and at the same time upending a glass of red wine which teeters precariously and deposits most of its contents on my dad's trousers.

Dad no longer sees the funny side of things and is blaspheming irreverently whilst trying to swat at Roland with a napkin. Roland, thinking this is all part of the game, plants both his feet on Dad's shoulders, effectively pinning him to the chair. Darcy looks completely nonplussed by the whole scene of all of us trying to guide the rambunctious dog back under some sort of control. My Mother, who has been a primary school teacher for long enough to know how to manage most eventualities, waves a nearby copy of *The Daily Mail* in the vicinity of the dog, who sensibly admits defeat and retreats obediently, stubby little tail between his legs, into the utility room.

'Do you like dogs, Darcy?' she asks casually, whilst giving him yet another damp cloth to wipe his trousers and ordering my father with a look, to get himself upstairs and change his wine sodden clothes.

'Erm, yes,' he says, 'my mother has a Pomeranian, but I like big dogs, although that one is a little lively.'

'Yeah, sorry about that,' Ben says glibly, he has barely left eating his pudding in all the chaos. 'Can I have some more Eton mess, Mum?'

Thank goodness, the rest of the afternoon goes without a hitch and I sort of feel we might have got away with things with Darcy. At least he is polite enough not to comment. That is until my dad, in freshly changed clothes, appears at the door.

'Phillip, what are you doing in those horrible old trousers?'

'I just need to shift the manure, dear,' he says from behind the safety of the door.

'Not now, dear, *pas devant les invités*.'

'Pardon?'

'Can't it wait until another day?' She gives him the kind of warning look that any of the rest of us normal human beings would appreciate is best to take note of.

But my dad as always is oblivious. 'No it can't, we have rain forecast for tomorrow and I spent £90 on that lot. In fact, it would be a lot quicker if someone could give me a hand?' He eyes Darcy hopefully, who is sitting still smart and smoulderingly handsome as ever on my mum and dad's old sofa.

'What do you need help with?' Darcy asks. 'I'm happy to do some lifting, I spend a lot of time fencing, so I have muscles.' I can vouch for that, he has a nicely toned physique.

'Don't think we need any fighting, but lifting would be great. Come on, Ben, no slacking,' my dad shouts up the stairs.

'I need to walk the dog!' Ben shouts down.

'He can wait until you've finished helping out.'

Before my mum or I have a chance to protest, my ever-resourceful dad has Darcy Drummond shovelling pig poo from the driveway into a bag, in his now slightly brown-stained Alexander McQueen trousers, and I don't think I'll ever be able to look him in the face again.

CHAPTER 7

'What sort of evening is this?' Ben asks looking around him with evident distaste, although the gardens are looking incredible, with tiny lanterns illuminating beautifully decorated booths.

'It's the kind of night out you're going to get if you belong to a Regency dating agency,' I mutter whilst smiling politely at a passing lady, handing her a drink of ratafia.

It was my idea to have a Regency speed-dating event, with the surroundings based on an evening at Vauxhall Pleasure Gardens. The history of these gardens has always fascinated me, ever since our long caravan journeys abroad as a child. Our old car was without air conditioning and the journeys through the dusty long French endless roads would have been unbearable had it not been for my dad's bright idea to borrow an audiobook from the library on the history of Vauxhall Gardens. Might have sounded a bit of a bore to the average teenager but for me, it was fascinatingly reminiscent of all the bodice ripping Georgette Heyer books I lapped up delightedly. Georgette Heyer's romances were like old friends, to whom I'd go when I was a little down or unsure of myself. *These Old Shades, The Grand*

Sophy, *Friday's Child* – all delightful romps through the happy world of Regency romance.

The paths of Vauxhall Gardens were notorious for romantic assignations and I had some crazy notion we could somehow recreate this. Emma and I painstakingly illuminated the walkways and bushes with lanterns and fairy lights, and the booths have paintings by Canaletto, prints of course, carefully hung on the walls.

I have to say I am pretty pleased with the effect we have achieved, even though I say so myself, and I make a mental note to suggest to Emma that we could do this again, but as a masked ball.

At least this project has taken my mind off the recent disaster of Darcy's visit to my parents' house. It was quite frankly one of the most embarrassing moments of my life and there have been quite a few of them. Of course I apologised after and he seemed fine on our date last night, but I can hardly bear to think of it.

'Good evening!' I am addressed by a gangly and rather goofy-looking young man with very slightly protruding teeth and a mop of ginger curls. 'This must be your charming sister you have been telling me about, Ben?'

'Yep, this is Sophie. Sophie, this is my friend, John.'

'Nice to meet you,' I say distractedly, horrified by the fact he has taken my hand and noisily kissed it with great aplomb.

'I have heard so much about you,' John waffles, but I can't take him seriously because his manner is so over the top and I wonder if he is being sarcastic. Being a friend of my brother's, he probably is.

'All of it hideous of course.' Ben snorts. 'John is Roland's owner.'

'Roland, the dog who jumped all over my boyfriend and trashed his trousers,' I say, glaring at John over the tray of drinks.

He helps himself, completely unabashed, and downs most of

the glass in one gulp. 'Yeah he's a real character, Roly, wouldn't have meant any harm though, he's just one big cuddly teddy bear.'

'A rather hairy, unpleasant and wet teddy bear,' I say drily.

Thank goodness, just at that moment, I'm rescued by a voice I seem to recognise from somewhere but can't remember where. 'Sophie, isn't it?'

I turn to see a young girl with a lovely smile. 'Freya, so good to see you.' Behind her is Edward, looking a little reticent as always. He shakes my hand and smiles but my eye is drawn to a couple of extremely elegant women at his side. They have got to be related, as they look so similar in spite of one having a flaming head of auburn hair tumbling down in a mass of curls and the other being brunette.

'Hello, Sophie.' Freya smiles shyly but then goes quiet leaving Edward to introduce his sisters.

'This is Amelia and Caitlin,' he says indicating politely to the young women. I would say they are in their early twenties, but are pretty sophisticated and apparently unimpressed with their surroundings. They murmur something at me vaguely, but their eyes are soon flicking around the gardens to suss out the competition, I rather suspect.

'Come on in, everyone. Do have a glass of ratafia.'

'Ratafia,' retorts the brunette, who I think is Amelia. 'Isn't there any champagne?'

'You could have had champagne at home,' Edward remarks drily, passing both women a glass. 'Cheers!' he says, taking a sip. 'It's not bad actually.'

'I should say so.' John, who unfortunately hasn't gone very far away at all, grabs a second glass from the tray, whilst giving a lascivious look at my cleavage.

'Do go and mingle. There are lots of new people here this evening,' I say politely.

'If you insist.' He sweeps the room with his beady eyes. 'Come on, Ben, there's some likely looking candidates over here.' He grabs my brother's arm and drags him off in the direction of an archway where some young women are dancing near the quartet in the corner.

Edward and his little party have wandered on into the floodlit walkway and left me to greet the last few newcomers. 'Is that everyone on the list?' asks Emma, who has been meeting and greeting the little gaggle of newbies.

'Yes except the Baroness Mayer,' I say, consulting my gold-embossed notebook. I have a real thing for notebooks and stationery at the moment. I think I must be a compulsive collector, every time I go to a shop I always seem to find a new one for something or other. Paperchase is currently a banned shop – Mel has forbidden me from going there as she says I won't have enough money for the next rent. Each and every notebook has to be exactly right for the sort of material I want to put in it. It's not just notebooks either; I adore brightly coloured pens, Post-it notes, highlighters and stickers.

'Oh, didn't I tell you? She's not coming, she has an appointment with the Shah of Persia.'

'Fair enough, I've been stood up for less reason.' I smile.

'Time to mingle.' Emma claps her hands. 'Can I have your attention, everybody? Okay, so for this Regency speed-dating night, we are swapping tables, having five minutes with each person to discuss genteel topics only. Each time a person should change, I shall ring this little bell, and I would like all the men to move to the right please. If at the end of the evening there is someone you would like to get to know a little better, you each have an embossed card, your calling card, on which you should write your name and phone number and your reason for the invitation, polite ones only please, this is the Regency era.'

There's a murmur of laughter and raised eyebrows as several

people, most notably Amelia and Caitlin, exchange sardonic glances. I'm not at all sure about those two.

Thank goodness, as host and Darcy's girlfriend, I get to meander around the paths supervising rather than mixing with perspective beaus.

I am quite pleased that we have a few eligible dates tonight, thanks to a sudden small flurry of young men. I notice for her first date, Freya has been placed with John Smith, not a good match at all. She looks terrified and he appears thoroughly bored, meeting my eye to raise his alarmingly bushy eyebrows and giving me a flirty look. I was hoping Darcy had broken my lifelong run of bad luck attracting complete and utter weirdos. Obviously not.

Ben has been matched with an attractive and bubbly blonde, her hair is almost white; it's so fair, really striking. I wonder if it's natural, she also has attractively scattered freckles, a honeyed brown tan and a very low-cut top. They seem to be hitting it off quite well and are soon laughing about something. At least she's single; or rather I hope she is.

Edward is chatting animatedly to a tall, elegant lady with a chignon and a nice smile, but I think she is far too old for him. Never mind, at least he looks happy. She might do for Sir Henry Greaves, who I catch sight of in a booth with some poor young woman I don't recognise.

I watch the Regency clock and wonder what Darcy is up to. At our date last night he had suggested we could take our Paris weekend trip in a couple of weeks and I feel ridiculously excited at the very thought. The Champs-Élysées with Darcy, Lacoste shirts, buying knicks in Le Petit Bateau and perhaps a racy little number at Yves St Laurent. Not that I could afford any of those. I wonder idly if he might buy me some designer clothes, but then remember with distaste our recent shopping trip in Knightsbridge with his mother. She bought herself vast amounts of various high fashion labels, Darcy purchased two pairs of designer shoes, and I ended up carefully examining various pricey items and putting them down again quickly as they were so expensive they felt as though they might burn my fingers.

At least if we go to Paris, Veronica would most definitely not be coming along.

'Sophie?' Emma disturbs my thoughts, she has her phone tucked under her ear and is clutching the small silver bell. 'You couldn't take over for me for a mo, could you? My father is having an existential crisis and I need to sort it out.'

'Okay.' I reluctantly take the bell, about to ask her how long is left, but she's already whizzed off remarkably quickly considering the height of her Louboutins. I gaze after her enviously, that girl has such style. I'm amazed she's not already been snapped up by some wealthy English lord by now. I meander round the avenue of booths, hoping everyone is getting on okay. They all seem to be coping; I give it another couple of minutes, then ring the bell.

'Okay then, everyone, time's up. Hope you enjoyed your little chat. It's now time for the men to move to your right, to the next partner.'

Amongst much chatter and banter, everyone appears to know where they are going. Everyone, that is, except Sir Henry Greaves. Of course, it would be him.

'Absolute shambles this, how in Jupiter am I supposed to know where I am going?' he grumbles.

'You move to your right, Sir Henry,' I say politely, gesturing with my right hand for emphasis.

'Quite ridiculous,' he says loudly, 'five minutes is barely long enough to boil an egg, let alone find out what someone does for a job or their position in life.'

'This is only a taster session, Sir Henry. If you like the

person, you can always request to see them again,' I say patiently.

'Utter rot,' he mutters, plonking himself down opposite Amelia who looks suitably disgusted with her proposed match. 'And who are you, m'dear?' he asks.

'I am Lady Amelia Smetherton – Lord Smetherton's daughter,' she says regally.

'Not the Chumley Smethertons?'

'The very same,' she says with a bored expression.

He visibly perks himself up, his back ramrod straight in his seat. 'I do beg your pardon, m'dear, terribly confused by the set up y'know, but anyway, ahem, delighted to make your acquaintance – used to be at Eton with your father, y'know.'

'Really?' she asks, totally disinterested.

I smile inwardly and meander on. Sir Henry was one of the clients who seemed to be my lot in life for the first few social events when I joined the agency and obviously due to my lack of fortune or title, I was not even worthy of his notice. I'm just sorry Lady Constance is no longer a member of the agency – she is the most perfect match for him, whatever she thinks. His daughter, Maria, is sadly unable to come tonight as she is getting married in a couple of months to her old flame, the lovely Charles and, after all, this is a singles night. I really miss the old gang, Izzy and Matthew as well, but they're coming to the Chawton Ball in a few weeks' time. It will be such a lovely reunion.

I am disturbed from my progress by a hale and hearty shout from the arch at the entrance to the gardens, 'Halloo? Miss Woodtree?'

I turn to be confronted by a larger than life, rather rotund character who looks a little like Billy Bunter crossed with Giant Haystacks, though rather smarter dressed than both of those redoubtable people. I hastily feel in my pocket for my list, I was sure all were present and correct other than the Baroness, but in spite of my uncertainty I rush to greet the newcomer as politely as possible.

'Good evening, Mr... er?'

'Lord Bamford, at your service, madam.' He gives a sweeping bow, which is all the more incongruous as he struggles to even bend slightly due to his rather tight waistcoat. I want to giggle as the buttons look fit to burst and I have an image of them pinging off one by one across the room like tiny fireworks. 'You must be Miss Woodtree.'

'No, I'm Miss Johnson. Pleased to meet you, Lord Bamford. Do come and have a glass of ratafia and join the throng.' I still feel at a complete and utter loss. How did he get omitted from the guest list? But seeing as he is a lord I guess we had better overlook this for once.

Lord Bamford trips along remarkably lightly for his size. 'I was so sorry to be late,' he bumbles, 'but Mummy would insist on my staying to talk to the butler about the arrangements for tomorrow's garden party.'

'Yes of course,' I say vaguely. Not another guy who calls his mother Mummy, I desperately try to consider who I should introduce him to, as he is like a rather overenthusiastic puppy and not exactly to many of the ladies' taste.

He follows me across to the nearest booth, which unfortunately is occupied by Amelia and a callow-looking youth, with rather protruding eyes, not unlike a codfish. I make as though to move on, but she calls to me, 'Miss Johnson, isn't it time we changed round?'

I look at the clock in the courtyard. 'Oh gosh, yes,' I ring the tinkly bell, 'everyone change round please – to the booth to your right again.'

'I don't appear to have a partner,' Amelia coos, looking at Lord Bamford speculatively.

'My chart says you would be moving on to Ben?' I say, as my

brother appears to be in the next booth, and I have quickly consulted my list.

'You are mistaken,' Amelia says primly. Hmm, I might have known Ben wouldn't be good enough for her but she's not his type anyway. 'I'm more than happy to make the acquaintance of this gentleman.' She lowers her eyes, having given Bamford a belting look and then gazes down again in mock piety. Wow – I need to take lessons from this girl. Although I'm torn between irritation at the way she has totally subverted my organisation and admiration of the ease with which she manipulates everyone around her.

'Goodness, yes, I mean...' Oh great, Lord Bamford is totally socially inept, with women anyway.

'Lord Bamford, this is Amelia Chumley Smetherton,' I say smoothly. In fact I'm quite proud of myself as it's a terrible mouthful really and actually the ratafia is rather stronger than I thought. Surprisingly the Regency drink reminds me of alcopops which, I believe since my misspent youth, were banned for the simple reason that they tasted like lemonade and slip down ever so easily and then after a couple of bottles you wondered why the dance floor seemed to be spinning faster than you were. Not a good thing.

I needn't have worried; Lord Bamford has seated himself opposite Amelia, who is doing a remarkably good job of looking as though she is interested in his every word. Strange, there's no way she can be attracted to him, but I guess they're an eligible match when it comes to title. For goodness' sake, has anything changed in the two hundred years since Jane Austen's birth? Obviously not.

CHAPTER 8

The evening seems to be going amazingly well and I wish Darcy were here to see it. The fairy lights twinkling from the vine-entwined booths add a magical touch and the air is vibrant, I can almost imagine the intrigues, the liaisons going on between new couples. I pass Edward, who is chatting away animatedly to an incredibly elegant woman with long raven curly hair piled high on her head. 'I learnt to play the harp at the Royal Academy of Music,' she is saying.

'I would love to hear you play more than anything,' he murmurs, and she smiles coquettishly.

'You will have to mark my name on your card then,' she says with a smile.

Another success story there in the making, I hope. Poor little Freya doesn't seem comfortable in her match, she's moved on from John Smith to my brother, Ben, and he's not even really bothering to talk to her, being rather more interested in the blonde who is giving him surreptitious peeks from under her suspiciously long and dark lashes whilst at the same time appearing to be listening to her partner, the googly-faced lad who had been with Amelia. She is totally out of Ben's league, he's wasting his time there.

'How's it going then?' Emma asks, bustling into the scene with her usual businesslike and assured approach. I'm glad she's returned, it makes me feel as though I have backup somehow, although I'm not quite sure what's going to happen on a Regency speed-dating night, but we don't want any drunken brawls. With my brother and his friend, John, in the vicinity, you never know. I remember their probably-much-exaggerated stories of their uni antics.

'Great,' I say, 'everyone seems happy and there appear to be some who are getting on really well.' I motion over to Amelia and Lord Bamford.

'Isn't that Lord Bamford?' Emma exclaims.

'Apparently.' We are interrupted by a raucously loud laugh; honestly his normal volume is as amplified as though he were on a loudspeaker.

'I'm not surprised he's here,' she says, 'his mother is desperate to get him married off. Who's that he's with?'

'Amelia Chumley Smetherton,' I say blandly.

'His mother will be pleased with that idea. She's determined on an advantageous match and I believe there's only a handful of women she feels might even be vaguely worthy of him.'

'He's certainly a bit of a character.'

Emma agrees with a smile as another blast of his voluminous talk deafens us again and all the other guests look over their shoulders at him. She puts her mouth to my ear. 'Rumour has it, he's actually gay, but his mother won't hear of it.'

'That's terrible.' Oops, that came out rather too loudly, I lower my tone. 'But surely he needs to put his foot down.'

'Mummy wants an heir and what Mummy wants, she gets.'

'Surely there are other ways these days, she has to accept it.'

'You've got to be joking, have you ever met the Marquess of Bamford?'

'No, funnily enough, I haven't.'

'A redoubtable woman.' Emma whips out her phone and brings up an image, which she shows me surreptitiously from behind the screen of a hedge.

'My God, she looks like a battleship with a tent on top.'

'Shh, she's one scary woman and makes Lady Constance look like a pussycat.'

'How do you know all these things, Emma?'

'Public school is a complete social education in itself.'

'How I have missed out,' I say, then smile. 'This is a whole new world and I thought I was escaping that, running away from Modiste.'

'Ha, this country is constructed of an entire class system as hierarchical as it ever was. Don't tell me within fifteen seconds of meeting someone, you aren't able to tell me their background, status and income.'

'I wouldn't really...' I flounder, as I feel out of my depth in this conversation. 'Anyway, how's your dad, is everything okay?'

'My father,' Emma rolls her eyes, 'is a complete and utter nightmare. He has pains in his stomach and is worried it might be his gallbladder.'

'How dreadful. Has he seen a doctor?'

'Sophie, my father has seen every doctor in this world and every quack, fake physician and scammer there is.'

'It sounds like he really has a problem then.'

'Yes, he has. He's the world's greatest hypochondriac.'

'Surely not.' I'm a bit shocked, Emma's father is quite an important man.

'He absolutely is. From a very young child a whole section of my father's library was taken up with great dusty medical tomes. He read them constantly and if any of us children were ill, they were the first thing he consulted. He marked out most of the diseases in there with comments on his symptoms, and even the things only women could get, he had a male version.'

I subdue an overwhelming urge to giggle. 'That is unfortunate.'

'Not as unfortunate as it is with the advent of social media, just think what he now imagines he has. Google is like a hypochondriac's crack cocaine.'

I don't need to; I've been guilty of looking up symptoms to an ailment on Google and it's a very bad idea. You're definitely at risk of having something incredibly serious or reading about someone who had the same symptoms and it turns out to be something dreadful. I've actually banned myself from Google, on my sister's advice, as it is a little addictive. And I've found myself googling all sorts of strange questions, like 'does your boyfriend like you even if his mother doesn't?' and 'how to feel more confident at social occasions' and 'what would have happened if Jane Austen had married Harris Bigg Wither?'

(It's no good, his name still makes me laugh – I'm sorry, Harris, you sounded a perfectly nice man too.) Worse still, I get totally caught up reading the answers and have had to give myself limits on how much time I spend on social media because you can end up sitting there staring at a blank screen for hours without even realising it when you could be doing all sorts of useful things like learning an instrument or Greek or something like that. Google has become the person you ask anything at all or maybe that's just me. But not any more. No more Google for me, well not for a while anyway until I cave in again.

'So do you think it's going well?' Emma asks me, her eagle eyes darting here, there and everywhere.

'I think it's quite successful for some of the guests so far, the two we have mentioned. Edward, the new guy, has someone he seems to be getting on very well with.'

'Oh yes, Miss Foxton, she's bubbly and very amusing. I would have thought she was a bit too much for him but they seem to be chatting away happily.'

Edward is sitting forward in his chair, his entire posture pointing towards Miss Foxton who is holding forth about her recent holiday in France. I feel a pang of envy. With her outfit and absolute assurance, she is one of those people who knows exactly what she is doing in any given situation.

'Stop it, Sophie,' Emma remonstrates with me. 'I'll set Mel on you.'

'I don't know what you mean.'

'Yes you do, I can sense you feeling all inadequate again. No one can make you feel inferior without your permission.'

I laugh. 'Whoever wrote that had never met Lady Constance.'

Emma snorts. 'But you need to listen to it, sweetie. You're dating Darcy!'

'Yes and hopefully going to Paris soon,' I say dreamily. 'And how about you, is there anyone here who catches your eye?'

'No. No one has ever been able to tempt me enough to give up my independence. I like my own space, can't possibly imagine ever having to put up with anyone's tantrums other than my own.'

I glance at her amused; I'm not at all convinced but assume it is because she hasn't met the right person yet. 'What about that chap, James, who was at the Regency Ball?'

'No, he's just a friend.' She laughs. 'We've known each other forever, ooh no that would be simply wrong.'

I shake my head, still puzzled, Emma is so lovely, but perhaps she is super-picky.

'What about Mel? Are we going to be able to persuade her to rejoin the agency again, do you think?'

'Not a chance with this vegan business going on.'

'Yes, it is a shame, as a vegetarian she was still fun, but this activism she's into is a bit worrying,' Emma says.

'I know, she's managed to force me into going to one of her protests soon,' I lament.

'You at a vegan protest march. Please tell me you're joking, Sophie, you're not even vegan.'

'I know, I did say to Mel that I'm not eligible. In fact, I'm positively underqualified for the job, but she won't hear of it.'

'But, Sophie, this could be an absolute disaster, you know the sort of people who get mixed up in these things.' Emma is serious and has one of her 'don't mess with me, I mean business kind' of looks.

'I know but it's about climate change too and that's really important.' It is as well, I read an article on the disappearing ice caps the other day and felt nearly as stressed about it as Mel. We all have to try to do something about it before it's too late. 'I'll just lurk on the sidelines, it'll be fine.' I think I'm trying to convince myself rather than anyone else.

'I'm sure the sentiment is valid, we all care about the future of the planet, but I don't want you getting mixed up in any trouble. I think you should get out of it if you can.' Emma firmly fixes me with a steely gaze.

Fortunately we are disturbed by a gust of laughter from a nearby booth, 'Ooh, Ben, you are *hilarious*,' squeals the blonde, whose top has, if it is at all possible, gone even lower, showing rather a lot of her creamy white chest. Ben has his arm around her and looks as though all his Christmases have come at once.

'More beer please, milady, and some for my girlfriend.' He peers at me squiffily, whilst tapping his glass with his finger.

I meander over to him as casually as I can, whilst in reality hurrying before Emma or some of our more salubrious guests notice.

'Ben,' I hiss under cover of removing his drink, 'this is my work, it's unfair of you to embarrass me.'

'Oh Bennywenny isn't embarrassing, is he?' simpers the blonde whilst spilling her own drink down her front, which Ben is only too happy to dab with his napkin.

I knew this was a really bad idea, Ben joining the agency. I'd tell my mum but she won't hear of her son being such a pain in public, she'd think I was exaggerating. I look about for John, who I hope might be a little supportive; he's in a raucous-sounding conversation with a lady in his own booth so no hope there.

'No more beer until you've eaten something else,' I say firmly.

'We'd love another helping of that sliced beef,' Ben says. 'The last one wasn't that big and I'm still hungry.'

'Okay, I'll ask the staff to bring you some,' I say as politely as I can, 'and I'll get you a jug of water.'

'Thank you. That would be lovely,' his companion lisps with a friendly smile. Okay, so maybe she's not so bad after all, and Ben does have a habit of bringing the worst out in people.

As I wander the path back to the kitchens, I notice there are rather too many women still without partners who are having a pleasant little chat together, but I'm worried this isn't what we are aiming for. We desperately need to find a way to attract more young men to these events.

The rest of the evening passes without much incident and I think in spite of the slight imbalance of men and women it was enjoyed by all.

'I hope you had a good evening?' I ask Freya anxiously.

'Oh yes. I love reading about Vauxhall Gardens and to have it recreated like this is magical. Did you know they would have had exactly the dishes you served here?'

'Yes I did some research before we started but was worried it might not be what people might expect.' I was quite pleased with myself.

'I'm glad the toilets weren't authentic,' Edward laughs, 'or some of the gambling.'

'No, I believe there were some dodgy goings on in the bushes in Regency times.' Freya smiles.

'Hopefully we managed to avoid any of those,' I say, giving my brother and his blonde friend a baleful stare. I guess they are only messing around and have managed to control themselves for most of the time.

'It was an extremely enjoyable evening.' Edward politely shakes my hand.

'It was,' Freya says. I catch her glance up at her step-cousin and I wonder for a moment, I could have sworn I saw a look, one that I recognised, but within moments it had gone and perhaps I imagined it. It certainly vanished as Miss Foxton appeared.

'Miss Foxton.' Edward drops my hand immediately.

'Edward, what a pleasant evening. I did so enjoy our conversation.'

'To be continued, I hope,' he says gallantly, fervently looking at her face.

I can't help but glance back at Freya who is apparently fiddling with her tiny bag, covered in beaded butterflies. It's gorgeous actually.

'Soph,' my brother comes blundering up, the blonde girl on his arm, 'John's looking for you to say goodbye.'

'I'm here,' I say exasperated.

'So you are. Thanks for a lovely evening, sis.' Ben gives me a beery kiss on the cheek.

'Yes, I actually enjoyed it,' the blonde girl says, sounding surprised, 'such a laugh.'

John Smith approaches at comical speed. 'Miss Johnson, Sophie,' he bends and kisses my hand noisily, 'would have liked a good old yarn with you. Maybe next time or better still, a bit of a boogie?' He looks at me hopefully. Has no one told him I'm with Darcy?

'Maybe,' I murmur, thinking, *not if I see you first*.

'Jolly good night,' Ben slurs, just as Amelia and Lord Bamford are approaching, and I try to usher them out of the door quickly. 'But it would be a damn sight more fun if we had a bit of sport or something next time, eh, Soph?'

Hmm, now that is a thought, Regency Sport – miracle of all miracles, I think my brother might actually be onto something.

CHAPTER 9

'*A*h, Miss Johnson, there you are!'

'Good afternoon, Baroness.' Hah! No more bowing and curtseying, merely a sensible handshake, I'm doing much better this time. Perhaps it was the Baroness's luxurious house that made me so nervous.

Rodrigo is following behind with his dark sunglasses. Why is it that security men always wear those? Do they think no one will recognise them behind a pair of shades, because I think I still would even if I met him without them, although I guess I wouldn't know what colour his eyes are. I can't make up my mind whether I should say hello, or ignore him in a casual way, as he is merely 'staff' – I don't want to put my foot in it with the Baroness. I content myself instead with an apologetic smile.

The Baroness Mayer, businesslike as ever, is oblivious to my dilemma. 'Shall we walk this path?' she asks, but like everything else she utters, it is a command, though politely put.

'Of course. It's a lovely day, isn't it?' I burble as we follow the gravel path through St James' Park. Rodrigo follows at a polite distance, but I can't help wanting to smile about it, or half hope for there to be a minor breach of security simply to see what he does.

'I believed it was nicer for us to meet for a walk, the house can be so formal sometimes,' she says.

'Yes I agree, I like the fresh air too and this is a lovely park.'

'Miss Johnson, I will be quite frank with you, I have not much time, as I have another meeting in the diary after this, but I am aware you are needing more information in order for me to join in events at your Regency agency.'

She pronounces Regency, with such a rolled 'r' that it somehow manages to sound super formal and actually slightly sinister.

'Yes of course.' I mentally run down the list of things I had prepared to ask her.

'Do you have an ideal man in mind?' I don't want to offend her, but I can't see her with anyone less than a very diffident and easily managed individual. Anyone dictatorial would instantly fail with this strong, independent matriarch.

'I will tell you something, Sophie,' she glances at me discerningly, 'you are young yet and inexperienced. You have your whole life ahead of you and a lot to learn.'

'But–'

The Baroness motions for me to be silent. I must not butt in; I do have a terrible habit of interrupting people before they've finished speaking. It's only because I am enthusiastic but it's not a good thing.

That along with finishing sentences, when people are slower than me. I'm trying to be better about it ever since I had a work colleague who once completely blasted me for it. She was one of the slowest talkers I'd ever met, she was so deliberate and I thought I was being helpful, finishing her sentences for her, finding the words she was obviously struggling to retrieve. How wrong can you be? Very wrong it turned out. It was the end of a lovely relationship. During a meeting when I had obviously finished her sentence one time too many, she'd turned to me and said, 'Sophie, can you please stop pre-empting what I'm going to say?'

I was kind of shocked and had immediately stammered, 'I'm so sorry, I really didn't mean to.'

And that would have been the end of it and we could have stayed friends had she not continued to annihilate me for an entire half of an hour. I had obviously really got on this poor woman's wick. She had gone on about it for a further ten minutes without stopping (probably too scared I would interrupt again). But ever since I have tried to be aware of this habit and be more patient.

Obviously not that well though as Darcy had brought it up a couple of weeks ago. 'You have two ears and one mouth for a reason,' he had said.

'Oh?'

'Yes, that means you need to listen to people, especially at social occasions, people want to talk about themselves, you need to let them.'

'But I do let them,' I had said indignantly, 'I like people talking about themselves and hearing about things they are interested in.'

'You do, but you have a habit of interrupting and it's best not at society events, it is better to speak little and listen more, especially if you're not used to such things and aren't sure of the etiquette.'

'You mean I should be seen and not heard,' I had muttered.

'Not at all, everyone finds you charming,' he had given me a little kiss on the nose, 'but you will always have those who will criticise and be looking for a reason to be rude about or exclude you.'

I was annoyed with him and a little hurt at first, but then as I try to be fair, I had a think about it and realised that I do get overenthusiastic sometimes and perhaps need to be a little less like a waggy-tailed puppy. Might make me a little less vulnerable I suppose to the criticism of others. So with the Baroness, I am on my very best behaviour.

'You have very little knowledge of the world,' she continues, 'you have been gently brought up, in a nice loving family and you can have no idea as yet of true love.'

I open my mouth to speak of Darcy, then think better of it and shut it again.

'My husband was the real thing,' she says after a silence.

I watch a nearby white dove flutter from a tree and into the blue sky high above the spires of the nearby dome of the military school.

'I adored him.' She stops to one side as a group of impeccably groomed, shiny-coated horses jog by, their breath coming in clouds in the cold air, the smart buckled guards mounted on them, expressionless.

'He was quite simply the one.'

I could imagine this, from her face when looking at the photograph on the table when I had first met her. I stay silent, partly because I'm unsure what to say, I can hardly comment that she will meet someone the same if he was the love of her life.

'Yet he was also probably one of the cruellest people I have ever met.'

I'm confused but keep my head down, silent. The Baroness appears to be gazing out over the lake where the birds are all fighting for crumbs from passers-by. A child stumbles over backwards as a swan gets too close for comfort and she starts to wail from her lowly position on the ground.

'You have no idea, Sophie.' The Baroness sighs and peers at me with her intense gaze. 'You and your seaside town, your agency, your happy place. You have no idea of "les mains sales", which have dogged my life. You have to play the game you see and then just when you think you are winning, you have nothing. You think I am rich, yes I am as rich as Croesus but at what cost.' She sighs and says half to herself, 'I don't even really know why I am telling you all this, I barely even know you.'

I smile lamely. 'My friends at uni said I should be a counsellor; people tend to tell me their problems. It's one of my skills, that and picking up losers.'

The Baroness gives a sudden shrill laugh, so out of keeping with her image, it makes me jump.

'I don't mean you, I...'

'I know what you mean, Sophie, and I'll tell you why people confide in you, it's because you are honest, and honesty is a rare occurrence indeed in this squalid world of vice and crime. Anyway, I digress.' She gives herself a little shake. 'I don't have a list of requests but I would simply ask you to find me someone kind.'

'Kind?' The way she put it makes it sound an almost-impossible task. Perhaps it is if you are obscenely wealthy, maybe everyone merely wants to be with you because of your money, you can't tell who likes you for being you. 'I don't think that will be too difficult,' I say cheerily.

The Baroness smiles and pats my hand. 'You are ever the optimist. Try to stay that way, my dear. Don't let the group you are mixing with taint your happiness. Don't become one of them.'

'One of who, or maybe that should be whom?' I ask, confused, but the Baroness looks at her watch and exclaims at the time.

She extends her hand formally. 'Duty calls as ever.' Her countenance returns to its original mask-like expression, the traces of a smile have faded into its habitual lines of hardship and her narrow face looks troubled once more. 'I have very much enjoyed our meeting, Sophie, thank you.'

'No problem,' I say politely, 'any time.'

I watch her tiny, but irrepressibly upright figure, dwarfed by the bulk of the bodyguard next to her, disappearing back to her luxurious mansion at Kensington Palace Gardens. After our conversation however, it seems little more than a gilded cage. I wonder what her history is. Was her husband a criminal? Who were they and how did they get such a vast amount of money? Having to walk around with a bodyguard constantly with you like that, had they done something very terrible? I give myself a little shake. My imagination is rather inclined to run away with me and I have got to the creepiest part of *Gone Girl*, it is keeping me awake at night, but I just can't put it down.

Back at the office, Emma is looking gorgeous in a new pink and white floral Yves St Laurent top. 'Wow, you look stunning,' I say.

'Thanks.' She smiles. 'Last night was a great success, wasn't it? So I thought I'd treat myself.'

'Yes it was, other than my brother being a little embarrassing.'

'He wasn't too bad, I've seen far worse!'

'His idea was quite a good one, don't you think, not that he really thought it through, but what do you think about Regency sports events?'

Emma ponders for a moment, the end of her sparkly Swarovski pen twinkling in the sleepy sunlight, reflecting through the diamond-paned window. It refracts into a million tiny crystal lights revolving around the walls and ceiling. I watch them fascinated. 'Do you know, I think it might work. What sports do you have in mind?' she asks.

'You know how I am on historical research.'

'Yes, a bit of a nerd!'

'Okay, anyway, I was thinking the first event could be archery, then maybe going on to some other sports such as clay pigeon shooting. We don't want to hurt any animals.'

'The real thing might be better,' Emma ponders. 'Remember, we are dealing with people of a certain class and they are going to want to act like Regency gentlemen.'

'Not my thing really, shooting birds,' I say, thinking with dread of Mel's potential response, as well as my own dislike of harming any feathered or furry creature.

'Happens all the time in the country,' Emma says dismissively.

'I guess.' We can argue about that little detail later. 'Anyway, what do you think about the archery?'

'I was wondering about Grensham Hall for the archery shoot? We have extensive grounds.'

'And people who have extensive grounds themselves are always pleased with anything in the same style,' I quote.

Emma laughs. 'Yes, Mrs Elton.'

'It's a great idea. Do you think your dad would mind?' Grensham Hall is Emma's father's country estate, which I would love to visit.

'No, he'd enjoy it, although,' Emma considers a moment, 'he's not always good with people he doesn't know, but I'm sure he'll be fine.'

'If not, we could go to Lutterworth House?'

'I'd like to do it at Grensham if we can; the grounds are so much nicer. How did you get on with the Baroness?'

'Fine, but all she can say she wants in a partner is kindness.'

'That should be easy,' Emma remarks, 'if only all our clients were so unexacting.'

'I guess, but surely you would think she would like someone

with specific characteristics, I don't know what, but like short hair, enjoys opera or something like that?'

'Not necessarily, maybe she wants a surprise?'

'I don't know, I think there's something strange about that husband of hers.'

'Ooh a mystery, how thrilling, do tell.'

'There's nothing to say yet, but there is definitely a backstory to the Baroness Mayer and I want to find out exactly what it is.' Speaking of mystery, I still haven't told Emma about the creepy incident upstairs the other day with the window. I hadn't mentioned it as she would have laughed at my overactive imagination and I must admit, I figured it was probably just the wind. When I had popped upstairs to grab some books the next morning however, I noticed something really disturbing. The edition of *Northanger Abbey* and *Persuasion* was on the floor again in exactly the same position as the night before, the pages open as though someone had been reading it. Most odd.

Emma continues to talk, breaking into my uncomfortable thoughts. 'Speaking of which, did you tell Mel that you aren't doing the activist protest with her?'

'Not yet,' I say casually, 'but I will, when the time is right.'

'It's probably better sooner than later,' she remarks. 'I'm off to the post, be back in a while.'

I smile, but my head is full of dreams of Regency wedding dresses and designer bridalwear. I still have the stash of bridal magazines under my bed. Just imagine if the agency had a double wedding, Maria and Charles and Sophie and Darcy? Just like Lizzie and Jane Bennets' double wedding with Darcy and Bingley. It would be the Regency wedding of the Year.

My phone blasts out. 'Hey, Miffy, how's it going?' I answer.

'Good thanks. So after our catch up the other day, which was gorgeous, by the way.' It was actually, the food was divine. 'This month we are looking at vegan alternatives, so I thought a feature on your friend, Mel, would be great.'

'Wonderful, I'll get some questions together and I'm sure she'd be more than happy to give me a preview of her designs.'

'Hmm, no, Soph, I don't think that's going to be quite enough. Can I be honest with you, darling?'

'Of course.' I'm a bit taken aback. I feel a bit like she's going to tell me I'm not right for this, not subversive enough. I've got that hideous imposter syndrome thing going on and I've wanted this for so long.

'That's a little safe. I need something controversial, groundbreaking. This is Modiste, if you're going to provide regular editorial, it needs to be something different.'

'Not like the stuff I wrote before,' I say quietly.

'Don't get me wrong, Sophie darling, that's great for an extra, for small pieces we might slot in amongst the other features, but if you want to work here you need to pull something major out of the box.'

I feel a little dejected and totally underqualified, I mean, I work for a Jane Austen Dating Agency. It's not exactly controversial or out there, it's romantic and conservative.

'You've got some old copies of Modiste, do some research.'

'Okay, of course.' I pull myself upright. I can do this, really I can. But there's a little voice in the back of my head, you know the horrible doubting one which is best ignored at all times and at all costs, but I can't help listening to it. The voice telling me that all the other girls who've ever done this job have been connected, they are all heiresses, living on the cutting edge of high society, like Emma and Miffy, Natasha and Bunty. They were all born to do this. I am plain old Sophie Johnson, who has managed to claw her way in, but I don't have the connections or the knowledge of society or fashion.

'Sophie, you can do this. I know you have it in you, otherwise

I wouldn't have asked you. You're not a sheep, you're a pioneer, think outside the box.'

Whilst she's talking, I turn the pages of the nearest Modiste magazine, glancing through the stalky models, with edgy make-up, designer brands blazing from the page, with models posing, razor sharp in warehouse car parks. They aren't looking for pretty or conventional.

'I am meant to be going to a protest march with Mel,' I say suddenly. 'Although, I was thinking maybe I shouldn't go, in fact I shouldn't go, but... it would be out there, more controversial. Her team are going to model her vegan range and...'

'That's it,' exclaims Miffy, 'simply perfect, it would be amazing.'

'I only hope it doesn't get too out of hand.'

'So what if it does? More publicity, darling. If you get arrested, even better.'

'I don't think Darcy would approve,' I say quietly.

'Darcy schmarcy. Sometimes that boy can be a right old stuff shirt and as for that hideous mother of his.'

'Yes, she is a little scary,' I say with a smile.

'For God's sake, Soph, you've been going out with him for a few weeks and you're already slave to what he thinks.'

'Not at all.'

'You are. You know what Mark would say?'

'I can probably imagine.' I smile. Mark was one of my colleagues in the Sales Team at Modiste. He was the best friend ever, but he and his husband have gone on a sabbatical to New Zealand and his emails are depressingly rare as he's probably far too busy living it up with his usual flamboyant party lifestyle. I miss him terribly, as well as our chats over the obligatory Modiste smoked salmon blinis.

'He would say, this isn't the Sophie I know and love, who walked up those stairs to Editorial, who smashed getting a plum job at the top of The Jane Austen Dating Agency. If Darcy wants a puppet, he might as well marry that airhead who simpers after him and his mother wherever they go.'

'You mean Tara? You've noticed. I guess she is more conventional than me.'

'Boring and like all the other girls he's ever dated.'

'I know, but I'm worried about losing him,' I say sadly.

'You can't be like that. That's no life for you, Soph, you're better than that.'

'Yeah right,' I say with a smirk.

'You are. Do you really think Lizzie would have put up with doing what Mr Darcy wanted her to do all the time? It's fine if you want to be Jane Bennet, all compliant and mousey.'

'I didn't know you'd read *Pride and Prejudice*.'

'Mark gave me his copy before he left.'

'I hope you enjoyed it.'

'I loved it. But you know what I'm saying about Darcy.'

'I guess, I'm just not sure any more.'

'If you decide to let Darcy's disapproval put you off bagging one of the most amazing articles Modiste has seen for the last however many bloody years, you're not the person I thought you were, darling.'

I ponder Miffy's words, long after she's rung off, and sit and stare out over the beautiful green lawns of Chawton House and mull over the dilemma of choosing between Darcy, The Jane Austen Dating Agency and my lifelong dream of writing the most incredible editorial piece ever.

The phrase about wanting my cake and eating it springs to mind. Quite honestly, it's a stupid expression anyway, who would want a cake and not eat it? Such a waste of perfectly good cake.

CHAPTER 10

'This is so nice,' I say happily. Walking along hand in hand with Darcy is the best thing ever. His hair flops forward slightly over his forehead and I stare at it fascinated. He is definitely one good-looking guy.

'It is.' He gives me that look which still makes my heart sing, and even now, when he talks, his deep voice continues to send shivers to places other men simply can't reach.

We are walking over the Millennium Bridge, looking out across the boats and avoiding the passers-by. It's sunny and vibrant, the sun reflecting dazzlingly off the clock face of Big Ben. I have almost managed to block out the face of the young Indian woman who had a sign at the front of the bridge – at the entrance to the walkway. '*Please I am starving. God bless you.*'

I had wanted to give her money, it had been my instinct to, but then the moment had passed as I kept walking. You know when you have an instant where you can walk up, but then I wasn't sure how much was in my wallet, you know the kind of thing, which then meant by that time, we had walked past. I figured maybe I could give her something on the way back, or buy her some food the other side of the bridge and go back with it. I know they say we shouldn't give money, so I try to buy thoughtful food items, which someone homeless would really need.

As we reach the other side of the bridge, an Indian man, dressed in a cacophony of colours, but in a tired kind of way, stands in front of the same sign, saying the same thing. I mention him casually, then Darcy remarks, 'All playing the game.'

'Do you think so?' I say. 'I was sorry for the woman the other side, she looked desperate.'

'Very clever acting, they probably live in a penthouse in Drury Lane.'

'That's a bit harsh. If they did, they'd hardly need to be begging here, would they?' I say indignantly.

Apart from anything else, Darcy is loaded. He could hand over a huge pile of notes from his wallet and not even notice they had gone. Whenever he pays for things, I have been unable to avoid spotting a large wodge of notes in his wallet. Not that I am looking of course, but it's in rather stark contrast to my purse, in which the only large wad is old receipts. Every so often I get fed up with them and pull them out, leaving them in a pile round the flat, until Mel gets mad with me and I recycle them. Those and vouchers, which tauntingly, every time I remember to use in a food shop, have inevitably gone out of date the day before. It seems to be some kind of sod's law – it wouldn't be so bad somehow if they had been out of date ages ago, but to miss a discount by such a small margin is so incredibly frustrating.

To be honest, I am a bit taken aback with Darcy and his mum's spending habits. They think nothing of buying a bottle of wine for £500, yet are really weird when it comes to spending on other things, like Christmas presents when they'll give each other something random from the cupboard or a box of chocolates someone else gave them, in Darcy's mother's case. As for stationery, Darcy didn't understand my need to buy two notebooks and some Post-it notes the other day at all. Then again, I guess as a businessman, they are a little superfluous; they're probably all provided by the firm; boring brown leather stationery with monograms on them.

I try to erase the sadness of the woman's face from my mind and meander along the South Bank. 'Ooh, can I look at the second-hand books?'

'I suppose,' Darcy says amused, 'though I would have thought you have enough already.'

'You can never have too many books,' I say in mock horror and peruse the trunks piled high with an eclectic mix of novels, under the arch of the bridge.

Many minutes later and with several precious volumes clutched under my arm, including a presentation edition of *The Secret Garden* and a couple of psychological thrillers, because I am completely addicted to them now, I look about for Darcy. He's on the phone and is totally distracted, I can see him pacing up and down, looking very serious about something. I busy myself going into Foyles because what is a girl to do? Besides, you can't go into too many bookshops, it's just not possible.

Finally Darcy is off the phone and comes to find me. 'Not another bookshop.' He smiles indulgently. 'You must spend your entire salary on books and stationery!'

'Not at all,' I say, although to be fair I probably do.

'So, lunch at Pierre's?'

'Oh, erm, we could, or we are right next to Wagamama's,' I say hopefully. I'm actually super hungry and the last time I went to Pierre's with Darcy, I felt a little on my best behaviour and the portions were kind of small. I'm in the mood for a quick satisfying nosh.

'Really, Sophie? I think we could do a little better than that.'

'I'm quite happy there, honestly.'

'If you insist.' Darcy sighs inaudibly.

We wander in and find a perch on the end of the table but I can tell he's not at all comfortable in his surroundings.

'Are you worried about sitting with everyone?' I tease.

'Not at all,' he says, but I don't believe him.

Fortunately our noodles and side dishes come quickly and are delicious as always. I actually think Darcy quite enjoys the food and finishes my huge bowl of soup, as I can't manage it all, the portions are so generous!

'I hope you like French cuisine?' he asks.

'Oh yes, I love most food, but I adore croissants, tartes aux fraises and steak frites.' I laugh.

'All on the same plate?' He laughs. 'Then I am going to take you to Maxim's when we go to Paris.'

'I'd love that, especially if there is seafood.'

'Fruits de Mer are their speciality, I don't think you'll be disappointed.'

'I'm going to have to plan what I'm going to wear.'

'I guess we might have to go shopping then.'

It makes me want to hug him, so I do. His immaculate suit looks rather crumpled after, but it makes him even more endearing.

Two hours later, we have shopped most of the high street stores in Oxford Street and I have a stunning new dress, which Darcy helped me pick out from Warehouse. It is a beautiful turquoise halter neck and I feel gorgeous in it. It certainly isn't designer, but it couldn't be any lovelier if it were. It's one of those dresses you can wear in summer for best or other times with layers over it, it's so gorgeously floaty. We meander along the Thames, eating hot nuts and laughing over the mad-haired crazy festival-goer shop assistant, who had been recommending Glastonbury and any other gig she had ever been to. Darcy's face had been a picture, I really can't imagine him in fields with wellies and public loos.

As we reach the bridge, his phone goes. 'Mummy,' he answers immediately.

Oh great, just what we need to dampen the mood.

'Yes, I haven't forgotten. I'll be along tomorrow then. No, is it formal dress? Right, no I hadn't realised...' He walks off under the arch where I can't quite catch his words. For some reason this troubles me, I mean this is his Mum not another woman. The fact he might want some privacy isn't a problem surely? He's ages and I figure I might as well make myself useful and there's something I need to do. There's just time. I whip into the nearest café, grab hot coffees and some warm filled rolls. Not the best fare, but they will do. I peer quickly over my shoulder, as furtive as any criminal. Darcy is pacing, talking into his phone.

Within minutes I'm back up on the bridge, the man at the entrance has gone and I feel a sense of frustration and a wave of guilt that I'm too late. I should have ignored Darcy and done something sooner instead of shopping for books. I continue to stride over the bridge, just in case the woman is still there. She is, if anything else, looking colder than she was earlier, the temperature has started to drop in the rapidly cooling winter afternoon air.

'Just a few things to help a little,' I say ineffectively, but place the hot coffee and snacks down next to her.

'Bless you,' she says and I see a glimmer of a smile at the corner of her mouth. Awkwardly I smile back, wishing I could do more. No one wants to have to stand here asking for food. Not in this day and age. Has nothing improved since the old days?

As I walk quickly back across the bridge, I see Darcy is off the phone and looking around for me. He doesn't look best pleased.

'There you are. Where did you get to?'

'Nowhere, just went for a little walk across the bridge.'

Darcy looks at my face. 'You went and gave money to that woman, didn't you?'

'No, not money. Just some food, nothing much.'

'You softie you. Honestly, you'll never have any money if you go spending it on every homeless person you see.'

'Never had much anyway. I know I have more than her in any case. Everything all right?'

'Of course.'

There's a silence because I'm kind of hoping he might say what his Mum wanted, I feel like if it had been me I would have said something like, 'oh Mum, just needed to know if I was going home for dinner...' But nothing, nada, rien. Sometimes Darcy is a bit too closed. He hadn't talked of his call at lunchtime either.

'Was that your mum?'

'Yes,' he says, but there's a terseness to his tone I can't quite put my finger on.

'Does she need you for something?'

'Just dinner tomorrow night, I had forgotten all about it.'

'Sounds nice, is it business?'

'Not really, although the crowd will be there from the other evening.'

Stop yourself, Soph... 'Including Tara?' It's no good; I can't stop myself.

'I think she might be there,' he says casually, far too casually to my mind.

I don't reply as there isn't anything to say about it really. The silence stretches out between us, as deafeningly loud as any blazing row.

'She's an old family friend, so she is at a lot of the social occasions I have to attend.'

'Right,' I say, trying to be firm, sure of myself. She's just a friend and surely that's okay. But I can't get the feeling out of my head that Darcy's mother is deliberately throwing the two of them together.

We take a cab to Maria's flat where I am staying the night and although Darcy kisses me before I get out and my stomach tingles traitorously at the touch of his lips, my head is full of irritating little misgivings.

'You're back early,' Maria says. 'Would you like a hot chocolate?' It's so nice staying with her again; it takes me back to last summer when we all lived together for a while. Maria, Mel and Izzy too. She is so motherly.

'Please. You're a total star.' I kick off my shoes, my feet are killing me as I had made the decision, perhaps unadvisedly, to wear my high-heeled pumps with my jeans and although they do make my legs look longer and I'm sure create a slimmer profile, they have totally annihilated my feet. I can't be bothered to change my clothes so slump down exhaustedly on the sofa.

Maria plonks the frothy chocolate down next to me. 'Come on then, spill.'

'There's nothing to say. Darcy and I had a nice day out, bought some clothes, had a walk along the river, it was all very romantic.'

'But...' Maria is far too perceptive for her own good, but then she always was the maturer member of our little group.

'Nothing, it was lovely really.'

'Really? Come on, Soph, this is Darcy Drummond, every woman's dream man. Something is obviously wrong in paradise.'

'It was nice, it's just that Tara.'

'Tara, the wealthy daughter of an old family friend?'

'That's the one,' I say sourly. 'The one who's all over him, looks perfect and is besties with Darcy's mother.'

'She wasn't on the date, was she?'

I laugh. 'Of course not, it wasn't that bad!'

'At least I've made you smile.'

'True and I'm sure I'm overreacting. Darcy got a phone call from his mum, which is fine in itself, it's just he went wandering off to take it. I felt as though I was being excluded, but I know that sounds horribly needy.'

'Probably he had some private business to discuss.'

'I know, but he seemed loath to talk about it.'

'Not everyone's as open as you.'

'I know, but it turns out Darcy is going out tomorrow with the same group as the other night, including Tara, and I'm not invited.'

'What, he said you're not allowed to go?'

'Not in so many words, but I haven't been invited and he knows I'm still in London tomorrow.'

'Couldn't you have asked?'

'I'd have felt so embarrassed, it's a bit like asking for your child to be included in a party they haven't been invited to.'

'I see what you mean.' She ponders for a moment. 'I think Darcy probably wants you to go, but is up against his mother.'

'I guess, but I feel maybe he should stand up to her, he's nearly thirty.'

'You'd be surprised how difficult it is for men to stand up against their mothers.'

'I thought you got on well with Charles's mum?'

'Yes. Teresa's lovely, but I know from speaking to our friends that they've sometimes been viewed with deep suspicion by their other half's mum.'

I think about how my mum is about my brother and can't help but agree with Maria. 'You're right, I don't think Darcy wants to be with Tara.'

'No because if so, why would he be with you? It doesn't make sense. He's probably unable to fall out with Mummy as she holds the purse strings.'

'I suppose so,' I say glumly. 'It's just not very appealing or romantic, is it?'

'What do you mean?'

'I'd rather he faced up to Mummy now, otherwise when will he ever do so? Also, Mr Darcy stood up to both Miss Bingley and Lady Catherine de Bourgh for Elizabeth Bennet. I need him to say, "No, Mum. Sorry but I'm going out with Sophie tomorrow night, or if you expect me to be there, you must invite Sophie, she is my date."'

Maria laughs. 'Not *his friend*, Sophie!' Then she sees my anxious face. 'It's early days yet, Soph, you've only been going out a few weeks, his family's way of doing things is probably all he is used to. And you have this amazing trip to Paris coming up in a few weeks where he can whisk you away and be as romantic as you like.'

'True.' It will be lovely to go to Paris with Darcy; every woman's dream come true.

'And after all, Darcy Drummond is not Mr Darcy, is he?'

'No, he jolly well isn't.'

CHAPTER 11

'Hold your bow a little higher, Lord Bamford.' Emma is in her element, she is wearing a beautiful peach-coloured dress which accentuates her slim but nevertheless statuesque frame, as she demonstrates perfectly how to shoot an arrow right into the centre of the target.

I meander across the beautifully striped, perfectly manicured lawn of Grensham Hall, surveying the scene before me. It's quite exciting actually, I didn't think I could ever be enthusiastic about sports, but Regency sports have a different atmosphere about them from your usual events. The memory of childhood sports days still fills me with dread, I was never much of a sprinter and although I tried my hardest, I would still be overtaken by half of the field well before the finishing line. I always used to feel as though I somehow looked hideous running full tilt towards that unattainable ribbon, my face hot and red, my chubby cheeks flapping in the breeze or that's what they felt like anyway.

I remember once winning a red badge from my junior school sports day sprint – with three black stars on for third place. I still treasure it. By senior school I became good at long distance, maybe I was built for endurance (no surprise there) and won a few stitched badges, which I don't value half as much as that third place, make of it what you will. But by my mid-teens I would carry a selection of Tubigrip bandages about my person, in preparation for sports lessons. The PE staff never seemed to notice I was always nursing another imaginary 'injury'. Mind you I'm not surprised, I was the most clutzy, clumsy child you ever met so they probably figured it was par for the course.

This feels different somehow, maybe it's the grounds with the oak trees dotted artistically along the horizon, the ha ha with the sheep grazing contentedly the other side.

Ha has have always fascinated me, ever since I was a child and my father explained they were called ha has due to the fact that if the owner of the estate absent-mindedly failed to warn a guest walking the grounds that there was a drop, they would fall down it into the field below and the Duke or whoever he was would shout 'ha ha'. It is kind of funny, but I believe the real reason for ha has was to provide a barrier to keep sheep in without the need for an unsightly fence or wall. This one is certainly picturesque, we are in the midst of a quintessentially English scene and it's pretty darn perfect. Days like this I adore my job.

Lord Bamford guffaws, glibly takes the bow and arrow into his hands and without further ado shoots his arrow into a tree. A nearby shaggy-haired lurcher, who had been basking at its foot in the sunshine, gives an anguished yelp and lopes off towards the house.

'Emma, my dear, I thought you asked Bentley to shut the dogs away, we can't have people shooting them,' Mr Woodtree states, sounding distressed.

'Yes, Father, I did ask, but you know what Fern's like, slips out of doors more effectively than the scarlet pimpernel. I'll ask Bentley to shut her back in, with the door locked this time.' She raises her eyebrows at me and paces towards the house where Bentley is handing out drinks to guests.

'So very worrying,' Mr Woodtree fusses agitatedly.

'I'm sure she is fine,' remarks a rather statuesque, ruddy-cheeked and slightly portly man in red hunting jacket, who is downing a large glass of what looks like claret clasped strongly in his surprisingly hairy hand. 'Anyway, you've got plenty more dogs where that one came from. I've got a fine bitch just about to whelp, won many competitions countrywide. Could get you a much better looking dog than that poor creature.'

'My dear fellow, that's very good of you, I know Fern may not be much to look at but she was my wife's dog and very fond of her we are too.' Mr Woodtree quite rightly looks more than a little upset.

'Are you going to have a go at archery, Mr, er...?' I flounder, in order to change the subject quickly.

'Baxter, General Baxter,' he says bluffly, 'and you are?'

'Sophie Johnson. I run the agency with Emma Woodtree.'

'And a good little thing she is too.' Mr Woodtree nods and scratches his chin absent-mindedly. I'm not sure if he's referring to me, or the dog.

'Ah and you're looking to join the agency, General Baxter?' I ask.

'Good God no, I've got enough bally problems with my offspring...' He catches Mr Woodtree's rather baleful stare and breaks off. 'Friend of Woodtree's, came along for the sport.'

'Well you're welcome to have a go, or we have some clay pigeon shooting over in the far corner.'

I excuse myself and saunter across to where Emma is

showing Ben how to shoot an arrow. Typically of him he's a natural and is crowing loudly about his prowess. He always was brilliant at every sport he tried his hand at. 'Come on, Soph, have a go!'

'I could I suppose,' I say, wondering if as one of the hostesses I should or not, but I have often fancied a go at archery. Very medieval and all that; I've always liked the idea of playing the part of the feisty princess in Robin Hood.

Emma passes me the arch or whatever it's called and I practically drop it, it's unexpectedly heavy and unwieldy. 'Come on, girl,' she laughs, 'you need to hold it up, next to your shoulder, that's it.'

I grasp the darn thing as strongly as I can and take hold of the arrow in the holder. It's definitely an exercise in multitasking, but I've got this, I can do more than one thing at once.

'Right, now then, pull back with your finger and release...'

I let go of the arrow and as the bow pings back it snaps onto my finger, pinching it hard. 'Ow!' I drop my shoulder and the arrow pops out of the arch, sails up in the air for about two seconds then falls rather disappointingly down onto the ground.

'Nice one.' Ben laughs. 'You're a natural.'

'Really?' I grumpily suck my finger, which is feeling quite bruised. 'No one told me it would hurt,' I moan at Emma under my breath.

'It's not supposed to,' Emma says politely. 'Have another go and you'll see.'

John Smith raises his head from where he's been bending down to stroke yet another dog, fortunately not his. 'I'll help you.' He starts towards me with enthusiastic intent.

'Would love to, but I've just noticed Freya is on her own,' I say hastily and speed walk to where Freya is wistfully watching

Edward with his arm round Miss Foxton, helping her rather unnecessarily, I feel, to aim her bow.

'Are you being looked after, Freya?' I ask kindly.

'Oh, Miss Johnson.' She seems to have been miles away. 'I'm fine, thanks. I was just watching Edward and Miss Foxton.'

Miss Foxton snaps back her bow finger and the arrow flies elegantly through the air and hits the target beautifully. I notice she's wearing gloves, very sensibly; my finger is still complaining from the pinch as an ugly-looking blood blister is forming.

'Not having a go?' I ask.

'Gosh no, not my thing at all, I'd make a fool of myself.'

'Not as much as I just did,' I say with a smile. 'Would you like a wander then, unless you want to stay here? There's a lovely walk down to the lake and a beautiful rockery which is well worth seeing.'

'I'd love that, thanks.'

We meander companionably down the walkway, away from the brightly coloured melee of tents and targets, into the quiet tranquillity of the shrubbery. I'm quite relieved; the sun is very unforgiving today for the season.

'So are you close to your family?' I ask.

'Yes and no.' Freya pulls absent-mindedly at a weeping willow branch above her head. 'I've grown up with Amelia, Caitlin and Edward, we're like family now.'

'That's so nice, I'm one of three.'

'Do you all get along?' Freya asks.

'Some of the time,' I laugh, 'until my mum insisted on my brother, Ben, joining the agency that is.'

'Is he embarrassing?'

'Yes very and my sister, Chloe, is lovely but she's away with her new man in New York.'

'You must miss her.'

'I do actually, very much. We facetime of course but it isn't the same.'

'Well I have Amelia and Caitlin, although they're step-cousins, well they're...' she breaks off awkwardly.

'They seem very smart,' I say politely.

'Yes they are, they're just very confident and...' Freya looks over her shoulder somewhat nervously, 'I'm a little bit scared of them.'

'You shouldn't be, you are an amazing young woman in your own right.'

'Yes,' she says, obviously not convinced, and I thought I needed assertiveness classes.

'I bet Edward sticks up for you though.'

'He does, when he notices.' She smiles at the thought.

'He *is* a man, they don't always notice things,' I say with a laugh.

'Edward does usually but he's a little distracted at the moment.'

I think I can guess the reason for this. 'So do you ever see your real family?'

'Not often no, I haven't seen my mother for years, my father you see...' she falters.

We continue walking and I stay quiet, hoping she'll feel able to continue.

'My father can be, though he was a, well he wasn't this bad before, but he has a drink problem.'

'I'm so sorry. That must be very hard for you.'

'Yes it is, my mum has left him twice but she takes him back every time.'

'Perhaps she loves him.'

'She does and I do too in a way, because he's my father, but in another way, I hate him!' Her sudden, unexpected vehemence surprises me. 'I know I shouldn't say awful things about my family. But it's the little ones I feel sorry for.'

'Oh, you have younger brothers and sisters?'

'Yes. Two boys and a girl and they are sweet, but I hardly see them. I really miss them though.'

Poor Freya, she seems such a timid little thing. I noticed earlier, that she was very jumpy; the slightest noise seemed to startle her. No wonder she's so reliant on the kindly Edward. Though I have a feeling his attentions are going to continue to be directed elsewhere.

I move on to more cheerful topics such as books and Freya perks up a bit. She loves poetry and is really into Thomas Hardy, not that he's very upbeat but I adore his descriptions of the Dorset countryside.

We have reached the lake, with the herons nesting high in the trees above and ducks milling quietly along the still surface of the water.

'This is beautiful,' Freya rhapsodises, 'so tranquil, I would so much rather be here quietly away from the socialising.' She catches my eye. 'Oh I don't mean to be rude.'

'I don't take it that way at all,' I say reassuringly. 'Much as I enjoy balls and glittering parties, I also love the peace and tranquillity of country walks. Why shouldn't we enjoy both?'

In the distance I can see someone approaching and as he gets nearer, my heart lurches as I realise it's Darcy. I knew he was coming, but didn't realise he would get here so soon. I have a total cathartic moment whilst watching his lithe and handsome form descend the hill.

'Isn't it Darcy?' Freya asks, her easy manner has been transformed once again into shyness.

'Yes, but don't worry his horrible mother isn't with him.'

Freya stifles a giggle. 'She was a bit scary.'

'Sophie,' Darcy approaches quicker than I thought, I hope

he didn't hear that, but he gives me a peck on the cheek, seemingly oblivious, 'I thought you'd be down here. Isn't it beautiful? Oh hello, Freya, isn't it?' He gives Freya a kiss too, much to her complete embarrassment. I am totally in awe of the way he can always remember people's names when he's only met them once. I am terrible with names, which is a big disadvantage in this job. To tell you the truth, I do spend a significant amount of time in the evenings writing down who's who from a client's point of view, next to their photos so I don't make a mistake. Sad, but true.

'I thought you'd be up at the house, trying your hand at archery?' I say, smiling.

'I thought I'd better give the competition a chance and of course, I wanted to join you first. We can walk back up together.'

We all meander the return path companionably and soon reach the lawns in front of the house. A girl I don't recognise with short red cropped hair is expertly shooting arrows in quick succession straight into the middle of the target. I'm most definitely not having another go, the first was embarrassing enough. Darcy leaves my side to speak to Mr Woodtree and Sir Henry Greaves. He is so polite to everyone, no one is beneath his notice and I rather like that about him. Most of the time anyway. You see there is a tiny rather selfish and childish part of me that wants him to stay at my side, as a couple. Not to hang on my words, that might be a bit too much, but perhaps for him to look for me when I'm not there. Though he did come to find me at the lake; that is pretty nice.

'Sophie! The Baroness has arrived, are you happy to go and greet her?' Emma calls.

'Of course.' I make my apologies to Freya, who says something about going to find Edward. He is nowhere to be seen and I have a feeling he's wandered off with Miss Foxton. Fortunately Amelia and Lord Bamford are nearby – Bamford is crowing so loudly at his prowess at fencing, I should imagine they can hear him in the city, but at the same time he is lamenting the fact that the kit won't fit him as he has too manly a frame. He is a complete buffoon, but at least he hails Freya in a friendly fashion and kindly draws her into the group.

The Baroness is standing in the sweeping gravel drive having just alighted from a large black Bentley with the ever-faithful Rodrigo at the wheel.

'Baroness!' I say politely and we shake hands.

'This is a beautiful scene.' She takes in the lawns, the brightly coloured tents and targets with a practised eye. 'I congratulate you my dear, very inspired.'

'It's Emma's country estate,' I say diffidently. Why can I never accept a compliment gracefully? Must try harder.

'Yes but I like the way you have arranged the vista, so colourful, quite charming.'

We meander across the lawn to where Bentley passes the Baroness a large glass of Pimm's, from which she sips gracefully. Everything about the Baroness is immaculate and effortless, her dark suit, snugly fitted to her slim silhouette. She must be boiling hot, but her make-up nevertheless remains flawless and in place. It would not dare to move, I think to myself.

Emma approaches, accompanied by a recent newcomer to the agency, who we both think is going to be perfect for the Baroness.

'Good afternoon, Baroness. Beautiful day, isn't it?'

'Spectacular, Emma, as is your home here.'

'We love it.' Emma smiles. The man next to her fidgets impatiently. 'Please meet Gene Weston. Gene, this is the Baroness Mayer.' Gene is in a cream suit and has sandy hair, slightly thinning on top, but is immaculately smart, with an open pleasant face.

'I am honoured.' Gene shakes the Baroness's hand and looks

suitably ready to admire her. I'm not surprised; she has a very commanding presence and is extremely handsome. 'I see you have a Pimm's, the perfect drink for a day like this.'

Emma cleverly moves to one side so Gene and the Baroness are next to each other. 'I must go and see what my father is thinking of doing about the refreshments,' she says, gives me a conspiratorial wink and disappears towards the nearest refreshment tent.

I feel like such a third wheel and it's always really embarrassing when people are thrown together. It's so awkward to watch. Like those television dating shows where the couple is painfully shy and the poor individuals 'erm and ah' at each other and you just want to help them out with a 'would you like a drink' or 'what book are you reading', or anything really to stop that horrible awkward silence that seems to go on forever. Now I'm there however, it is difficult to think of anything to say at all. 'This is a beautiful setting, isn't it?' I offer. I guess it's better than nothing. 'Reminds me of *Downton Abbey*.' Oh good grief, where am I going with this?

'It is lovely,' Gene agrees pleasantly. 'This is the first time I've been out in the country for weeks.'

'Are you not keen on the countryside?' the Baroness asks.

'Oh yes I like it very much,' Gene replies, 'just too busy working and socialising tends to be within the capital.'

'I understand,' the Baroness replies, 'it is much the same for me, I am forever rushing from one appointment to the next.'

This is more like it, time for me to make a hasty exit. 'Gene, would you like to show the Baroness the clay pigeon shooting or the fencing?'

'Nothing would give me more pleasure.' Gene is quite a gentleman in spite of his businesslike, slightly over-groomed appearance. He offers his arm to her and she puts her surprisingly tiny gloved hand on it and they wander down to the woods where the regular bangs betray the location of the clay pigeon shoot.

I think he might be a perfect match for the Baroness; I believe they will probably understand one another and he seems like kindness itself. I feel quite pleased with my matchmaking actually, with skills like these I could give Emma Woodhouse a run for her money.

CHAPTER 12

I take full advantage of my escape and leg it out of the tent to where Darcy is chatting to Edward and Miss Foxton. 'Of course, I was hoping for a career in education,' Edward is saying, 'but my parents don't exactly approve.'

'I'm not surprised.' Miss Foxton laughs. 'How very boring, surely you can think of something else you'd rather do. How about finance or banking?'

'I'm totally unsuited to anything so competitive,' Edward says shyly. 'I just don't have the personality for it.'

'Utter rot,' Miss Foxton protests hotly. 'There are all sorts of positions in London in accounting and it's far better paid than being some poor teacher in a backstreet somewhere, preaching lessons to kids who don't want to even be there, sat in long droney lectures thinking about what's for tea.'

'I think it's a wonderful vocation,' I say, coming to Edward's defence, 'teachers have an extremely important job, inspiring the next generation.'

'Can't abide most children, they're rude and obnoxious and poor Edward will be constantly surrounded by hideous groups of try-hard parents who want to get their little darlings into the village school,' Miss Foxton says tartly.

'There's enough of that going on in London, let alone in villages,' Darcy states. 'Parents are by their nature always looking for the best schools for their children and who can blame them, this is a competitive world we live in.'

'Absolutely and that's why we simply can't let the delectable Edward here throw himself away on being a measly teacher. Just like Austen's clergymen, Mr Elton and Mr Collins, awful young men.'

'They were,' I say, smiling, 'but there are plenty of people who can be that annoying who have nothing to do with the clergy.' I am thinking of Rob Bright, one of my hideous ex dates who was the closest living person to Mr Collins I've ever met.

'Perhaps you should try the city, Edward,' Darcy suggests, cleverly moving the subject away from my debate with Miss Foxton. 'There are some great apprenticeships going at Goldman Sachs for a person with the right amount of drive.'

'I'm not sure... I...'

'Oh yes do, Edward. That's an amazing opportunity, Darcy. If you would be happy to recommend him. We could meet in London for dinner. Darcy could come too I'm sure.'

'It could be arranged,' Darcy says politely. 'Do you have a card, Edward?'

Edward passes his card across having rummaged in his jacket pocket. Miss Foxton looks like the cat who's got the cream, her full charm offensive with the two men reaping rewards for her, but I can tell Edward isn't happy with the idea at all.

'Would you like to come and see the fencing?' I ask Darcy, hoping to escape Miss Foxton for a while. She is far too up together and overbearing for me, rather like Mrs Elton.

'Of course, excuse me,' Miss Foxton simpers in response. I'm amazed she doesn't drop a curtsey and offer her hand to be kissed.

'Did you notice that Edward wasn't very keen on the idea of Goldman Sachs?' I ask Darcy as we walk hand in hand down the gravel path to the lower part of the gardens.

'No, he wasn't overenthusiastic but then he's a good, steady fellow, I think he'd do well in the city.'

'I guess, but I don't think that's what he wants to do.'

'What he wants to do and what he ends up doing are two very different things,' Darcy states. 'He might have some dream he could be a teacher, but it's unlikely he will be, and if he wants to have any kind of chance with Miss Foxton, he will have to change his ideas rather quickly.'

'But surely she isn't the right person for him if she doesn't support his ideals?'

'Not at all, I would say the opposite, that she is exactly the sort of woman he needs to help him move forward, instead of dragging him down.'

That told me then. Should a woman encourage a man to be ambitious? Is that how Darcy sees me, someone who will help him further his career? The thought makes me want to laugh; it's so incongruous. If that's the case, he's going to be very disappointed. At any rate, the more I see of Edward, the more I can imagine him being a great headmaster, with a lovely wife and several children all living in a picturesque village somewhere.

'I'm just not sure Edward has the cut and thrust attitude of a businessman,' I persist.

'Like me you mean?' Darcy turns to face me and I blush.

'Perhaps.'

'Because I'm so tough and aggressive,' he jokes, his brown eyes twinkling.

'Something like that.' I smile enigmatically.

'Speaking of which, I'm afraid I do have some news,' he says rather awkwardly and I can kind of sense the mood changing, which is a shame as I was enjoying the romantic walk through these beautiful gardens.

'Sounds ominous,' I joke, trying to keep the mood light.

'It's not really, just a minor setback,' he says as I carry on walking, thinking, *Please don't let it be something serious.* 'We are going to have to postpone our trip to Paris.'

'Oh, that's a shame, why?' I try to keep my voice steady, calm.

'Unfortunately it's been brought to my attention there is a clash of dates.' He looks studiously at a pair of squabbling magpies in the branches overhead.

'But it's booked, the tickets and everything,' I protest. This is all going horribly wrong.

'It can easily be changed,' Darcy says. A little too easily I feel.

'When were you thinking?'

'Only a few weeks. Until this deal is sorted with our Swiss colleagues.'

'A few weeks,' I squeak. I thought he meant a week or two.

'This deal is super important, if I take the pressure off now, we could lose everything.'

'I know it's important and I guess at least we can go later,' I say, but inside I'm distraught. The romantic trip to Paris with Darcy is no more, finished; it's totally unbelievable. I bet his horrible mother is behind this and is it just me, but he doesn't exactly sound disappointed? Maybe he's putting a brave face on it in a manly way. 'As long as the weather is still reasonable,' I say, thinking of my new turquoise dress with its long layers, ready for autumn in Paris.

We are shielded from view from the rest of the world by beech hedges, but are suddenly interrupted by the sound of laughter. Darcy lets go of my hand immediately as though I am forbidden fruit and we walk side by side as though nothing has happened. I know we can't be constantly smooching, but I don't see why we have to act as though his mother is round the corner the whole time.

It's frustrating; he is so formal and straight-laced, just like his namesake. But Darcy changed by the end of the book, he was meant to become more accessible, less uptight, thanks to his 'dearest loveliest Elizabeth'. Perhaps it's me, I need to help him find his more touchy-feely side and after all, it took Lizzie some time to bring out Darcy's true personality and it's only been a few weeks.

We approach the roped off area where a couple are fencing. To my inexperienced eye, it looks rather aggressive and full on, the tiny figure on the right appears to me to be in full-attack mode, the rather larger man on the left is flailing backwards towards the hedge. He gamely manages to throw his opponent's sword to the side and regain his position near the centre. 'Well played, sir,' calls out the assistant fencing person. I'm not sure what you call someone who manages swordplay, but that will do.

The man acknowledges with a comical little salute with his sword-free hand, but barely has a chance to recompose himself as the small figure is at him again, driving him once more to the hedge, upending him to the floor in one masterstroke of the sword coming down to put the blade at his chest. He lies there rather like a beached whale, trapped and flailing helplessly on the sand.

The small figure turns away, having neatly withdrawn their sword and handing it to the assistant, removes the face guard in one swift movement.

'Baroness,' I gasp as I realise it is she who won and her opponent who turns out to be Gene, a rather panting and exhausted Gene it has to be said, who drags himself to his feet and removes his visor.

'You've done that before,' he says to her, with a smile. He is a sport, this guy.

'Just a few times, but I thought I had forgotten.'

'You certainly haven't,' remarks Darcy. 'I haven't seen swordsmanship like that for years. Was never very good at it at public school, but I reckon you could have given most of the masters a run for their money.'

'I give most people a run for their money,' the Baroness replies and I swear she raises one of her eyebrows slightly at me, but I could have imagined it. 'Your turn now, Sophie.'

'Oh no, I wouldn't know what I was doing at all.' I back away.

'Come on, Soph.' Darcy smiles. 'I reckon you could pack quite a punch and I can be your opponent.'

'But you know how to fence.' I take back what I was thinking at the beginning of the day, this is like all my nightmare sports days packed into one.

'Not very well, I'll go easy on you,' he says with a boyish grin.

'Okay then.' I submit myself to putting on the hideous top and headguard, it feels heavy and horrible and smells slightly sweaty and malodorous.

'Glad I made it in time for this,' Ben says, arriving on the scene with his usual hideous sense of timing. You've got to give him points for fast work.

The red-haired girl is on his arm. 'I'd like a go,' she says enthusiastically.

'Of course.' Darcy hands her his sword and gear politely.

This really takes the biscuit. It was bad enough having to fence with Darcy but at least there might have been some kind of frisson about it, but this girl – she was flipping marvellous at archery, I'm going to get thrashed.

'Right, you need to keep your eye on her at all times, have your right arm ahead on guard and be nimble on your feet,'

Darcy coaches in my ear. That's kind of cute I guess, but I really want to run away.

The redhead and I stand opposite each other in the grassy area, eyeing each other up warily.

Next thing, she thrusts her sword forward, catching me right across the side.

'Ow!' That takes me by surprise but makes me incredibly mad. I wave my sword angrily towards her and hit hers across the front so hard, it makes her drop it. Hah. That showed her.

'Well done, Soph!' Darcy shouts, which makes me flush with pride. It was a total fluke though. Unfortunately, whilst I'm basking in the sunshine of a word of praise from Darcy, the redhead has picked up her sword and wacked me hard in the stomach, which takes the wind heavily out of my sails and I sit down hard on the ground. 'Oomph,' is all I can say.

'Are you all right, Sophie?' Darcy asks, bending over me. I feel such a fool; I'm all right, just winded.

'I'm fine.' I struggle to my feet in a totally unladylike manner, and rub my stomach. 'That really hurt.'

'Well yes,' Darcy laughs unsympathetically, 'it does a bit, this is fencing, not Regency dancing.' Huh. I'd take Regency dancing any day. I was so not designed for this.

'I thought the protective gear meant you didn't feel anything,' I say.

The girl laughs. 'It doesn't really hurt,' she says, peeking at Ben from under her eyelashes. How does she do that? If I try, I just look as though I have something stuck in my eye.

'That's what you think,' I mutter under my breath.

'Another round?'

'Maybe not,' I say firmly.

Darcy stays to have a fence with Ben, but I make my way back up to the refreshment area under the pretext of checking the guests but actually my stomach still hurts. I think in the current situation another large Pimm's is the order of the day.

I approach the tent, a hand gingerly on my stomach, when I'm surprised to see John Smith in conversation with General Baxter. I didn't know they knew each other but I suppose he's just being polite. As I approach they look in my direction and I can't help but feel as though they're talking about me. I take my Pimm's in any case and return to watch the archery with Freya and Edward. It feels a little safer as long as I stay at the opposite end from the targets.

'What's the Baroness's history?' I ask Emma as we are clearing the cloths away, later that evening.

'I don't really know in any detail. Why?'

'Just interested. Who was her husband? What happened to him?'

Emma carefully removes the flowers from the vase at the centre of the table. 'It's all rather hush-hush. Her husband fled from somewhere abroad with rather a lot of money. They say he is worth billions and that is why she lives in Kensington Palace Gardens.'

'What happened to him though?'

'I thought she said she was a widow, so I assume he died.'

'How odd.'

'Not really.' Emma is businesslike as ever, folding cloths perfectly and passing them to me. 'I know you're trying to make a mystery out of this, but there is none. The Baroness's husband died, he was probably ancient, and she now wants to find another man to keep her company in her old age. It's not surprising, is it? She must be lonely in that great house.'

'Yes I was thinking that. But...'

'But what?'

'I don't know, there's something odd about the atmosphere; there was a sadness. I could sense it.'

'Of course there was some sadness, her husband had died.'

'It's not that, it's just... some of the things she has said.' But Emma hasn't heard as she is walking steadily towards the house, expertly balancing cushions and flowers, piled high in the air.

There *is* something odd about the Baroness, I'm sure of it. I am still pondering the matter, whilst carrying a couple of champagne coolers and leaflets across the lawn. Darcy has already left as he had a business dinner he needed to go to and I am still down about the whole situation. I know it's only a blip and it's not as though he's said we won't go to Paris at all, but it's taken the wind out of my sails somehow. As I approach the house, General Baxter appears. 'Ah, Miss Johnson.' He makes me jump with his hearty address. I wasn't expecting him to talk to me at all after his manner earlier.

'Good evening, General Baxter,' I say politely, feeling at a disadvantage with my arms full of wine buckets and papers. 'I hope you enjoyed your visit.'

'Very much so,' he says, falling into step beside me. I wish he wouldn't walk so close, he puts me on edge, but I can't tell you why exactly. He is a creepy sort of guy with his expressionless face and there is something about him I just don't like. He's cold.

'Are you aware I have a son and daughter, Miss Johnson?'

'Yes,' I say vaguely, 'I think I met them recently.'

'Did you? Ah right, Henry and Eleanor?'

'Yes.'

'I believe they should join your agency.'

I'm totally amazed. Why would General Baxter want his children to join our agency? But it's a good thing of course; I liked both Henry and his sister.

'That's wonderful.' I take the card the General passes me. 'I shall send you the details tomorrow.'

The General bows formally and disappears off into the night, which almost makes me want to giggle, if it weren't all so strange. I would never have imagined him wanting his family to be part of the agency, but I suppose he is friendly with Emma's father so perhaps there is some scheme at play here.

Once inside the house, I enter the large drawing room, to drop off the flower stands and cloths. Emma is nowhere to be seen, but two people are in earnest conversation and I feel unaccountably as though I am intruding.

'Ah, Sophie!' It's Mr Woodtree. 'I was just discussing the gardens with the Baroness.'

'How nice,' I say, taking in the two of them sitting comfortably on the old and shabby sofa, the Baroness for once not upright as a poker but sitting properly in the seat, the long-legged lurcher, Fern, with her head on her knee.

'I became rather lost,' the Baroness rises to her feet, disturbing the happily sleeping dog, 'and Mr Woodtree most kindly rescued me.'

'Don't mind me, I'm just leaving,' I say hurrying back towards the door.

'I must depart in any case,' the Baroness says, following me out. It's as though the mask, which had momentarily slipped, has been firmly put back in place.

'Thank you both for a most enjoyable afternoon of Regency sports, I don't know when I have enjoyed myself so much, it made me almost forget...'

'Forget what?' Mr Woodtree asks. 'You haven't left something, have you? You ought to be wearing a coat, the evening has become quite cool now.'

'I am used to the temperatures in the far north, Mr Woodtree, this is like a spring afternoon!'

With that, the Baroness steps into her great black car, driven by the solemnly faithful Rodrigo. He reminds me rather of a loyal spaniel and disappears into the night, along with my romantic dreams of snuggling up with Darcy in the leafy bower in the garden, with him telling me how ardently he admires and loves me.

CHAPTER 13

'So, the trip to Paris is off?' Mel asks, spilling her whole packet of pins on the floor.

'Yep.' I scrabble around, picking up pins and putting them back in the container. 'Though Darcy says we can go next month maybe.'

'Maybe?'

'That's what I thought; I understand he has work but I'd feel happier if the date were booked in the diary. It would make it feel more real somehow.'

'I know what you mean, but I'm sure Darcy will rebook; he sounded keen.' Mel begins to methodically pin the hem on the sheer piece of fabric in front of her. How she manages not to tear it I don't know, as she's pretty clumsy usually but give her a piece of fabric and she magically transforms it with deft fingers.

'I guess.'

'Come on, Soph, he's obviously nuts about you. Look what he's done for us when it comes to giving out low-rent accommodation.'

I smile. 'I know, it's just I can't help but feel his mother has something to do with this.'

'No doubt she has, but if his mum can stop him going to Paris with you, then it's not much of a relationship.'

'True. How long is it until the girls get here?'

'Oh God, I'd forgotten they were coming this morning. Wasn't it about ten?'

'It's 9.45 now, we'd better hurry.'

Mel throws the fabric to one side. 'I'm totally up against it, this show is next week, surely you can check out the grounds without me?'

'I s'pose, but I wanted you to be thinking of the table designs and the ballroom. Also I still have a few last-minute preparations for Maria's hen do tonight.'

'Okay, okay I'll make time.' Mel throws everything to one side. 'But only because you're featuring me in the next edition of Modiste.'

'Great friend you are,' I joke. 'It might be a rubbish article and you'll have to cope without.'

'No I won't.' Mel laughs. 'You're a bloody good writer, so don't let me down.'

I throw the nearest piece of net over her head and she yells at me, tipping even more threads and bits all over the floor. She manages to chuck some yarn at me, which hits me on the cheek, so I retaliate with a roll of fabric.

'Can anyone join in?' a voice asks. It's Izzy, standing in the doorway, looking gorgeous in a delicate strappy top and skinny jeans.

'Hey.' I rush and give her a big hug, closely followed by Mel who is doing a convincing impression of the Loch Ness monster covered in gauzy fabric.

'You look like the ghost of Chawton House,' says Maria, who was following close behind.

'Don't even go there,' Mel says. 'Sophie has already bumped into her a couple of times.'

'Yeah right,' I say, trying to cover my embarrassment. I have had a couple more incidents with the banging window upstairs. Both times it has been swinging open, the curtain blowing in the wind when I could have sworn I shut it, although this time the book appeared a couple of times on the bureau in Jane Austen's reading nook. What's really odd though is it's always open on the same page of *Northanger Abbey*.

It's also extremely puzzling as I've confronted Emma about moving the book but she's adamant that she hasn't touched it and is so convincing I believe her. But then how does *Northanger Abbey* get there? Unless it's Mel, but I wouldn't have thought she'd bother. It's all a bit creepy, and I've taken to leaving Emma to lock up on dark evenings to be on the safe side. 'There is definitely a presence in this old house.'

We leave Mel's room, to tidy up later, and wander out into the courtyard.

'It is old.' Maria is staring at the house, which is looking pretty beautiful in the early October sun. 'There probably are plenty of stories for this building to tell.'

'Lots of ghosties.' Izzy shivers. 'I wouldn't want to be in there alone at night.'

'See it's not just me.' I smirk at Mel.

'Izzy, you should be backing me here,' Mel says indignantly.

Izzy laughs. 'Nope, I agree with Soph. Anyway, I'm reading *Gone Girl* so I'm having to leave the light on at night at the moment.'

'Not another one!' Mel snorts.

'Well we'll all get a chance to find out how many ghosties there are tonight as we will be spending the evening in the upper gallery,' I say.

'Can't wait,' says Maria, lifting her long pink skirt from the morning dew.

'You look lovely, Maria, new dress?' Mel asks.

'Yes. I've been buying a few bits ready for the honeymoon.' Maria smiles. 'Father has miraculously finally come around to the idea of Charles and has funded quite a few nice outfits. Make me look a little younger, he said.'

'As if you need to look younger,' I scoff.

'Perhaps your dad needs to look in the mirror!' Izzy chuckles. She hasn't changed at all.

'He looks quite good for his age,' Maria says shyly.

To be fair, Sir Henry Greaves does look quite spruce considering he must be at least in his sixties, but he's one of the most judgemental, male chauvinists I've ever met and probably spends a fortune on his appearance, fake tan and Botox notwithstanding.

Emma jogs across the grass at the front of the house to join us. 'Hey, it's like old times. Are we all set for tonight? I've got plenty of delicious goodies and Sophie has decorated the room with Mel's help.'

Izzy nods. 'Ooh sounds fun, I hope there'll be some surprises for Maria.'

'Definitely,' Emma says, 'with the addition of Regency games as well as a Jane Austen movie marathon.'

'You're the best,' Maria says. 'I can't believe you've organised this for me when you've got a Regency Ball to plan as well.'

'It's no trouble,' I say. 'It's a privilege to be able to host Regency events. Besides, this is the first ball I've been involved in arranging and it has to be perfect.'

'No pressure then,' Mel mutters.

'It'll be fine,' Emma says, 'it's only a matter of organisation.'

'That's right.' I whip open my new stationery book with Regency figures on the front.

Mel eyes it suspiciously. 'Is that a new notebook?'

'No, it's an old one,' I say quickly, covering the price label I've left on the back of the book. 'So, I was thinking we could have lanterns up the front drive, in the trees, arranged all the way along?' We turn to look down towards the horses grazing at the entrance gates.

'That would be lovely,' remarks Maria, 'I wouldn't mind that for my wedding as well.'

'Okay I'll make a note of that,' I say.

'Then the carriages will drop guests at the front of the house, where they will be greeted by a butler, just one, or actually maybe Sophie and I could meet and greet everyone, to make it more personal, where they will pass their cards to be checked.' Emma likes to deal with all the practicalities.

'So do you want any flowers or decorations outside?' Mel asks.

'I don't think so, but in the entrance hall it would be nice to have some, perhaps leading the way to the upstairs gallery where we'll be serving refreshments.'

'Dancing will be in the great hall on the left, it's compact but there's another room next door for chatting and mixing with couples as well as the lawn outside if it's warm enough.'

'It won't be in late October, I don't think,' Mel says categorically. I think she's right. 'Maybe we should have a marquee.'

'As long as it's heated,' I add.

'So an autumnal ball theme?' Mel suggests.

'Yes I think so. Don't you, Emma?' I respond.

'Absolutely, I like the idea of the brown colours, perhaps the flower arrangements should include berries and fruit.'

'Apparently, balls were often held when there was a full moon in Regency times to help with lighting, but at least we don't need to worry about that these days. We could however have gas-type flickering lights to look like candles?' I suggest.

'If it's practical,' Emma replies.

'It would be so romantic though,' Maria says.

'And candlelight is flattering.' I laugh.

We tour the rooms, planning out the refreshment ideas and the decorations. There could be a quiet area upstairs, where I like to think of Jane sitting and writing her novels. I might even make it look pretty with candlelights arranged with autumnal berries and leaves on the evening, and I'll double-check *Northanger Abbey* is locked away for safe keeping.

'I'm so excited about it all,' Izzy says. 'Have you girls decided what to wear?'

'I shall be wearing the same dress I wore to the last two events you dragged me along to,' Mel says.

'Spoilsport,' I retort.

'Not really, how many Regency dresses do you expect me to own?'

'Yes but it's nice to wear something new,' Izzy says. 'I've got my eye on a beautiful pale blue gown I saw at the Bath costume hire.'

'I'm totally frustrated with that company,' I say. 'They have the most tantalisingly gorgeous dress in stunning blue and white but they only have it in a size eight.'

'Don't they have any other sizes?' Maria asks patiently.

'No I checked, not a twelve in sight.'

'What about Mel? She can create anything.'

'True. Mel is a genius when it comes to designing and creating clothes.'

'Absolutely not.' Mel strides out in front resolutely. 'Besides I've got all the wedding outfits to create yet.'

'You might owe me one,' I say.

'Huh!'

'You'll never guess who I saw the other day when I was in London?' Izzy abruptly changes the subject.

'Not Rob Bright,' I say.

Mel laughs. 'You have that man on the brain.'

'I'm not surprised, after my hideous experience with him last year,' I say indignantly.

'No, not Rob Bright, nor Lady Constance before you suggest her. It was someone I used to have a real crush on.'

'Josh?' Emma asks, horrified.

'Yes, isn't that amazing?' Izzy says casually twirling her hair in her hand.

'Not really,' I mutter.

We all exchange glances as Izzy trots on oblivious. Last time I met Josh was after he had broken Izzy's heart earlier this year and I didn't want to ever have to see him again.

'What's he doing these days?' Maria asks.

'He says he's got a successful new job in the city as a stockbroker.'

'Oh,' Mel says, 'doesn't surprise me.'

'No, he was always determined on being a high-flyer,' I retort.

'I hope you were reserved and aloof around him,' Mel says.

'Definitely. I think he got the message I'm not interested in him anymore, I have Matthew now, he's so sweet and really considerate.'

It's a beautiful day and in such a setting, it's a shame to let any shadow cast itself over proceedings, but I can't help feeling a sense of unease around this casual mention of Josh. Somehow Izzy's tone was a bit too forced and the thought of him being in contact with her at all is alarming.

CHAPTER 14

$\mathcal{A}$s it turns out, I don't have time to brood on Josh and Izzy or anything else for that matter, as everything is temporarily forgotten in our evening of Regency fun and games for Maria's hen night, which is a total riot. It went incredibly well, with the bride-to-be dressed in an over-the-top Regency dress mocked up by the ever-talented Mel with all sorts of fun accessories such as a sparkly tiara with 'Bride-to-Be' written on it and a 'I've found my Regency hero' sash. We danced exuberantly to an eclectic mix of music, both traditional and modern, Regency and romantic. It sounds strange but bizarrely it worked.

The food, delivered by a local company, was incredible, an amazing-tasting menu, accompanied by champagne and luxury chocolate making to finish, which we did in the flagstoned kitchen, then served in the gloriously decorated upstairs gallery.

I had really enjoyed myself with the colour scheme, pale pink and blue confetti hearts were strewn everywhere, with garlands of ribbons and cascades of lace over the wall, placed there by Mel's magic.

We played Regency games like spillikins, which Maria

turned out to be surprisingly good at, and battledore and shuttlecock, during which I'm surprised we didn't break something, as the game became more and more outlandish.

Finally after apple bobbing, which meant we all got soaked, we curled up in our cosies, eating the delicious truffles we had made and watching *Pride and Prejudice*, *Emma*, *Sense and Sensibility* and *Mansfield Park*. There was a bit of a kerfuffle initially because we hadn't been able to decide which version of *Pride and Prejudice* we should watch, but in the end everyone had to concede to the 2005 Keira Knightley film, for the simple reason it is shorter, with the agreement we would have a 1995 *P and P* party in the near future. For me Jennifer Ehle and Colin Firth as well as anything by Andrew Davies has the slight edge as being nearest to Jane Austen's writing. Yet I love the 2005 version in a different way. In any case, it was total heaven, a great chance for us all to relax and have fun together, the original members of The Jane Austen Dating Agency reunited at last.

The only thing is, I don't think I've yet recovered as we were up most of the night drinking champagne and eating far too many chocolates and popcorn and several days later, I'm still exhausted, which is not good timing considering the fateful day of Mel's climate demonstration has arrived. Somehow I've managed to keep it secret from Emma, which is quite tricky, as she usually knows my movements in the diary. I've had to pretend I'm going to London on business without actually telling her fibs, as the protest *is* in London. I do feel bad though because it's about as far from agency business as you can physically get.

I haven't mentioned it to Darcy either for obvious reasons, as he would totally disapprove and not only that, I'm still a bit annoyed with him for not standing up to his mother. I know it's difficult for him, but in bowing to his mother's wishes, he is seriously struggling to live up to my Darcyesque ideals.

I make it to Parliament Square at 9.45am, which isn't bad considering the train was delayed past Winchester due to leaves on the line or some such nonsense. I had only just made the train in time as I had a complete dilemma of what to wear. I had thought of rocking the geography teacher look, you know, a sort of checked shirt and some jeans and hiking boots, to fit with the environmentally friendly theme, but then I fortunately remembered that Mel is needing images for a design shoot and I need to look more like a member of editorial from Vogue, not The National Trust.

So in the end I opted for my cool blue striped shirt, faded out skinny denim jeans and my Dune London duffel slung over my shoulder, topped off with a chunky grey sweater in case it gets cold. I am glad I was practical in my choice of shoes as I've had to run from the tube station, Mel was adamant I should be there well before the crowds she is expecting.

'Finally,' she says to me grouchily as I arrive. She had gone via her offices to meet the models and sort out the clothes.

'Train was delayed,' I huff. 'Outfits are looking good.' I need to try to get back into Mel's good books. I peer at the models, who are all holding placards but unlike your usual protestor, they are posing artistically with their boards, beautifully painted with 'Save our Planet' and 'This is what Democracy looks like' etched on them. 'Won't they get cold in those outfits?' I ask. The clothes are fabulous; all the girls are dressed from head to foot in white, contrasting starkly with the red painted signs. The fabrics look flimsy and cold, however.

'Maybe, but you know how it is.'

'Yes I do, *il faut souffir pour être belle*.'

'Soph, you know how I feel about that hideous expression,' she snaps.

I do actually; Mel has expounded for long periods about the

ridiculousness of women having to manipulate their feet into high heels, or go through dyeing their hair to look a certain way.

'Why should we change for men or anyone else for that matter?' she always says.

She has a point of course, but in my limited experience, both male and female models seem to have to put up with all sorts of unseasonal discomfort on photo shoots.

'Right, if you can get some photos before any more people come along, with The Houses of Parliament in the background.' Mel thrusts the large-zoomed-lens camera towards me.

I take some quite good shots I think, with Mel rearranging skirts and scarves, against the backdrop of red slogans. At least there aren't too many people about yet; the square piece of grass is filling up with protestors with various placards, all garbed in student-type clothing.

'Can you get some stuff out on Instagram?' Mel asks from the floor where she is trying to pin up a beautiful black model's trouser leg. It looks a bit weird actually, why would you have one leg longer than the other on a pair of trousers? I never understand that about fashion, or art for that matter. Like artists in the Tate Modern who put a plate and a fork in a box and that's art.

I'm probably going to be in trouble for this, but I've seen school children's copies of Van Gogh's *The Sunflowers*, which look far more like sunflowers than his did. Perhaps I just don't appreciate art, I try to, but I prefer landscapes and creations that look like the things they are painting, like Monet and Constable.

I put out some arty-looking shots on Mel's Insta and Facebook and make sure I have all the images I need for the start of my editorial. 'I'm hoping to get some others with more protestors in as well,' I say.

There are certainly plenty of people milling into Parliament Square and as Big Ben chimes 10am, the chanting starts up.

There seems to be a militant group in the centre who are very lippy and admittedly resourceful, who start shouting this kind of chant. 'People listen up!'

Everyone repeats, 'People listen up.'

'The world is dying,' all shout along. 'Politicians are lying.'

Mel and I join in because, well what else are you meant to do when you're at a demo? You can't just stand there and besides, Mel is well into this and appears to know a couple of the organisers. She waves cheerily at a couple of hairy, beardy obviously vegan protestors who to be fair are quite friendly looking. At first I feel rather self-conscious, but as I continue to chant, even the models are joining in, it feels sort of revolutionary and cathartic somehow.

The chant leader changes to a more frantic shout. 'What do we want?' This girl really does not need a megaphone.

'Climate action,' we all roar back.

'When do we want it?' she blasts.

'Now!' we all shriek.

I'm having so much fun; I wonder why I haven't done something like this before. Perhaps I've had a repressed childhood or something but the whole shouting at the top of your lungs thing is quite stress relieving.

'We're trying to get this world to end!' I respond with the rest of the crowd.

'You idiot, it's we're trying *not* to let this world end,' Mel shouts.

'Oh.' Oops. I think I might have shouted the wrong words; I get some dodgy glares from a few of the protestors around me. I'd better be careful, I'm seriously outnumbered here and things could get messy. I concentrate to make sure I get the next line right.

I am in complete mid-shout when a large black Bentley swooshes past, the windows are tinted so I can't quite tell who is inside and I hope fervently that it is not the Baroness. I suddenly begin to feel a little uneasy, maybe this isn't the best idea after all; it's hard to be incognito on the fringes of a vegan climate protest at a busy time of the morning in Parliament Square.

I voice my concerns to Mel.

'You're a laugh a minute,' she remarks. 'The whole reason we're here is to be seen.'

'I suppose,' I hiss, 'but you have less resting on this than me.' I add under my breath. I shift further behind the edge of the crowd and try to shield myself within the anonymity of the heaving wave of people. By now there is hardly room to move at all, the whole square is crammed. All I can see is a sea of heads, interspersed with boards waving wildly in the air in time with the chant.

'Hello, can I interview you for Vegans for the Future?' a man in cords and a reddish beard asks.

'Erm, not really, I'm only here on a photo shoot,' I mumble, looking around for Mel, who seems to have got swooshed away by her team of models, looking slightly more dishevelled and warlike by now and is sitting on someone's shoulders still chanting wildly.

'Are you vegan?' he asks unperturbed.

'No I'm not,' I say cheerfully, 'so I won't be any help to you I'm afraid.'

'Yes you will, I want to know why you aren't a vegan?'

'I'd like to be,' I prevaricate, 'and I go without meat once a week,' I add proudly – sometimes twice actually cos living with Mel we try to reduce our impact on the planet and besides Mel won't cook meat so on her nights to cook, vegan it is.

'That's a start, why do you do that?'

'We're trying to reduce our impact on the planet, of course, and my friend Mel is a vegan, in fact she's over there, maybe you should go and interview her?' I add hopefully. I've lost visual on

Mel and am beginning to wonder where she has gone. Typically, she's disappeared and left me to this perfectly nice, but annoyingly persistent, guy.

'But you still aren't vegan?'

'No but I am thinking about it,' I say suddenly. 'There's so many good vegan alternatives and I love Linda Macartney sausages.' He peers at me as if to see right into my head. 'And I don't eat pork either.'

'Why not? What's the difference with pork?'

'It's since I went for a walk in the local woodland and we came across two pigs who were eating the acorns and I called "here piggy, piggy," as you do and they came running up with their tails wagging like little dogs. Made me feel desperately upset at the thought of eating them.' That and watching a programme years ago where scientists did an experiment with pigs and they turned out to be at least as intelligent and affectionate as dogs.

'But what's the difference?' the man persists; boy, he is totally not giving up. 'Why would you cuddle one and eat the other?' I look at his shirt and realise one side is a puppy's face and the other half is a pig – it reads 'no difference'. I suppose I can see his point. There isn't a difference really.

'Obviously there isn't one,' I say awkwardly, 'but people are used to eating certain animals, it's what they are used to, how they're brought up.'

'Absolutely,' says the guy, 'and that's why we're here today educating people about the reality. Have you seen the footage of a slaughterhouse?'

'Gosh no,' I exclaim backing away nervously, 'I don't particularly want to either, thanks.'

I've already had Mel showing me conditions in a factory farm and it's disgusting. I was so upset I do try not to buy anything but free range organic meat, but then Mel showed me this picture of a cow standing at the entrance to the abattoir, one side says free range and the other says factory farmed, but the fact is they both end up in the same place.

'It's just that my friend has already shown me them,' I say quickly.

'Yet you are still paying for it to happen?' This man is beginning to get on my wick now.

'No. I've decided to become vegan.'

'So what are you waiting for?'

'My GP – needs to check my vitamin levels and then, then I will be becoming vegan.' I proudly do a sad little fist bump in the air, not that anyone would notice, there's so much chaos going on around me.

'Right,' says the guy, 'so can I add you to my list of people who are making the change and going vegan?'

'Absolutely, thanks very much.' Without further ado I turn quickly into the crowd, anything to escape this persistent man. He had a way of getting under my skin and making me feel bad about my choices.

I meant what I said too, I would like to become vegan, it's just I enjoy eating meat. And I did once go vegan for about three days and gave myself such a bad pain, I thought I was seriously ill. When I spoke to the doctor he said it's best to ease gradually into large amounts of fibre, but the experience was so unpleasant it kind of put me off. Maybe I'll give it some thought again though, as their argument does make sense or I could at least give going veggie a go.

Drat, I can't find Mel anywhere, even her models seem to have vanished and I charge through the crowds, trying to spot her.

After half an hour or so, I have totally had enough and whip out my phone. It takes several tries, but eventually I manage to get through to her.

'Mel, where the heck are you?' I shout over the deafening din.

'I'm on my way back. Just had to pop out to pick up our vehicle.'

'What vehicle?' I ask, completely confused.

'You'll see.' There's a load of noise in the background and before I can respond, Mel's gone.

At least I know to walk near the road as she must be coming from the direction of Knightsbridge, but I have no idea why she's getting a car. I'm quite relieved however, as I've had enough of the protest thing now, the throbbing crowds and the vegan interview guy has put me off. I meander along, trying to keep myself out of trouble. With Mel gone I feel a bit lost and vulnerable.

There is a steady stream of cars going past, but I can't see Mel in any of them. 'Are you all right, love?' asks a policeman in a reflective jacket. How sad, I must look pretty lost. He's quite sweet actually.

'Yes, fine thanks.' I guess I don't exactly look as though I belong, all alone and with no placard. 'I'm just waiting for my friend to pick me up.'

'What car has she got?' he asks helpfully, peering at the road.

'Erm, that's the thing, I don't really...' I break off, as I can't believe what I'm seeing. Driving towards us is a huge red fire engine and in the front seat is Mel, waving frantically.

'Oh my God.'

'That's unusual.' The policeman smirks. 'Oy, George, look what's coming!' he shouts to his beardy colleague.

Men are so obvious; I guess a fire engine full of attractive girls is a bit of an unusual sight but even so. The truck is driven by a young woman in overalls and pigtails, who is obviously one of the protestors.

'Come on, Soph. Hurry up.' Mel swings open the huge door of the truck, as it pulls up right by me.

'You can't stop there.' The policeman closes his mouth, which had been hanging open.

'Sorry. We're just going.' Mel slams the door behind me and before I can say a thing. I'm sitting in the cab of the fire truck on our way to goodness knows where.

CHAPTER 15

'What the heck are we doing?' I splutter at Mel.

'Isn't this amazing. Soph, this is Betty, she's managed to get hold of this little beauty for us.' Betty is petite and blonde, with an arresting stripe of blue down one side of her hair and the sort of expression around her mouth that means business.

'What are we going to do with this? Is there a fire?' I ask.

'No, silly, it's part of our demo. Have you made sure you've got all the gear?' she asks Betty.

'Course, it's all been planned for days.'

'I wish someone had told me about it,' I mutter.

'It's a surprise,' Mel says, 'and you must admit it's the most wonderful idea we've had yet for promotion.'

I look back at the models all dressed in white around me, the effect is quite dramatic, contrasting beautifully with the red snazzy interior of the fire truck. I take a couple of photos.

'I think it would have been a better surprise if you had stolen a truck with the fit firefighters in it,' I comment drily.

'You're so shallow.' Mel laughs. 'Besides, it isn't stolen, Betty bought it.'

'I didn't even know you could buy a fire engine,' I say.

Betty turns to talk to me. 'Yeah, it cost a few quid on eBay but worth it.' I wish she'd keep her eyes on the road; I'm concerned she's going to take something out, like the corner of a building, or a person, or something terrible.

'So what are we doing with this thing?' I ask. 'Is it for a shoot?'

'Yes it is, I need you to get some shots of the models but there is a bit of a twist.'

We pull up on double yellow lines on Horse Guards Road.

'Isn't this the Treasury?' I ask.

'Yep,' Betty says. 'Right, Mel, we'd better get a move on before we're noticed.'

'I think we'll have a bit of a job not being noticed in this huge thing,' I remark.

'Come on, Soph. Quick, I'll go up the top with the hose, you get down on the street with the girls and get some shots.'

Before I can answer, both Betty and Mel have gone. The models all pile out. It seems they have all been briefed. Horribly embarrassed, I gingerly climb out of the cab and practically fall out on the pavement; quite honestly, these things are far too high up. I don't know how the crew manage; I guess they get used to it.

'Okay then, girls, arrange yourselves and the placards to the side of the building or you're going to get sprayed. You need to be in the foreground of Sophie's shot but you won't want to get caught in the fire.'

'Caught in the fire? Spray?' I'm really confused but help get the girls arranged, whilst Betty and Mel climb on top of the fire engine.

'Right. On the count of three.' Mel looks totally crazy, her curly hair has gone all frizzy and is standing up round her face where she is positioned, clutching the huge hose of the fire engine.

Before I have time to react, the fire engine roars into life and the hose swells ominously like a giant inflatable snake. It bunches horribly and then belches its load to where Betty and Mel are aiming it – all over the side of the building, but instead of water, which would have been bad enough, it is blasting the walls with vivid blood-coloured liquid.

I'm not usually at a loss, but I really am. 'What the hell is that?' I shriek.

'Don't worry it's only beetroot mixed with a bit of food colouring.' One of the nearest models is smiling at my horrified face. 'You'd better get going with the shots or they might run out.'

As if in a trance I start to take photos of the models, each looking eye-catching in front of the red-spattered Treasury, the fire engine in the background. I warm to my task, these are amazingly striking actually; my article is going to be incredible. Although I'm not even going to stop to think for a second what anyone I know who has a rational mind is going to say about this.

Suddenly there's an almighty bang and the hose shoots away from Mel and Betty's grasp, covering them in red from head to foot. The pump, even more horribly snakelike now, forcefully retracts and lands on the pavement next to me, writhing and reeling whilst simultaneously shooting blood-red liquid over the pavement and anyone and everything in the vicinity. I am covered, as are the models, I try to run from the whirling, spouting hose and end up tripping over my feet.

'Take photos, this is brilliant!' Mel shouts at me above the din. She has gone totally mad.

I pull off the shutter and start snapping at the models who are squealing and shrieking at the red spattering from the hose all over their beautiful white outfits. 'They're ruined!' I shout at Mel.

'It's bloody wonderful publicity!' she shouts back, drunk on the excitement.

A short sharp screech of sirens announces the inevitable arrival of the police. Sadly it's not the cute guy who was at the protest. Typically these are the older stern and long beardy variety, not that I want any type of policeman at all right now. This is all going horribly wrong, I just want to be back at Chawton chatting to Emma within the cosy rooms of our office, sipping hot chocolate. I'm not designed for this demo malarkey.

'For God's sake, turn off the ruddy hose,' blasts a police officer with a pot belly and a definite lack of humour.

'I can't!' shouts Betty.

'Bill, you'll have to get up there and help them. Bloody women with machinery, shouldn't be allowed anywhere near it.'

I am so horrified by this blatant sexism, I stand quietly and am even more distressed to find an approaching officer place handcuffs on my wrists. This cannot be happening. 'I have nothing to do with this,' I protest. 'I'm just a passer-by taking photos and I got covered.'

'That's what they all say.' The officer reminds me of PC Goon in *The Five Find-outers and Dog*. Stolid and unable to understand anything.

'I'm innocent!' I shriek. 'I'm a fashion editor and I'm taking photos of these models.' I motion towards the girls who are also being handcuffed and are looking most dismayed.

'Leave it out!' one of them shouts. 'This is a violation of my rights.'

'We can talk about that at the station,' the implacable PC Goon states.

A sodden and bloodied Mel and Betty come down off the top

of the fire engine. Of course they are cuffed as well and we are all led to a police van.

'Can I have a last request?' I ask pitifully.

'What's that?' Goon asks.

'Please, for God's sake, don't tell my mother!'

CHAPTER 16

'What were you thinking?'

I sit at my desk with my head half-hidden behind my hand, I can barely look Emma in the eye and I feel awful. In front of us, *The Mail*, *The Telegraph* and *The Times*, all with headlines splashed across the front:

'Militant Vegan Activists Spray the Treasury with Fake Blood!'

Emma stares at me with disbelief and I feel bad, really I do. I couldn't have imagined this might happen.

'I didn't know that Mel was going to borrow a fire truck, it was meant to be one little demonstration. I had no idea it was going to go viral.'

'You could have not gone, as I asked you. You could have said no like a normal person.'

'But I owed Mel one, and we're mates,' I mumble feebly.

'What about our friendship?' Emma asks miserably. 'What about your job here at the agency?'

Thank goodness the phone rings, I feel as though I'm truly saved by the bell because I don't know how to answer her.

'Good morning, The Jane Austen Dating Agency, Sophie speaking. How may I help you?'

'Ah, Sophie, the very person I wanted.'

'Morning, Baroness.' That's great, the Baroness is not the person I want to speak to; she's probably phoning to say she is leaving the agency.

'I am surprised you are in work this morning after your recent exploits,' she says.

'Yes, well,' I stammer awkwardly, 'I can explain, you see...'

'It was quite remarkable,' she pronounces emphatically. 'This is exactly what I meant by "les mains sales". It means quite literally, "dirty hands". You've proved what I always knew about you, Sophie, you have, what is it they call it? Guts?'

Guts? I don't think I've heard anyone say that for years. Do people actually say that anymore? Obviously they do. 'Yes well, it was certainly an experience.' I glance at Emma, who is filling out forms in a businesslike manner. I've never seen her upset with me like this and I feel terrible.

'Of course you are totally right, human greed is certainly putting an end to this planet and we won't have one left if we don't stand up for ourselves.'

'Absolutely, yes you're right, I mean that is precisely what we were trying to say.'

'What a way to get the message across too, a fire truck!' She gives an expressive chuckle. 'You certainly know how to get attention, wonderful.'

I'm unable to respond except with stunned silence. 'That is not why I was phoning of course,' she continues, 'though obviously I wanted to congratulate you on your newly discovered fame! But also I was going to request another date with, I forget his name, erm...'

'Oh you mean Gene Weston, yes of course.'

'No, no not Gene, though he is a very nice man. I meant the other gentleman who owned the property?'

'Mr Woodtree?'

Emma looks up questioningly as she hears her father's name.

'Yes, charming man,' the Baroness says.

Okay, this is awkward. 'He is, isn't he?' I burble. 'But the thing is, he's not really a member of the agency.'

'Oh? He was at the event so I thought he must be.'

'No, it was just by his kind permission we were allowed to use the gardens.'

'What a shame, he was so pleasant and I rather thought...'

'Will you be attending the Chawton House Ball?' I ask suddenly, desperately trying to change the subject.

'Yes, I am looking forward to it. I have never been to a Regency Ball, I am sure it will be most interesting.'

'Should be fun,' I say enthusiastically, 'and it will be amazing, dancing into the early hours. We have a few surprises as well.'

'Sounds perfect. I won't keep you then, Sophie. Just remember, to do anything worthwhile, you have to do as you have done already. This is the case with anything in life, if you truly want to live, you will have to put it out there and you may lose some people along the way, but it will be worth it for the end result.'

I'm about to reply, although I'm not sure what as I'm so taken aback at the Baroness's words, but merely end up thanking her and getting off the phone.

'That was weird,' I say, momentarily forgetting Emma is angry with me.

'Who was it?' Emma asks.

'The Baroness,' I reply, still stunned.

'Is she all right? Why was she asking about my father?'

'That's the funny thing. She wanted to go out with him on a date.'

'How odd.' Emma nibbles on the end of her pen contemplatively. 'I didn't even realise she had met him, except for a few moments at the Regency sports event.'

'Well no, they were chatting when I left but she was leaving at the same time as me.'

'I thought she was getting on well with Gene in any case.'

'Me too, but apparently it was your father she has her eye on.'

Emma smiles wryly. 'I didn't see that one coming, but then I seem to have been doomed to blindness.'

'I'm really so sorry. I honestly thought we would go and do a bit of chanting and then come home, having taken some snaps for Mel's work.'

Emma looks at me and sighs. 'I understand, I assure you I do and goodness only knows I support the climate strikes. It's just so awkward in this line of business, you have to be above reproach for anything outside the law. At least if it had been a small local protest, that would have been something but this is hardly the best publicity for the agency, is it?'

'No, although,' I brighten slightly, 'don't they say there's no such thing as bad publicity?'

'Whoever said that obviously hadn't sprayed the Treasury with fake blood.'

I guess she has a point.

§⚘

I try to work doubly hard the rest of the day, putting together some flyers for the agency and some extra social media campaigns ready for the Chawton Autumn Ball and Regency Christmas event at Chatsworth House. But all the time, I have a horrible knot of anxiety in my stomach. What if I have ruined the agency's reputation with my involvement in Mel's ridiculous stunt?

The phone goes and my mum's number flashes up on the screen. Perhaps I'll just ignore it. I really can't face her – she is going to go berserk and it's not going to be pretty. Although, maybe... that's a thought, perhaps she'll decide I'm a bad influence on Ben and insist he leaves the agency.

'You can't avoid your mum for the next ten years.' Emma points out 'You're going to have to face her sometime.'

She's right. I take a deep breath and pick up the call. 'Mum?'

'Sophie, you there?'

'Yes. Where else would I be?'

'I just don't know anymore with you.' She giggles almost girlishly. 'I can't believe you're in all the papers – it's incredible!'

'Yes I know, I'm sorry – it's just that Mel–'

'Sorry? I think it's amazing. You've really made a stand.'

'But... I thought...'

'Your dad said everyone's talking about it at the golf club, didn't you, Phillip...?'

'Yes, but... I was worried that...'

'And word is that reducing our intake of meat and how we treat the planet is going to be discussed at the next parliamentary discussion,' she announces triumphantly. 'Whose idea was the fire truck?'

'That was Mel,' I say weakly.

'Inspired, you'd never have got such media attention without it. Good for Mel. Do say "well done", won't you?'

'Erm, yes.' I can't believe it. I thought my mum would go crazy about this development and instead she's congratulating me. My whole world's turned upside down.

After a little more discussion during which I've returned into the office where Emma is typing away still in a slightly aggressive manner, my mum rings off. Too late I realise that this means she won't be going back on her decision for Ben to join the agency, darn it.

Emma looks up briefly from her keyboard. 'So, how's your mum?'

'Bizarrely, over the moon.' I slump down in the chair, still bemused.

'That's surprising, I thought she would have been horrified.' She gives a small shrug.

'Hmm, you and me both.' I randomly pick up some papers on my desk and leaf through them.

'And what about Darcy?' Emma asks quietly.

'Darcy?' I ask casually, as though it hasn't even crossed my mind. But it has. Of course it has. Darcy is going to be horrified, angry; ashamed of me even.

'Yes.' Emma sighs. 'I have a nasty feeling he's not going to be too happy about this, both as our boss and as your boyfriend.'

'I know. I don't know what to do. What if I've completely messed everything up?' I sit with my head face down on the desk, my forehead pressing into the wood.

I feel a reassuring hand on my back. 'Come on, Soph. You've been through worse than this. I'm sure it'll be fine and Darcy obviously loves you. We'll get through this.'

I come out from my position of despair and give Emma a hug. She's such a good friend, I know I shouldn't have got involved with Modiste or Mel's march, but life is complicated and maybe it will sort out in the end. Things usually do. My mum always says it all comes out in the wash, but this time I'm really not sure.

Later that evening, I am slumped in my chair feeling nicely full as Mel cooked a delicious meal of vegan meatballs, mashed potato, veg and gravy. She obviously still feels slightly guilty, although neither of us has mentioned it, beyond a terse exchange.

'How was work?' she asked.

'Fine,' I replied whilst chewing a mouthful.

'Emma all right about, you know?'

'Not really, but I'm sure it'll be okay.'

'Hopefully.'

'Have you spoken to Darcy?'

'No but we're going out tomorrow so I expect I'll hear from him.'

'Oh.'

So as you can tell, it had been a slightly tense meal. Mel is never very good at apologising and I'm annoyed with myself more than anything, so we were a right pair of grumps.

Since then I've been snuggled in my chair, wrapped in a *Pride and Prejudice* cosy blue blanket for comfort. Is it just me, or do you find blankets incredibly reassuring when you're feeling a bit cold and sorry for yourself? Many a time I want to hide under a throw with a cosy book into which I can escape to avoid the grown-up decisions of the real world. I sometimes think there should be a get-out clause, maybe a sign we can put up, saying 'day off from adulting, please try again tomorrow'.

I peer half-heartedly at my phone. Nothing from Darcy, but then he could be busy, or maybe he hasn't heard the news. That would be best; with a bit of luck he might not realise I was a part of the whole protest thing. I glance across at the various images Mel put up in pride of place on the kitchen noticeboard earlier, erm then again maybe not. I think I'm going to have to ask her to take them down, I hardly need reminding on a daily basis of my misdeeds, and if Emma or Darcy visit, it's really not going to help matters. In a couple of the papers, I am pictured looking suitably rebellious, mostly because I was furious at being sprayed with revolting beetroot paint spouting from the hideous out-of-control fire hose. Unfortunately however, my expression could be misconstrued as the face of someone with violent and angry intentions. They say photos never lie, but they obviously can. In this case, I had just wanted to get out of there, but my face doesn't quite convey this message.

Maybe I'll brave it and text Darcy myself. I know I'm trying to be more cool and aloof these days, but we have been going out for a while, so why should I have to play hard to get. I type, *Hi, just wondered if you are still okay to meet up tomorrow afternoon? Xx*

I press send and try not to stare at the screen or keep rechecking for the next few minutes. Goodness only knows how they coped in Regency times when they had to wait for days to receive a reply to letters. These days, minutes can seem like hours. I peer disconsolately at the screen. Nope, nothing. I try to distract myself by opening my latest book, *The Hunting Party*. That will definitely take my mind off Darcy; that's the good thing with thrillers, they keep you on the edge of the seat. I'm totally addicted.

I'm lost in chapter four, when my phone bings the arrival of a message, making me jump. That's the downside with exciting books, they can make you a bit stressy, or maybe it's just me.

Not really, something's come up at work. Sorry, Darcy

Oh, that's a bit abrupt and there's no kiss. Although, sometimes he doesn't put one anyway. I must admit, that did upset me at first, although I put it down to his more formal personality. He says he doesn't put kisses to other people, especially at work, so he's not used to it. I tried to understand, but it doesn't seem that difficult to me. Surely he can remember when he's messaging me to put a kiss at the end, it's not exactly rocket science.

I'd pointed this out to him a few weeks ago and since then he'd been putting a small kiss after his messages. I peer at my previous texts from him; yep there is a kiss on all of them since we had that conversation. The fact he hasn't put one today does not bode well at all; he's obviously totally hacked off with me.

That's a shame, do you fancy going out in the evening? Sophie

I don't put a kiss in my reply, but soften it with a smiley face. Too placatory probably but I still find it difficult to be remote. It feels too abrupt somehow to not even put a kiss or an emoji. It's weird, but there's a whole social etiquette to texting, well I think so anyway. Maybe Darcy's never learnt it.

I'm just getting back into chapter four of *The Hunting Party* when my phone goes; it's Darcy. Thank goodness, it's all going to be okay.

'Hey,' I say in an upbeat and cheery tone.

'Hi.' He sounds rather like someone who has won the lottery and then discovered he's lost his ticket, or accidentally put it in the washing machine in his trouser pocket or something.

'That's a shame you can't meet up tomorrow.' I can't help gabbling but when I'm nervous I spout words rather like one of those annoying over-wound singing Christmas toys. It's something I have tried to work on and I think I'm better than I was, but obviously not today. 'It sounds as though work is being a bit full on and you need–'

'Sophie,' he interrupts.

I stop abruptly mid-flow. 'Yes?'

'I saw the photos in the papers.'

'Oh.' There's a deathly silence, during which I desperately

try to think of an excuse. I am actually really tempted to flick the phone off, shove it under a cushion and run away at top speed, but I don't, I can't, I have to face the music like an adult. 'Yes, that was rather unfortunate.' I remark in a blasé tone. That's it, Sophie, just blag it, mature attitude on, matter of fact. In a sort of 'it happened, it was a shame but never mind, let's move on' sort of way.

'Unfortunate,' he utters loudly. Oh God, this is not going the way I want it to.

'Yes, I was only there to take photos, it's only I got caught up in things,' I mumble like a little kid. I don't know why but his sternness takes me back to being caught out at school for not bringing in the right maths equipment or something.

'But you shouldn't have. You shouldn't have been anywhere near any protests. Not in your position.' He sighs heavily. 'You have responsibilities, Sophie. You're not the heroine of one of your romance novels.' Actually I've told him I don't read those anymore, but he's obviously forgotten. Maybe now's not the time to mention it. 'You're a managing director of a successful company. What the hell were you doing getting involved in a vegan protest? You're not even vegan.'

'But Mel...'

'Mel!' he shouts. I don't think I've ever heard Darcy shout before. 'Bloody Mel and her activism.'

'She is an incredibly good person actually. She's just trying to make a difference to the planet. Trying to get people to change.' I don't know what I'm saying, I mean it's not like I'm a vegan or a climate change protestor but Darcy's making me so angry. Telling me what to do, controlling my life. I'm not a kid, I'm a free person and yes it wasn't a sensible thing to do in my position, I realise that, but it wasn't meant to go this wrong. Besides the planet is important after all, it's where we live; it affects all of us.

'She's a danger to the public and herself. You know how ridiculously extreme she's got in her views. In any case, you simply can't go round spraying buildings, unless you want to get arrested.'

'I know, I know,' I mutter. 'I was asked by Modiste to write an article and...'

'You're working for Modiste? I thought you stopped writing for them now you're managing the agency?'

'I had, but then they wanted me to write this article and Miffy needed it to be raw, edgy, alternative.'

'Sophie, you're quite ridiculous. Has it never occurred to you that firstly, you are none of those things and secondly, even if you were, they're totally incompatible with you being a managing director of a Regency dating agency?'

'Yes. I mean, no. Of course I was worried, it's just sometimes it's hard to make choices between two things that really matter to you and Mel's a good mate.'

'What about me? Doesn't our relationship mean anything to you?' He pauses for breath and I desperately want to explain that he means everything to me, that I really care about him. To try to tell him that I've been feeling pushed aside by Tara and his mother, but before I can articulate anything he continues. 'What about the agency? I asked you to be MD because I thought your heart and soul was really in it.'

I am silent for a moment; he couldn't have hurt me more if he physically punched me. 'I love the agency, it means the world to me as well as you, us, I mean...' I say in a trembly voice.

'It obviously doesn't. Did you ever think how this would affect me and my family?'

'No, I didn't, because I thought you supported my writing. In any case I had no idea about the fire truck. That wasn't what Mel had said. It just kind of happened and I got caught up in it. Besides...' I suddenly register what he means by his family...

'you're just angry because Mummy didn't like it, it might upset her friends.' I didn't mean to be so mocking, but my pent-up frustration has made me sarcastic.

'No she didn't like it. In fact she's having to do a lot of damage limitation at work, that's partly why I can't meet with you tomorrow. Life isn't simple, Sophie. You can't just do what you want. Not when you're involved in business. Not that you'd understand.'

'I do actually. I'm perfectly capable of knowing what I'm doing.'

'Then maybe you should have hesitated for a couple of seconds before you got in that fire truck, thought for a moment what you might lose.' I don't like to point out to him I was standing on a roundabout at the time, but it no longer seems relevant. 'That you could lose both your job and me.'

There's a silence.

'Are you firing me?'

'No, I've managed to persuade Mummy that it was a mistake. You weren't a willing part of it and although she is still very upset, I have got her to agree to you remaining as MD. Emma knows her job and will manage to somehow pick up the pieces. Maybe we can try to keep this quiet. But you can't get involved in any of Mel's bloody mad schemes from now on.'

'I guess,' I say, torn between shock and relief. 'But surely it's not up to your mum who runs the agency.'

'No, it's my decision although of course I like to have her approval. And I've decided to give you another chance. I know you love this agency, so don't screw it up.'

'You won't regret it,' I burble with relief, 'when we catch up, I've got some really amazing ideas...'

'That's the thing, Sophie, we won't be catching up.'

'But...' I can't believe what I'm hearing. This can't be happening.

'Look, I just don't think it's a good idea. I don't think this is going to work with us. Do you?'

'I don't know... I thought...' *Keep calm, Sophie, don't cry, whatever you do don't cry; hold your head high.* 'You mean, you don't want to go out with me anymore?' I'm totally devastated. I'm being dumped by Darcy. This is the end.

'It's not that simple, it's not a matter of want. Not in my position.' Does he sound a bit choked up or has he got a frog in his throat? 'Look this just isn't going to work. I'm going to have to go. I can't talk about this now. Maybe if we were living in a romantic story everything would be okay. But we're not. This is real life. I'm sorry. Bye, Sophie.'

And like that it's over; he's gone. I've got my job, thank God, which is probably more than I deserve after messing things up so badly.

But I've lost Darcy, my Darcy Drummond, my dream man, who I love. This is so not supposed to happen. Jane Austen would be tearing up her manuscript and changing her career for good. Lizzie being dumped by Darcy was definitely not part of the plot. But as Darcy pointed out, this isn't a Regency romance, it's reality, and there's simply no running away from it.

CHAPTER 17

'*S*ophie...'

I can vaguely hear someone calling my name and in my dream, my boat is being bobbed about like a cork on the ocean. Darcy is shouting to me, from his luxury yacht, his mum and Tara are either side of him trying to pull him away from the tiller. We appear to be in some hurricane, the waves are huge and in spite of Darcy's best efforts my boat is turning over slowly, oh-so slowly but in a deadly manner. Oh my God, I'm falling out into the water.

There's a bang and I open my eyes to find that I seem to be on the floor. 'Ow, this water's hard,' I exclaim blearily, looking round my reassuringly familiar room.

'Floor's usually are,' Mel says, standing over me. 'Come on, you've overslept and we're meant to be seeing the guy about the marquees at ten.'

'Can't you see him for me? I don't feel like getting up.' I reinforce this thought by climbing back into bed along with the duvet, which I pull over my head.

'No.' Mel yanks the duvet off with one swift tug. 'Look I've brought you a nicely caffeinated coffee. Have some of that and you'll feel more like facing the day.'

'I don't feel like facing anything ever again,' I groan, pulling the sheets back over my head.

'Come on, Soph. You can't go to pieces just because of a man.'

'I can.'

'I know you can, but please don't.' Mel drags the duvet and sheets off my head yet again and passes me a cup of steaming coffee. It smells delicious actually. 'Come on, have a sip.'

With a sigh and some difficulty, I struggle to a sitting position and drink some of the coffee. It's lovely, warm and reviving. 'I know it seems pathetic, I feel such a failure. I messed everything up and it's just I did really love Darcy, I still do. He was so gentlemanly and quite honestly the first decent man to ever go out with me.'

'He was the only decent guy to go out with you!' Mel snorts.

I give a rueful grin. 'True I guess.'

'I reckon Darcy still likes you and given a bit of time, he'll miss you and come running back full of apologies.'

'If he doesn't run off with that Tara girl first,' I lament.

'He won't. He has any number of girls like that running after him and he doesn't like any of them. He'll change his mind. Honestly, he'd be a fool not to.'

'Thanks, Mel.' I smile weakly at her.

'It's the least I can do, I feel so bad. This is partly my fault. Darcy would never have dumped you if it hadn't been for the whole fire truck incident.'

Partly? It feels mostly her fault actually, but I don't point this out, it's as near to an apology as Mel gets.

'He's just trying to keep his mum happy. For now, she's got what she wants, but in time he'll realise how controlling she is and come running back.'

'Do you think so?'

'If he doesn't, he's not worth bothering with. Who wants to be married to a mummy's boy?'

'Hmm, yes true, that would be a complete nightmare.' I sip more coffee.

'In the meantime you need to throw yourself back into work. Keep busy. It's been two weeks now, I've heard "All By Myself" so many times I could scream and you must have sung yourself hoarse shouting out the lyrics to "Without You" a million times. Any more and you'll never be able to speak again. You, girl, have got to move on.'

'I guess.' I s'pose I *have* been a bit difficult to live with since being dumped by Darcy. Drifting round the flat in my pyjamas and belting out tragic romantic ballads at top volume has been my only solace. That and a huge investment in a large and steady stream of chocolate on demand.

'You know it. In any case, Darcy probably isn't pining away for you right now so why would you stay in moping for him?' My eyes start to fill with tears yet again at this awful thought. 'Have another sip of coffee, Soph. Come on, he's not worth it and you so are. You've got to get yourself back out there. Besides I hate seeing you like this. Where is the Sophie Johnson we all know and love, the shining ray of sunshine and optimism?' I give her a baleful look. 'In any case, The Jane Austen Dating Agency can't run without you. It's just not possible.' Mel throws the invitations for the Chawton Ball at me. 'Apart from anything else, you've got a ball to organise.'

Mel, satisfied she has done her job and managed to motivate me to actually do something, wanders off to start cutting out one of her latest designs and with an effort, I haul myself out of bed.

❧

Some time later, after an invigorating shower, which does make me feel a little better, combined with a smart trouser suit to really look the part, I stalk into the office at Chawton House, looking more confident than I feel.

Emma looks up from her pile of papers, obviously pleased to see me. 'Hey, Sophie, how's it going?'

'I'm back, so that's a start I guess,' I say with a small smile.

'Of course it is, though you look like you need a nice hot cuppa.'

Within minutes she's bringing me a steaming cappuccino.

'That's perfect, thanks.' I take a grateful sip, although soon I'm going to be totally wired after this much caffeine. 'Right, so is everything set for tomorrow night?'

'All looking fab. The caterers are arriving at 5pm, the gazebo is going up this afternoon as well as the tables.'

'That's great, you're super-efficient.' I glance through the paperwork.

'The girls are so excited about seeing you tomorrow.' Emma smiles. 'It should be an amazing night. The Baroness is looking forward to talking all things revolutionary and we have a good number of guys.'

'Sounds great,' I say as enthusiastically as I can. 'Except I think Ben and his horrid friend, John, are coming.'

'Yes they are,' Emma consults her list, 'but so is Lord Bamford, some of his friends and Edward and Freya. It's a fabulous turn out – I think Darcy will be very impressed.'

'I guess, although I don't think he's ever going to speak to me again.' I bite my lip to stop myself from crying for the thousandth time this week. 'I miss him, you know.' My voice breaks treacherously.

'I'm not surprised, but honestly, darling, this is just a blip. He adores you. Mummy is obviously throwing her toys out of the pram. He'll realise in the end that he can't live without you. I give him a couple of weeks at the most and he'll be back.'

'It's been several weeks already and it sounds as though he's fine.'

'He's hardly going to write and tell you how terrible his life is without you.' She laughs. 'He'll be back in no time, you'll see.'

'How come you're such an expert on men?' I ask with a faint smile.

'Years of practise, so no arguing with the professionals. Tomorrow night's ball is going to be amazing and you will be there with your hair done, make-up perfect, wearing that gorgeous lilac gown you showed me last week and it will all be a fabulous success. Darcy will soon be along hotfoot to congratulate you on your sheer talent and brilliant organisational skills and we will all live happily ever after!'

'Yeah right!' I laugh, which is a miracle considering I have a broken heart, but I'm grateful to her all the same.

The next day, like all long-awaited events, arrives far sooner than we imagined; we have been planning this ball for months. Emma and I are buzzing about from early on in the morning, making last-minute touches to the swathes of fabric adorning the morning room and checking the cloths and place settings in the marquee. The colour scheme works perfectly from various shades of soft browns, to reds picked out with sky blue.

Mel flits here, there and everywhere, pinning fabric and stitching beautiful autumnal shades of cloth, which subtly skim sheer net backgrounds. Over the conker brown material, delicate autumn leaves appear to be casually strewn, but are in fact painstakingly sewn on. The completed effect is quite breathtaking.

By dusk, cars begin to crawl down the lantern strewn driveway to Chawton House. Emma and I are positioned in the entrance hall to welcome guests individually.

'Sophie!' I am enveloped in a huge bear hug before I can even register who it is. Of course it's Izzy, she always loves to be early, her blonde curls tickling my face as she gives me a kiss on the cheek.

'You look gorgeous, Izzy, totally fabulous!' Emma greets her warmly.

'She always looks amazing,' Matthew remarks, ever faithful at Izzy's side. He had entered the hall with firm strides, only slightly hampered by his rather obviously too large riding boots, the picture of a Regency gentleman. 'Can I leave my cane here? They're all very well but I'm never sure what to do with them.' He brandishes a long black walking stick in the air as if to emphasise his point, narrowly missing Emma with it.

'Pop it in the umbrella stand,' she suggests helpfully.

'Champagne and canapés are served in the front room, if you go through, we'll join you when everyone's here,' I say hastily, as Regency couples are arriving thick and fast in a flurry of satin and leather, separately of course, not in combination otherwise this would be a very different party.

'Lord Bamford, how nice to see you.' I smile at him as he greets us both cheerily, his florid cheeks vibrant in the candlelight.

'And Lady Amelia Chumley Smetherton, welcome.' Emma extends a gloved hand in greeting.

Amelia touches our hands with a featherlight waft of her expensive satin gloves and returns the full wattage of her smile to the object of her attentions, Lord Bamford. He, with the air of a male spider, willingly but nevertheless firmly ensnared in her web, blunders his way through to the refreshments. I raise my eyebrows at Emma, but there's no time for remarks as the Baroness has arrived in her huge limousine, driven as usual by the ever-faithful Rodrigo.

'Welcome, Baroness.' I give a small curtsey, as she alights from the car. The curtsey seems appropriate for the era we are dressed in.

'Good evening! No riots or protests tonight?' She smiles ironically, the breathtaking diamonds around her neck dazzling in the candlelight.

'Best not, terribly unladylike.' I smile conspiratorially.

Emma rises above this reference to my transgression and welcomes a man in smart tux and boots, who turns out to be Gene.

'She obviously likes him after all,' I hiss to Emma as I watch them walking arm in arm into the drawing room.

'Looks like it,' she replies under the pretence of smiling at a couple of young women in matching white muslin and swathes of glimmering white pearls in their hair. The effect is lovely and I make a mental note to ask how they managed to place them so they would actually stay in. My hair is so fine and slippery that even a grip tends to fall out within minutes of placing it, let alone beads.

I am still contemplating the bead issue when General Baxter appears before me, taking my hand and bowing formally at just the right height above it. I must admit he cuts quite an imposing figure with his bright red officer's jacket with gold braiding. 'Miss Johnson,' he says gruffly, 'charmed.'

Close behind him I'm pleased to see Ellie, looking gorgeous in a cream dress with dark-blue ribbon threaded at the bodice and the sleeves. 'I'm glad you could come,' I say, meaning it.

'Henry persuaded me,' she says with a wry smile. 'But it does look lovely, I adore the lanterns, they're so atmospheric.'

'Took ages to arrange, but I felt they made the whole Regency theme. It gets dark so early now.' Whilst I'm babbling inanely Henry catches my eye and grins. He's very smart in a dark jacket, blue cravat and polished boots.

'Miss Johnson,' he says. It's nice to hear his voice again, I noticed when I met him before, it's deep, gravelly almost, and I find myself wondering randomly if he can sing, but as always it's touched with a slightly tantalising air of mockery. 'We meet again.'

'We certainly do,' I say brightly. 'Do go on through for some refreshments, there's no ratafia here, just champagne.'

'What a relief.' He laughs and steps forward with his sister at his arm to greet Emma.

Within what seems like minutes, the house is full of music, laughter and conversation, with just the delicate tinkle of the harpsichord in the background and I glance round the room, feeling goosebumps at the fact that this must be one of only a handful of times Chawton has seen such a Regency gathering since Jane Austen's day.

For a moment I wonder what Jane would think if she could look down from her writing table in the sky and see this wonderful sight. I fervently hope she would approve.

For once, all our arrangements seem to be working smoothly and I begin to relax and enjoy the evening. I feel as though I am overdue some good fortune after the stressful reality of recent events. Perhaps I belong in Jane Austen's refined and escapist world after all, rather than in our real one, for all the Baronesses comments on les mains sales. After all I do rather prefer having clean hands, it's so much more pleasant.

Shortly after the reception, the musicians gather in the marquee and the brightly lit autumnal swathes of fabric flicker with the movement of dancers gently parading to and fro.

Even Ben seems to be behaving himself in a reasonable way for him, talking and laughing with the striking redhead from the Regency sports event, 'You are a scream.' She giggles, patting his shoulder and peeping up at him endearingly.

Emma skims elegantly across the floor, effortlessly scooping up another champagne glass at the same time, without spilling a drop. I follow, trying not to look too awkward, smiling at a waltzing Maria and Charles on my way. They look so happy in spite of the fact Maria's father, Sir Henry Greaves, is marauding in the corner.

'Enjoying yourself, Sir Henry?' I ask, offering him a glass of champagne.

'Dom Perignon, I hope?' he asks gruffly.

'Of course.' It's cava actually, but hopefully he won't notice the difference.

I follow his gaze across to Lady Amelia Smetherton, who is dancing with Lord Bamford. 'Darned silly business this dancing, far too energetic.'

'Supper will be served in a moment,' I say cheerfully. 'So I am sure you will have a chance to mingle some more then.'

'Huh, if there's anyone worth mingling with.'

'Have you met the Baroness yet?'

'The Baroness?'

'Yes, the Baroness Mayer.'

I want to giggle at the rapid change of expression on Sir Henry's face. You can actually see him mentally calculating whether a baroness might be a greater catch than a lady. Brilliant.

I lead him to her. 'Sorry, to interrupt your conversation,

Baroness. Please may I introduce Sir Henry Greaves. Sir Henry Greaves, the Baroness Mayer,' I say politely.

'Delighted,' the Baroness says.

'Are you one of the de Rothschild Mayers?' Henry Greaves asks. It's comforting to think this man doesn't change. I can imagine him mentally combing his much-loved, well-thumbed tome of Burke's Peerage for the origin of her name.

'Excuse me.' I turn away to leave the Baroness to deal with him. Somehow I feel as though she's more than capable of coping with the task.

Henry Baxter appears at my side with a welcome glass of cava. 'Hey.'

'Thanks.' I take the glass and sip it gratefully.

'So, do you enjoy reading or don't you talk about books in a ballroom?'

'No, unlike Elizabeth Bennet, I'm perfectly happy to talk about books even in a ballroom. In fact pretty much anywhere anywhen! Yes, I'm addicted to psychological thrillers. They make a change from romantic novels.'

'I bet, I haven't read many of those but Ellie loves them.'

'I don't believe you when you can quote from Austen.' I smile at him. 'But in answer to your question, yes they're great, but maybe they can give slightly unrealistic expectations.'

'Definitely. Ellie certainly has some very strange ideas of what an ideal guy should be like.'

'They're all so perfect in romance novels and it makes it tough, when the reality is so far removed. *Pride and Prejudice* is especially so. Some modern men can be rather inadequate.' I glance meaningfully across the room at Ben who is doing a horribly good impression of dad dancing. 'He's my brother, by the way.'

Henry follows my gaze and laughs. 'Brothers are especially trying, to be fair. My older brother is horrible.'

'I'm sure he's not that bad.'

'Hmm, he really is.' Henry twinkles at me. 'He's always been rude and obnoxious, goes with being the eldest son. They get all the privileges and constantly blame you for everything; breakages, spillages, even for forgetting to replace the loo roll.'

I laugh. 'I can relate to that. Being the youngest in my house I was always blamed for everything that went wrong.'

'The perils of being the baby of the family, hey?' He smiles. 'Although, actually, Ellie is younger than me. I'm the middle child.'

'Hope you don't suffer from a constant feeling of being ignored and left out then.'

'Not really. I always enjoyed sneaking under the radar and getting away with things. Being the middle child is great.'

'I'll have to take your word for it,' I say. 'But there are advantages of being the youngest, my siblings say I always got away with more because Mum and Dad had given up by the time they got to me!'

'Brilliant!' I like his grin, it's warm and friendly. 'Are you busy or would you like to dance the next with me?'

'I would actually, that would be, er, nice?' I finish my champagne, then look around for somewhere to put my glass, that's the only trouble with these occasions. Henry notices my dilemma and takes the glass in a gentlemanly manner and passes it to a nearby uniformed footman.

I follow Henry to the centre of the marquee, where everyone is lined up ready to start and we stand opposite each other. He looks at me smiling as the violins strike up a rousing tune.

As we are at the top of a row, we dance towards each other, meet in the middle, bow and curtsey, to go back again after. This is followed by linking arms with the person to the right of us, then we return to link arms with each other. It's fun and I feel relaxed with Henry, he's easy-going and makes light conversation, whenever we are near enough to talk. Izzy and Matthew whirl past and at one stage I am dancing with Charles, who is of course opposite Maria.

'This is great,' he says enthusiastically. 'If our wedding is half as brilliant as this evening you've organised, I'll be more than happy.'

'Glad you're enjoying it,' I say with relief. Perhaps things will be all right after all. Maybe Darcy will see what a great success I'm making of the dating agency and he will realise I'm not a revolutionary and everything will be fine.

Speaking of revolutionary, I suddenly notice the Baroness at the end of the row with Sir Henry Greaves. I have to quickly look away again because I have an overwhelming urge to giggle; he is so upright and pompous, peering down his rather large aquiline nose at the other dancers, forbearing to touch anyone without his long white gloves.

The Baroness as always, gives nothing away other than to give me a conspiratorial wink as she waltzes smartly past. It is so subtle, I wonder whether I imagined it, her expression is always so imperceptible.

Henry Baxter and I meet and waltz together in the centre. 'I'm glad now I practised before I came along,' he says. 'There's so much dipping in and out, I'm always concerned I'm going to go the wrong way or stand on some poor unsuspecting damsel's feet.'

'I can tell you've been trying hard, my feet and dress are still remarkably intact.'

'So far!' He laughs. 'The dance isn't over yet.'

'True, there's still time,' I reply, then catch sight of Ellie in the corner, talking to Mel. 'I'm glad your sister came along, I was worried she wouldn't want to. Doesn't she like dancing? There's plenty of eligible men here tonight.'

'I don't think she had much choice. For some reason my

father thought it was a good idea,' Henry glances at my face, 'although for once I happen to agree with him.'

'I'm glad you rescued yourself, before I got really offended.'

'Me and my big mouth.' He gives a wry grin. 'Of course she looks like she's enjoying herself and in answer to your question, she does love dancing, but I don't think there's anyone here she wants to dance with.'

'Fair enough. Maybe she'll change her mind.'

'Speaking of which, I thought you'd be here with Darcy.'

There's an awkward silence, during which I occupy myself with adjusting my glove whilst dancing round my partner before I am close enough to Henry to talk again. 'Darcy?'

'Sorry have I put my foot in it? I thought you were dating Darcy Drummond, the oil magnate.'

'I was,' I reply shortly and waltz round in a circle with Ben who is slightly worse for wear already, but oblivious to everything apart from the tipsy and giggly girl next to him.

'But no longer?' Henry raises his eyebrows slightly.

'No.'

'I'm sorry,' he says seriously. I notice him studying my face. 'But if I'm totally honest, maybe not that sorry?'

I peek at him from under my lashes as I retreat down the line of the dance. I'm not sure how to take that. It had crossed my mind that he might like me, although I'm still not very good at spotting the signs. I guess of course, he wouldn't ask me to dance if he didn't. Trouble is I don't feel anything about anything anymore. After recent events I'm done with it all.

We finish the dance and walk together to the table where canapés are arranged neatly. 'Plate?' he offers, passing me one. 'I didn't mean to offend you back then. Just forget I said anything about Darcy.'

'It's okay. I wondered if you know him?'

'Not really, no. I've heard of him of course, who hasn't?'

I smile. 'True. Good things I expect, the Drummonds are renowned in the city?'

'Maybe some. But I don't think he can be as smart as everyone says.'

'I think you'll find he is. He owns half of London, or at least his family does.'

'That doesn't mean anything, except they're loaded.'

'You cynic!'

'Not really, it's just I've seen enough of the world to know money can change what people say about a guy.'

'Fair enough. But he's pretty switched on.'

'Hmm.' Henry adds another mouthful of beef and Yorkshire pudding canapé.

I look at him enquiringly. 'You don't sound convinced.'

'He let you go, didn't he?'

I stare at him for a moment. 'Yes, I guess he did.'

'I rest my case. The man's an idiot.'

The dance ends abruptly, which is fortunate, because several couples leave the dance floor allowing me time to alter my expression, which is one of surprise, and I don't want anyone to see it.

The next dance starts up pretty quickly and I excuse myself from Henry under the pretence of needing to check the arrangements for hot drinks for later in the evening. I'm not sure how I feel about anyone being rude about Darcy; the wound is still raw. I wrap my stole round my face to keep out the biting air, as I venture back into the house, to speak to the staff in the kitchen.

As I wander across the grey flagstones, my heels clicking on the unforgiving surface, I hesitate at the foot of the wooden banisters, I could swear, well, I could swear I can hear a noise upstairs. There shouldn't be anyone up there; the staircase is railed off, to prevent idle stragglers or the inquisitive from exploring until later when it might be used as a quiet area to sit and rest. Perhaps it's simply my imagination. I shake my head and continue along the corridor into the kitchen whereupon I'm startled by a familiarly large head poking suddenly around the door.

'Miss Johnson! Just checking if there are any more of those delicious sausage things on offer.'

It's Lord Bamford, sporting a large tray of canapés. I think I must be standing there with my mouth open, but promptly shut it with a click. 'Thought I'd take them back to the dance floor, in case anyone else is a little peckish!' He chortles, as a small glob of sausage meat flies from his mouth and wavers unpleasantly on his chin.

A figure appears next to me. 'Lord Bamford, I seem to have lost you.' It's Lady Amelia. The forced composure on her carefully made-up face makes me want to laugh out loud. I can't really imagine her losing anything.

'There you are, sir.' One of the waiting girls tips some more sausage canapés on the tray balanced on Lord Bamford's hand. 'Here let me take it, there is plenty more food coming out, you know, sir.' She carefully manoeuvres the tray out of Lord Bamford's tight grip, it's almost comic as the two appear to be wrestling for control of the tray, until he finally concedes that he is not being very gentlemanly and surrenders his booty.

After the initial tussle, where he simply pouts like a naughty boy, his good manners triumph and he chortles. 'Simply can't have too many canapés, can you, Amelia!' He manages to stuff another canapé whole into his mouth that he's pilfered from the tray, whilst he talks. It's quite a talent really.

Lady Amelia smiles politely in return, but firmly placing her arm through his, she accompanies him in the direction of the entrance to the house.

The long-haired waitress with plaits gives me a

conspiratorial grin and I smile back. 'Are you happy with everything?' she asks.

'Yes, you're all doing a wonderful job, thanks. Oh and at the end of the night, you're all more than welcome, if you're not too tired, to stay on for a hot chocolate and marshmallows.'

'Ooh lovely.' The plump cook pauses from taking another large tray of canapés out of the oven and offers me a steaming pork and apple dumpling to sample.

I wander out the back door, nibbling the delicious mouthful and relishing the cool air and a moment of quiet before returning to the melee of whirling satin and lace.

As I reach the front of the house, I catch a glimpse of someone slipping across the lawn and up towards the rose border. All I can make out is a pale blue skirt and the gleam of the sole of a pair of slip-on satin shoes. The path is lit with tiny lights and I instinctively follow, just to make sure everything is okay. I mean why would a young woman run into the trees in the dark of night? Seems a very dodgy business.

As I reach the top of the path, I round the corner to where the red brick of the flower/rose garden juts out, just in time to see Ellie look behind her and slip through the huge wrought-iron gates at the entrance. Odd as I always keep those locked, but strangely they opened easily enough and I watch her hurry on down the empty winter rose and vegetable beds to the apple orchard.

As she arrives at the far wall, where in the summer the cordoned fruit trees share their bounty, I notice the figure of a man. He isn't dressed in Regency, merely a modern dark jacket, though it is hard to quite make him out. His lack of costume makes me assume he isn't at the party, but from Ellie's manner of meeting him, he is no stranger. The couple are standing very close together, Ellie on her highest tiptoes, arms stretched round his neck, pulling his head in for a passionate embrace.

Their intimacy and the sudden hoot of a very enthusiastic owl, jolts me from my observation and automatically, I stealthily turn and make for the house. Without the distraction of the pursuit of Ellie maybe needing my help and the sudden realisation that any murderers could be lurking in the bushes, I half run towards the house as my fears have completely taken over.

'Sophie, are you okay?' It's Henry Baxter, who appears to be standing in the courtyard by the house.

'You made me jump,' I say accusingly before I can stop myself. My heart is racing, I really should take up jogging or something, I'm totally unfit.

'Sorry, but you startled me too, I was hardly expecting a Regency lady to come sprinting round the corner at full whack.'

'I just remembered I'd left some food in the oven.' I improvise.

'Really? I hope it's not all burnt.' His sardonic eyes look teasingly into mine.

'No. I've realised of course that the catering team will have managed it fine.'

'What a relief. Should Regency ladies be running anyway?'

'Maybe not.' I smile, it's impossible to take Henry seriously.

'Unless they are making some kind of secret assignation?' He raises an eyebrow.

'Definitely not! Who would think of such a thing? It's dark out there.'

'Yes plenty of scope for all kinds of vagrants, murderers and scoundrels.'

'Nonsense. I'm sure they've got better things to do than lurk in the bushes here at Chawton. You must have been reading too many thrillers.'

'Isn't everyone reading them at the moment? *Girl on a Train*, *The Girl on a Platform*, *Gone Girl*.'

'I do enjoy a psychological thriller.' I shiver whilst I'm talking, not because I'm scared, but because I'm super cold.

'Come on, we'd better go in or you'll freeze to death. The perils of the outdoors on a winter's night for the unsuspecting female!' He flicks me a grin as he places his long jacket around my shoulders and I follow him towards the house. 'So which one's your favourite so far?'

'Oh I don't know, I love all the ones you mentioned, as well as *Rebecca*, which I guess has got to be the best.'

'Last night I dreamt I went to Manderley again...' he quotes, his breath frosting atmospherically in the cold night air.

'You've read it,' I squeak.

'Of course. It's an amazing book, although I never really understood why Max de Winter kept on that hideous Mrs Danvers. Terrifying woman.'

'Yes she was,' I laugh, 'but the whole book is so atmospheric. And I love the way we never know the narrator's name, yet Rebecca always dominates the whole narrative.'

'True, it's a great story, I never saw that twist coming at all.'

'They're always the best. Take you by surprise. I can still remember where I was when I read that part of the book and it was years ago.' I smile.

'Me too. I was on the train to Paddington and I can remember the old man opposite me gave me a very strange look because I exclaimed something unmentionable out loud. I think he thought I was talking to myself. Most unsettling.'

'That's brilliant – you could have explained you were reading a great book.'

'I don't think he'd have understood. He was scribbling away on some document, so maybe I disturbed him.'

'Perhaps he was a writer.'

'If he were a writer, he'd have had sympathy with anyone making exclamations about *Rebecca*!'

'Good point.' We both laugh and walk companionably into the marquee. Everyone seems to be having a good time; Sir Henry Greaves is dancing with the Baroness. They appear to be locked in a fierce battle as to who can be the most formal and upright. It's hilarious; I wonder why I never thought of matching them before. Although I think the Baroness would probably eat Sir Henry for tea.

Maria, Charles, Izzy and Matthew are dancing in the centre and are joined by Freya and Edward who are dancing happily together in the absence of Miss Foxton, who I don't believe was able to come this evening. In another circle, Lady Amelia is skipping delicately along, her fragility emphasised further by the contrasting nearby hulkingly bulky form of Lord Bamford, who is ridiculously puffing alongside like a prize penguin.

I feel a pang of anxiety as I notice Ellie is still absent, her father is standing formally in the corner of a marquee. I notice the General flicks a glance in Henry and my direction, but I can't make out his thoughts as he's got one of those expressions that is hard to read. He just seems so stern and remote. He'd make an excellent comedy villain. 'Have you seen Ellie?' I ask Henry.

'Not for a while. She's probably popped out to the ladies or something.'

'I guess,' I mutter, unsure whether to say anything to him or not.

Mel appears breathlessly from nowhere. 'Soph, it's the phone for you. It's Darcy!'

'Darcy?' I utter stupidly as though it's the first time I've ever heard his name.

'Yes, duh, the guy you've been moping about for the last however long.' I love Mel, she always has to rub it in and doesn't care what she says in front of other people. Henry looks at me questioningly, but I'm already rushing to get to the phone.

'Okay, sorry, Henry. I'm just, er...' I call over my shoulder.

'That's fine, you go...' he says politely.

Mel accompanies me across the lawn into the house. 'I told you he'd be back,' she declares triumphantly. I take the phone from her, giving her a look, which encourages her to retreat hastily.

'Hello?' I mutter into the handset.

'Sophie?' Darcy's voice gives me goosebumps the moment I hear it. He sounds embarrassed actually. 'I was wanting to speak to Emma.'

'Oh,' I sink down into a nearby ornate Regency chair. 'She's outside actually.'

'I wanted to know how the evening is going.' He sounds flustered. 'But of course you can tell me that.'

'No.' I draw myself up out of the chair. 'That's fine. I'll go and get Emma now.'

'No don't... I...' I don't stop to hear what he has to say. My face is aflame with embarrassment. How did Mel get this so wrong? I half-throw the phone on the dresser and stalk off in the direction of the marquee.

Emma, who is dancing energetically with John Smith, is happy to extricate herself from his rather sweaty attentions and wafts off to speak to my ex-beloved and I am left to nurse my emotional wounds in the corner of the marquee. I feel like going home, but there are still a couple of hours left so there's no chance of that happening.

'You look like you need a stiff drink.' The Baroness appears noiselessly at my shoulder, passing me a glass of something strong smelling, which I think might be gin.

Nevertheless I take a revitalising sip, the scalding liquid burning down my throat. 'Wow that's potent.' I try desperately not to cough.

'Does the trick though,' she remarks with a stern laugh. 'And goodness only knows this evening between Sir Henry Greaves and Gene Wilder over there, I need some myself.' She takes a swig from her own glass.

'I hope they're not stopping your enjoyment.'

'Of course not, I have come up against far worse than a couple of over keen older men dressed in Regency clothing.'

'I guess you have.'

'So you're still struggling with the after-effects of the protest?' She looks at me speculatively.

I stare at her. 'I don't know how you know that, but yes I am.'

'Not much gets past me, child, and I'll tell you this. The one thing I truly know is, life is short. Very short. God only knows I have been made rudely aware of this in my time. If Darcy is half the man you deserve, he will speedily get over this ideal he's been told to believe in and realise he has a wonderful young woman within his reach and every moment he is not with you, is a total waste of time.'

Before I can answer, she raises her glass, mutters 'Tschüss,' downing the fiery liquid in a manner bound to put hairs on the chest and gamely marches towards Sir Henry Greaves.

Ben saunters to join me, only he manages to barge into my arm, making me spill my drink. 'All right, sis?'

'Yes fine,' I say with a fake smile, hoping my slightly reddened watery eyes don't give away my inner turmoil after Darcy's call.

'I'm bloody glad *you* are. Look at that.' He gestures randomly over to where the tipsy, dishevelled, but somehow still sultry looking redhead is dancing pretty closely with a couple of good-looking Regency dandies.

'Oh,' I articulate as I stare momentarily at the dancers. 'I expect she's just being friendly.'

'Friendly! She's bloody well all over them.'

'Shh, don't make a scene. I'm sure it's nothing and anyway it's not as though you're going out with her? You've only met her recently.'

'Not the point.' He's drunkenly lurching in her direction. I seriously hope there isn't going to be a punch-up; that would be the last straw.

'Hey, Ben.' It's Henry, who I hadn't noticed nearby at all. He takes Ben gently by the arm. 'Why don't we go out for some air?'

'What the...?' Ben slurs, but he allows Henry to help him outside. He's a decent guy. A scene is the last thing we need and I feel grateful to him.

A couple dance past in perfect harmony and I think how handsome they look together, until I suddenly realise with a jolt its Freya and Edward. She's positively stunning tonight, her cheeks are flushed pink, and I try to think what's different about her. Then I catch sight of her expression, gazing up adoringly at Edward. Of course, she's in love with him. How awkward, even though they're not technically related, I worry he probably sees himself as an older brother. He's fond of her; I can see that. But I can remember all too clearly how he was looking at Miss Foxton at the sports afternoon. Why oh why is love always so complicated?

I notice Ellie stealing back into the room, obviously trying to look as though she's been here all the time. She manoeuvres behind her steely looking father, slipping effortlessly into the dancing besides a laughing Izzy. She's obviously no stranger to sneaking about behind her father's back. There's definitely something strange going on there. I just don't know what. Why didn't she invite whomever it was to come along? I guess he isn't a member of the agency, but surely he could join.

Matthew appears at my side. 'Great evening,' he says pleasantly, adjusting his trouser above the gleaming top boots.

'Isn't it?' I agree politely. 'Izzy is certainly enjoying herself.'

'She is.' There's something about Matthew's tone, a slight unease that makes me peer at him a little.

'Is everything okay?'

'Yes. I think so, it's only, there's something different about her. I'm just worried... maybe it's nothing.'

'But you're both happy together, aren't you?'

'Of course, I adore her. It's just, I heard that...'

General Baxter appears imperiously at my side. 'Miss Johnson?'

'Yes, General?' General Baxter is one of those imposingly formal people who make you feel bad when they interrupt as though it's entirely your fault, not theirs. Matthew makes a small bow, vanishing into the heaving throng, and I feel a sense of frustration as there was obviously something he wished to tell me.

But General Baxter is not to be discouraged. 'I was hoping to speak with you before the end of the evening.'

I fix him with a polite smile, goodness only knows what he's about to say.

'My son and daughter are accompanying me next week to reside at our country estate, Dreyfus Manor. We always go every year at this time, it makes a break from London and we would be delighted if you would consider being our guest for a few days, Miss Johnson?'

'Me? Stay with you?' Okay I was not expecting this at all.

'Yes, Henry and Eleanor always find it a little quiet after the city. You would be very welcome as our guest. I know you have a busy schedule but we would be honoured if you would join us.'

At that moment Henry appears at his father's side and I look at him questioningly. He looks surprised, but then he grins. 'It would be an excellent opportunity for more discussions on *Rebecca*.'

'Put like that, how can I refuse?' I swallow another sip of the

Baroness's firewater and give the General my hand, which he seems to be expecting. 'Thank you. I would be delighted.'

And just like that, I've agreed to go and stay goodness knows where in an old and probably deserted manor house with an extremely strange guy who I hardly know. But what did the Baroness say? We need to seize the moment and make the most of things. Darcy is obviously not missing me in the least and I've made a mess of every romantic opportunity I have ever had.

Besides, I like both Henry and Ellie, although there is definitely some mystery going on there. All is not as it seems and I feel a few days away could be the distraction I need. Maybe I can do something useful for once. This might not be *Northanger Abbey*, but then I am no Catherine Morland, so Dreyfus Manor will do just as well.

CHAPTER 18

'You're going to Dreyfus Manor?' Chloe shrieks on the other end of the phone.

'Seems like it.' I rub my ear, I think she's deafened me. 'Have you heard of it then?'

'No, but it sounds amazing. Really old and romantic.' There's a rustling in the background, she's obviously trying to multitask.

'Do you think so? I tried googling it but there aren't any photos. I'm beginning to wonder why I'm going when I hardly know these people. But Mel and Emma think it would do me good to get away from it all for a while.'

'I totally agree,' Chloe says briskly, 'you need to get that Darcy out of your head for a bit.'

'Easier said than done,' I lament. 'He's the nicest guy I've ever been out with and trouble is, I love him. You just can't turn that off.'

'Nope it's not that easy.' I hear Chloe take a moment and can understand. 'Kian had me hook, line and sinker in spite of how horrible he was. For a long time I struggled to stop having feelings for him. But I got over it in the end.'

'I know, and in any case who wouldn't with someone like Nick around. How is he?'

Chloe's tone becomes dreamy. 'Great. He's so sweet and he's doing incredibly well at the office out here. Darcy's very pleased with the increase in revenue. But then it's effortless for Nick, everyone likes him, he's so easy-going.'

'Yes I can imagine that. Unlike Darcy.'

'I know. But Darcy is still a lovely guy.'

'I guess. I suppose I worry he's as arsey as his namesake. In any case he's so over me now since that stupid protest.'

Chloe sighs. 'Yes that wasn't great. I only saw the pics on the internet but it was pretty full on. I suppose you can see his point, spraying the Treasury doesn't exactly fit in with the whole genteel Regency romance thing does it. I'm totally behind saving the planet, it's just a shame you couldn't have simply handed out flyers or something.'

'I know it was crazy, although I wasn't expecting to be defacing anything. I honestly thought I could quietly join the protest to help Mel, get some pics for the editorial for Modiste and everyone should have been happy.'

'Did you seriously think that though? It would have been a pretty mundane article, which from what you were saying wasn't really what Modiste wanted anyway.'

'True, I've finally finished the piece and I'm quite pleased with it actually. If there's one thing I can say, it's certainly not boring.'

'Fair enough. You've got to stand up for what you believe in. But you do give out pretty mixed signals sometimes.'

'What do you mean?'

'You kind of go at everything at a hundred miles an hour.'

'Thanks a lot.'

'I don't mean it like it's a bad thing, it's just you need to make your mind up – you can't be a famous editor, run a Regency dating agency and be a militant vegan activist all at the same time.'

'I guess not. Though you can remove that last one. I never did want to be an activist, although did I tell you, the chanting bit was quite fun?'

I can tell Chloe is rolling her eyes even though I can't see her. It's funny how you can know someone so well, you can sense what they're thinking even several thousand miles away. I wonder if I could ever get to be like that with Darcy. Maybe not, he's so remote and self-contained. 'It'll do you good to get away for a bit.' She continues. 'Maybe try to think about your priorities, what matters most to you.'

'Sounds a bit heavy.'

'Okay then have a good relaxing holiday anyway, let everyone else look after you for a change.'

After a bit more chat and promising to keep Chloe posted, I meander back into my room and contemplate my slightly pitiful looking pile of clothes ready to pack. I've got a few bits, which I think will do for most occasions, but I'm not sure how posh the General's family will be. Perhaps I'll ask Emma, she always knows what to wear.

'Are you ready yet?' asks Mel, drifting in whilst noshing a piece of marmite on toast and perching on the end of my bed.

'Oy, you've dropped crumbs on my covers!' I brush at the bedspread aimlessly.

'You're not going to be sleeping in it for a bit,' she says stuffing the last bits in one large mouthful. 'Have you thought any more about becoming vegan?'

'What?'

'After that YouTube clip with the interview guy at the protest. You made a pledge.'

'A pledge?'

'Yes, you said you were becoming vegan.'

'Oh that, yeah well, as I said, I'm considering my options.'

'I guess it's a bit difficult when you're going to stay with people. Maybe look at it when you get back. I've got some great new recipes.'

'Right I'll take a look. I think the General is likely to dine off pheasant and venison from his estate so if I don't want to starve I think I'll have to stay carnivore for now.'

'Yuk.'

'It's probably their way of life. Has been for centuries,' I say dismissively, which is ridiculous really as I don't know anything about them. But I imagine this is a proper country estate with all the accompanying traditions. I wonder if they have horses, that would be amazing and at least if I get fed up trying to make conversation, I can slope off to the stables and talk to the animals. I haven't ridden for years, but I would love to. That's a point. 'You don't think they'll make me go hunting, do you?' I ask anxiously.

'Probably. You know what the country set are like. You'll be bloodied before you know it.'

'I'll refuse.' I sink onto the bed, panic stricken. 'Besides I don't know what I'd wear anyway. I haven't got anything suitable.'

'Then you're totally safe. Unless you want to be like Lady Godiva.'

'Ha ha, not. Don't think anyone would want to see that!'

'Definitely not.'

My phone rings out and the room fills with the sound of 'Dance Monkey'.

'Is that loud enough?' Mel retorts as I grab it.

'I love that song, it's brilliant,' I reply boogying at the same time as pressing the green button.

'Soph, how are you?' It's Miffy.

'Hi, Miffy. I'm fine thanks, just packing my bags for a little trip.'

'Ooh romantic weekend away with the delectable Darcy?'

'No actually.' I swallow and slump back down onto the bed, desperately trying to regain my faux-cheery tone. 'We broke up.'

'I'm so sorry, darling; I had no idea. What happened? You were so loved up, I was totally jealous.'

'Life got in the way I guess,' I say as cheerily as possible.

'Often does, sweetie, often does. Well...' She hesitates as if waiting for me to elaborate, but as I have no intention of doing so, she continues anyway, 'Maybe this will cheer you up. I've been speaking to Penny and she's extremely impressed with your editorial piece. The whole slant on vegan identity and crisis within the backdrop of the vegan climate protest was stunning. Fabulous work! And she's not easily impressed.'

'Wow that's great, I'm so glad.' Maybe something good is coming out of this whole protest thing after all.

'Great? It's incredible! Penny is giving your piece an entire four-page feature in this month's Modiste. You totally nailed it!'

'Whoop, whoop, that's so exciting.'

Mel, in the kitchen ladling more marmite on toast, watches dumbstruck as I do a victory lap of the flat, waving my hands in the air.

'So...' Miffy waits a moment for me to calm down a little, 'we would like to commission you to write a feature on Vivienne d'Artois for the next magazine.'

'Vivienne d'Artois?' I gulp at the mention of the scarily named Vivienne. She's the sister of one of our most terrifying ex-clients Lady Constance Parker, who I had a dramatic tête-à-tête with last year. It's a long story, but Lady C accused Mel of stealing her sister's dresses to make copies. In fact Mel actually borrowed them to get some design ideas, very different ones of course, her designs are nothing like Vivienne's. It was more to see the standard she needed to reach. To be fair I think she did say they were going to be exhibited in the V & A museum, which was a teensy bit of a fib, but even so, Lady C was totally out of order in her behaviour to all of us.

'Yes, it's quite a coup actually.' Miffy is still talking away, oblivious to my negative vibes. 'Vivienne rarely grants interviews to anyone these days, but surprisingly she's agreed to meet you on eighth December. You'll need to travel to her house in Chelsea, but I'm sure you won't mind that. We will obviously reimburse all expenses.'

'No of course not, but I mean...' I'm distracted by Mel making faces in the background, I know her well enough to be able to translate them. I put on my can-do attitude immediately; damage limitation is necessary here. Besides this could be a good plan. 'That would be great. I'm going away for a few days, but will be back by December.'

'Fabulous, darling. Where are you off to anyway, if you aren't with Darcy?'

'To stay with General Baxter and his family.'

'General Baxter, gosh. One is mixing in terribly elevated circles, isn't one?' She does sound surprised. 'He usually only invites royalty to stay or those, shall I say, with private means. Don't know how you've managed to wangle that one. Another article in the offing? Let me guess, I bet you're planning on writing about his daughter, Eleanor Rafferty Baxter. She's one of the most eligible young ladies in the country.'

'Ellie?'

'Ooh, on first name terms too. You are a dark horse, Soph.'

'I don't really know her or the family very well,' I confess awkwardly.

'I'm sure you soon will. Never known you to fail at anything yet. Anyway got to dash. Lunch date at Harvey Nicks with the gals. And don't forget to prep for Vivienne Artois, bit of a stickler by all accounts. Tootle pip.' And just like that she's gone, leaving me to panic even more about what I'm going to wear to the Baxters' mansion.

§

Several hours later, a sparkling midnight blue Rolls Royce Phantom ascends the driveway to Chawton, looking every inch at home with the beautiful surroundings.

'Is that the car they're planning for the wedding?' I call to Mel.

'No, you goose, it's the Baxters for you!' Emma calls from down in the hallway. 'Madam, your chariot awaits!'

'I can't believe it! I've never been in a Rolls!'

'They're very comfortable,' Emma says. She's probably been travelling in them since she was born. 'You'd better hurry. Great people do not like waiting.'

Mel waves me out the door. 'Terrible for the environment those things.' She frowns at the beautiful car.

'I don't expect they take it out much,' I soothe, dragging my case over the cobbled driveway.

A smartly suited and booted chauffeur is already out of the car to take my bags. Of course the boot opens effortlessly on its own.

'Miss Johnson.' General Baxter alights from the front.

I spot Ellie who opens one of the rear windows to say hi. She's half-hidden by an alarming tower of band boxes.

'I'm sorry we're late,' the general continues, 'there were a few urgent matters I had to deal with.' He still manages to look, if it's possible, more annoyed than he usually does. 'Ah, here's Henry.'

A smart little two-seater appears, bowling up the drive. It's one of those gorgeous classics with a runner alongside, I note as it purrs to an abrupt halt at the top of the drive.

'Morning, Sophie!' Henry Baxter's face crinkles into its usual smile and the anxiety which had been building up in my chest subsides a little.

'If you would like, Miss Johnson, you are more than welcome to travel with Henry in his car, or if you would prefer you may spend the journey with us. It's totally up to you,' the General says politely.

It's a no brainer really, one glance at Henry's cheery smile, combined with the chance to escape from the General's stifling formality and I'm decided.

'If you don't mind I am happy to keep Henry company,' I say casually, my slightly reddened cheeks belying my tone.

'Way to go, Soph,' Mel mutters as I give her a hug goodbye.

Emma gives a regal wave from the open diamond paned office window. 'No thinking about work or anything else,' she calls in a mock stern voice.

Within minutes I'm tooling along at a reasonable speed with Henry amongst the Hampshire country lanes and am feeling pretty cheery with life. I'm only a tiny bit disappointed about not travelling in the rolls, but I'll get over it.

'So you've got a fair few bags with you. Hope you haven't brought any work to do. Sounds as though you need a holiday,' Henry comments, his hair going crazy in the breeze.

'Yes I do actually. Although the bag thing is just because... well...' I break off not wanting to explain.

'Because?'

'I wasn't really sure what I would need to wear. I mean I do normally, because it's quite simple, depending on the weather and where you are. But visiting a large rural estate, I feel a bit out of my depth.'

'Not used to country piles then?' He laughs.

'Not really. I come from a seaside town called Bampton on the south-west coast. It's nice, but no stately homes to be seen.'

'How disappointing,' Henry says mock seriously, 'but it doesn't seem to have stopped your enthusiasm for them?'

'Not at all. I love old places. They are all so romantic and I can just imagine myself in the old days, parading around in long dresses.'

'No wonder you need so many bags.' Henry chuckles.

'It's okay. I've only brought three ballgowns and two state gowns.'

'Oh.' He looks concerned. 'You might need three state dresses if the Queen and Prince William come to call.'

'Darn, do you think we can go back? I left my other three state dresses hanging in the wardrobe at home.'

We both laugh and Henry offers me a chocolate éclair.

'These bring back memories,' I only just manage to utter, as my teeth are slightly gummed together. 'My dad always brought them on car journeys.'

'Yes they're the best, except they do tend to stop you talking.'

'Hmm, I see the method in your madness.' I smile.

'Not at all, I like to hear you chat away. That's why I suggested to my father you might like to travel with me.'

'Does Ellie not mind? I mean...' Oops, never cool to suggest to someone that you can't imagine how anyone can bear to be stuck in a car with their dad.

But fortunately Henry doesn't seem to mind. 'No, she's pretty used to him by now. I think half of it goes in one ear and out the other, though she's had a tough time of it. At least I can get away as I have a property of my own so I have to go down there and do maintenance.'

'So what do you do?' I ask shyly as I can picture him being a landowner and nothing else.

'I pretty much run my own farm as well as helping my dad out with his estate.'

'Sounds perfect. Do you have livestock or mostly fields?'

He laughs. 'Some of each. We do have a dairy herd as well as some sheep. But it's mostly arable farming.'

'You must be super busy then.' I have visions of him out in all weathers, toiling up the hillside, James Herriot-style, to help with the lambing.

'No, I have a farm manager,' he admits sheepishly.

'Sounds like a good plan.' I hope fervently I might get a chance to visit the farm. It sounds far more interesting that Dreyfus Manor, but I don't like to ask. He might think I'm after something that I'm not.

'Anyway, how about you? I hear you're a writer as well as the MD of the dating agency?'

'Yes. I write articles for Modiste. I've always wanted to talk about contentious issues and make a difference.' I become silent, not wanting to talk about recent events.

'Good for you. I'd like to do the same, but I can't. You're lucky. I presume your parents don't mind.'

I picture my parents in their cosy flowery wallpapered dining room that they decorated that way in the nineties and now left in the hope that it would eventually come back into fashion if they wait long enough, and feel a wave of affection for them. 'Yes they're pretty supportive. Embarrassing but lovely, if you know what I mean.'

'Don't even start talking about embarrassing when it comes to parents. It's in their job description, isn't it?'

I laugh. 'True enough.'

There's a silence.

'Did Darcy get on with your mum and dad?' he asks, his eyes concentrated on the road.

'Well he didn't really know them. They tried very hard when he came round, but our backgrounds weren't very similar.'

'No?'

'Not at all. My parents live in a house in suburbia. Darcy

resides in several properties in the metropolis and his mother thought I was some kind of fortune-hunting little minx.' Oops my mouth has run away with me again so I break off. Perhaps I've said too much.

Henry shoots me an amused glance. 'It's always difficult when it comes to family. I think most peoples are pretty strange.'

'Yes you're right, I think we just get used to our own kind of weird, then maybe can't cope with someone else's.' We both laugh.

'Speaking of strange, I hope you'll enjoy staying at Dreyfus. It's a big old place, chock-full of dark draughty corridors and strange noises in the night.'

'Sounds perfect,' I say flippantly. 'A perfect place for a murder.'

'You could say that.' Henry smiles. 'I don't know its full history, but you never know. It's hardly romantic, unless you like being cold twenty-four-seven and needing to wear thirty layers just to stay vaguely comfortable.'

'I'm sure I'll be fine.' I think with satisfaction of the thermals Emma insisted I borrowed from her ski collection. 'Old houses are always cold and draughty,' she'd said, when she had noticed my startled expression. Thank goodness Emma obviously grew up with a great deal of experience of these places.

We drive on through the sun-speckled country lanes, the kind you get at this time of year where the light stays low in the sky throughout the day. Every so often, Henry hums or sings along to a good song on the radio and I feel inspired to join in, softly at first and then louder as I feel more confident. I'm loving this actually because I like to sing randomly at times and it's usually shocked most of my potential partners.

It's great to hang out with someone and just be friends for once. I don't think I've ever had a male friend. I've started out that way with several in the past, but they always wanted more, unknown to me, or I guess in other cases I started to fancy them and they didn't like me in that way. Maybe losing my romantic ideals, I'm finally growing up. Here's to platonic friendships and plenty of them. Henry Baxter is certainly a really nice guy and I'm enjoying being with him.

CHAPTER 19

*D*reyfus Manor looms before us, an imposing grey building with wisteria growing up the front of its vast crumbling walls. No doubt it would probably be stunningly beautiful in the summer, adorned with tumbling white or purple flowers, but in the bareness of November, it is a barren looking monstrous dwelling. I love the sash windows, which are large and open looking, but other than that it looks generally rather cold and I inadvertently shiver as we approach along the length of the twisty driveway.

'I didn't realise you lived at Manderley,' I joke to cover my slight unease.

'It is a little like it,' Henry smiles, 'but you will be relieved to find there's no Mrs Danvers here.'

'That *is* a relief.' I smile back.

'As for Max de Winter's, I'll leave that to you to judge,' he adds with a twinkle.

Maybe I don't feel quite so okay after all.

The feeling of unease fails to lift as I reluctantly leave the warmth and ease of the fading winter sun and Henry's easy company to stand in the cold and damp entrance hall to Dreyfus

Manor. An equally grey and sombre butler stands in the doorway, drooping rather like a wilting spaniel.

'Afternoon, Gregson. Please could you remove Miss Johnson's baggage from my car. My father will be arriving shortly. Will dinner be ready at seven?'

'Chef has it all under control, sir.' The butler is, in spite of his appearance, totally professional.

Before I can turn to Henry and comment, I spot the dark flash of blue between the trees. He follows my gaze.

'My father is always punctual.'

'That's good,' I say non-committally.

'Depends if you are on time yourself.'

'No, never, in my case.' I smile at him and he grins back.

The General alights from the elegant car; Ellie follows close behind. 'Well what do you think, Miss Johnson? Not a bad old pile, eh?' he asks.

'It's very grand,' I say politely, trying not to catch Ellie's eye.

The General doesn't seem to know how to respond to my comment, so merely continues. 'Eleanor will show you to your room. Henry, I need to talk to you about the boundary wall at East Weldover.'

I watch the General and Henry disappear off round the side of the house and think, not for the first time how very dissimilar they are in appearance. The General, obviously an older father, is an upright, large jowelled man with a slightly receding hairline. Henry is altogether narrower in build, not that he isn't quite fit looking, but he's taller and less broad. He also has a sense of humour. Sadly, General Baxter was obviously missed out of the queue when they were giving those out.

Ellie glances at me, looking relieved that he's gone. 'Shall I show you your room?' she asks with a smile.

'Please. I'm really excited to see it. Your house is enormous, like a hotel!'

She laughs. 'I suppose it is. I never thought about it like that. To me it's just our winter home. I've never known anything different. The rest of the year we spend between our London house and touring in Le Touquet and Granada.'

'Wow. That's pretty impressive.' I feel awkward and gauche saying this, but don't know how else to put it. My parents have spent their whole lives trying to pay off their mortgage on our 1930s house. I'm sure my dad said it would take him until he was seventy. It always seemed a depressing thought and wealth at this level is just a different world. Although, maybe the General has problems of his own. Most people do and he doesn't ever seem very cheerful to be honest. You'd think owning all this he would be the happiest man on earth. Although I've never heard about his wife. I didn't like to ask.

Looking around at the décor, it's quite outdated and a bit of an acquired taste. I follow Ellie up the stately staircase that goes up in one large flight and then splits on a second landing into two more flights. At the top we follow the huge landing round to the right. I try not to gawp at the spears and shields along with family crests adorning the walls, or the vast dusty-looking tapestries that line the way to the bedrooms. On our way, heavy Tudor-style chests suggest secrets hidden within, as well as possible human dramas already unfolded but long buried. All of this waiting, Agatha Christie-style, for some detective to solve their riddles and explain it all to unwitting family members.

'It's all a bit old fashioned up here,' Ellie waves her hand in casual dismissal of the wall hangings, 'but my father likes to celebrate the family history.'

'I don't blame him,' I say, although I kind of do actually, as it's pretty creepy, but when it's all your ancestors' stuff there's not a lot you can do about it. If you took it all down and tried to hide it in the cellar, your ancestors might come back and haunt you forever in revenge, like on the sitcom *Ghosts*. I love that show, it's hilarious.

'You're just through here.' Ellie leads the way through an archway where there is yet another chest, I guess they didn't have wardrobes, and into a vast square bedroom with a huge picture window overlooking the grounds.

'It's lovely,' I say, 'gorgeous views.' I had no idea we were so high up. I can see for miles, right across the grassy grounds, past the rose garden and the obligatory obelisk surrounded by a stone path and over romantically arranged trees and grassy slopes, delicately kissing the roots of trees and the wooded hills in the distance.

'Yes you can see for miles. You can sometimes spot red kites swirling high above – we have a pair that nest in nearby woods. We are totally in the middle of nowhere here; it's really wild. Is there anything you need, by the way? My father is a complete nightmare if any of us are late for dinner so please can you make sure you dress quickly otherwise it puts him in a foul temper.'

'Of course, it's no problem. Thanks, Ellie.'

'No probs, if you need me I'm just down the corridor or if you prefer, it's quicker to text.' She waves a shiny purple iPhone at me and leaves with a grin.

I am left to explore my room, which is huge and a bit draughty if I'm honest. At least someone seems to have lit a fire, which is gorgeous, crackling and atmospheric. It feels like a real luxury to have a fire in a bedroom, all to myself. I push the great reinforced door with the heavy latch closed, so I can start to unpack my clothes.

I notice another large door to the left of the window. Unable to stop myself, I go and carefully turn the handle. It won't open; it's locked. I rattle it more firmly, but it won't budge. I'm not sure whether that's a good thing or not. I hate having a second door in a room like this. I would feel safer if I had the key. The lack of key or bolt means that anyone else who happens to have locked this door some time ago, still has the key and I do not. It also means they could walk in at any time, whenever they want to. I involuntarily shiver and return to my unpacking. I really do need to stop overthinking things. Why would anyone want to get in my room in the night?

Just like the pink elephant effect, my mind immediately begins to think about exactly why someone would want to break in. I shake my head and hum under my breath in an effort to be cheerful. It's a perfectly nice room, not creepy at all. The woman in the painting on the wall above yet another of those chests looks a bit miserable, but perhaps she is missing her home, or has just been dumped by her boyfriend.

I examine the painting more closely. It's very brown. And the lady is all dressed in a sort of dull ditchwater dark green, with a white apron. She is peering downwards to the side, slightly over her shoulder, with a soulful expression at her hand, or maybe she has a splinter or something. I don't know, but either way, I would never have chosen this image, it's hardly prepossessing.

The other painting on the far side of the room portrays another woman, who is holding on to the iron railings of an old-fashioned garden gate. She's also whimsically staring into space as though she's looking for something or maybe contemplating her life and where it is going. Again the painting is dark, a sort of muddy brown and not very enlightening.

I stand there for a moment and then realise, it's no good; I'm going to have to look in the chest. I can't let it get dark and then wonder what's in there. Already, shadows are beginning to form in the dim late afternoon winter light and the fire is flickering strips of what looks like shadow grass up the wall. I glance at the chest again. There could be anything in there. It could be a body, or some important papers, or... that's it, I'm going to have to have a look. I squat down and lift the lid. It's ridiculously heavy and I struggle upwards with it and it slams back against the wall with a thump. For a second I wait, statue-like, breathless, in case someone comes along the corridor. They'll wonder what I was doing, for goodness' sake.

A minute or two tick by and no one comes. That's another thing about old houses, who on earth puts an extremely loud clock on the wall in a bedroom? They're so creepy. Is it just me or isn't there something really medieval about an inordinately loud antique ticking clock in a bedroom in an old scary house. It's as though someone has gone through this room with an itinerary. Old cobwebby beams? Tick. Two doors, one of which is locked and some unknown person has the key? Tick. Creepy chest? Tick. Extremely loud ticking clock? Tick. They have left nothing to chance for the person within to fail to be totally creeped out.

I rummage about in the chest and there's nothing I can find except a pile of thick woollen blankets, which I can tell would be horribly rough and harsh on the skin but are probably warm. I lean back on my heels, how silly of me. The room is perfectly normal. Nothing strange to be seen here.

In defiance of my overactive imagination, I put on Spotify on my phone, blasting out 'Dance Monkey', just to up the mood a little. It works like a charm and with a confident sweep, I draw the heavy curtains against the gathering darkness. That's another thing about living in the countryside; there are no street lights. I busy myself getting ready for dinner.

I think the Monsoon gossamer grey dress for this evening, with delicate silver beading, the one Emma lent me earlier. As long as I can walk in the matching grey strappy sandals that is. I haven't worn them for ages and they are a little too large, then again someone once told me most celebrities wear shoes that are slightly big for them. There's probably a reason for it, but that currently escapes me.

❧

By five to seven I'm ready to descend the stairs for dinner and am quite proud of myself. This needs to go in the diary, Mel will never believe me, I don't think I've ever been this punctual.

I make it to the hall safely, feeling quite complacent for once, although I am pretty nervous and have no idea where we are meant to be eating. The depressed-looking butler, appearing, if it's actually possible, even more depressed, materialises from nowhere. 'Dinner is currently being served in the dining room, modom.'

'Thank you,' I reply, but before I can ask where that might be, he has vanished as quickly as he appeared and I am left to teeter on my impossible-to-walk-in shoes down a corridor to my right in the hope the dining room might be in that direction. The first couple of doors appear to be more rooms and then a broom cupboard, but just as I'm about to give up the idea of eating before midnight, I stumble into a vast great hall.

I only have a chance to take in the sight of an irate and red-faced General standing at the top of a huge wooden trestle table, flanked on right and left by Henry and Ellie. Ellie looks stressed but Henry gives a surreptitious grin.

'I'm so sorry, I couldn't find the dining room...' My voice trails off in embarrassment.

'Please serve us,' barks the General, tight-lipped. 'Miss Johnson, there's no hurry, you need not have rushed. We do not stand on ceremony in this house.' He sort of smiles, but his words belie the fact that lateness really is a problem.

A servant pulls out the chair for me on the right side of the General's, Ellie is on my left and Henry opposite.

The first course appears to be a consommé, but I have never seen such an array of cutlery with which to eat it. There's got to be at least five knives and forks on each side, not even counting spoons. Henry notices my discomfort and under the pretence of reaching for his napkin, knocks the second spoon in on the floor. At least I think that's why he does it, it could be he's just clumsy and this isn't the right spoon after all. Although, looking at it, of course it is, it's a soup spoon. I knew that. I want to say something but in view of the General's presence decide against it, but as I take a mouthful of soup, Henry smiles at me conspiratorially across the table.

'I would think you are used to much bigger rooms than this at Darcy Drummond's place,' the General barks.

'Erm.' I struggle not to choke on my soup as I wrestle to think of an appropriate answer. 'Yes he has large rooms, I believe, but I don't think he has any bigger than this.'

The General appears utterly mollified by this information. 'I am sure his are very elegant even if they are not so large.'

What is it with some men and their obsession with size? It's quite unfathomable to me. I continue to concentrate on eating my soup without dripping it down Emma's grey dress. It was totally the right choice. I notice Ellie also wears a floor-length gown and looks lovely. Good old Emma, what would I do without her. There still remains a complicated and unfathomable social code at work in this country; no different from the one Jane herself would have been dealing with. Clothes, manners, hairstyle, jewellery, choice of hobbies, all would be part of being a member of a select club, an instantly recognisable sign of status. Of the difference between belonging and just not being a part of the elite. Simply not being quite the thing.

Throughout dinner I try to fit in, answering the General's questions as best as I can, without sounding too awkward and embarrassed. The conversation is embarrassingly stilted, Ellie is unusually quiet and even Henry is not his usual chatty and cheery self. The General seems to put a spell on everyone and everything around him, expelling an air of constraint and heavy formality.

❧

After dinner, the interminable courses of which seem to go on forever, thank goodness, he mutters that he has to go and attend to business and leaves us in peace.

'Anyone got room for toasted marshmallows?' Henry asks.

'Might have a little.' I smile. Actually I love marshmallows; they're my favourite. Soon Ellie, Henry and I are seated round the roaring fire in a cosy sort of snug/lounge toasting marshmallows on great long forks. They are always the best, the resulting bronzed mallow, crunchy on the outside and gooey within, absolutely perfect. Soon we have a system going, Henry passing me beautifully toasted mallows to scrape onto my plate, whilst he carefully places more on the fork.

'I've just remembered, I need to ask Lily, my maid, something.' Ellie gets up abruptly and disappears from the room, her blonde ponytail swinging behind her. Strangely I feel awkward left alone with Henry but as always he fills the silence easily.

'I hope you don't mind our tearing you away from Chawton. It's pretty quiet here, you know.'

'Not at all, it's lovely.' I sit back in my chair and sigh contentedly, my legs pleasantly warmed by the gently flickering flames. I don't think I can move, I've eaten so much. Then I pluck up courage to add, 'I hope Ellie's okay, she seems very quiet?'

'She is always here.' Henry pulls another marshmallow off the fork and takes a surreptitious glance at the door. 'My father is not the easiest of company and she and he don't always see eye to eye.'

'Often the case with parents though,' I say with a shrug, 'the whole generation gap thing.'

'True, but it sounds as though you get on pretty well with your mum and dad?' Henry smiles at me.

'I'm lucky I guess, there's no real pressure as such. Although my mum did want me to be a teacher and was very disappointed I didn't choose to go that route.' Somehow I manage to force down just one more marshmallow. They really are too delicious.

'But she let you go the way you wanted.'

'Of course. This isn't the Middle Ages, is it?'

Henry grins. 'You'd be surprised. In this house, it pretty much still is.'

'I guess you have got the décor to match.' I think of the artillery in the hallway.

Henry laughs. 'We have. My father likes to keep hold of all the antiques. He also has some strong views on how things should be run.' Henry becomes serious at this.

'I can understand that,' I say tactfully. After all I'm his guest here, I'd better not be rude about him. 'I guess this is a big estate to run for him. It's a lot of responsibility.'

'It is. I don't envy my elder brother taking all this on one day. Not that he cares. He's too busy enjoying his army training and the freedom that gives him away from my father's beady eye.'

'But he's got to be twenty-something, surely. Can't he do what he likes?'

'Not with my father around. He has ways of dealing with things,' Henry states categorically.

I can't help a shiver reaching down my spine. What sort of man is General Baxter? Why is everyone so scared of him? There is definitely something strange going on here and I am determined to get to the bottom of it.

CHAPTER 20

The next day I phone Mel to catch up on the gossip. 'Hey, Soph, how's it going?' she asks, sounding suspiciously pleased to hear from me.

'Great, I've only thought of Darcy a few times a day, which isn't bad for me and I'm missing you and Emma of course.'

'No surprise there! What are they all like?'

'Henry and Ellie are lovely, I'm really enjoying being with them. The General is definitely a bit strange.'

'What kind of strange?'

'Scary to be honest. Everyone seems afraid of him, including me.' I am whispering now as although I'm safely ensconced in my room, I don't want to be overheard.

'Yeah but it doesn't take a lot to scare you though, does it?' Mel remarks.

'Ha ha. Ellie is definitely very wary of him and even Henry. Their older brother, Captain Baxter, spends most of his time away from home, as far away from him as possible. And we don't even know what happened to his wife.'

'There's probably a reasonable explanation. She maybe just left. Plenty of people are divorced, aren't they?'

'I know, but what if it's something more sinister?'

'It's good to know your imagination is still being ridiculously overactive. Don't let it run away with you!'

'Just a mo, Emma is calling, I'll put you hold. Bear with!'

'Hey, Soph, how's it going?' Emma sounds very cheerful.

'Good thanks,' I reply.

'It seems very quiet here without you, your desk is strangely empty and there's still loads of chocolate biscuits in the snack tin.' Emma laughs.

'Don't worry I'll soon sort that when I get back. I'm having a great time thanks, though I'm missing our chats. The General is a bit weird though, do you know anything about him, like was he ever married?'

'I'm pretty sure he was, why?'

'Just trying to work out why everyone seems so scared of him.'

'Hmm, definitely a mystery then. I think his wife left him years ago. Caused a right old scandal at the time, she ran off with the Duke of Bedford's son.' Emma as always is well informed on the exact details.

'How dramatic.'

'I don't think anyone who knew them blamed her. By all accounts General Baxter has always had a bit of a hot temper. Perhaps she just had enough.'

'I'm surprised she left her children though.'

'They'd have had a governess anyway to manage them and now they're older, I believe they go and stay in Granada with her and their stepdad every summer.'

'No mystery there then,' I say, disappointed.

'Don't get involved in digging up family secrets, Soph. You'll only get yourself in trouble. By the way you didn't clear up that book you left on the floor upstairs. That's the second time you've left it there and it's a first edition. Should be locked away.'

'Which book?'

'It's a first edition of *Northanger Abbey* and *Persuasion*. I'm surprised at you leaving it on the floor. Anything could happen to it.'

I feel a creeping sort of shiver down my spine. 'I didn't leave it there. Why would I do that with any book, especially one so precious. I thought you must have got it out and forgotten to put it away.'

'I told you it wasn't me. Why would I do that? I never touch the listed books unless cataloguing. And if you didn't, who did?' Emma sounds genuinely puzzled.

'That's what I've been wondering. It's a mystery. I've found it there several times. What page was it on?' I ask.

'I don't know. What difference does it make?'

'Just an idea I had, I'm trying to work out what's going on. Both times I've found it on the floor, it's been open on the same page, which is even more bizarre.'

'There's nothing going on. Must be Mel or someone playing a trick on you.'

'Wouldn't surprise me. Oh no I forgot, I've left her on hold. I'll ask her. Hi Mel, sorry about that, Emma's on the other line.'

'Charming!'

'She says that book is on the floor again upstairs.'

'You must have left it there then. I'm always telling you to clear up and stop leaving things round the place.'

'I didn't though. It's quite valuable. I do have respect for books.'

'You are horribly messy. Are you sure you didn't just get distracted?'

'Definitely not. It's no good pretending, Emma and I have found you out. Trying to make us think there's a ghost in the house.'

FIONA WOODIFIELD

'I wouldn't do that, though it is quite funny.' Mel sounds quite serious, but you can never be sure.

'Huh, well we're onto your little game now!' I remark.

After some more chat with Mel and a hurried goodbye to Emma as she had an important call, I meander down to find Henry. He's asked me to go to the stables and Ellie kindly put out some of her old jodhs, which seem to fit quite well. In fact I don't look too bad, although I'm super nervous as I haven't ridden for years and don't want to make an idiot of myself. The General makes me anxious on the ground let alone when I'm on a horse.

As I wander down the stairs, I hear shouting coming from the left side of the house and stand uncertainly where I am, worried about intruding on any kind of argument.

'It's not much to ask!' It's the General and he sounds pretty mad.

I hear a murmured voice in reply, I think it's Ellie but I can't be quite sure. Perhaps it's a servant instead. I can't believe the General would shout at his daughter like this.

'The man is perfectly acceptable, houses like this don't look after themselves. You think our money just grows on the trees in the garden? You, my girl, have a lot to learn.'

Again I can't quite make out her reply, but I freeze where I am as there is the sound of a door opening. Without even thinking, I instantly crouch down behind one of the large chests on the landing.

'You've got the rest of this week and after that I'm putting out the announcement of your engagement, or you'll be dead to me.'

'I should think that would be a bloody relief.' It's Ellie; I recognise her voice. She comes running up the stairs and thank goodness, probably because she's so stressed, doesn't notice me, flounces into her room and slams the door.

Now I'm in a dilemma, do I follow and try to comfort her? Or do I carry on towards the stables and talk to Henry? Either way, I don't dare to move until I'm sure the General has gone. After what seems like an age and my legs have gone to sleep, I hear his heavy footsteps in the hall, they seem to approach in my direction and I freeze, not daring to move a muscle. Until finally he continues some way along the corridor and I am left to scramble out from my hiding place.

Henry looks up as I approach the beautiful old stable block. He's firmly brushing a large bay horse with long sweeping strokes. 'There you are. Thought you'd got lost again.'

'No, I'm fine.' I manage to muster a smile.

'Are you okay? You seem a little flustered.'

Yeah I've just been hiding from your dad behind a large chest. Don't think I'd better tell Henry that.

Instead I say, 'Fine, thanks. I was worried about Ellie, I think she might have had a row with your dad. Sorry, I wasn't prying, I couldn't help but overhear.'

'I wouldn't worry. They row all the time at the moment. I'm sure it will sort.' Henry's words belie his expression however. He seems uneasy, worried even. 'Perhaps we'll just go for a shorter ride and I'll have a chat with her when I get back. I don't like it when my father gets on at her. It's not fair.'

I'm struck once again by Henry's obvious concern for his sister. 'Do you want to leave it and go to her now?'

'No, my dad will still be on the warpath. Better to wait a while until he's got distracted with business. Ellie's tougher than you might think. Or don't you want to go? Got cold feet?' He grins at me cheekily.

'Of course not.' I smile back.

'You'll be fine,' he says, and I believe him. There's something very reassuring about this guy. 'You're riding Meg, she's a very sweet mare. She'll look after you.'

I stand anxiously, trying to think if I can even remember how to get on a horse, let alone hold the reins. It's fine, I'm sure it's like riding a bike. A smartly dressed groom appears leading an extremely tall dapple grey horse.

'Miss Johnson?' he asks politely. 'If you'd like to climb on the mounting block...'

I scramble up, take the reins in my left hand and place my left foot in the stirrup. Once astride, I feel a little better. Meg has a really sweet expression in her eye, there's something dependable about her. Bizarrely not having ridden for many years, it is rather like riding a bike, there's a familiarity about the saddle and Meg responds promptly to my gentle nudge for her to move away from the block ready for Henry to mount a large bay he introduced as Dom.

As we move off, a wave of sheer happiness breaks over me unexpectedly, the sunshine of the day, the freshness of the dew on the grass in spite of the chill winter air, there's such a feeling of optimism as we ride out across the adjoining track and onto a grassy path. I haven't ridden for so long and it's a part of me that had become forgotten. Our horses seem to get along, making the ride so much more enjoyable. I remember the few horse-riding lessons my mum managed to afford for a short while when I was a teenager, scraped together with Christmas and birthday money. The moody pony I used to ride ambled at a ridiculously slow pace, which would have made a snail look speedy, unless he was rowing with one of the other horses in the line, when he would suddenly lurch at them in a manner perfectly designed to make me lose my stirrups. In spite of this, I had loved every minute; just being with horses had been a privilege. This however, I think satisfactorily to myself, is how wealthy people must live all the time; riding stunning horses, on a weekday, not having to work or stress about anything.

Although they do have worries really, my reasonable self adds. I think of Ellie. 'Will she be all right? She seemed pretty upset.'

Henry brings his horse to jog alongside as he answers. 'She'll be fine. I'll talk to her when we get back.' There's a silence as I pat Meg on the neck, enjoying the feel of her warmth. 'My father... is used to his own way and God help anyone who tries to stop him.'

'I'm sorry,' I say, as our horses jog companionably together. 'I guess I thought you all had it pretty easy, huge house and an estate to inherit.'

'No such thing as a free lunch,' Henry says lightly. 'We may appear to be well-loaded but my father is extremely good at spending it in his club, and unfortunately this puts pressure on the rest of us to marry into money. Not a bit either, we're talking huge amounts. And my older brother will inherit the estate.'

'That's tough and I guess there's nothing you can do about it. But, what about love?' I ask before I can stop myself.

'Love?' He laughs. 'I guess we'd better hope we all fall in love with wealthy people.'

'I'm sure you will. There's plenty of gorgeous heiresses out there, ready to be snapped up.' I go silent as I think of Darcy and Tara. Who was I trying to kid that there was any other possible ending in real life? Darcy had been trying to tell me all along and I had been determined not to see it.

'Maybe I don't want a gorgeous heiress,' Henry says lightly. 'Fancy a canter?' He nudges Dom into a fast trot and Meg quickly follows.

'Okay. I'll give it a go!' Flinging my usual caution to the wind, I sit down and ease into Meg's easy canter. It's terrifying and exhilarating all at the same time and I feel incredibly free from all the stress that's been building up over the last few weeks.

The ground rushes past in a heady blur of green and brown and all too soon we are trotting again as we reach a stream.

Henry is waiting for me in the shelter of the bare trees. 'Everything okay?' he asks, his eyes on mine and gently, he touches my hand on Meg's bridle which has gone pretty white from clinging on.

'Hanging on for dear life?' He laughs.

'Maybe.' I laugh too. 'It *has* been a while.'

'Do you know, I get the impression that's how you live your whole life.' He smiles at my quizzical expression. 'I love that, you jump in with such enthusiasm for everything. It's amazing.'

Is it? I think randomly, gazing back at his chiselled brush of stubble. I squash down any feelings of excitement, which I felt at the touch of his hand. There's something so warm and vibrant about Henry Baxter, but I guess I'm just missing Darcy.

'I don't think I've enjoyed anything as much as this for a long time,' I say, surprised even at myself for admitting it.

'Good,' Henry says, 'we'd better get back, but same time again tomorrow?'

'You bet,' I reply and we push our horses on and canter homeward across the fields, as I have dreamed for more years than ever. We could be two figures in a Regency romance, out together on horseback, although I'm glad we skipped the side-saddle, I would have ended up in a hedge.

CHAPTER 21

*T*ime passes and I realise as I go down for breakfast that I've already stayed three days at Dreyfus Manor. The hours seem to have flown. I feel as though I'm in some period drama, far away from all the stress of the agency or Darcy or anything else. Although it has to be said the atmosphere at Dreyfus is far from comfortable, unless I am out walking or riding with Henry or Ellie.

I've also had a terrible time sleeping; I seem to hear every tiny creak and grumble of the building and every hoot of an owl. Although it's been better since I managed to wrap the annoying ticking clock in a blanket at the bottom of the cupboard. I really couldn't bear it bonging out every hour of the night for one more minute.

'You'll stay on a few days longer, won't you, Miss Johnson?' General Baxter makes me jump as he barks out the surprising invitation at the breakfast table.

'Well, I...'

'Oh yes, please do,' Ellie pipes up for once. 'I enjoy our walks together.'

Henry's smile adds more pressure and I would like to, I really would. 'It's only I have the Stourhead walk tomorrow so I should be back for that.'

'But Stourhead is hardly any distance from here,' remarks the General. 'Henry would be only too pleased to drive you, and Ellie could go as well. In fact, it's a good plan, I'm sure Sir Henry Greaves will be there.'

Ellie's face falls and she glares mutinously at her plate.

'Yes I think he is going actually.' I'm surprised General Baxter should take an interest. He has never shown any friendship towards Sir Henry Greaves before. 'Do you know him well?'

'Er, yes.' The General gives a sideways glance at Ellie. 'Our families have known each other for some time. He comes from a very renowned and virile line of great men.'

I have to pretend to be seriously studying my scrambled egg at this point before I snort with laughter. Virility is not a word that should even be used in the same sentence as Sir Henry Greaves.

'I could make some calls today to see if Mel and Emma can spare me a little longer if you honestly don't mind my staying on.'

'That's settled then,' the General remarks. 'I shall be driving to the city this morning and returning with some friends tomorrow, so will unfortunately be unable to join you.'

I heave a silent sigh of relief. Everything is so much more relaxed when he's not around.

Having phoned Emma and agreed that I can go straight to Stourhead tomorrow and all the arrangements are okay, I meet Ellie in the rose border to start our walk. Her long blonde hair hangs in a neat ponytail. She's so elegant, but in a casual unpretentious way. Her eyes have a wary expression as she watches her father's blue Rolls slowly wend its way out of the drive.

'Thank God he's gone,' she says with feeling.

'I guess it's not easy for you with him here,' I reply sympathetically.

'Not at all. He just sees us as his meal ticket out of any kind of financial difficulty.'

'Surely that's a bit outdated?'

'Not in his eyes. Ask my mother.'

'Do you get to see her often?'

'Not as much as I'd like. But I don't blame her for getting out of here. It's not a happy place to be. As soon as I'm old enough I'll be off and never looking back.'

'You must be eighteen already?' I ask; Ellie seems so much more mature somehow.

'No,' she smiles, 'I've always looked older than I am. My father has a strong grip on my bank accounts. He's totally determined that I'll marry some rich old codger and secure everyone's future.'

'That's ridiculous, like something straight out of a Regency novel!'

'It is, but I'm afraid in my experience things don't seem to have changed much. That's why I hide in the world of Regency romance.'

'Oh, me too. It's such a happy place to be, everything always turns out well in the end. Although, be careful, it can set you up with high expectations and a long way to fall.'

Ellie looks undeterred. 'I have no intention of falling or marrying some old man. I still have everything to play for... as long as...' she breaks off.

'As long as...?' I continue for her.

'As long as my father doesn't find out.' We both shiver even though the air is less cold today. I get the impression that none of us want to come up against this guy; he's got a whole side I don't want to know about.

'But surely, there's not a lot he can do? He can't exactly take your phone away, or cut off your allowance? You're no longer a child.'

'You'd be surprised.' Ellie is serious for a moment. 'He has his ways.'

A chill goes down my spine and not for the first time, I glance back with a shiver at the foreboding bulk of the grey building behind me.

'Your mother got away,' I say.

'Only just. You have no idea.'

Now I'm really creeped out. Surely she's exaggerating? Ellie's probably just a rich kid who's used to getting what she wants and although I can understand she doesn't want to marry someone her father arranges, especially not Sir Henry Greaves, I can't imagine he can force her to marry, can he? Surely not in this day and age?

We are interrupted by the cheery arrival of Henry who suggests a boat trip on the lake, which we enjoy in spite of the fact it starts raining part way through and we all have to run back to the house in the teeming wet.

'Here, take my coat.' Henry wraps me in his long fleece jacket and as he pulls it close round me, not for the first time lately I feel warm and cared for. He meets my look with his endearing smile and I bask for a moment in his gaze. I've never noticed before, but his eyes, are a warm shade of hazel. Sort of green mixed with brown. They remind me of the familiar green countryside, there's a gentleness about them. I wonder if anyone ever feels sad for long around him.

We arrive panting and sodden at the doorstep. He passes me a towel from the boot room. 'Go up and have a hot bath.'

'Are you always this cheerful whatever happens?' I ask, amused.

'Of course,' he laughs back, 'it's given you a healthy glow.' His hand brushes mine, so so gently, and with a shock I realise the pleasure of the touch of his skin, but before I can even consider how I feel, I blunder upstairs and am soon basking in a scalding hot bath with gorgeous scented bubbles and a glass of wine, brought up by a blushing housemaid. This is the life.

I just wish I felt more settled, everything is still so up in the air, Darcy, the agency, I've still got the dreaded interview with Vivienne d'Artois and to top it all although I've been having a social media break from my phone, this morning a magazine gossip column came up showing a photo of Darcy out with his mother, a snapshot of him at a dinner with Tara. Darn the cleverness of social media recognition. So I guess that's it, nothing has changed.

Darcy has realised it's best for him to stay where he's comfortable and I just need to move on. But it's easier said than done. I did so like him, I was in love with him, even though it probably wasn't sensible, in many ways we were so incompatible, but it's impossible to switch off. And then there's Henry. Hmm, Henry, I'm so confused how I feel about him. I must admit; I really like him. He's funny, kind, I've yet to see him in a bad temper, although he can't always be easy-going of course.

He makes me smile and I can tell him anything I think... obviously I don't like him in that kind of way because I still love Darcy, but that look Henry gave me yesterday... and the excitement I felt when he touched my hand earlier. I wonder if... but it was probably accidental and there's no point in thinking about it anyway. Life is far too complicated as it is.

৪৯

The next day I am back in work mode, I have my list ready. In fact I am super interested to discover more about a new recruit, Miss Foxton's brother, Alistair, who is coming along so it will be good to have another new Regency man on our books. We soon arrive at the gardens after a pleasant drive across to Stourhead, in yet another car. A comfortable Range Rover with heated seats and cream leather. I mean who has one of these as their spare car? I'm relieved General Baxter hasn't reappeared since yesterday morning, otherwise he would be here, no doubt asking me how many vehicles Darcy owns and how big they are.

We arrive nice and early so I can go to the entrance of the gardens to check members of the agency are all here, as we have the whole place exclusively to ourselves for the day. More than anything I'm incredibly relieved there is still an autumnal hazy sunshine peeking from behind the clouds and enough leaves on the trees to still make the garden truly spectacular, adorned in its raiment of golden colours.

'Sophie, is it really you? You're on time!' Emma rushes forward and gives me a big hug.

'I know, it is possible after all. Although I'm not making a habit of it.'

Henry laughs next to me. 'You've been on time to every dinner so far, except for when you first arrived and lost the dining room, but that was understandable!'

Emma smiles. 'How much wine had you drunk that night, Soph? Although I think food is the one thing Sophie is usually on time for. Just like Maria in *The Sound of Music*.'

'Thanks, Emma!' I laugh. 'Anyway, food is important.'

'It's nice to have a guest who enjoys eating.' Henry smiles at me in that cute way he has.

'Thanks, you're too kind!' I shove him in a friendly manner.

Emma glances at him, then back at me with a knowing look in her eye.

'No one with the habit of being late would survive for long at Dreyfus Manor; my father can't stand anyone not being punctual,' Henry remarks.

Ellie, who is close by, rolls her eyes and mutters under her breath. 'Amongst a whole list of other things.'

Oblivious, Emma carries on with her preparations, dragging me off to check lists and make sure everyone who we thought was coming, is present and correct.

Soon we are all walking down in slightly scattered groups, through the beautiful entrance to Stourhead, past the tiny quaint lattice-paned cottages at the gateway.

All the usual suspects are here and I am delighted to be walking with Maria and Charles who are full of their wedding plans.

'It's only two months away. It seemed only minutes ago it was a year to wait.' Maria is positively glowing.

'After waiting all this time, the last bit will go in a flash,' Charles reminds her. The way he looks at Maria makes my heart melt. It's so sweet. These two met when they were young and were kept apart by the machinations of Maria's horrible father, Sir Henry Greaves. Now Charles has a good job, he's relented and has even agreed to show up to the wedding, although I'm sure we'd all much prefer it if he didn't.

Speaking of Sir Henry, I notice he is walking alongside Ellie, who looks very unhappy to be anywhere near him and is obviously standing as far apart as she can, whilst replying in monosyllables. We are approaching the trees to the right of the lake, but as the path bends, I lose sight of them.

'Your father seems on top form today,' I say to Maria.

'Yes, although I'm not sure he's going to be very successful there,' Maria replies and we both laugh.

'I don't want to offend you, but he's got to be about thirty years too old, hasn't he?'

'And the rest. Of course I'm not offended; you know how I feel about my father. But I've heard that he and General Baxter have been planning some kind of arrangement between them. I thought you'd know all about it as you've been staying with them?'

'I heard things were difficult between the General and Ellie, but surely he wouldn't be trying to persuade her to marry Sir Henry Greaves?'

'I'm afraid that's exactly what he's trying to do. My father has this strange idea he could finally produce a male heir, effectively cutting out my cousin who is currently down to inherit the whole estate.'

'But she's far too young and besides, surely you should inherit. I thought women could these days? That's positively medieval.' I protest, trying not to look too revolted. 'And I know age doesn't matter in a relationship, but only if both parties are happy. Ellie isn't suited to him.'

'I gave up the whole arguing with my father about the fact women can run an estate every bit as well as a man, a long time ago. As for Ellie, I'm afraid I can believe it all too well. And the General apparently...' Maria looks over her shoulder.

'Is pretty used to getting his own way... yes I've heard. But this is all so prehistoric. Besides,' I lower my voice, 'I've heard he is extremely scary to come up against. But what can he do in this day and age?'

'Plenty,' the normally gentle Maria says with vehemence.

I look over my shoulder; Henry and Charles are deep in conversation a few yards back.

'What do you mean?' I shiver involuntarily even though the air is warm for the time of year.

'I've heard he has a group of men who operate, shall we say beneath the law. They're pretty much untouchable and have their own unique ways of threatening people and getting them to do what he wants. He's a very powerful man and is mixed up in all sorts of things. Because of his importance, I don't think anyone's been able to pin anything on him in a court of law.'

'That would make sense, I did see some dodgy-looking guys around the estate the other day, but hardly thought they could be anything to do with the General. In any case, surely he won't use ruthless criminals against his daughter?' I stumble. 'He wouldn't, he can't?'

'I don't know.' Maria speaks so quietly I can hardly hear her. She continues a little louder. 'But I think a lot goes on that we know nothing about. You've been staying with the General. How does he seem to you?'

'Scary, sinister. Perhaps a bit threatening. But what can we do about it? No wonder Ellie is so unhappy.'

'I'd try to persuade my father otherwise if I could, but he doesn't listen to anyone, most especially me.'

'I know, you're in an impossible situation. We'll just have to think of something. A distraction,' I suggest.

At the back of the group I spot the Baroness picking her way carefully down the path in her usual direct, but precise manner. 'I've got an idea at least for the short term,' I say to Maria, and hurry off in the direction of the Baroness.

'Ah, Sophie,' she says as I huff and puff up the hill towards her. 'How are things?'

'Good thank you, I've been having a bit of a holiday.'

'Yes you look more relaxed, it suits you.' She peers at me with that unreadable expression she so often has.

I blush. 'I just wondered...'

'So you need my help.' She follows my gaze in the direction of Sir Henry. 'Hmm, that's not a great match, is it? Or perhaps it is a very great arrangement for certain people.' She narrows her eyes. 'I was that age when I married my husband you know. He was over thirty years older than me.'

I must look shocked as she continues. 'It could have been worse; I survived the experience even though he was not a kind man. Besides I was in love with him. In any case, I'm still here to tell the tale, though I'm not sure Sir Henry is cruel. Ignorant and vain perhaps, but there's no real harm in him.'

'Are you thinking of dating him yourself?' I ask daringly.

'Absolutely not! He would drive me crazy, forever gazing at his reflection at all the mirrors in my house. I'd have to take them all down or we'd never get anywhere. Good God. No not after my hard-won freedom. My thoughts have been following a very different direction.' She looks over to where Emma and Gene are walking together.

'I'm glad to hear that.' I've often thought the Baroness and Gene would make a good pair. He is a savvy man of the world, but has a gentlemanly way about him. 'But would you mind just to help things, temporarily adding a little distraction for Sir Henry. You're the only person he would rather speak to than Ellie and she really doesn't like him. If you might just interrupt a little, you would give her a chance to get a break. A little of Sir Henry goes a long way.'

'As I already know, to my own cost.' The Baroness still seems distant, but snaps her attention back to me. 'Very well, but you know you owe me one, Sophie.'

'Thanks. I will repay you.'

'I know,' she says simply. 'You would never do anything else.' And with that she stalks off in the direction of the clump of trees into which Sir Henry and Ellie had disappeared several moments ago.

By now the group behind me has caught up, consisting of Freya, Edward arm in arm with Miss Foxton and a laughing Amelia and Caitlin who seem to be on a full charm offensive, giggling and flirting furiously, either side of a jaw-droppingly good-looking young man with almost black hair and a very clean-shaven face. He has a startling square cut chiselled jaw and a charming smile. He really could be a model in GQ.

'Miss Johnson.' Edward steps forward immediately, as always, he has excellent manners. 'Have you met Miss Foxton's brother, Alistair?'

'Pleased to meet you,' I say pleasantly, trying not to be distracted by an arresting pair of steel-blue eyes. Surely those are contacts? His teeth too when he smiles are a perfect pearly white.

'Miss Johnson, lovely to meet you.' Alistair Foxton holds my hand politely for just the right amount of time; squeezes it slightly as though he is absolutely thrilled to meet me and lets it go. This guy really does put the charm in charming.

'You were telling me about your tennis match,' Caitlin simpers; she has her arm tightly around his.

'Yes of course, well in the end I came second, but how was I to know my old chum Winston had set me to play against Roger Federer's nephew.'

'Oh you are a scream,' Caitlin titters loudly. It's amazing actually, I hardly heard her talk at all before this. It's as though someone's put money in one of those horrible creepy fairground character slot machines and they've come to life, chortling and chirruping away, until you wish you hadn't even thought about it.

Alistair looks round at Amelia. 'You aren't amused, then?' He asks her.

'Of course, I am, it's *très amusant* that you should have been pitched against someone so talented and still came second in the whole tournament? Very impressive.'

'You're always so serious, Amelia. She's such a realist,' Caitlin tootles, gazing up into Alistair Foxton's handsome face, 'not like me, I like to have fun. Who wants to be boring?'

'As the eldest, I've had to be a little more sensible, especially when I've ended up getting you out of scrapes,' Amelia says seriously. Touché one:all. Quite honestly, she has a point; her father is probably yet another ambitious matchmaker who expects her to marry well.

'Where's Lord Bamford anyway?' Caitlin squeaks. 'I thought he was walking with you today, Amelia.' Okay, two:one to Caitlin.

'No, unfortunately he was out late hunting yesterday and has caught a cold, so he wasn't able to come,' Amelia says with a slight smirk.

'His loss is my gain then,' Alistair says politely, ignoring Caitlin's scowls. Two:all, new balls please. Blow tennis, this dialogue is far more entertaining. I don't fancy much for Lord Bamford's chances now the gorgeous and suave Alistair Foxton has arrived on the scene; he's as practised and charming as his sister who is currently walking over the picturesque Stourhead bridge arm in arm with Edward.

Shrinking behind the girls, Freya looks miserable I notice, although Gene has kindly come to walk with her. He's a nice man and is exactly the sort of person the Baroness needs. It's a shame Freya likes Edward so much, I don't think he's ever going to notice her in the way she wants him to.

Emma comes hurrying alongside, her clipboard at the ready. 'So, everyone, if you can just stop here. This is the gorgeous bridge that Keira Knightley ran across whilst filming the 2005 *Pride and Prejudice*. They say that the scene had to be shot five times, as the rain was so heavy during filming. Apparently, Keira said she was incredibly nervous playing the role of Elizabeth because *everyone* loves *Pride and Prejudice* and to a certain extent everyone believes in some way that they are Lizzie Bennet.'

Emma carries on talking and leading everyone over the famous Palladian bridge. 'This way please, we are extremely fortunate as this bridge is usually closed off to the public, but we are lucky enough to be allowed to actually walk on it. If you wish to take photos, we need to take it in turns.'

'Ooh yes.' Caitlin squeals, dragging Alistair along.

'We must wait for Amelia,' he insists, giving his arm to the lady in question, who shoots her sister a triumphant look.

But I am lost in thought. It was something in Emma's or rather Keira Knightley's words, *everyone believes that they are in some way Lizzie Bennet*. I guess that's the point, we do all believe in some way we are Elizabeth. There's a part of all of us who longs to be Lizzie.

Jane Austen created a heroine not only to escape from her own life, but for all of us. Little did she know what joy Lizzie Bennet would bring for generations to come. We all want to be part of her wit, her vivacity, her fine eyes, her ability to attract a wealthy, proud man like Darcy. It may be that some of us might be more like Jane, or Kitty or even Mary but in our hearts we want to be Elizabeth Bennet.

And I too have got caught up in this dream. I have dreamt of being Lizzie and of course as part of this, I wanted Darcy. But what if I'm not Lizzie? Maybe I'm Catherine Morland or no, actually I'm not that naïve. But I could be a little like her, with a dash of Lizzie and a small bit of Jane's easy-going nature – I'm a mixture of all of them.

In that case, which man would suit me? Does such a man exist? Is there a man who is vaguely normal out there who might be right for me? Other than Darcy of course, because it's become glaringly obvious we aren't meant to be together. It was all a dream, *une belle* image. I can't even blame the vegan protest, if I'm honest with myself; it was more than that. Perhaps Darcy and I were never suited in the first place.

CHAPTER 22

'Left behind, Sophie?' Henry arrives next to me, looking amused.

'Yes, I was just checking everyone had finished taking photos and...' I look over the bridge and realise even the stragglers at the back, the Baroness and Sir Henry (she is taking her duties extremely seriously) have long since gone and are walking round towards the other side of the lake.

'Lost track of time?'

'Maybe. I was just pondering on things.'

'Sounds serious.'

'Not really. I was just wondering if maybe it's possible to lose yourself in pipe dreams, which are never going to become reality.'

'I should think most of us try to escape from reality. It's a human trait to want to get away from the problems in your own life.'

'I suppose. Some of us do it more than others.'

'What's wrong with that? I like to watch *The Grand Tour* just to get away from my life when I'm fed up with it. I can pretend

I'm some TV presenter who can choose whichever car I like with a huge budget and travel the world with some great mates.'

'Yes I suppose that's a healthy thing. I prefer books myself.'

Henry nods. 'I know where you're coming from, I like books just as much as the screen.'

'You do?' I can't believe I've found a good-looking guy who is actually nice and likes books as much as staring at the TV. I should be sitting down, not meandering over the bridge, which Keira Knightley ran across in the 2005 *Pride and Prejudice*. In fact I should be running across this bridge. 'Henry hold that thought, but do you mind doing something for me?'

'Depends what it is.' He laughs.

'Would you film me running over the bridge, Keira Knightley style?' Unsurprisingly he's staring at me as though I've lost my mind. 'I know I'm not in Regency Dress, but I do have a long trench coat, which is similar to Keira's – it's actually dark blue. But I feel the need to have a cathartic moment.'

'Fair enough.' He smiles, good humoured as ever. 'I'll take it from the other side of the river. It might take me a while to walk there though. It could be raining by then.'

'That's fine I'll wait. Then signal to me when to run.' This should go in my diary; I very rarely run anywhere. In fact I'm one of those people who decide once a year to get fit and go for a run. I get in all the gear, lycra, trainers, headband, the lot, and start off jogging enthusiastically, hoping the neighbours notice me looking all keen and sporty. I might just about make it round the corner at the end of the road, realise I've got a stitch and can hardly put one foot in front of the other. Think I'm going to have to stop, then one of my friends drives by in their car and I smile and wave or rather grimace, whilst having to keep running, in spite of the fact I feel I might collapse, until their car drives out of sight. It's quite sad really. But at least the length of the bridge is not very far, even I should be able to do this and there's no lycra in sight.

I wait patiently whilst Henry walks all round the other side of the island. In fact I'm not that patient, hopping from one foot to the other as I'm terrified an angry swan might run at me, or some annoying passer-by might get in the shot, or something irritating like that. Finally, after what seems like ages, but is probably only about five minutes, Henry waves his arm at me and I run across the bridge, quite fast actually and I don't fall over which is a huge achievement in itself as I'm generally really clumsy.

'How was that?' I shout across. He's making some kind of signal but I can't understand it at all. He's waving his arms in a flat line. 'Shall I do it again?' I yell.

He nods so I walk back over the other side of the bridge and get ready to run again. He waves and I leg it across the bridge, but nowhere near as enthusiastically as before. Actually I'm getting quite tired now and hope he's got the shot. In fact, sod it, even if he hasn't I'm giving up, this bridge running thing isn't much fun after the first time. Besides they probably paid Keira Knightley a fortune and what do I get? Nothing except muddy shoes and for goodness' sake, it looks as though a bird has pooed on my best London coat. 'This would never have happened to Keira,' I complain.

Henry laughs as he appears from the other side of the bridge. 'Oops. Did you know that was lucky?'

'Doesn't feel very lucky to me.'

'That's what they say,' he says, dabbing the bird's calling card from my shoulder with a smart blue hanky in a gentlemanly manner. 'There's a bit in your hair.' He gently dabs at the back of my head. 'It's all gone anyway.'

'Thanks.' I smile at him. 'Did it look ridiculous?'

'What, your running, or the bird poo?'

'Both,' I comment wryly.

'No of course not, in both cases.' He shows me the video on his iPhone. I just look like a random woman running across a bridge.

'Well I don't look like Keira Knightley but at least you can't see how out of breath I was.'

'Nonsense, maybe you just need some atmospheric music in the background or something? It was very elegantly done!' Henry says politely but the twinkle in his eye belies his words and I think we'll leave it at that. We meander companionably up the hill towards Apollo's temple. Everyone else seems to have gone on and we chat about this and that.

'It wasn't as romantic as it looked on the screen.'

'It never is though, is it? If you watch the behind-the-scenes footage on any movie, it's never quite the same when you see Miss Elizabeth Bennet eating a hamburger between takes and Mr Darcy taking a call on his iPhone. It's all an image.'

'I guess you're right. But it's that image, that escape that we all need. That's what we buy into.'

'True.' Henry takes up a nearby branch and swipes the ground with it. 'We all want to escape.'

'Where would you go if you could choose?'

'I don't know. Abroad somewhere probably, to get away from my father, but then I'd only be running away from my duties. I have a farm here to run.'

'Yes responsibilities.' I sigh heavily. 'We all have them.'

'What would be your most romantic escapist dream, Miss Sophie Johnson?' Henry gives me his hand, as I'm struggling up a particularly steep bit of the path.

'You'll only laugh at me. As you usually do.'

'I'll try not to. I've heard Ellie's wish list anyway so it probably won't be worse than hers. Let me guess, dancing with a handsome masked stranger at a Regency Ball, or being married under an archway of swords, or I know, walking along the beach leaving nothing but footprints.' He looks at me with a grin. 'Can't be more mushy than any of that lot!'

'Okay, well, here goes. It's a scene from *Northanger Abbey* where in her imagination, the handsome hero aka Henry Tilney rescues Catherine from his father and John Thorpe by gathering her up on his brave steed and galloping off into the sunset.' I turn to face him. 'So laugh away.'

'I'm not laughing.' He turns to me trying to keep a straight face but he can't quite and his lip twitches a little at the corner.

'Yeah right,' I flounced back.

'I do approve really. For a romantic fantasy that's fairly normal I guess, except it's hardly practical. Imagine the horse trying to carry both people's weight and she would obviously have to be wearing a dress.'

'Obviously. It would never work if she was wearing jeans and a T-shirt, would it?'

'Absolutely not. Sorry, I was only thinking of the practicalities.'

'Practicalities are never very romantic though, are they?' I laugh. 'Anyway I've given up reading romances and have moved on to psychological thrillers. They're far more realistic.'

'A little too realistic I should think in some cases.' Henry laughs too. 'Skeletons in closets and everyone plotting everyone else's downfall and it's nearly always the boyfriend whodunnit anyway.'

'Not always,' I say. Then I laugh. 'Okay so most of the time it is!'

As we have been climbing the hill, the clouds seem to have descended and together we run the last few metres, as we are quickly completely soaked by sheets of rain.

We shelter under the temple's large, imposing columns, as

the heavens open and it chucks it down, the rain racing past the ancient stones in great sheets.

'Very romantic, a torrent of rain. Happens in all the best movies. Didn't it rain in the proposal scene of *Pride and Prejudice*, the one with Keira Knightley and Matthew whoever it is?' Henry says flippantly.

'Macfadyen. Well remembered. How do you know that?'

'Ellie made me watch it about ten times, I think I probably know the whole movie off by heart.' He turns towards me and gives a smouldering look. It's working for me actually. 'This is the bit where I need to tell you how ardently I admire and love you.'

I stare back at him through rain sodden lashes and wonder absently if my mascara has run. It's really not that romantic in real life though, is it? I mean it looks all sultry and damp on screen, but the reality is you're just cold and wet and in November, it's flipping freezing actually.

'And then?' I ask because quite honestly I can't think of anything else to say and in my defence, I am distracted by the rain.

'I would ask you if you would agree to marry me, even though I know that I am going expressly against the wishes of my family and am lowering myself in doing so.'

'In that case, I would say, sir, I am sorry for any disappointment you may be feeling, but I hope it will be of short duration.' I'm really getting into it now. 'It was unconsciously done.'

Henry smiles and takes my hand, stepping nearer, I can feel the warmth of his palm in mine, see the rain drops resting on the slight scattering of stubble smattering his cheek and gaze into the deep green of his eyes. They're so intense; I could really lose myself in them.

He continues, 'I'm sure it was, but, Sophie, joking apart... I wanted to tell you.' He looks into my eyes and I stare back into the warm green of his and I feel as though we might...

'What the hell?' He jumps back as something large and wet seems to have thrown itself on him, showering drops of water on us both.

'Roland!'

Out of nowhere the hideous Roland has appeared, soggy and wet mouthed as usual and has taken a total fancy to Henry's clean chinos. From a nearby path comes the just as overenthusiastic and annoying John Smith, closely followed by an angry-looking Ben. For goodness' sake, this couple of clowns weren't even supposed to be coming today, not according to my list anyway.

'Get here now, Roland!' John shouts and Roland, for once, finally getting the message that he really isn't wanted by anyone in the vicinity, slinks back towards him. After that is of course a couple of false starts where the naughty dog pretends he isn't actually sure which way his owner wants him to go. Finally John has him back on the lead and meanders up with him dragging behind, having now decided he's too anxious to come anywhere near us, as he's afraid of columns. This dog really takes the biscuit.

'Sorry about that,' John says cheerfully. 'Total mind of his own, Roly.'

'He obviously has.' Henry is more than usually rattled. I feel exactly the same, I'm not sure where things were going when Roland burst on the scene like an extra from *The Hound of the Baskervilles*, but it was something I've never experienced before, not like that anyway. The rain tumbling down, I can't forget the intensity of Henry's eyes, looking into mine. It had felt new and exciting and I can't help wondering what would have happened if Roland hadn't made his stupid entrance.

'Room for a small one?' Ben asks, jumping up under the

columns for shelter as the rain looks as though it has no intention of lessening.

'I suppose so. This is Henry. My brother, Ben, Henry.'

'Nice to meet you.' Henry is perfectly polite and shakes hands with Ben, who is giving me a bit of a look.

'So you're a dark horse, Miss Johnson,' John says matter of factly, joining us with his horrible wet hound, 'lurking under Palladian columns with anyone other than Darcy Drummond.'

'We were just sheltering from the rain,' I say with a fake smile on my face. I can't stand John Smith, quite honestly it may not be very Jane Austen, but I would like to push him off the step he's arrogantly idling on and shove him back down the hill.

Evidently Ben is feeling something along the same lines, as he suggests rather tersely, 'Would you like to walk Roly back down to see if the others have made it to the main house?'

'Not really,' John says rudely. 'Why don't you?'

'Because you're the one with the dog and I want to have a word with Sophie a moment. Maybe Henry will go with you and we'll catch you up in a minute.'

'You can tell a chap when he's not wanted,' John grumbles. 'Come on, Roly.'

'I'll walk with you,' Henry says obligingly, although he doesn't quite meet my concerned look. 'I need to check on Ellie.'

We watch them meander back down the path towards the lake and I feel frustrated about the interruption and unfairness of life. Romantic moments are so few and far between; they should be nurtured. Interrupting them should be a federal offence along with disturbing someone when they're reading a book.

Now we are alone, Ben says to me, 'I just don't understand why Mum insisted on me joining this agency.'

'No, well...'

'It's not my thing. John's all right, he's a bit of a laugh, and there's some fit girls.' He gazes across in the direction of Amelia and her group. 'But they're all so...'

'So what?' I say defiantly.

'So picky. They won't give me a second glance,' he grouches, kicking at a stray fir cone with his shoe.

'They might if you bothered to find out what interests them. It's not all about looks.'

'God, you're not back to reading those blasted romances, are you? I've never heard such tosh. It's because I'm not Lord someone or other, with a million pounds in the bank. That's the fact.'

It isn't a very pleasant walk back towards the gatehouse; Ben is super morose and it's cold and damp. Everyone else seems to have made it back to the stables in surprisingly good cheer, happily sipping hot chocolate and enjoying cream tea in the shelter of the old beams. It looks very cosy and I sit gratefully with Emma by a roaring log fire.

'Such a shame it rained,' Emma looks round pensively, 'but everyone seems to have had a good time.'

'Hmm.' I really can't agree. Amelia is after Alistair when Lord Bamford likes her best, Caitlin also likes Alistair who seems to prefer Amelia. Edward likes Miss Foxton and fails to notice that Freya is in love with him. Sir Henry is after Ellie who is far too young for him as well as the Baroness who doesn't like him. Ben likes several girls but they're obviously not interested. I still want Mr Darcy, well I think I do anyway, but I also have feelings for Henry. I just don't know anymore.

'Is this how love always works out?' I muse out loud as I walk along up the steep hill back to the car park. 'Everyone always attracted to people who don't like them back. Like Jane with Harris Bigg Wither or even before that her first love Tom Lefroy? She liked him but she wasn't wealthy enough for his family. What a tangled web we weave.'

'True,' Maria says brightly. I hadn't even noticed she was walking along next to me. 'But it can work out. Look at Charles and me.'

I laugh and give her a hug. 'Thank goodness for you both. I think I'd give up on Regency romance altogether if it weren't for you two.'

'Yes but look how many issues we had along the way. The course of true love never did run smooth. This will all sort, Soph, don't you worry.'

'I just don't think I thought through how complicated it would be trying to get the right people together,' I say dispiritedly.

'But your job isn't to control everything and everyone,' Maria says, sensibly. 'It's to introduce people and then stand back to let things take their course. True love will find a way.'

'I guess you're right,' I ponder as I shift my picnic basket from one hand to the other. 'But sometimes I don't even know what I really want anymore. I'm so confused. I grew up thinking Mr Darcy was always the man for me but...'

'Now you're not so sure?'

'Well, Darcy Drummond obviously doesn't want to date me.'

'More importantly, do you want to date him? That's what matters.'

'Yes. No. I mean, I don't know. I'm confused.'

'Be patient, give it time. All will become clear in the end. And stop matchmaking, we've already got–'

'Me. That's my job,' Emma says, coming up in perfect timing behind us. 'Ever the matchmaker. Don't give up, Soph. I'm determined to have a higher compatibility success rate than last year. The next event is a tour of Luckington Court, the Bennets' house – what can possibly go wrong in such a beautiful location? I'm sure we will get the right people together in the end.'

Maria raises her eyebrows at me and laughs.

'I'm just going to stop off at the house to collect the last couple of things,' I say to the others. 'I'll catch you both up.'

I drop off the umbrellas I'd borrowed from the main house and am striding back up the hill, when I hear a familiar voice loudly blasting into the ethos. A horribly familiar voice actually. I must be mistaken or hearing things. I haven't heard this person's voice for months. It can't be her though; I must be imagining it. Although, I haven't even thought about her for ages. I hold my nose and blow out – a good tip to get rid of annoying blockages in the ears, by the way, although it only really works if your ears are congested. Nope, I can still hear her.

I check my phone is on silent. Once I thought I was hearing people talking when there wasn't anyone there and it turned out I had accidentally pressed something on my phone and YouTube was playing in my pocket. No, my phone is fine and the voice is getting louder.

I reach the top of the path and then hurriedly crouch back down so I am hidden within a small area of densely planted trees and shrubs. The voices are coming from the Baroness's car, which is parked on the edge of the car park.

'I was hoping you'd give me an update on the latest progress,' the voice was saying.

The Baroness replies. I can hear every word, she must be on the car phone. 'I told you, we aren't able to confirm numbers until next week.'

'This week was at the very top of our schedule. Daniel won't be pleased, he needs to speak to the guys to get the connections sorted out.'

'You know I keep my word.' The Baroness's voice is steely. I wouldn't mess with her.

'Fine,' is the tight-lipped reply. 'We'll speak again, at the weekend. On schedule to start the new plan next week.'

'No problem our end.' The Baroness appears to ring off and I watch her car slowly pull away out of the car park and ponder for a moment, still hidden in my tree-lined hidey-hole. I would recognise the person on the other end of that call anywhere. It was none other than Jessica Palmer Wright, my arch-enemy from last year. She had been Head of Membership at the Dating Agency and in addition to generally making my life pretty miserable when I first joined the agency, she ran off last summer with my first proper date, Daniel, along with most of the profits of the agency.

It had turned out Jessica and Daniel as well as a couple of others from Modiste had been running an illegal gambling ring under the pretence of the Regency gambling. Darcy managed to recoup a lot of the money, but he's never been able to catch up with Jessica or Daniel since. And now here she is again, up to something, infiltrating the agency through the Baroness.

I feel completely betrayed, I knew the Baroness was up to something, but I believed she was one of the good guys. I kind of felt a connection somewhere along the line. Maybe I had just been flattered by her attentions but I'm shattered, my instincts aren't usually so wrong. There's something about her I'm drawn to, that I really like. And here she is in cahoots with Jessica and by the sound of it, Daniel as well, all involved in some new scheme, which could put the whole company into jeopardy again.

What am I going to do? I can't tell Darcy. I don't feel like speaking to him, even about this. Besides he wouldn't believe me anyway, he's decided I'm a maverick, some vegan revolutionary. I feel as though I'm on my final warning. What if I lose my job over this? Besides, the Baroness is one of our most prestigious clients.

This is a very awkward situation. I'll have to talk to Emma, but even then what evidence have I got? I should have pressed record on my phone, but it wouldn't have picked up the conversation at that distance. It's no good; I'm going to have to get a whole lot better at this detective thing if I'm going to get to the bottom of this mystery. Perhaps rather than psychological thrillers, I should read Sherlock Holmes instead; it would be far more useful.

CHAPTER 23

There's no time to brood over recent events the next day, as the General arrives in the morning with a large party of guests. I haven't seen any of them yet, which is kind of a relief, but I believe they must be important, judging by the amount of baggage that seems to be being transported from one place to another, by a multitude of porters and servants. I try to contact Emma and leave her several urgent, babbled voice messages, but I think she's at a management conference today, so that would explain her unavailability.

I haven't seen Ellie this morning either, she didn't show up for our usual walk, not that I blame her, she's probably depressed after Sir Henry's persistent attentions yesterday. I noticed in spite of the Baronesses' intervention, he still insisted on walking her back to the car at the end of the afternoon. As a distraction, I decide to walk to the stables to talk to the horses, I always feel relaxed there.

One of the General's array of spaniels seems keen to accompany me. She is often to be found pootling along at my feet, a little Blenheim Cavalier King Charles, not one of the larger spaniels. She doesn't seem as much part of the pack as the others and often follows me about the place; she's a sweet little dog actually and the complete opposite to the rambunctious and inevitably soggy Roland. I love stroking her curly ears and she gazes at me with her slightly protruding eyes. I realise I don't even know her name, but she doesn't seem to hold it against me and follows me towards the stable block.

I love the smell of stables, fresh hay, sweet grass and leather mixed with manure, which has a country-ish aroma. Whilst I am talking to Meg, giving her a piece of carrot I managed to pilfer from the kitchen on my way, the little spaniel at my feet, munching on any leftover morsels, I am disturbed from my monologue by Henry.

'Morning,' he says with a smile. I try not to stare at his snug-fitting britches over long country boots. He's seriously fit actually.

'Hi, I was just, er...'

'Chatting with the horses and Widget, the greedy dog?' he asks completely straight-faced.

'Yes that's it. They're good company and I talk to animals all the time. If they're not available, I sometimes even talk to myself,' I confess with an embarrassed smile. There's something about Henry which makes me feel as though I can tell him anything.

He laughs. 'You probably get more sense out of either of those options than most people.'

'True, I'm glad you agree. I know I talk too much, but then there's always so much to say. And to be honest, it's only a small amount of what's going on in my brain.'

'That doesn't surprise me.' He leans across me to stroke Meg's soft grey neck. Unwittingly I inhale the smell of his aftershave. It's nice actually, tangy and masculine and I find myself wishing he'd stroke my hair like that. For goodness' sake, what's wrong with me? It has to be Darcy I'm missing, not Henry. I need to stop this.

That's another thing, I've been having some slightly disturbing dreams about Henry the last week or so. I feel like a teenager again who has a crush on their first hot guy. He turns to look at me, breaking over the unwelcome thoughts. 'I like your chattiness, it's cheerful, you make me laugh anyway!'

'In a good way I hope? Some people say I babble too much.' At least Darcy does at any rate.

'Then they don't know what they're talking about,' Henry says and I grin at him and we walk companionably down the path by the stables, leading to the woodland beyond. It's picturesque, overhung by trees, bereft of many of their leaves now, but some still managing to cling on by a thread, dotted in beautiful russet and gold, drooping down above our heads. A passing squirrel scrounges for chestnuts and the green meadows of the fields beyond beckon us towards them in a friendly manner. This is countryside I really feel like exploring.

'I'm sorry about my brother, Ben, and his annoying friend, and even more obnoxious dog, Roland.'

'Why? You need to stop apologising for things you can't do anything about.'

'It's an occupational hazard of being British, isn't it?'

'Yes, but you seem particularly good at it. I don't think it's fair to hold anyone's family or their friends against them, do you?'

'No,' I laugh, 'and if everyone did, Elizabeth would hardly have married Mr Darcy, would she?'

'Definitely not. Although I suspect her family continued to annoy him after they married.'

'You cynic,' I joke, as a distraction from how secretly impressed I am by the fact he's not only actually read *Pride and Prejudice* but can also hold a conversation about it.

'No I'm just a realist. And look at my family. A total mess.'

I peer at him; it's so unusual for him to be serious.

'Not a total mess. I expect all families have their challenges. Do you see your mum much?'

'Not as often as I'd like. And I'm not fussed about my stepdad. He's okay, but one overbearing father figure is enough in my life.'

'I can imagine. Do you all have to do what he says?' I say, then wonder if I've gone too far.

'Usually, it just makes more sense that way.' He looks uneasily over his shoulder. 'Actually, I've got to go and look at some business with him now, but I'll see you at dinner.'

'Have you seen Ellie this morning, by the way?'

'No, I expect she had a headache or something and needed a lie-in,' Henry says abruptly. He seems in a hurry to be off and I hope I haven't offended him in my usual style that Mel is always laughing about. With reluctance I watch him disappear into the distance.

As I look back towards Dreyfus Manor, I notice a couple of men walk round the back of the side gate, towards the rear entrance. They are very heavily set, somewhat like powerfully built bodyguards, seemingly rather out of keeping with their surroundings. I wonder who they are? I guess they could be gardeners, but they look a little smartly dressed for that.

Maybe they are delivery drivers, or what if they are hit men? Maria said she had heard that there were gangs of men employed by the General. A chill trickles down my spine, but then I give myself a little shake. Maybe I need to give thrillers a bit of a break; they make me see perfidious plots everywhere.

I decide to phone Mel for a comforting dose of reality as I cross the field on the way back to the house. She picks up quite quickly. 'How's life amongst the landed gentry?' she asks in a mock posh accent.

'Nice,' I say, 'I wish I had some land like this. It's amazing and the horses are just gorgeous. I've also made a little friend.'

'Has Darcy been replaced then?'

I laugh. 'Pretty much. She's small and furry, follows me everywhere and fails to complain when I interrupt, or go on climate strikes. She's called Widget and is a spaniel.' I look down at her fluffy white head with its brown spot, sniffing in a nearby rabbit hole. I can't help but be flattered that she wishes to stay with me rather than heading back to the warm and cosy house with Henry. 'Doesn't smell too good though.'

'You'll have to bring her back with you, Chawton could do with some animals to make it more homely.'

'I don't think they'd part with her. Anyway, I have something serious I need to talk to you about.'

'Okay fire away. I've missed our gossipy chats.'

'This isn't gossip, it's incredibly important.'

'Ooh, hark at you.' She breaks off, obviously realising from my abject silence that I mean business and abruptly goes quiet.

I briefly repeat what I overheard last night from my hiding place by the Baroness's car. As I'm talking however, I hear a twig crack from the edge of the woods near the path I'm walking along, and cursing my over-imaginative mind, I quicken my steps and lower my voice to tell the rest.

'That's terrible if the Baroness really is involved with Jessica Palmer Wright, the snake! But then what if they were talking about something innocent?'

I sigh. I can't argue with Mel, she's only voicing the same doubts I have had. 'I agree. So you don't think I should tell Darcy. Especially not after how things have been between us?'

Mel is silent for a moment. 'I guess not. Hasn't he contacted you at all?'

'Nope, nothing, nada... It's okay though,' I say after a pause, in a falsely bright tone, 'I've totally moved on.'

'Really?' Mel doesn't sound convinced.

'Yes,' I say with a firmness I don't feel and simultaneously pushing the constant daily wonderings over what Darcy is doing to the back of my mind. 'So do you think I should tell Emma?'

'I'm not sure there's much you can tell her at the moment,' says Mel thoughtfully. 'I mean you've not got any evidence of what's going on. You're going to have to do some snooping.'

'Please not after the Lady Constance incident last year. That didn't end well.'

'I don't mean that kind of snooping. Just some investigating. What about Chloe?'

'What *about* Chloe?'

'She lives in New York, that's where Jessica is supposed to be. Maybe you could get Chloe to look into it.'

'I suppose I could, although New York is a huge place.'

'True, but Jessica and Daniel are bound to have made ripples wherever they went. They're both such divas. I'm sure they'll have left a trail of some kind.'

'It can't be a very obvious one if Darcy is unable to catch them.'

'Even so, it's worth a try. By the way,' Mel adds, before I could leave the conversation, 'you know that book? The one about an abbey.'

'Yes *Northanger Abbey*,' I say distractedly as I'm nearly back at the house and don't like to be on the phone at someone else's place. It feels rude somehow and as though the walls have ears.

'That's the one. Back on the floor again last night.'

'How odd. How do you think it got there? You can't blame me as I was here, miles away.'

'I realise that, duh. But it must be Emma. Anyway I thought I'd tell you so when she phones you can tell her I'm onto her! She's the only one with the key.'

'Okay.' I laugh. These two are hilarious, I still miss them though, pair of idiots that they are. I miss the cosiness of our chats and my little reading nook at Chawton. In the daytime that is.

'By the way,' I add.

'Yes?'

'Next time, can you just let me know what page the book is open at?'

'Why would I do that?'

'Please?'

'Okay but I'm sure there won't be a next time. I've put the book in the downstairs library, but in a completely different place.'

'Surely Emma can easily find it there.'

'Not where I've hidden it.'

Honestly, these two are a laugh a minute. But I miss them all the same. I text Chloe, but can't get her but I guess it's early morning there and she's probably busy. I also have to make final arrangements with some of the suppliers for our grand Regency wedding, which is now only a month away. There's so much to check through and I can't wait for Maria and Charles to tie the knot. They're such a lovely couple. The unwelcome thought that Darcy would have gone to the wedding with me flits into my mind, but I dismiss it instantly, brushing it aside like an annoying sticky bit of spider's web. It obviously wasn't meant to be.

A reply bings up from Chloe.

Hey how's life in the fast lane? Did you want me – I'm up now if you want to chat? Cx

Great, thanks. Calling now! Sx

It's so good to talk to Chloe. She sounds as loved-up as ever and is even helping Nick with the business. It's lovely to hear how motivated she is.

'I do need a favour, Chlo,' I say once we've got the preliminary conversation over. I've deliberately left out the latest events especially Henry, because it's just too complicated to know where to begin.

'Fire away,' she says tearing into a chocolate bar, well at least I think it is, there's so much rustling. 'That's what I'm here for.'

'You remember Jessica Palmer Wright?'

'Euch, how could I not remember her? I love Nick, but I can't understand how he can be related to such a hideous woman. And the way she ran off with that slimeball, Daniel Becks.'

'Word is she might be back in circulation again, up to her old tricks.'

'I thought she'd disappeared without a trace.' Chloe finishes her chocolate bar and noisily scrunches up the wrapper.

'They have, but apparently to New York.'

'Hmm, but New York is a huge place, Soph.'

'I know, but you're pretty good at research, and I need someone to do some digging around to find out exactly where she is and what she's up to.'

Chloe sighs. 'I guess I can use my contacts within the business to do some questioning, is this a Nick thing or does it have to be confidential?'

'No,' I hiss, 'it's definitely not a Nick thing. There's no way he can know anything. I haven't told Darcy either.'

'That's not great. I know you're feeling bad about Darcy but what are you hoping to achieve with all this secrecy?'

'I'm trying to save the agency. You know I was telling you about the Baroness, our most prestigious client?'

'Yes it sounded great, you did incredibly well recruiting her.'

'It *was* great or so I thought, but I overheard her on the

phone to Jessica. I think they're up to something dodgy. They were talking about some arrangements for a plan happening this next week, to do with setting up connections, and anything to do with Jessica Palmer Wright has got to be bad news.'

'Ooh, the plot thickens. Adventure never stays very far away from you does it, Soph? Although that doesn't sound much to go on. They could be just setting up a manufacturing business or something like that.'

'I don't believe anything Jessica is involved in is legit. But I need to sort it out. We can't risk the future of the agency; it means everything to me as well as Emma and all the others.'

'Okay of course I'll look into it. I could hire a personal investigator, that's how everyone finds out stuff over here, although they're pretty expensive so I don't know how I could afford it without telling Nick.'

'No,' I exclaim, 'definitely not. The thing is I don't want this getting out and besides, Darcy will have already thought of that I'm sure, if he's been looking for them all this time. Think how much money he's got to hire people for him.'

'True, we're going to have to think outside the box.'

'I know how good you are at getting in with people. I'm sure you must have connections who keep ears to the ground.'

'Hmm, mostly boring business people, but I'll have a think about it.' She pauses a moment. 'In fact, I do have a couple of people in mind, Mrs Van Hayler, she has a lot of contacts in the city and Anya Stepler, they're the two biggest gossips in the whole of New York. With them around, the place might as well be the size of a Regency village. Okay leave it with me. I'll get back to you as soon as I can.'

'Thanks, Chloe, you're a star. But I don't want Darcy hearing about it or anyone. Keep it low profile. Maybe this way, we can find out what's going on and then tell him when it's all sorted.

Meanwhile...' I pause for a moment. 'Meanwhile... I'm going to do some investigating of my own.'

Although how I'm going to snoop about behind the back of someone as well protected when it comes to bodyguards as the Baroness Mayer, I don't know, I add silently.

CHAPTER 24

*T*he evening comes around long before I want it to. I've been dreading this as I still find formal dinners awkward to contend with. At least Henry and Ellie will provide some kind of familiar company, although Ellie still hasn't appeared all afternoon.

I walk down the stairs promptly just before seven and am delighted to find Henry waiting in the hallway for me. 'My father suggested I accompany you in to dinner,' he says with a mock gentlemanly bow, belied by his familiar grin. 'Although I'm sure you could find your own way by now.'

'Just about.' I smile, placing my arm on his. 'But it's kind of you to make sure I don't get lost.'

'I would have told him that you are perfectly capable of looking after yourself,' he says. 'But we are having drinks to start in the drawing room.'

'Too right, I can as well. But I'm glad you're walking in with me all the same.'

'They're all right really,' Henry sighs, 'although you might just die of boredom.' I give him a conspiratorial grin and we walk into what appears to be a room crammed full of people.

'Ah there you are,' General Baxter says with a smile unnatural to his usually stern features. 'Miss Sophie Johnson, I should like to introduce you to our worthy guests, Lord and Lady Tremmick, Mr Bertram Basset and his fiancée, Bebe Gutherington, and last but by no means least, Lady Constance Parker.'

Everything seems to go into slow motion as I hear the fateful words. Lady... Constance... Parker... I don't believe it. This is hell on earth.

I greet and shake hands with the perfectly pleasant people who are introduced to me until I'm standing in front of Lady Constance Parker. 'Who's this?' she utters to General Baxter. 'She looks bally familiar. Who did you say she is?'

'Miss Johnson,' General Baxter repeats and I marvel at his fake patience, which he never shows with his children, although those who know him well can sense the tension simmering beneath the surface.

'I'm perfectly certain I've heard that name before. Do I know you?' Lady C thunders at me. How can it be she doesn't recognise me? It was not that long ago, we had a blazing row after she accused Mel of stealing clothes from the spring collection designed by her sister, Vivienne Artois. But then I realise, of course, my hair is up for once in a chignon and I am wearing Emma's designer evening gown. In this environment, I am perfectly camouflaged. Long may it last.

Thank goodness I manage to bumble my way through pre-dinner drinks and actually Bebe turns out to be nice and chatty and although we come from totally different backgrounds, she's a debutante with the inevitable engagement announcement in *Country Life* (I know, we're back to that again) and she grew up on an estate in Surrey, with ponies and dogs and oodles of free spending money to buy gorgeous clothes for her model like frame, she at least likes animals and seems happy to include me in the conversation.

'Oh good I'm glad, you're next to me,' Bebe utters when I am shown to my seat next to her and I give her a smile. To my great relief, Lady Constance is placed at the far end of the table.

On my other side is Henry, but so far this evening he has been very quiet and totally unlike his usual self. 'Where's Ellie?' I ask, under the pretence of dropping my napkin, 'isn't she supposed to be here?'

'Yes, my father says she has a headache.'

'Oh I'm sorry I would have gone to see her, if I'd known.' I would much rather sit quietly upstairs with Ellie than stay at this dreary dinner table.

'No,' Henry says, almost snapping my head off with the force of the word. 'It's fine. My father's instructions are to leave her alone.' I peer at him alarmed, so he softens it with, 'She's had some medicine and it's best she sleeps it off.'

'Okay. As long as she's all right.'

Henry remains quiet and I can't help but feel a little uneasy.

'Isn't Eleanor joining us this evening?' Bebe asks and I wonder if she overheard our whispered conversation.

Before Henry can reply, the General interjects. 'Sadly, Miss Eleanor is unwell and unable to attend this evening, but she will be at the Hunt Ball next week.'

'I'm so glad, I was looking forward to talking tactics ready for Badminton,' Bebe utters.

'I hear she is potentially going to be betrothed to Sir Henry,' Lady C booms, shovelling in a mouthful of potatoes. There's a pause as she chews vigorously. 'Not that I agree with such ideas, a large age gap is bound to cause issues. Whatever the breeding. Especially if she is sickly.'

'My daughter, Lady Constance, is an extremely healthy young lady.' The General interjects. 'An occasional headache is hardly a problem. She's a very fit young woman.' It's as though he's talking of one of the brood mares in his stables. 'She rode the point-to-point in record time last week.'

'I'm jolly pleased to hear it,' Lady C remarks, undeterred. 'I hope it isn't issues with alcohol either. No debutante should be unable to hold her drink.'

To my amusement General Baxter's face begins to go an interesting shade of puce, which I think has little to do with the large glass of red wine he has by his place setting. 'You will discover when you meet Eleanor, Lady Constance, that she is a well brought up young lady and has all the manners which go along with her position.'

'Let's hope so. It would be nice to believe that some young women still set an example to all the drunken forward hussies which seem to litter society these days.' I'm sure it's no coincidence that Lady Constance fixes me with a steely look between narrowed eyes, whilst ruthlessly forking another spoonful of the delicious duck into her mouth. I begin to wonder uneasily if she has recognised me after all and is merely biding her time, like a wolf stalking its prey.

'Wow, she's pretty hard work, isn't she?' Bebe whispers to me sotto voce.

'You could say that,' I whisper back.

Henry gives me a conspiratorial smile, but his attention is taken by Lady Tremmick on his left, who seems to have plenty of conversation about her flower arranging and kitchen garden.

The company is generally not that bad, other than Lady C, but I am in a state of nervous anxiety throughout dinner, terrified any moment that she might suddenly remember where she knew me from and start on me in front of the whole room.

Three courses pass and I can't help but be in a hurry to get through the dinner. Besides, I've made a plan. Ellie is obviously struggling and I've decided that I'm going to find out exactly what's going on. If she has a headache, I'm Lady Catherine de Bourgh.

The drinks and chat seem to go on interminably. Finally the men withdraw to swig port and smoke cigars, Henry apologising to me sotto voce for the antiquated habit, which he says they only do on formal occasions. I'm just relieved they are all going and hope to goodness the ladies will start to tire and go to bed, or figure I can make some excuse that I need to go and powder my nose or something.

After an intolerable half hour of talking about a whole group of society people I know nothing about, totally dominated by Lady C's conversation mostly about who's due to have a baby and who is next in line to be presented to the local Huntmaster, I decide now's my chance. 'If you'll excuse me, it's lovely to meet you, but I do just need to attend to some business.'

Attend to some business! Now I sound as though I've swallowed a Jane Austen novel, but it seems to do the trick as the ladies smile and nod, with the exception of Lady C who regards me rather like someone might an earwig on the bottom of their shoe. Either way, they're probably relieved to be left to talk about their entire acquaintance without the inconvenience of an interloper.

I walk smartly along the corridor, hoping to quickly make good my escape, before I glance through the window and catch sight of a car crawling up the drive. The headlights flick around the cold stone creepily lighting the old panelled walls. It's a familiar silver Vauxhall Corsa. I stand and gape. It can't be, surely? But, I really think it is. A small man with spiky over gelled hair steps out and walks towards the main entrance.

It is, I can't believe it! It's Rob Bright, the bane of my early dates with the dating agency. But he's not alone. I watch fascinated as a young woman gets out from the car. I notice typically of him, he hasn't bothered opening the door for her. I expect he's too busy trying to get inside to Lady Constance as fast as he possibly can to open the door for his friend. I'm sure that's the reason he's here.

I hope the girl comes round this side of the car, as I'm desperate to know what she looks like. She hones into view, following after Rob like a lost sheep. She is the perfect match for him with her shoulder-length lank hair, part tied into a topknot, large unflattering glasses and slightly protruding teeth. She's wearing flat brown shoes, which were simply never in fashion, a long coat apparently completely incongruous with the rest of the outfit and a particularly annoyed expression. Brilliant.

I don't have time to linger though, they're obviously coming in and I don't want to get caught, Rob will definitely recognise me.

I creep as fast as I can up the stairs before I'm disturbed by the General or even Henry – I have a strange feeling he might not want me to speak to Ellie. This family has major secrets; I can feel it in my waters. It's not right at all.

I reach the top of the stairs, looking over my shoulder the whole time. This creeping around thing is really stressful actually. I'm nearly at Ellie's bedroom, which is along the corridor from mine, when I hear footsteps. It's a maidservant. Quick as a whiz I leg it along the passage and back into my own room.

A few moments later, I peer round the door frame. The coast is clear and I tread carefully back towards Ellie's room. Quietly, oh-so quietly, I knock on her large heavy oak door. 'Ellie,' I call softly. No answer. 'Ellie? Can I come in?'

Still no reply, but then the door is quite solid; perhaps she hasn't heard me. Gently I put my hand on the solid iron door latch and turn it. It clicks loudly, so loudly I look back down the hall, half expecting to hear running footsteps coming to stop me. Gently, I push open the door and peer round. The room is... completely empty. Well, apart from the furniture. The bed is neatly made but bare, the sheet perfectly turned over. There is nothing on the tops, no clothes left out or shoes on the floor. You'd think Ellie is a tidiness freak, but I went in her room to sit and talk to her the other day and there were things strewn everywhere. This is very odd.

I walk softly across the plush cream carpet and push open another door, which is obviously an en suite. Again it is clean and tidy, but empty except for a bottle of soap. There's no razor or hairbrush or any sign at all that Ellie was ever here, that she ever existed even.

It's as though Ellie has vanished without a trace. But people don't suddenly disappear, not without a word. Or do they?

CHAPTER 25

I am startled by a noise. Someone is coming along the corridor and I can't, I really can't, be discovered in here. It would be too embarrassing or maybe in view of what might have happened to Ellie, disastrous? My mind is racing with hideous thoughts. What if she's been murdered? And now the killer's going to come back and he will have to silence me, because I'm the only one who will know what has happened and that will be it. The end.

No one will think of looking for me, not for several days anyway because Mel spoke to me earlier and Emma is at a conference. Oh God, I start panicking. Where can I hide? I feel as though I'm on a movie set but there's no creepy music, although there's a hefty bass banging in the background. Actually I think that's my heart, it's going through the roof.

I peep in Ellie's room again. Good there's a huge wardrobe. I think it's big enough; I'm getting in. By some sheer luck, it's totally empty and I fit easily into the bottom, squidging up against the back wall, wondering where Narnia and Mr Tumnus or even some big thick furry coats are when I need them. Even the white witch might be a better option than a murderous hitman who's willing to kill or kidnap his own daughter to force her marriage to a hideous old man. Then there is silence.

This is like a nightmare. I hear Ellie's door creak open and the footsteps sound out on the floorboards of her room. I hear them hesitate. Then they move on into the bathroom. I hear the light go on and I imagine the hitman, dressed all in black of course, probably with a balaclava over his head, touching the switch with his black leather gloves. He's far too clever to leave fingerprints. Odd, it sounds as though he turns the tap on. Oh God, perhaps he's going to drown me. I read that in this thriller where they made it look like an accident and then... Wait, he's coming, I can hear the footsteps coming back; he's getting nearer the wardrobe. It's like one of those hideous games of hide and seek where you find a great hiding place, then you discover you need the loo. Involuntarily I scrunch myself closer to the back of the cupboard as though that's going to make any difference.

Slowly, slowly, horribly slowly, the wardrobe door creaks open and for once I am too terrified to speak at all. But actually, wait a minute, I'm face to face with none other than a very surprised-looking Henry Baxter. Oh please God, don't let him be in on this, it would be terrible.

'What are you doing?' he asks angrily.

'Erm, I'm looking for Narnia...' I say randomly. Oh this just gets worse.

'Narnia?' he hesitates. 'I think you might have the wrong bloody wardrobe.'

I want to laugh but am still so shocked and stressed I think I merely gape at him like a startled hen. I manage to recover myself but when I speak, my voice is dry and comes out like a strangled squeak, 'I was looking for Ellie.'

'In the wardrobe?' He sighs heavily.

I shrug, I mean what else can I say?

'She's not here.'

'I think I realised that. But I was worried and wanted to ask her how she was and then I heard footsteps so I hid.'

'You hid?' He offers a gentlemanly hand to help me scramble out of the wardrobe in some kind of vaguely dignified manner. Okay so a murderer probably wouldn't politely help you out of a cupboard. That's a relief.

I feel really stupid now. 'Yes, I did because... because I felt as though I was intruding being in someone else's room.'

'Even though we all know you?'

'Yep.' There's an awkward silence. 'Anyway that's not the point, where is Ellie? She can't just vanish.'

'No she can't, she's left.'

'Left? But where's she gone? Is she okay?'

Henry walks to the door, looks round it into the passageway, then comes back in and shuts the door firmly. 'She's gone somewhere safe.'

'From your father?'

'Yes, where else?'

'Oh that's such a relief, so he doesn't know where she is? I thought... I was worried...'

'You thought what?'

'I was just worried that maybe...'

'Maybe...?' Henry advances ominously towards me and I feel a bit embarrassed, I mean what was I thinking?

'That maybe your father had taken your sister somewhere to try to make her marry Sir Henry Greaves...' I should stop now, Henry's face is a picture... but I can't stop... 'or...'

'Or what?'

'Or something worse...'

'Worse?'

I feel so stupid. 'Worse.' I falter.

'What could be worse than a father who would do that to his

own daughter?' Henry demands angrily. He pauses and stares at me a moment, his dark brows drawn together in a frown. 'Wait a minute. You thought he's kidnapped her or even more unforgivably, murdered her because she won't marry the man he wants her to, didn't you?'

'I was just worried... that maybe your father wasn't very kind and...' Oh God it's out there now.

'You thought my father might murder his own daughter because she wouldn't marry Sir Henry Greaves?' Henry repeats. Okay so when he puts it like that it does sound pretty fantastical.

'Of course I know that isn't the case now, but I guess I...' I look at Henry's angry face and falter... 'I guess I got a bit carried away.'

'I should think you bloody well did. I know my father has a nasty temper and can be a little aggressive at times, but a murderer?' Henry strides across to the window and looks out over the gardens. 'How do you think he'd have got away with it?' He turns back towards me. 'Where would he have hidden the body?'

'Lots of places actually.' I'm warming up to my defence now, the relief hitting me with a wave of almost hysteria. 'I read this one book where...'

'Bloody psychological thrillers have got a lot to answer for. Maybe you should stick to reading Regency romances.'

'I think I got warned off those as well,' I say miserably.

'I never thought I'd say this, but maybe for someone with an imagination like yours, novels should come with a health warning.'

CHAPTER 26

J am totally embarrassed and have barricaded myself in my room. Well not literally but at least no one seems to be disturbing me. This is a disaster, I've admitted that I basically suspected Henry's father of plotting to murder his own daughter and put Henry off me for life. I really liked him too, not as a boyfriend obviously because I'm beginning to figure, I'm totally unsuited to go out with anyone. But as a friend; a really decent, kind, funny friend. I've never had a guy who was a good friend before and now I've blown it.

There's no doubt, I, Sophie Johnson, am still officially a dating disaster area. In spite of running a dating agency. I can imagine the headlines now, *Spinster sad and alone, living off nothing but romantic novels, runs dating agency shock!* I am a total joke. I sit in the yoga child position on the floor, hunched over so the world is completely shut out. I've always wondered why they call it that. I guess it's because you can hide in it like a little kid and that's what I feel like.

Here I was planning this year would go so well, dating the most gorgeous man in the universe, Darcy Drummond, running the agency, writing inspirational copy for Modiste and now look at me. Single again of course after a pathetic few months, dumped by Darcy, no idea where Ellie is, suspecting a perfectly nice family of terrible crimes they weren't about to commit, and I still haven't managed to do anything to stop the Baroness's plot with Jessica Palmer Wright. I lift my head from the floor. There at least I can do something, although I'm not sure yet quite what. Just as I'm picking up my mobile, it rings.

'Hi, Sophie. How's it going?' It's Maria.

'Hi, good to speak to you,' I say desperately. It really is, I am so relieved to hear her familiar voice.

'Are you okay, Soph? You sound a little flustered?'

'Yes I'm fine.' I try to pull myself together to sound as normal as possible, 'It's nice to have had a break from everything here at the Baxters'.' There's a faint scratching at the door, which makes me jump, my nerves are all over the place at the moment.

I'm almost beginning to sympathise with Mrs Bennet and I don't even have five daughters to try to marry off. I walk softly to the door and open it. Thank goodness it's only Widget, who comes trotting in as though she owns the place (although I guess she does), she leaps on the bed and makes herself comfortable. 'Hello, little dog,' I say sitting next to her and ruffling her ears.

'Are you talking to yourself?' Maria asks.

'Sorry no, the dog has come to sit with me,' I say, smiling and feeling better. 'At least she likes me.'

'Soph, everyone likes you. What's wrong?'

'I've been getting myself into scrapes again,' I say sadly. 'I thought it was bad enough with the vegan climate protest, but this is even worse.'

'Anything I can help with?'

'Not really.' I hesitate, although Maria is an incredibly kind person and I need to tell someone. Mel would combust with laughing over this one and say I told you so. Maria is far less judgy. 'The thing is, I suspected the General had done something terrible and unfortunately I told Henry, and now he probably hates me.'

'The General? Why did you think he'd do something awful? Although he does have a bad reputation I guess, all those bodyguards and dodgy men hanging around. Perhaps the rumours are true?'

'Long story and I was totally wrong, but now I've messed up with Henry.' I sniff, trying hard not to let Maria know I'm crying.

'Henry Baxter? He always seems really laid-back, I don't think he could be cross with anyone for long.'

'He is with me. I've never seen him so furious.'

'I don't expect it will last. Look, Soph, I feel like I've known you all my life, there's no way anyone can stay mad at you for long.'

'What about Darcy?' I point out.

'That's different,' she says carefully. 'Anyway, I don't think Darcy is mad with you. Just being controlled by his mother and other responsibilities. Every time I saw him with you, I could tell he was totally smitten. In any case, what does it matter with Henry? I didn't think you felt that way about him?'

'I didn't. I don't. I mean, I just don't know anymore, I'm so confused. It's just that we've got really close, I've enjoyed our chats and I don't want him to think badly of me.'

'He won't. I promise, Soph. Nothing you can have said or done will be that bad. And don't worry, it will all become clear in the end. Give it time.'

'Thanks, Maria. You always make me feel better.' And perhaps she's right, maybe Henry will forgive how silly I've been and we can go back to being friends. He's the only guy I've ever felt like talking to, telling him about my family and everything without feeling he was going to judge anything. 'So enough of my sad personal life. How's the wedding plans going?'

'Really well.' Maria becomes animated as she talks of her

forthcoming nuptials. 'All sorted, slight issue with the groomsmen's suits as my father didn't want to wear neckerchiefs, but he seems to have come round to the idea.'

'With bad grace I should think, knowing him.' I laugh.

'Pretty much. He's complained that this would never have happened if I were marrying a lord!'

We both laugh. 'I did want to just mention something to you though, Soph. Have you heard from Izzy?'

'No, nothing, not even a text, which is a bit weird, as she usually messages quite a lot.'

'I know, me neither. Also she's been acting a bit strange. I phoned her at the weekend as I hadn't heard from her and she was very cagey about meeting up.'

'Perhaps she's just busy?'

'I would think that, but Mel says she asked her to have a chat about some surprise she was considering with the décor for the wedding and she seemed distracted, furtive even. Also, she's usually pretty transparent.'

'That's true.' I ponder for a moment. 'I hope it's nothing to do with Josh. I hate even suggesting it, but I know Matthew did try to talk to me at the Chawton Ball, but we were interrupted by General Baxter. I think Matthew was hinting that he was worried she was acting a bit strangely, but with one thing and another I forgot all about it.'

'That's what I was concerned about. She just seemed pretty edgy after mentioning meeting Josh again and I wondered if she might be thinking of getting back together with him.'

'Surely Izzy wouldn't do that. She adores Matthew.'

'I don't think she would, would she? Although she was totally crazy about Josh when we first met her.'

'That was a long time ago though, wasn't it?'

We are both silent, each hoping against hope that Izzy

wouldn't be so silly. Besides there's nothing we can do about it at the moment.

'If I could but just know his heart, everything would become easy,' Maria quotes.

'Nobody says it better than Jane Austen,' I say, and it's true, they don't.

CHAPTER 27

I peer outside my bedroom door to make sure no one is about. I don't feel like facing anyone right now. I've had enough of being inside however and have decided to make a break for it and go for a walk in the grounds. Henry isn't here, I saw him drive off in his little sports car earlier, and I haven't heard a sound from any of the household for some time. The coast is clear, so I leg it down the stairs and out into the fresh air. The little spaniel follows close at my feet; she really is sweet. As I breathe in the smell of countryside, I ponder my next move. First I definitely need to get out of here, there is no reason for me to stay. Ellie has gone, although I'm worried where, but I guess if Henry knows about it, she must be fine.

Also I can't face him again, not after what I said, so I need to leave as soon as possible. I kind of wonder if I can just go and leave a note. Perhaps that's best, but then it would look so rude and I don't want to offend the General any more than it will already if he gets wind of what I suspected of him! Secondly I need to meet with the Baroness, or at least try to find a way to discover what is going on. Or I could confront her, but that's going to have to be a last resort as she's probably a pretty formidable adversary. I haven't forgotten how she completely thrashed poor old Gene at fencing and I don't fancy my chances even in a verbal confrontation.

As I approach the stables, which have become my favourite go-to thinking place, I overhear the General talking. He's the last person I want to see. I start to walk away from the entrance, but can't help but overhear a few words of snatched conversation, 'Good God, Rigsby, if the systems aren't working, there's going to be a delay and I told Skeller the lines from Antigua would be working by Saturday.' There's a silence as I presume Rigsby, or whoever the other person is, is talking at the end of the line. I'm sure he was some weird, miserly landlord on the seventies sitcom *Rising Damp*. I don't expect this is the same one however.

I can hear the General continue angrily, 'Then sort it out, that's what you're paid for, man. Every day it's not working I'm going to start deducting from your fee.' There's a noise indicating that someone's coming out of the stable and I flee back into the nearby woods. There's no way I want to be caught eavesdropping .

As I get within the trees, I hide behind a thick heavy trunk and some dense undergrowth and watch as the General leaves the stables. For a moment he stands peering down at his phone, then he looks up and I could swear he stares right at the spot where I'm hiding, but I must be mistaken as he then strides away in a purposeful manner towards the house. Enough of this imagining things, I have no intention of accusing this poor man of one more thing, even if his conversation did sound dodgy. It's nothing to do with me. No more over-imagining. I'm done with psychological thrillers, no more conjuring up of criminals lurking within the shadows.

I return to the house, still not having found a solution to my quandary on how to leave. I think the best option is to make my apologies and go. Just as I am rummaging in my bag for a pen and paper, I know there's one in here somewhere, I can't be that disorganised, I'm disturbed by a polite cough behind me. It's Gregson, the droopy spaniel-jowelled butler who looks as miserable as ever. 'Excuse me, madam, but the General has asked me to mention that he has suddenly recalled an urgent business meeting in town and he is therefore unable to entertain you any longer.'

'Oh, don't worry,' I say cheerfully, 'that's fine, I don't need entertaining, there's plenty for me to do.' For goodness' sake, why've I said that? I should just agree and leave.

'Ahem, the issue is, madam, that the General cannot have guests in the house in his absence so requires you to leave...' I gape at him '...immediately.'

Okay so that's told me then. 'That's no problem,' I say breezily, having scraped my chin off the floor and trying to gather any crumbs of self-respect I can muster from very low reserves. 'I will pack my things, which I'm just doing by the way,' I indicate my suitcases with an impressive sweep of the arm, 'as I also have a very important meeting I need to get to. I was actually about to summon you to give this message to the General.' Gregson looks at me balefully. Who am I trying to kid? I am convincing no one. 'What time can I expect the car?'

'Madam will have to arrange her own transportation,' he replies glumly.

'But I don't have a car here, because I was driven by Henry, that is Mr Baxter and now... I'm kind of stuck.'

'I can phone for a taxi if that will help, madam?'

'No, it's fine thanks.' I sigh. That would cost a complete fortune. 'Although, Gregson,' I call at his departing back, 'is there a train from Stanton?'

'I think so, madam. Where do you wish to go?'

'Chawton.'

'There will be a couple of changes, but it's possible.'

So I am to be evicted from Dreyfus. Without a goodbye from the General (which I don't care about) or any word at all from Henry who is still out (which I *do* really care about, and feel like blubbing and singing 'All By Myself' at top pitch about) which would probably just get me evicted even quicker.

❧

The shameful journey home takes all day, taxi, train, another train and a bus and it is dark by the time I limp exhaustedly down the long drive at Chawton bumping my large pull-along behind me and staggering under the weight of the other bags on my back. The lights of the familiar house shine out brightly into the night and I can't help feeling my spirits lift a little.

I'm home. Chawton represents a beacon, not only for me, but for women's literature, for Jane and women on their own everywhere. We don't need men, just a cosy nook and a jolly good book.

As I reach the top of the drive, the door opens and Emma comes wandering out with pile of papers in her arms. She throws the documents back inside the door and legs it toward me. 'Sophie, what a lovely surprise! How come you're back on foot?'

'Long story,' I gasp, 'which I'm not fit to tell until I've been revived with good wine and plenty of chocolate.'

'Same old Soph,' Mel shouts from the upstairs window of the apartment. 'We could order take out to celebrate?'

'Sounds perfect,' I say happily. Sometimes you can't beat a tasty takeaway. 'Coming up, Emma?'

Emma follows behind with my heavy case, Mel swings open

the door, gives me a huge bear hug, which leaves me reeling and grabs my other bag. 'Glad to be back?' She smiles.

'You bet I am.' I laugh. This girl has had enough adventures to last a long time. Just give me a cosy fireside and a good book and I'm happy to stay home.

CHAPTER 28

The next day I awake feeling slightly refreshed and, for once, inspired by the tiny sliver of weak early morning winter sunlight filtering through the diamond panes of my bedroom window. I'm never particularly great in the winter months, I swear I'm solar powered. If it's sunny, I feel like getting up and at it. If it's cloudy I turn primeval woman, wanting to curl up in front of the fire with consolatory reading matter, whilst steadily comfort eating for several people. Although I'm not sure cave women had books.

What a relief it is today, no stressful people to sit at breakfast with, although hmm, no butler to fetch my coffee in the morning either. Maybe there were some upsides to staying in a smart country house. I miss the wide lush green fields, Widget's sweet little face and floppy ears staring up at me, and if I'm honest, Henry too.

I enjoyed our chats, he made me laugh and our rides out over the countryside were something I've always dreamed of. But I guess that's all it was, an enjoyable dream. Now it's back to reality and I'm still left with the fact that I really don't think I'll ever be able to look Henry in the face again. I'm even more embarrassed to see him after my ridiculous suspicions, than I was with Darcy after the manure incident at my parents' house and that's saying something.

'Morning, sleepyhead.' Mel comes blundering in with a nice hot cup of coffee. 'Don't expect this treatment every day, I just thought you might be missing the butler service at Dreyfus.'

'You obviously read my mind, we really must do something about hiring staff for this place.' I laugh.

Mel snorts. 'Yeah, right.'

'How's the bridesmaids' dresses going?'

'It's all under control.' Mel's unusually calm and I wonder if she's telling the entire truth. 'They're nearly finished anyway. Final fittings next week.'

'I can't wait; I'm so excited to see everyone again. I hope Izzy's coming.'

'Yeah, it's a bit weird about Izzy; she's kind of gone off the radar, which is really unusual for her. She's been texting, but when I asked her to meet up she was full of excuses about how busy she is.'

'Maybe she is,' I say casually, absent-mindedly scrolling through my phone. 'As long as she's there for the fitting I guess it's all good. Oh my God.' A reminder has suddenly pinged up on my phone. 'Of course, it's today I'm meant to be interviewing Vivienne Artois!'

'It can't be, I thought that was next month.' Mel is pleasantly unperturbed.

'Nope it's today and I'm due in London in just over two hours.' I jump out of bed and start running around the room like a crazed thing, pulling out potential outfits and turning on the shower, all at the same time with the result I forget to pull the shower curtain across and completely flood the floor.

'You've not changed one little bit.' Mel throws a towel at me. 'By the way for your info, I've caught Emma red-handed.'

'With what?' I ask from within the shower, frantically lathering soap everywhere.

'That book. *Northanger Abbey*. It was back on the floor again last night, open on page 183.'

'What?' I shiver in spite of the warm water. 'What did it say? The person be it gentleman or lady, who has not pleasure in a good novel, must be intolerably stupid.'

Mel thinks for a moment. 'It could have been something like that. I can't remember.'

'If it had been Greta Thunberg's book you would have remembered exactly what it said.'

'That's different, she's got something relevant to talk about.'

'And Jane Austen hasn't? Philistine!' I protest, legging it out of the shower into my warm towel. 'What did you do with the book this time anyway?'

'As I obviously didn't use a good enough hiding place in the library because Emma must have found it, I've now put it somewhere no one will ever discover it.'

'Good for you. Though I hope it's a safe place, because it's a first edition and extremely valuable.'

'All the more reason why it shouldn't be left on the floor of a dirty old country house.' Mel smirks and leaves the room.

I can't really argue with that.

A couple of hours later and I'm trotting down the street in Emma's Dune pumps towards Vivienne Artois' house in Kensington. The buildings are so white, I'm grateful for my sunglasses to cut the glare. I feel rather like a mole in the winter in this country whenever the sun comes back out. It's as though I've become more used to existing in the dark. No wonder rich people escape abroad until at least March and return for the spring. Vivienne Artois lives at one of the attached houses at Palace Gardens Terrace and thank goodness I arrive at her front door just before 11am. I give myself a couple of seconds to pick some fluff off my smart cream coat (River Island – high street I know, but it has a lovely faux fur collar which looks incredibly expensive) and check my dark navy heels with the red bows are still looking shiny. Yep all good.

My ring on the doorbell is answered by a surprisingly conservatively uniformed maid. 'Good morning, Miss Johnson. Mademoiselle Artois is expecting you.' She opens the door wide and a little surprised, I walk on in.

The entrance hall is also traditional, the parquet floor tiles attractively mosaic and I am shown up an elegant flight of stairs to a front room with a bay window which seems to run completely from the front to back of the house, with a large dining room table in the centre and an incredibly cream, modern sofa with metal props, like something out of the seventies.

From round the corner, which is a frighteningly expensive-looking white marbled kitchen area, prowls an elegant woman in a long, brightly chequered trouser/lounge suit, mixed with platform pumps and a large and flamboyant hair slide with a dragonfly appearing to be perched on the side of her head. Her hair is natural, parted in the middle and flicks back either side, Farrah Fawcett style, just coming down to merely touch her incredible cheekbones.

'Miss Johnson, do sit.' Vivienne smiles, showing an even and enviably white set of teeth and I sit down at the seat she indicates at the table, reassured by the warmth of her brown eyes which are wide apart and surprisingly lacking in make-up. Altogether she is beautiful, but much more naturally so than I expected. I cannot believe for a minute that this pleasant woman is the impressively successful Vivienne Artois, the sister of Lady

Constance, who quite frankly is one of the scariest women I've ever met and has a slightly hairy chin.

'Thank you,' I say, hoping my face isn't showing my complete and utter surprise. It probably is, Mel always tells me she can read me like a book. Oh crap.

'Coffee, Miss Johnson?' Vivienne asks with an elegant hand gesture. Everything she does reminds me of a dancer, she is so long and lithe. She really is the antithesis of Lady Constance.

'Yes please, that would be lovely.'

Within minutes I'm sipping a deliciously long latte in a tall elegant glass. Very nice, I'm beginning to remember how much I love my job. This is far more up my street than driving fire trucks and filming protests, even though it was for a good cause.

'So you want to ask some questions?' Vivienne sits opposite me, her long legs tucked under her. I don't know how she can sit like that; it would give me a terrible backache.

Yes, like how on earth a nice person like you is related to a horrible dragon like Lady Constance. That's the question I'd like to ask. But somehow I manage not to mention this and ask her how she got started into fashion and all the usual questions she's probably been asked a million times. She's very polite, but I notice she sighs and shifts a little in her seat, and I feel as though we ought to change it up a bit.

'Do you mind telling me about your early years, what inspired you to get into fashion and family life, because you're related to Lady Constance, aren't you?'

'I am.' She laughs. 'I understand you know my sister.'

'Oh,' I falter, this is awkward ground. 'Yes I do, a little.'

'She has mentioned you a few times actually.'

I'm not sure whether to be flattered or horrified by this, so I just smile. 'I've met her at the dating agency, when she was a member that is.'

She really laughs now. 'I couldn't believe it when I heard

she'd actually gone along. My sister at a Regency dating agency. Too funny!'

I pull at my top which is lacey and very stylish but the collar is a little scratchy. 'I was rather surprised when she came along. She's lovely of course, but quite...' I search for the polite word sifting through the options, *difficult, fussy, downright awkward*, 'discerning.'

'She's a bloody nightmare,' retorts Vivienne. 'Another coffee?'

I accept and she gracefully peels herself off the chair and flicks on the machine.

'I must admit I do find her a little intimidating.'

'Caustic Connie? Bark's far worse than her bite. You just can't let her get the upper hand.' I'm still reeling from 'caustic Connie', so remain speechless apart from to gratefully accept the steaming fresh coffee. 'She's twelve years older than me. Would you like some apricot and pistachio biscotti?' They look delicious. I take one and nibble it politely. 'Always thought she could boss me around, tell me what to do, how to dress.'

I recover myself enough to ask, 'So how did you cope?'

'Waited until she went off to finishing school, pinched all her clothes, hideous though they were, and remade them into something decent. Father was horrified and she was furious when she came home, but my mother thought it was wonderful. Mother was very bohemian, had poetry parties and meetings with the best literary minds of the day. It was a wonderful atmosphere to grow up in. Connie hated it; she was a born horsewoman, rode hard to hounds, tally hoing round the countryside. You could hear her from here to Basingstoke. And all the while I quietly got on with creating things. Old vintage fabrics from the roof. I loved the colours, the textures, being able to create something completely new from some old discarded gown. It's still the most exciting thing in the world.'

'That's amazing. Can I see some of your design books and are you happy for me to take photos?'

'Of course, darling. I have cupboards full here.' She wafts out of the room and soon returns with huge pattern books, swathes of fabric spilling from within and soon we are lost in another world of creativity, different textures and a universe where anything goes. Just like on the surrounding walls, there are images of animals, but they are created out of anything. Wire, net, pieces of rubber. All surreal, but incredibly clever.

'My friend, Mel, is an aspiring fashion designer and would give anything for one moment with you,' I say, wonderingly gazing at the cacophony of colours and textures.

'What is she interested in?'

'Anything and everything but her line is strictly vegan. She's created all the dresses for my friend, Maria Greaves' wedding, which is happening in a couple of weeks, Regency style of course, in keeping with the dating agency. I wrote a feature on her in last month's Modiste.'

'One moment.' Vivienne flits out of the room and I take the opportunity to gaze at the strange but beautiful sculptures, one in the large bay window of a ballet dancer balancing on pointe. 'This one?' She returns and places my article open on the image of the fire engine and Mel's models all emblazoned in red paint. 'This was really something. I loved the contrasting styles, simple but yet so striking.'

'Yes she's super talented.'

'She's welcome any time. I would be pleased to meet her.'

'Thank you so much.' I can't believe how lovely Vivienne is. Then again I remember my dad saying that truly great people are always the humblest. I think he has a point. 'She won't believe it when I tell her, she's one of your biggest fans.'

Vivienne smiles and flicks the magazine page over. 'She's got a big career ahead of her. I like the way you've written this article too, you've got voice.'

'Thanks.' I blush. 'It cost me a great deal to write that, especially on a personal level.'

'Always the case with art. It's painful and requires great sacrifice. Believe me, I know.' She picks at a biscotti. 'You have to decide what matters most to you. I have gorgeous friends who have reached the dizzying heights of success, yet are now paying a fortune to their therapists in an attempt to understand why it hasn't made them happy.'

'You're right; I guess it's what you love that matters. My problem is I find it hard to decide. I envy you having this incredible talent, I feel as though I enjoy doing lots of things not that well.'

'I'm sure you do most things extremely well. Maybe you simply need time to realise what really matters to you. From meeting you today, I see someone who has a whole world of possibilities in front of them. Take your time and it will become clear.'

'I wish it felt that way.' I take a sip of coffee. I'm supposed to be interviewing Vivienne and it's turning into more of a therapy session. 'I feel as though I've made a mess of everything, work, relationships.'

'Don't talk about relationships. Complete nightmare, although I'm deliriously happy now with Gina, but it's taken several messy break-ups. I hear you were dating the gorgeous Darcy Drummond. God, I bet you've been positively beating women away from him.'

I would laugh if her picture weren't so painfully accurate. 'Yes, especially those arranged by his mother!'

Vivienne laughs. 'I heard he's back available again. Must have been a tough gig.'

'It was, it is, I mean yes, although I'm not sure I'm right for him.'

'What do you mean?'

'He was upset about the whole editorial protest – too messy.'

'Don't see what's wrong with that.' She gets up and peers inside the large spaceship-style fridge. 'Champagne? It's midday, so not too early.'

I hesitate, but not for long. 'Why not?' Therapy with wine sounds perfect. 'He said it didn't fit with the agency image. Especially not getting arrested.'

She laughs again. 'I can imagine that. Terribly straight-laced the Drummonds. But you didn't exactly do anything wrong. No such thing as bad publicity anyway. It probably gave the agency a boost.'

'Maybe,' I say doubtfully.

She passes me a terrifyingly delicate fluted glass full of champagne. 'Cheers, darling. Here's to living dangerously.'

'Cheers.' I take a sip of the gloriously cold bubbly liquid. 'Perhaps it is more fun after all.'

'You bet it is. Do you think I could have become a world-class fashion designer if I hadn't taken risks? And do you believe I'd have given it up for anyone?'

'No, that would have been a real waste.'

'Quite. You need to have faith in yourself. To hell with the lot of them! If you want to write controversial articles in your spare time, so be it. If Darcy doesn't like it, he's the wrong guy for you. All this, you're not right for him – total rubbish! You're too good for him and that irritating mother of his. You, my girl, need to have faith in yourself. We'll drink to it.' She pauses and raises her glass to me. 'To having faith in yourself.'

'Having faith in yourself,' I echo then slug down some more bubbly.

'By the way, I feel I have to say, because I like you a lot, my obnoxious sister, has been spreading it around that you're a penniless fortune hunter, first taking advantage of Darcy and now she's on about Henry Baxter.'

'What? How can she?' I hesitate a moment and say almost half to myself, 'Then she did recognise me the other night.'

'You bet she would have done, she's many things but she's no fool. Were you staying with the Baxters then?'

'Yes, the General invited me, but I never did understand why. I don't have a fortune and have never pretended to be anyone I'm not, believe me.'

'Someone must have made him think you are an heiress.' She leans forward and whispers conspiratorially, 'You didn't hear it from me, but everyone knows the General's in debt up to his eyeballs and is always onto the next get rich quick scheme. His plans usually involve marrying his children off to wealthy billionaires to make up for his own gambling debts.'

'What the heck did he want with me then?'

'I've no idea.' Vivienne laughs. 'He obviously got it totally wrong... but it sounds as though my horrible sister soon put him right.'

'It all makes sense then because...' I break off suddenly, I don't even want to admit to Vivienne that I was evicted from Dreyfus. But I wonder who made the General believe I have a lot of money and even more to the point, did Henry think I have money too? Worse still, is that the only reason he was kind to me?

CHAPTER 29

'Sophie, I have a breakthrough.'

'That's great.' I rummage out of the covers and try to sound more awake than I am. I will never get used to the different hours in the US. 'Fire away, I'm listening.'

'Sorry, did I wake you?'

'No it's fine. It's great. Have you found out something?' I take a sip of drink from beside my bed in a desperate effort to get my brain fully functioning.

'Well I managed to get talking to both Mrs Van Hayler and Anya Stepler. Anya has her own business and I thought she might have some news, but nothing from her so far. But Mrs Van Hayler knows of an English woman who has recently started a company over in lower Manhattan. It's a new start up and I am pretty sure it's Jessica. She obviously won't be using that name, but I think I would recognise her anywhere.'

'That's great. But how can you be sure it might be her? Any Brit could be starting up a new business.'

'True. But it sounds her sort of thing. Anyone renting in this part of Manhattan has got to be seriously rich and the whole thing smacks of Jessica. I haven't of course mentioned it to Nick. He hasn't heard from his sister in over six months, so there doesn't seem much point and I don't want him to let anything slip to Darcy.'

'Fair enough, that makes sense. So what's the next move?'

'I've got the address, I'm going to go down there and try to spot her.'

'But that's not going to work, you'll be there ages and hardly likely to see her. Also what if she recognises you?'

'It's okay, there's a park opposite so that's no problem, I've already checked the area out. And I'm going to wear a disguise.'

'Ooh, what sort of disguise?' I have visions of a comedy moustache and wig.

'I haven't planned it totally yet, but it will be good.'

'Thanks, Chloe, I owe you one for this.'

'It's okay,' she chuckles, 'I'm actually enjoying myself. I'll keep you posted.'

'Thanks and be careful, won't you?'

Having rung off from Chloe, I try with little success to get back to sleep. My mind is full of Jessica Palmer Wright, Darcy, Tara, and what happened with Henry.

❦

The next morning comes around and I'm feeling tired and not entirely in the mood for our day at Luckington Court, the Bennets' house in the 1995 *Pride and Prejudice*, which is a shame as I've been looking forward to it for ages. Fortunately an invigorating shower seems to help a little and I arrive downstairs, my excitement about the visit restored.

To my surprise, Mel is sitting at the table eating a bowl of fruit and muesli. She's not usually a breakfast person. 'I thought

I might come along today,' she says before shoving in a large mouthful of blueberries. 'Might be useful for me to get a look at the furnishings, to make sure any finishing touches for Maria's wedding are absolutely perfect and in keeping with the period.'

'Great, I'm sure you'll enjoy it,' I say.

'Muesli?' she pushes the packet towards me.

'Er, no thanks, I think I'll stick to a bowl of Oatibix.' I always find muesli so dry, it's like eating a mouthful of dog biscuits with no gravy. Not that I've tried eating dog biscuits, with or without gravy because that would be weird, but you know what I mean.

The journey to Luckington is quite uneventful as Emma drives us in her very smooth Mercedes coupe and it's a lovely trip across country, although we do stop halfway so Mel and I can swap seats. There's not much room in the back so to avoid bickering we decided to take it in turns like grown ups.

Luckington is a picture-book village, just perfect for reliving an Austen novel and as we arrive, I feel ridiculously excited. I can't believe we're going to be walking where Jennifer Ehle and Colin Firth were filming. Okay so it was over twenty years ago now, but even so, the magic lingers on.

As we arrive at the house, a mature-looking lady appears on the doorstep, dressed in a lightly patterned Regency dress, with a white pinafore. 'Welcome, welcome. I am the housekeeper, Mrs Hill, and you must be the lovely visitors from The Jane Austen Dating Agency for the Bennets. Shall we just wait here for the arrival of the rest of the party?'

'That would be perfect.' Emma, ever organised, produces her list of attendees and we hover and admire the scene before us.

'This is amazing, the wall, the house, it all looks exactly as it did in the series.' I touch the pale yellow stone with a reverent hand.

'What do you expect it to look like?' Mel snorts. Sometimes, for a creative person, she has no imagination whatsoever.

I ignore her. 'I'm sorry there aren't any flowers out though.' I look across at the border where in one scene, Jane is cutting blooms and Lizzie goes out to talk to her about Mr Bingley. I can remember the words implicitly, 'You're not happy, Jane,' Lizzie says and is reassured by Jane, who replies sadly, 'It's only I did like him more than any other man of our acquaintance and I did think he liked me too...'

I sigh and wish that somehow they could recreate that scene here and now. I look back towards the beautiful house, and then out over the lawns, with the circular steps leading up enticingly to the fountain, and wonder what it would have been like to watch the filming.

I am disturbed from my reverie by a flurry of arrivals, Miss Foxton with Edward, closely followed by Freya, who is walking next to Alistair Foxton, who is arm in arm with Lady Amelia. Thank goodness John Smith is unable to come and I should imagine in that case, Ben won't be appearing any time soon either.

A few moments later however, I'm amazed to see Ben arriving, smartly dressed in his chinos and a shirt. Although he is pretty much hiding in his oversized warm jacket. 'Hello, sis,' he mutters.

'I didn't expect to see you here?' I say surprised. 'Didn't think it was your thing at all.'

'It isn't. Mum made me come.'

I suppress a laugh. That doesn't surprise me. 'Never mind, you might actually find you enjoy it.'

'I doubt it.'

'Lord Bamford, welcome!' Emma greets the bumptious Lord with a friendly handshake and he rushes over to take his place at Amelia's side, apparently oblivious to her obvious connection with Mr Foxton.

Everyone else seems to arrive at once and there are soon over thirty of us, all standing in the large driveway.

'Maria, Charles.' I give them both a hug and kiss.

Emma smiles. 'Only a couple of weeks to go until the big day.'

'I know, after all this time, I can't believe it's this close,' Charles says good-humouredly, 'although all these preparations – it's exhausting, I'll be relieved when we're finally married.' He takes Maria's hand in his and she smiles up at him.

'You'll enjoy it when you're there and it's all sorted,' Maria says.

'I know, I'm looking forward to it.' He smiles back at her.

We are interrupted by the approach of Sir Henry. 'Not talking about the wedding again, are we?'

'Yes, Sir Henry,' I say pleasantly, 'we are. You must be excited now it's nearly here.'

'Humph, being excited at my age is a danger to one's health.' He wanders off to inspect a nearby family stone crest.

Maria and I suppress a smile. 'He's looking forward to it really,' I say to his retreating back.

She laughs. 'I'm sure he is.'

The Baroness approaches along with Gene. 'Good morning, Sophie, Emma. What a charming little place.' I want to laugh at her easy dismissal of the size of this estate, but along with Lady Catherine de Bourgh, I guess she is used to much larger properties. Although, I'm not sure I can find anything to laugh about in relation to the Baroness now I know about her involvement with Jessica Palmer Wright.

I suddenly feel a nudge in my ribs. 'Soph,' Mel hisses. 'Turn that frown upside down,' she whispers.

'Oh, thanks.' I make an effort to relax my expression into something more pleasant. Why do I have to have a face that reads like an open book? I had no idea I was glaring at the

Baroness. She carries on chatting to Gene, apparently oblivious and I sincerely hope I got away with giving her the evils when she wasn't looking.

'Are we all here?' Mrs Hill asks.

Emma indicates we are.

'Well, good morning, everyone, and welcome to Luckington Court, my mistress, Mrs Bennet, is within and is looking forward to meeting you all.'

We all file in through the legendary doors of Lizzie Bennet's house and I want to close my eyes and imagine I am wearing my Regency dress, removing my bonnet and coming in to speak to Mr Bennet in the library.

'What are you doing?' Mel asks.

'Just having a cathartic moment,' I reply dreamily.

Mel raises her eyebrows at Ben who happens to be next to her and he gives a supportive snort. Great, that's all I need, those two ganging up on me.

A matron in a lace cap, bustles out to greet us. 'How lovely to see you. I am Mrs Bennet and I am simply delighted to meet you all. You will have to forgive me this morning, as I am all of a tither. You will have heard my eldest daughter, Jane, was recently married to Mr Bingley and her sister, Lizzie, to Mr Darcy of Pemberley and they are all to visit us next Saturday week. Such excitement as was never to be seen! I shall have to ask cook to prepare such a feast and hopefully,' her tone becomes conspiratorial, 'there will be more handsome young men calling to court Kitty and Mary soon, although I see some fine young lads here.' She gives my brother, Ben, a wink, which makes him squirm and me want to laugh out loud.

'Five girls all married,' Mrs Bennet continues undeterred, 'and I shan't know what to do with myself. Now, Hill will show you around the estate, for if you will excuse me, these preparations do so tax my poor nerves. I bid you good day and hope to mayhap see you again one day soon.'

Everyone stands entranced as Mrs Bennet ascends the staircase to her room. I wish it could have been Alison Steadman, but this actress is very convincing and I can almost imagine that any minute, Mr Bennet will come wandering out of his library to ask what all the fuss is about.

Everyone seems to be enjoying the experience so far and we follow Mrs Hill into the front drawing room. 'This is where many of the scenes for the production were filmed. As you can see, we have a different arrangement of the chairs, as this is in reality a private house.'

In spite of the change of furniture from the television series (there is an attractive Regency sofa in front of the fireplace) the room is still reassuringly familiar as the place where the Bennet women sewed and talked and met to discuss the day's events. Also where Mr Darcy and Mr Bingley were received when they visited. I wander across to the classical Georgian paned windows and gaze out over the view. I would love to live somewhere like this. It's utterly perfect and I begin to understand Mrs Bennet's utter frustration that upon her husband's death, this should all go to Charlotte Lucas. That is pretty upsetting. At least now after the events of the book, she can go and live with Jane; I don't think Lizzie will have her.

I smile to myself. Honestly I'm talking about these characters as though they are real people, but then to Jane Austen fans they truly are real and better companions through thick and thin than the majority of people who actually exist. Through sickness and in health, whatever happens in the wider world, Lizzie and her sisters live on to cheer us through their ups and downs in *Pride and Prejudice*, along with the safe predictability of knowing all will end well. The same with Jane Austen's other heroines, Marianne and Elinor Dashwood, Catherine Morland, loyal friends waiting for us within the pages of a book, and that is a truly comforting thought.

We visit the library which is gorgeous and I wish I could linger a while, to browse through some of the large decorative books. But we are whisked on to the glamorous upstairs bedrooms then into the beautifully decorated kitchen below with the butler sink and lovely modern appliances.

'The original owner of the house, Mrs Angela Horn, was of course unable to use the entire house throughout the long shooting schedule, so was relegated to the kitchen, the housekeeper's room and the nursery. These were all beautifully decorated for her and when filming was over she was able to afford many of the alterations, which were needed to maintain the house.'

Mrs Hill continues, 'Mrs Angela Horn had lived here for forty years all alone and it must have been quite a shock having her rooms filled with costumed actors and crew.'

There is some appreciative oohing and ahhing from the listening group. 'However apparently Mrs Horn said she cried when everyone left as she felt quite forlorn.'

'I can imagine that,' I say sympathetically to Emma who is standing next to me.

'Now, come along then,' Mrs Hill says. 'Who would like to come and explore the gardens? I'm sure you'd all love to visit the prettyish kind of a little wilderness' that was the scene of the altercation between Lizzie Bennet and Lady Catherine de Bourgh.'

'I can quite see myself here,' Miss Foxton says in her high clear voice. 'With servants of course and all the necessities of life.'

Edward laughs. 'Jolly nice too, though how on earth would you pay for it?'

'By marrying a rich husband of course,' Miss Foxton says

glibly and everyone laughs. I don't know if I imagine it, but I can't help sensing Edward's amusement is a little forced. 'That's why you, my dear, will have to take up that offer of Darcy Drummond's friend to work at Goldman Sachs. A few years there and this property would be a mere snip.' She hangs on his arm ingratiatingly.

'I didn't think,' Edward begins. Then he tries again, 'I didn't particularly want to work there. I turned down the interview. I already have a job, you see.'

'How wonderful. Where? Morgan Stanley, JP Morgan? No I know, Evercore?' Miss Foxton positively gushes.

'No, it's at St Hilda's.'

'St Hilda's?' Miss Foxton sounds as though she is pained by the very words.

'Yes, it's a small primary school in Hampshire.'

'But you can't be serious about that. No one actually wants to teach these days, do they?'

Freya who had been silently walking behind them, pipes up, 'I think Edward would make a very good teacher. Children love him and he's very patient.'

'But he could do something so much more important, Freya. Come on help me persuade him. Edward, you must think about it. No one can live off a teacher's salary.'

He doesn't meet her eyes. 'Actually, I was hoping to eventually become a head teacher.'

'Even so. Please have a rethink, Edward, for me. You could do so much better.'

'Better,' Edward splutters. It's as though something inside him has finally snapped. 'Better than inspiring children to learn, become something amazing when they're older?'

'Give them wings to fly,' Freya says enthusiastically.

'I'm convinced,' I say politely, but then shut up again as I can see Miss Foxton is unamused. However if Edward really wishes to become a teacher, it's a calling, a vocation and I must admit, I think he would be a good one.

We all continue into the garden, admiring the old stone walls and the shrubbery in front of the house where much of the action took place. I notice that Amelia and Mr Foxton have disappeared somewhere and Lord Bamford is walking with Gene.

'I never knew you were keen on birds?' Gene says.

'I've been following the red kite numbers on our estate for years. Totally fascinated by them. Mummy's always saying I should forget the silly old birds, but to me it's vital we preserve them,' Lord Bamford states enthusiastically.

'Absolutely, I've been a member of the Red Kite Association for twenty years,' Gene replies.

'I'd love for you to come and visit the hides with me...' I listen, amazed at the two making arrangements to get together the following week. Yet I would never have guessed they'd have ever had anything in common.

'A match made in heaven,' the Baroness comments in my ear with a tight smile, as unbeknown to me she has appeared alongside. For once I'm completely speechless.

We continue along the path and I stand heart in mouth, gazing back at the house through the wilderness to the triple arches. It was here Lady Catherine infamously confronted Lizzie Bennet. I always adored that scene. I feel as though I would never have been able to deal with Lady Catherine so absolutely and concisely as Lizzie. I did make some kind of attempt when confronting Lady Constance earlier this year, but it was nothing in comparison. Sometimes I think I'm more like Jane than Elizabeth; far too meek.

I drift on further into the garden as I'm enjoying walking alone, imagining the scenes replaying in front of me, the others having moved on towards the church. Then I spot Miss Foxton coming this way with Edward. I have no desire to hear any more of her haranguing.

There's no escape however, due to the design of the path, and I can't help overhearing a snatched part of the conversation. 'Doesn't your brother realise Lady Amelia is going out with Lord Bamford?' Edward asks earnestly. 'I've heard they've skipped the rest of the tour and gone off on their own.'

'What Alistair does is his own business. I can hardly tell him what to do at his age, can I? I'm not his mother.'

'I'm not asking you to. It's just I've noticed he often flirts with Caitlin as well as Amelia. They're my sisters and I care about them. To my mind, it's going to end in tears.'

'Not my problem or yours,' Miss Foxton says dismissively. 'It will sort in the end and you can't seriously think Amelia is genuinely attracted to Lord Bamford. She's obviously after his money.'

'I admit that,' Edward replies, 'but it doesn't mean I approve of it. Does your brother really like one of my sisters, or is he merely messing them about?'

'He likes women. That's how he is. And what's wrong with a bit of flirting; doesn't do any harm. Anyway,' she pats his arm persuasively, 'I wanted to talk to you about your career.'

For a moment Edward stares at her and then, stepping away from her touch, he says abruptly, 'Do you know what, I don't want to talk about my career to you. I've had enough of my parents not agreeing with my choices and the last thing I need is a partner who wants me to be someone else as well.' And to my and Miss Foxton's amazement, he storms off towards the house, much like Lady Catherine de Bourgh, although obviously he's far nicer and I agree with him actually. I feel like coming out from my obscure vantage point and saying 'well done' and giving him a round of applause, but obviously I don't.

Miss Foxton, left to her own devices, merely remarks to no

one in particular, 'I suppose I misread that situation,' and walks slowly towards the house in Edward's footsteps, wrapping her pashmina round her shoulders in a businesslike fashion.

I heartily hope Edward's discovery of Miss Foxton's true personality might make him twig that he's got the perfect partner in his step-cousin, Freya. After all they're not even vaguely related and she obviously adores him. But since when in real life did the path of true love ever run smooth?

CHAPTER 30

*S*everal days later, we are all in the midst of wedding preparations. The drawing room at Chawton House is a splash of coloured fabrics and muslins. It's absolutely gorgeous, if a little chaotic.

'Wait!' Mel shouts, trying desperately to move a pin from the sleeve of my dress. 'If you all just wait a minute. I think it's best I come to you one at a time. In fact if you each walk in front of the mirror, do a slow rotation and then come back and stand in front of me, I'll be able to see if your hems are straight and what else needs doing.'

'What about yours?' Maria asks, twirling girlishly in front of the mirror.

'I'll look at my dress last. I can always ask Sophie to help me pin any finishing touches later,' Mel replies.

'Yes that's fine,' I say, 'although last time you told me off for pinning the hem wonky.'

'Well, you did.'

'I didn't mean to,' I protest. 'Ow! You've stabbed me.'

'If you stood still for two seconds together, I wouldn't have done.'

Obediently I stand still in front of the mirror and let Mel finish pinning the bodice on my dress. I love it; it's high-waisted, of course in true Regency style and a luxurious pale blue satin, which contrasts nicely with my long dark hair and blue eyes, with a thin tulle net reaching down from the waist.

Mel's dress is pale green, picking out her dark curls and Izzy's is a soft sunshine yellow which perfectly complements her blonde locks. If she turns up that is. Emma is at a work appointment this morning, but her dress has already been fitted. It's a beautiful rich lilac and suits her willowy elegance.

'So our final dress fitting is next week, Maria,' Mel comments. 'Then we should be all ready for the big day.'

Maria is looking out of the window. 'I hope it's going to be sunny. Or a white wedding.'

'We never have snow down here at Christmas, too far south,' Mel says.

'There's always a first time. You never know.' I wink at her.

There's a commotion in the doorway. 'Izzy, you made it!' I squeak.

'I did.' She breezes in and hugs us all, every inch the old Izzy we know and love.

'Hey, we've missed you,' Maria says. 'I'm so glad you made it for my fitting. Now we can crack open the champagne.'

'Definitely,' Mel says, 'I'm gasping.'

'Well you're doing all the work,' I say, passing the bottle to her. It's no good, I can master opening most bottles of wine, but with bubbly I'd be lethal and in a listed building it's unthinkable. Soon we're sipping champagne, once we're all out of our dresses that is, Mel is far too protective of her precious creations to let them be marked by spilt drink.

'Come on then, Izzy, you next.' Mel is up again and within minutes is pinning Izzy's dress at the hem, where it is slightly too long.

'So,' I remark casually, 'how's Matthew?'

'He's fine,' Izzy replies. 'Not that I've seen that much of him lately.' She pouts at her reflection in the mirror. We all exchange collective glances.

'That's a shame,' Maria says tactfully. For goodness' sake, we're going to be here forever.

'You're still together then?' Mel wades right on in, obviously feeling emboldened by the presence of pins in her hand.

'Of course.' Izzy looks at our expectant faces. 'Why wouldn't I be?'

'It's only that,' I start then wonder where I'm going with this, 'it's only that we wondered as you've not been around and we were worried...'

'Worried about what?' Izzy lifts her hair above her shoulders. 'Do you think it would look better up or down?'

'Looks lovely either way,' Maria says. 'We've been worried that maybe you still had feelings for Josh, as you said you'd seen him the other day.'

'Josh?' She laughs. 'You're not serious.' Then she gazes back at our earnest faces, all peering at her intently. 'I can't believe you really think that. However would you have got that idea? I don't feel anything for Josh. He's an idiot. I love Matthew. You all know that.'

'We do, not that we mind of course,' Maria says soothingly. 'It's up to you, we just didn't want you to be hurt again.'

'But in that case,' I'm confused now, 'why've you been avoiding us all the last couple of weeks?'

'Oh that,' Izzy says, 'well I have been hiding something, or perhaps I should say someone.'

Mel stops pinning and stares at her. 'Someone?'

'Yes, for the last couple of weeks, Ellie Baxter has been staying with me.'

'Oh... my... gosh!' I stutter. 'That's where she went.' It's all beginning to make sense now.

'Yes, her dad, the General, hideous man, shouldn't be surprised if he's some kind of ex-convict, he's so horrid...' I squash down a smile, it's obviously not just me then, 'trying to force her to marry that dirty old snob, Sir Henry Greaves. I happened to notice she stole away the night of the Chawton Ball to meet someone. It turns out she loves him, he's called Chris, by the way, but his family business has recently crashed and the General has forbidden them from seeing each other.'

'That's who I saw then,' I remark. It has all started to make sense now. 'I followed Ellie out on the night of the ball and saw her with some guy.'

'That would be him. She confided in me and I said if things ever got too much, she could always come and stay at mine. It's in London and well out of the way of the General.'

'I would have helped if I'd known,' I say sorrowfully. 'I would like to think Ellie could have asked me.'

'She would have liked to, I know she thinks the world of you, but Chawton is one of the first places the General would have thought to look.'

'True,' Mel says, 'it's far too obvious.'

'You could have told us,' Maria says gently, 'we would have kept your secret and I think Matthew has been worried by your behaviour. He thought that maybe you were avoiding him too.'

'It's fine,' Izzy says easily, 'I've told him all about it now. We're as loved up as ever. He says once Ellie has managed to find somewhere else, we're going away to Paris.'

I feel a twinge of envy as I think of Darcy's offer to take me to the city of love, but push it away. 'I'm so pleased for you, Izzy,' I say, giving her a hug. 'He's such a nice lad and how kind of you to look after Ellie, I was really worried about her.'

'I'm sorry I couldn't tell you. I was too worried it would be awkward for you as you were staying at the Baxters' house. You might have let something slip. Besides it all happened so suddenly, Ellie contacted me and Henry agreed it was a good plan, so he drove her to the station, she hid in the back of his car, and I picked her up in London.'

'Clever you,' Maria says, 'and to think it wasn't so long ago you needed rescuing but now you've been the one getting someone else out of a scrape.'

'I don't know about that,' Izzy says modestly, 'but I was happy to help, I know how I felt with my dad and stepmum. Obviously I don't need to tell you to keep it a secret, we can't let the General know where Ellie is.'

'Surely he'll be so worried, as a parent he has a right...' Maria, soft-hearted as ever, protests.

'Maria, you have no idea what a cretin this man is,' interrupts Izzy. 'You haven't heard the things Ellie told me. Believe me, he has no rights at all.'

Maria looks uneasy, but I add, 'Izzy's right, he's a pretty unpleasant man.' Even if he isn't actually a murderer, I add silently.

We manage to finish the fitting even to Mel's perfectionist satisfaction and I spend the afternoon sorting out final arrangements, as well as a couple of surprises Mel, Emma and I have up our sleeves.

Later, I am sitting in the office, sipping at a nice cup of tea and eyeing up another digestive biscuit... is it just me or do you find that once you've eaten one, you just have to keep eating and one becomes three, which becomes several. I have no self-control when it comes to biscuits. Maybe I shouldn't eat them at all. Emma has gone on a visit to preview somewhere we could maybe run another sports event so I have the whole place to myself.

Suddenly my phone goes. 'Chloe!'

'Hey, you're not going to believe this, I've found her!' Chloe struggles to get the words out she's so excited. 'It is her, at the new outlet in Lower Manhattan.'

'Jessica Palmer Wright? That's brilliant, did you recognise her then?'

'Yes she didn't even bother wearing any kind of disguise.'

'Did you?' I ask with a smile.

'Of course, I posed as a very large stuffed teddy selling balloons.'

'Oh my gosh, Chloe, that's hilarious.'

'I know, it was a brilliant disguise; no one could possibly have known it was me. The only thing was that kids kept coming up and wanting to buy balloons, which was a bit of a nightmare. But hey, it made it look even more convincing.'

'Clever you. So did she just turn up?'

'I hung around first thing in the morning, then went back at lunchtime and planned to return later at sort of five-ish. I knew that way I would see if she came along at some point. Although I thought I might have to do this for several days and it was going to get kind of awkward as Nick would wonder where I've gone.'

'Yeah I can imagine he would,' I add.

'Sure enough, nothing in the morning, but during my lunchtime shift, she appeared. Same old Jessica Palmer Wright, wearing a long moulded trench coat over a darling little designer suit. Hair in an immaculate chignon, I almost didn't recognise her though as I'm sure she was dark before, but now she's a kind of honey blonde.'

'Wow, I guess that's as much of a disguise as she thought she needed.'

'I suppose. Anyway, she went up to the office, I could see the lift moving from the outside. It's a huge glass building, very stylish actually. Since then I've gone back, obviously without the teddy suit, but wearing that blonde wig.'

'Not that one you wore for my twenty-first?'

'Yep that's the one.'

'I'm surprised it's still going after it got flung over the hedge at the end of the night!'

'It's fine, I gave it a wash and brush.'

And removed some spiders and a few bits of takeaway rice, I think.

'Anyway, I made some enquiries at the desk. The company they are supposedly working for is called Protech and is on the third floor. Run by three members of staff, Steve and Bella Coonan and a secretary, Sammy Cushman.'

'That's fantastic. Have you done any internet searches yet?'

'No not yet, but that's next. Give me a bit more time, but I could do with getting an investigator in now. I'm no spy woman.'

'You could have fooled me; you've done an amazing job. But fair enough.' I take a deep breath. 'Do what you've got to do, Chloe. We need to get to the bottom of this.'

'Okay, I'll report back tomorrow. Oh, Nick's back, gotta go, bye bye.' She disappears abruptly, leaving me to smile to myself at the slightly American accent she's started to pick up. It suits her actually.

I google Protech Holdings but don't seem to get much except a load of account holders and not much else. I wonder if I've done the right thing in encouraging Chloe with the investigator. But I don't suppose we have much choice.

By the end of the afternoon, I feel as though we're pretty organised for the Regency wedding. Maria has kindly invited all the members of the dating agency and as I consult the guest list, my heart skips a little as I notice Henry Baxter's name. Silly really.

As always in the winter, it has begun to get dark early, so I make my tour of the house, checking the windows are all shut and the doors locked. I shut the office door and wander back upstairs to make sure the lights are off. On impulse, I step into the alcove, where sure enough the book is back on the floor. For some reason I fully expected it to be there and it's open on page 183. Gently I bend down and pick up the book *Northanger Abbey* and *Persuasion* and sit down on the embroidered window seat cushion and begin to read. 'Catherine at any rate, heard enough to feel, that in suspecting General Tilney of either murdering or shutting up his wife, she had scarcely sinned against his character, or magnified his cruelty.'

These words strike home as an absolute truth. Okay so I was absolutely wrong in blaming the General for trying to murder his daughter, but that doesn't mean he's totally blameless for controlling his children, trying to force them into marriages that are so unsuitable for them to be happy. He's obviously a tyrant of the first order, and those men I saw at the back of the house were dodgy, I'm sure. Even Maria said he was not to be trusted. I just need to try to work out what he's up to.

'Thank you, Jane.' I smile and carefully close the book and place it on the table. There's still a mystery here to be solved and I, Sophie Johnson, am determined to get to the bottom of it.

CHAPTER 31

*T*here's no time for dwelling on General Baxter's mysterious goings on the next morning as I am due at the Baroness's at eleven. I am determined for better or worse to beard her in her lair. I know it's foolhardy and Mel tries to talk me out of it, but I refuse, quoting the Baroness's words back at her.

'Nothing is ever achieved if you don't get your hands dirty. To advance in life, you need to have "les mains sales", the Baroness herself told me, Mel. It means "get your hands dirty or get stuck in" and she's right, kick up a bit of fuss and you can manage anything. Look what I achieved from your protest,' I state.

'Well yes,' Mel replies doubtfully. 'Although you did get arrested, nearly lost your job and were dumped by Darcy.'

'Thanks for bringing that up again,' I retort. 'The point is, we're never going to get to the bottom of this business with Jessica Palmer Wright unless I go and do some snooping myself.'

Mel starts to fiddle with the box of pins left on the top. 'I still think you should tell Emma about all this.'

'I know what you're saying, but she would go straight to Darcy and I want to sort this myself.'

'Like some kind of vindication, you mean? I think you're trying to prove your worth and teach Darcy what an idiot he was to dump you.'

'Not really,' I say casually. 'Who says I even want him back now anyway?'

Mel pauses for a moment. 'Don't you think the Baroness could be dangerous? If, as you say, it's big business, surely she won't think twice about dealing with you firmly if you get in her way.'

'Maybe,' I say grimly. 'But faint heart won no woman and besides I have no intention of getting caught.' I walk with determination to the door of our little flat at Chawton. 'But if I'm not back by 2pm, call the police.'

By the time I arrive at Kensington Gardens much of my bravado has left me. I feel a bit shaky actually. Even my phone ringing suddenly, the dulcet tones of Sean Mendes' 'Nothing Holding Me Back' (extremely appropriate song for this moment actually), makes me jump.

'Miffy, nice to hear from you. How are you?' I answer.

'Great thanks, sweetie. I'm calling to congratulate you.'

'On what?' I'm totally confused now.

'On what? Good grief, darling, there's politely modest and there's you!' She snorts. 'On your amazing feature on Vivienne Artois, such incredible pics and the story is fabulous.'

'Oh that.' I had totally forgotten, although I had worked late into the night finishing the piece.

'The director is simply blown away, has insisted on my phoning you immediately to offer you a permanent position in the Editorial Team at Modiste.'

'Oh my gosh, that's... just, I mean, I can't believe it.' It's what

I've always wanted, what I've been working towards. A job in editorial and I've nailed it. I want to dance and sing and…

'Hello? Are you still there, Sophie?'

'Yes, sorry. I'm just so happy! Thank you so much.'

'That's okay. So is that a yes? Or do you need to think about it?'

'Of course I want the job. Although, maybe I should just talk it through with everyone.' I falter to a stop. That's the only thing; much as I want this position, there would be a high price to pay. No more gossipy chats with Emma in the office at Chawton over the merits of Regency underwear. In fact that's a point, I'd have to leave Chawton altogether and I've got so many ideas about how we can utilise the library and there's the agency as a whole. It's my baby and I feel as though all the people involved are family now.

'That's fine. I thought you might,' Miffy says breezily. 'Just give me a call when you've had a chance to think about it.'

'I will and, Miffy, thank you so much again. This is down to you.'

'Nonsense, darling, it's all you.'

She rings off and I gaze around, having been so engrossed in the call I can't even remember where I am for a moment. Passers-by continue to rush through the park, a child skips next to her mother with an innocent happiness that makes me long to be young again. It's all so much simpler when you're little and the most serious thing that happens is you forgot to learn your spellings in time for the test at school the next day.

I keep walking through Kensington Gardens, hardly noticing the scenes around me, which I usually drink in with pleasure. I love to think of Queen Victoria playing with her spaniel, Dash, in these grounds, even though it wasn't the happiest place for her.

But look at me! I still can't believe it.

I have finally been offered a job in the Editorial Team for Modiste. Wait until I tell my mum. Although how am I going to turn my back on The Jane Austen Dating Agency? Could I possibly bear to do so?

§♠

Surprisingly the slightly weedy security guard sweeps to one side as soon as he sees my card and I stalk down the grandly decorated avenue towards the Baroness's vast residence, half as if I own the place. I feel more confident than last time I was here, it's as though something has changed. I've changed.

As I pass the magnificent houses, I smile to myself at my naivety last time I visited, now having organised several events, been attacked by a fencing pro and dumped by Darcy, paradoxically for once I feel in control of the situation. Odd, but somehow I believe that I can do this.

I arrive at the imposing gateway to the Baroness's summer palace, as I would call it, and walk up the steps. Okay so I do feel a little like Julie Andrews at the start of *The Sound of Music* and find myself humming 'I have confidence in confidence alone', but it's only for a few minutes and I'm fine really. I've got this.

Instead of my mafia friend, the door is opened by the butler. He seems to be expecting my arrival, so bids me to come through and await the Baroness in the spacious lounge I visited last time I was here.

In spite of having already witnessed the stunning fountain and startling white embellished trellises en route, I can't stop myself from staring in wonder. The beauty of this incredible house never gets old and I wonder how the Baroness ever gets anything done. I'd want to sit and stare at the gorgeous fountain for hours and dangle my fingers in the water.

For once, fate seems to be on my side, the butler leaves me to my own devices and having offered me a cup of coffee, which I decline politely. Since my first visit I have heard exactly where Kopi Luwak coffee comes from and believe me, you really do not want to know. I can't believe my luck, apparently the Baroness is unavoidably detained a moment and I'm more than happy to make the most of this opportunity for a good old snoop.

The room is silent apart from a very loud and ornate ticking clock with golden cherubs, both reclining and seemingly blowing birds into the air, which sits in between the two religious triptych scenes. Silently, like a prowling tiger, I pad around the room, peering behind ornate picture frames and under the tables. I don't really know what I'm looking for. I stare at the photo of the man, who I assume was the Baroness's husband. He stares back, his face hiding any secrets he must have had. It's a cruel face actually. I wonder what he was mixed up in. He was obviously some kind of criminal, so I suppose it's no surprise the Baroness should turn out to be a baddie as well.

In the corner of a room is a bureau carved in heavy scrolled mahogany and I gently pick up papers and place them down again. There's a card from Gene, no doubt thanking the Baroness for taking him out for dinner or some such thing. I scan the room with frustration. Of course, the Baroness is hardly going to keep her private papers out on full view; I'm being ridiculous. Gently, quietly I feel along the edge of the desk until I come to a drawer. I press softly at first, then more firmly in the hope it might open but unsurprisingly it doesn't, it's locked.

'Did you want the key?' asks a voice, making me jump violently. I must have looked a comic sight if only the situation weren't so serious. And serious it is indeed, as walking towards me with an ironic smile, is the Baroness herself.

CHAPTER 32

'Er... I was just... absolutely fascinated by the beautiful wood detail on your lovely desk,' I blather, in a last-ditch desperate attempt to save myself.

'I am extremely disappointed in you, Sophie,' the Baroness utters. 'Bright girl like you should be able to do better than that.' She produces a key from her pocket. 'Here, I think this was what you were looking for.'

'No I really don't need to, it's fine,' I prattle as though I'm politely refusing a second apple puff at an afternoon tea.

'Come on, take it,' the Baroness insists and obediently I do, there is little choice and with a trembling hand I unlock the drawer. Inside there are various papers.

'Take them out.'

'No it's fine, I really don't...' I catch sight of her expression and think better of it; I take out the sheets of paper.

'Read them out loud.'

'Subscription to The Jane Austen Dating Agency,' I read, shamefaced and then, 'your phone bill with BT.'

'I don't always keep my papers separate,' she says, 'but I do have a PA who will be going through these things. Drink?'

'No thanks, I've already had a coffee before I arrived.'

'I think we can do a little better than that, don't you? And after this I think you will need a drink.' She rings a small bell by the fireplace and within seconds the immaculate maid comes in. 'Two vodkas.' The maid nods simply and disappears. Any hopeful thoughts that if I needed help at least I could enlist the staff fades as I realise they are all working for the Baroness and would obviously be too afraid to assist me. This is not good, not good at all.

'Please sit.' The Baroness indicates a chair opposite her and I sit where I did last time, hopelessly wishing I could just rewind the clock on the mantelpiece to when I was simply trying to enlist her as a client for the agency.

The maid returns and hands us small shot glasses, I take a restorative glug of mine, then realise too late that it could be poisoned. I really don't think I'd make a very good detective. I go round accusing innocent people of crimes they haven't committed, then walk right into the lair of real convicts, having been caught red-handed, poking my nose into their business.

'I have to give you credit for at least being onto me,' the Baroness says with a tight smile. 'But,' she reaches up to the triptych nearest, 'if you were looking for these, you weren't even close to discovering their whereabouts.' She presses on the halo above the Madonna and the painted image springs forward, revealing a safe behind. She deftly types in numbers and produces a sheaf of papers.

'Here, take a look at these and they'll tell you what you're so desperate to know.'

I try to stop my hands shaking as I peer at the lines of numbers on the documents in front of me. 'Bets placed,' I read. 'Account numbers... paid in from... Antigua. So you're involved in some kind of gambling scam?'

'It is gambling, yes,' she says. 'Why not? It's an extremely profitable business and most people want to take part. And on this level, it's so easy, like taking candy from a child. No one really gets hurt.'

'But I don't understand,' I stammer, looking at all the pages. 'These are all different account numbers and come from various betting sources. Gift cards, Bitcoin.'

'Offshore gambling,' the Baroness says. 'So much more profitable, bogus accounts set up in various locations, untraceable by the Feds.'

'Wow, so that makes sense.' The fog begins to lift. 'General Baxter, he's on here – this company, SportsBet, it's listed in the General's name and his address. Dreyfus House.'

The Baroness smiles again. 'You always thought there was something odd about him, didn't you?'

I blush. 'I did, although I was totally off-piste when it came to what he was really involved in. So he runs this show.'

'He does and is making a tidy little profit out of it too. This latest cluster should earn him the best part of $2 million and that's just the tip of the iceberg.'

'But, what I don't understand is where Jessica and Daniel come into this.'

'They work with him, under the pretence of Protech Holdings, which is the legitimate face of the business. Daniel outsources hubs on obscure islands offshore where the lines can be set up, untraceable by the authorities. You were getting there, I know you had your sister, Chloe, onto it.'

I take another sip of my vodka. Poisoned or not, I need something restorative. 'How did you know about that?'

'It's my job to know about everything,' she remarks coolly.

'Then you must know, Baroness, that I was beginning to suspect you.' There's no point in hiding this now. If she's going to get rid of me, it's too late anyway. Darn it, the clock only says one o'clock, there's time enough for the Baroness to kill me before Mel even notices I've gone.

'I realised you knew something wasn't right about me, I would have been disappointed if you hadn't, you're an intelligent girl.' She begins to laugh. Oh God, she's going to be like Klebb or one of those other Bond villains who cackle as they taunt their poor victim, before they kill them.

Maybe not so bright, I think, as I contemplate the doorway and try to work out how quickly I could attempt to make an exit.

'But the thing is you've completely got the wrong end of the stick.' She gets up and walks towards the fireplace. Is she going to pick up a poker or something more high tech? I peer at her trying to vaguely gauge if anyone who uses such quaint expressions as 'wrong end of the stick' could be a bad person. 'Unlike my husband,' she picks up his photo and gazes at it wordlessly for a moment, 'I am not the villain of the piece.' She takes his photo and places it face down on the small table.

'I made my choice some time ago, for better or for worse, even though this house and many things in my messy, corrupted life were originally funded by crime, to be no more a part of it. I'm trying, Sophie Johnson, to right some wrongs. Dirty hands can become washed clean again, or at least, I hope they can.' She looks at me intently and laughs again, almost girlishly. 'You don't get it, do you?'

'Not really.'

'The truth is, Sophie, I'm working for Darcy. He recruited me earlier this year to trace Jessica Palmer Wright and Daniel Becks and help him bring them to justice. He was aware that I work undercover and there's not much I don't know about the criminal underworld.'

'What?' For a moment, I gawp at the Baroness like a hare caught in headlights. 'Maybe I could have another vodka?' I blurt.

CHAPTER 33

'So all this time, you've known what's going on, with the gambling?' I stumble, sipping my next restorative glug of alcohol.

'I've had my suspicions, but it's taken me this long, to piece it all together. Jessica and Daniel were carefully hidden, like weevils in a burrow. But I knew where to look. Offshore gambling has become big business. It operates beyond the law because it's so easy to hide within a corridor of false paths and doorways. Most gamblers will have their credit cards declined if they try to deposit funds online. US regulations prevent gambling businesses from accepting credit card payments. But the cryptocurrencies, like Bitcoin, make it possible. So the only way to get funds to gamble is via an offshore site. Jessica and Daniel knew that and decided to set up a network, but they needed funds.'

'So that's where the General came in.'

'Exactly. He had stacks of cash, or at least access to his children's trust funds and he's due to make millions. It suits him as he already has a network of very unpleasant men he surrounds himself with.'

'I thought those men looked suspicious outside the manor, but wasn't sure if I was imagining it.'

'You were onto something. We have only just realised the link as I've had my connections bugging the lines. I posed as an investor willing to combine my knowledge of gambling with extra funding.'

'That's pretty smart.' I think for a moment. 'But I can't believe Darcy hired you! So that means I didn't recruit you for the agency at all?'

The Baroness smiles. 'Of course you did, with your charm and friendly outgoing personality.'

'But you were already a member, sent by Darcy!'

'I was but with your persuasive personality, I would have joined anyway!'

'So that's what Darcy was working on so secretly with his mother. And I felt rejected and left out all that time, when really he was busy with something so important. Why didn't he tell me that's what he was doing?'

'It would have been confidential company business. Even if you are brilliant at keeping secrets.'

'So I wonder if Tara was meeting with him about the same thing?' I muse to myself. 'Although there was no mistaking what his mother wanted, horrible woman. I just don't know what to think anymore. But I guess I needed to trust my gut. I knew there was something strange about the General, although of course I should never have suspected him of...' I break off awkwardly.

'What did you suspect him of?' the Baroness asks, perched on the edge of her seat.

'Oh nothing really. Just some silly misunderstanding,' I blather, trying not to blush. 'And it would never have worked out with Darcy anyway, not when he's someone who doesn't confide in me. It's important to have an open, honest relationship.'

'Very true, in an ideal world. But then this isn't one, is it? Personally, I have every intention this time round of getting it right.'

'So will you leave the agency now? When it's all sorted?'

'No, I have greatly enjoyed my time with you all. Besides I have my eye on someone who I think might just be the kind man I have been looking for.'

'That's wonderful,' I say, trying to think who that could be. 'So it might just work out after all.'

At that moment, there's an altercation at the door and the maid stumbles in, closely followed by a hot and bothered Mel and a slightly stressed and uptight-looking Emma.

'I'm so sorry, madam, I couldn't keep these two out.' The maid is distraught.

'Mel, Emma! What are you doing here?' I shriek.

'Rescuing you, of course,' Mel pants.

The Baroness smiles. 'From the evil baroness?'

'Absolutely not,' Emma says politely. 'We were merely passing and wanted to check your transport arrangements for Maria and Charles's Regency wedding. It's only a week away and we need to make sure we have everything organised.'

'Absolutely,' Mel says, recovering herself, obviously having now realised that the Baroness is not actually planning to assassinate me.

'You might as well both sit down. Bring a couple more vodkas, Collins, unless you would both prefer coffee?'

Mel and Emma sit down on the ornate sofa having unsurprisingly requested vodka. 'So I am supposing that you are both aware of this whole business?'

'Not really,' Emma says, 'I only heard about it this morning from Mel.' She gives me a look and I try to smile back apologetically.

'I am sure I can trust you all to keep this to yourselves, no doubt it will all come out shortly in any case,' the Baroness concedes.

My phone rings out loudly. I answer it. 'Chloe?'

'I have news,' she says. 'My source has discovered that Jessica is running a website, attached to an 0800 number to book bets and organise payments. They then use bank deposits, even gift cards to take payments out to Daniel at his set up in Antigua.'

'That's brilliant, Chloe, well done you! Do you have any evidence of this though?'

'Oh yes,' she says, 'that's the best bit. My investigator has enough numbers and links to provide evidence, against these two at any rate. We just don't know too much about Protech at your end.'

'That's all right, I think we do.'

§♠

Half an hour later, Emma, Mel and I leave the Baroness's apartments like old friends. She says that with the addition of Chloe and the private investigator's input, there is enough evidence to convict the whole group. She was quite impressed actually.

'Maybe I was right about the Baroness,' I say casually as we leave Kensington Palace Gardens. 'She is a kindred spirit after all.' Ignoring Mel's snort, I remark, 'How did you guys get past the security guard?'

'You don't want to know,' Emma says drily.

'At least you're in one piece.' Mel slaps me on the back, nearly knocking me off my heels. 'Annoying though you are.'

'Thanks, I really appreciate you both rushing in there like that, risking life and limb.'

'We're a team,' says Emma putting her arm around me. 'The Jane Austen Dating Agency, where friends matter even more than dates, but don't tell the clients, we obviously try to manage both.'

I smile as we walk together down the busy London streets. I may continue to consistently chase away any potential love interest, but as Jane herself would say, 'Friendship is certainly the finest balm for the pangs of disappointed love.'

CHAPTER 34

A couple of weeks later and after all those months of planning, the day of Maria and Charles's wedding has arrived and at 6am I'm blundering sleepily out of the shower. Outside it's pitch dark, but inside it's a hive of activity.

'Soph, Emma says the snow machine is just arriving,' Mel calls through the door.

Within minutes I am dressed and peering out the tiny diamond-paned window at two enormous trucks, which are steadily making their way up the drive. I'm so intrigued to see how they are going to do this, I rush downstairs and out onto the drive with a light jacket on and rush back in to get an extra jumper. It's so cold.

A whole team of snowmen (couldn't resist calling them that – how is it not properly funny?!), who are dressed rather ironically in black, start to unpack large flat bags, rather like growbags, full of snow.

I watch fascinated as they lift huge tarpaulins and lay them over the grass. A couple of other men pull down huge hoover-type tubes from the lorry and start to spray the ground and the walls with realistic looking white snow.

'I hope this is environmentally friendly,' remarks Mel icily.

'Yes, I checked of course. The blanket snow is biodegradable and made from renewable sugar cane. Even the nozzles on the snow machines are made from recycled plastic. Actually the company I found used scientists at a top British University to develop environmentally friendly snow material. They're so gentle that the Eden Project uses them to decorate their biomes. And they clear everything up afterwards and it doesn't damage old buildings.'

'All right, all right. Anyone would think you've got a degree in snow machinery!' Mel retorts.

'You asked,' I remark glibly. 'Anyway, I'm pleased with these guys, it took me weeks to find such a good company.'

'It's going to look amazing,' Emma says briskly, arriving from the office. 'So we need to just make sure everything else is organised. Sophie, you ready for a quick run through of the order of the day?'

Within a few hours, a weak winter sun is making its presence known in the sky and the outside of Chawton House is transformed into a snow scene worthy of a Charles Dickens Christmas card. The team have even sprayed St Nicholas's Church and swept drifts of snow gently up against the tombstones.

The trees themselves have a fine dusting. It's as though the snow queen I failed to find in the back of the General's wardrobe has worked her magic, but instead of evil, she has spread goodness and an angelic beauty everywhere, illuminated by the weak rays of sun. Unlike real snow this will not melt and I begin to feel as though the day is going to be perfect.

I just wish I could sweep one or two tiny worries under the

snow and leave them there to rest along with the other secrets I'm sure are also hidden underneath. Top of the list is the fact that Darcy is coming today and also Henry Baxter is on the guest list. How I'm going to face either of them I don't know, although I guess at least it gets it over and done with in one day.

I have no time to brood over this or anything else, however, as the guests are beginning to arrive. So as not to disturb the snow they have all been asked to park in the lane, so in dribs and drabs they begin to filter in through the gates and into the church. I feel as though we have been transported back in time, as brightly coloured Regency dresses and capes stand out in relief against the white snow, the men all smart in their top hats and tails, the women bedecked in bright colours.

I am as ready as I'll ever be. Maria kindly sent her make-up artist on to us at the great house and I actually look half decent. The talented young woman has worked her magic and for once I have not only cheekbones but also a dewy glow most would long for. How I wish I could do this every day. My hair is actually behaving itself and after some wrestling with Mel's GHDs, it is smooth and elegant. After one final glance in the mirror in the hallway of the great house, I am ready for whatever today throws at me.

'Wow,' Emma says. 'You brush up pretty well after all, Sophie Johnson. And you, Mel. I don't remember the last time we saw you in a dress.'

'Huh, make the most of it,' Mel snorts. 'It was the Regency Ball actually.'

'Shhh, Mel, look who's coming.' I elbow her hard. 'Try to close your mouth.'

We are silenced by the majestic arrival of Lady Constance who is arm in arm with none other than Vivienne Artois.

'Sophie,' Vivienne smiles, 'lovely to see you.'

'And you,' I smile back, 'and this is Mel.'

'Hey, Mel, I've heard a lot about you.' Vivienne shakes Mel's hand warmly.

'You have?' Mel squeaks, looking as though all her Christmases have come at once.

'Absolutely.' Vivienne leans in slightly. 'Hope we might be able to have a little chat later about fashion.'

'That would be... er... I,' Mel stutters. I don't think I've ever seen her like this with anyone.

'She means that would be lovely!' I say.

'Come along, Vivienne. We need to take our seats,' Lady C commands.

Vivienne raises her eyebrows, giving us all a very expressive look and I have a job not to smirk.

Suddenly there's a kerfuffle at the gate and we all stand transfixed as a familiar sight meets our eyes. It's none other than Rob Bright who comes scuttling up the driveway, wittering as he goes, 'Hurry up, Gwen. We're going to be late and I must sit as close as I can to...' He's dragging the poor unfortunate girl I saw him with on the evening at Dreyfus except today she is at least a little smarter, but her hair still hangs lank and miserable, and she's wearing flat red shoes with a pink satin dress, which clash rather horribly. 'Lady Constance,' Rob Bright falters, dropping an extremely low bow and nudging his drooping girlfriend to do the same, practically knocking her off her feet.

'I suggest you hurry along in, Mr Bright,' Lady C barks, 'tardiness is a very unattractive habit.' Obsequious as ever, he rushes off into the church, followed by the unfortunate Gwen.

'Stupid boy,' Lady C mutters, and for once I jolly well agree with her. I'm glad she's beginning to see it.

It's nearly time for the bride to arrive and yet still no sign of Darcy. Charles is already waiting in the church with Matthew, who, as his best man, is trying to keep him calm and prevent him wearing a pathway in the ancient stone floor with his constant pacing.

Speaking of Darcy, suddenly he's here, striding towards us, his Regency clothes fitting him perfectly and I wonder absently if they create suits like this by hand at Savile Row. Before I know what to say, he's already greeted Emma and then moves swiftly to me, 'Miss Johnson,' he says with a quick bow and before I can react, he kisses my cheek in a heady whiff of Calvin Klein, which is so familiar that my whole body responds with a surge of electricity.

Before I can reply, catch my breath even, he's gone, on into the church and I find myself laughing at absolutely nothing, whilst trying to recover the lost tatters of any sangfroid I may have had. The others give me sympathetic looks, but there's no time to react, as next up the drive is Gene, who rather surprisingly is ambling along hand in hand with Lord Bamford. I didn't see that coming, but I'm so glad because I don't think Lady Amelia really liked him and although he's a bit of an idiot, he's a nice one and I don't like to think of anyone marrying him purely for his money. They both look so happy. I just hope he manages to stand up to his fearsome-sounding mother. With Gene supporting him, maybe he will.

They are closely followed by Edward and Freya, walking arm in arm and talking and laughing easily, an air of bubbly and infectious happiness about them.

'Sophie,' Freya says, 'it's so lovely to see you again!'

'It is.' I smile and return her hug. 'So how are things?'

'Wonderful,' Freya says, smiling up at Edward, who looks down at her fondly. Arm in arm they walk on into the church.

'Have I missed something?' I ask Emma.

'Probably.' She laughs. 'I told you it would all work out in the end.'

'You did, but I wouldn't have believed it. What about Miss Foxton?'

'Not been seen for some time,' Emma says casually.

'Probably something to do with the fact you wrote to your father and asked him to make sure she was offered an event management position up on the Chatsworth Estate by his friends, the Duke and Duchess of Devonshire,' Mel remarks.

'Emma, you're a genius. And Mr Foxton?' I ask.

'Went too. Closely followed by Amelia and Caitlin. They can bicker over him just as well up in Derbyshire as they can down here.'

I am laughing when a familiar voice interrupts, 'Miss Johnson?' It's him. I've missed his voice so much. It's been as though a part of me has been lost all this time.

I turn slowly towards him. 'Hello, Henry,' I say awkwardly, barely daring to meet his eyes, but at the same time inexplicably drawn to them. He looks great in a navy jacket, a green cravat and tight britches, topped off by shining black leather riding boots, which I studiously avoid.

'It's good to see you,' he says, but then I'm unable to reply as I'm being enveloped in a hug.

'Ellie! I'm so glad you're back,' I say happily. 'And you look really well.'

'It's called escaping paternal tyranny. We'll talk later, I've got so much to tell you.'

'You'd better hurry in,' Emma says. 'The bride's arriving.'

She is as well. At the end of the drive, a large yellow Rolls turns in and steadily approaches in stately fashion. In the back, Maria looks radiant, positively sparkling and next to her is Sir Henry, who is for once appearing quite proud and even more regal than he usually is. If his nose goes any further in the air, it will get frostbite.

I surge forward as quickly as my dainty heels and long skirt allow and open the door for Maria.

'You look simply stunning,' I say, and she does. Her dress is sleeveless but she has a mock fur stole skimming her shoulders. The dress is Regency of course, high waisted, with a square neckline edged with delicate lace. Under her chest is a silver band, which is fashioned in delicate fabric and is complemented by tiny silver droplets on the top of the bodice. The skirt drops elegantly to the floor, in cascades of sheer lace, which hang straight to the ground, there's no meringue to be seen here. In keeping with Regency brides' etiquette she isn't wearing a veil. This was mainly because lace in Regency times was handmade and beyond the reach of most brides, but actually we all thought Maria looked perfect without.

Emma passes Maria her bouquet, a gorgeous mass of roses, peonies and a stunning spray of sweet peas, which complement perfectly the colour of our bridesmaids' dresses.

'The snow!' she exclaims. 'It's simply beautiful, however did you manage it?'

'A touch of magic.' I smile.

'It's amazing, thank you so much.' She looks as though she's going to cry.

'We loved arranging it,' Emma says.

'Well here goes,' Maria says, hitching her skirt up elegantly. 'This is it!' She waits for Sir Henry to adjust his cravat, which is obviously still bothering him. He's immaculately dressed in a pristine red jacket and cream britches.

'You look very smart, Sir Henry, every inch the father of the bride,' I comment generously.

'Who else would I look like, girl?' he remarks, brushing an imaginary speck from his jacket. But I have to hand it to him, his vanity serves its purpose for once. He's one of the smartest fathers of the bride I've ever seen.

'Maria, that dress fits you to perfection.' Emma comes forward to kiss her cheek.

'Thanks to Mel.' Maria smiles and we all walk sedately, but full of pride, to the church behind her.

The whole scene is magical, surreal; I almost feel not quite here, as though I am an actress on a movie set. I have never attended a Regency wedding before and it's the most amazing experience. Inside the church is adorned with swathes of flowers and ribbon decorating each pew and Maria and Charles look so happy throughout.

There is such an understanding between them like two old friends, I feel quite emotional and have a job not to cry. Thank goodness for waterproof mascara. This must be the first time in over two hundred years that Jane Austen's church has been filled with people wearing Regency dress, perhaps looking much as they would have done then and I wonder in one of my more fanciful moments if she is looking down on us.

The vicar is suitably ponderous, in the style of all the best Austen clergymen. He has this habit of emphasising one word in each sentence more than any other with suitably comic results. I don't know how to keep a straight face, but Charles and Maria just smile and make their responses in clear tones, they are so wrapped up in each other.

Sir Henry Greaves turns out to be extremely well behaved, considering, and plays his part to the letter, with pomp and ceremony, then returning to sit next to Lady Constance, which makes me want to nudge Mel, but I just about manage to control myself.

We stand in the aisle behind the happy couple, the colours of our dresses perfectly imitating the bunch of sweet peas in Maria's bouquet.

During the signing of the register, to my utter astonishment, Emma leaves her position at our side and seats herself at a piano in the corner of the church. I knew there was going to be a musical interlude, but I had no idea Emma was such a talented musician.

Within minutes her fingers are flying over the keys, as she plays a selection written by Jane Austen's favourite composer, Ignaz Pleyel. The music is simply beautiful and adds to the Regency feeling perfectly. It's as though we have all been transported back in time.

'You're a dark horse,' I whisper as she returns to us.

'I know, I'm full of surprises.' She smiles back.

On the way into the church I had walked down the aisle behind Maria along with the other bridesmaids, resolutely facing the front, avoiding both Darcy and Henry as much as possible, yet I can't help catching Henry's eye on the way out and his face lights up with that irresistible grin, which makes my stomach leap and I walk out of the church full of doubts and confusion, my head in a whirl. As if this isn't all enough of a quandary, deep in the back of my mind is the knowledge that I still need to give Miffy an answer about her job offer. It's been well over a week and it's getting really rude that I'm avoiding speaking to her, but I just don't know what to do.

The wedding breakfast is soon in full swing. The marquee placed on the lawn to the side of the great house, is simply incredible. Pockets of ribbons and flowers adorn every corner and we are soon tucking into hog roast and an array of vegetables and delicious sauces.

Someone, and I don't know who, but I strongly suspect Emma, has seated Sir Henry Greaves at the top table next to Lady Constance. But whoever it was knew what they were about (I am sure it is Emma, she is every inch as brilliant a matchmaker as her namesake) as they seem to be talking about something that they actually agree on for once and are getting along like a house on fire. This really is a magical day, the influence of which seems to be spreading its charm over everyone present.

'Have you seen the Baroness?' I ask Mel, who is seated next to me at the end of the top table.

'No, I thought it was odd she wasn't in the church.'

'I hope she's okay.' I have visions of her getting into difficulties with the gang and us all having to go on a rescue mission to sort them out, dressed in Regency gowns. The thought makes me want to laugh. 'What's the vegan roast like?'

'Very good actually,' Mel says. 'Although I really am thinking I'm going to take the food pledge after this.'

I make a mental note to stock up the freezer. It's a lovely idea, but I'm not sure about forgoing my hog roast for a while longer. Although I should try to help Mel out here, she's a good friend. 'I guess we could give Veganuary a go,' I say reluctantly.

'It's a deal. Hey, look who's here.'

I follow her gaze and notice the Baroness arriving through a side entrance of the marquee.

'Sorry I am late,' she says. 'I had some business to attend to.' And I swear the Baroness, the formal, uptight Baroness, gives me a wink and goes to her place, closely followed by Emma's father, Mr Woodtree, who sits down next to her, cheerfully accepting a glass of champagne and plate of food.

'Hey, Emma, I didn't know your father was bringing the Baroness,' I say to her, as she is seated the other side of Mel.

'Neither did I.'

And then it dawns on me. Of course, that's who the Baroness was talking about, not Gene. I had thought there was something between them at Emma's estate, at the end of the Regency sports event. I had never seen the Baroness so relaxed as she was sitting in Mr Woodtree's drawing room.

'Look at that,' I say to Mel, 'I think she's found her perfect match after all.'

'I'd have never guessed it,' Mel replies.

'I had no idea my father liked her,' says Emma, looking worried. 'But I guess if she makes him happy and he certainly looks it, then I'm happy too.'

'You said everything would sort and it certainly seems to have,' I say.

Maybe for everyone except me.

'It does,' Emma replies, 'of course it does, this is The Jane Austen Dating Agency.' She rises to her feet, 'To the bride and groom!'

We all stand and repeat, 'To the bride and groom!'

'And to happy ever afters!' she toasts.

'To happy ever afters!' we all repeat, raising our glasses high in the air and somewhere deep down, I feel the glimmer of a tiny spark of hope, and finally I begin to believe that maybe, just maybe, they might be possible after all.

CHAPTER 35

'Sophie, wait!' I turn, to discover Darcy almost jogging after me.

'I'm taking these to the kitchens.' I rearrange my armful of wedding favours, which had decorated the tables and now need packaging up to be taken home by guests at the end of the day.

'I'll help.' He carefully removes some of the cloth bags and walks alongside me. 'I need to talk to you.'

'Okay, although we've not got long until the afternoon celebrations start. I'll have to make sure the marquee is set up properly for the first wedding dance.'

'It won't take that long. Maybe we can just go outside where it's more private?' My heart leaps at his mention of the word private, but I continue to the kitchens, where we leave the favours in brightly coloured piles on the large wooden tables.

'I do have to check the walled gardens are ready for Maria and Charles's photos. You can walk with me if you like?' I suggest casually.

We wander round the side of the great house, up the steps, where earlier this year Darcy had taken my hand and told me he had saved Chawton House. He had done all this for me, for all literary and independent women for posterity. He had swept me off my feet and offered me the job to run the agency. Now it feels like years ago. I vividly picture how he had taken me in his arms and kissed me and I had believed we would live happily ever after. And if we had stayed here away from the real world, who knows? Maybe we would have done.

'Soph.' He turns to me as we walk up the grass towards the walled garden. It's quiet as most guests are taking a rest, relaxing and chatting inside the great house, Maria and Charles happily mingling between them. 'I owe you an apology.'

'What for?' I ask, surprised.

'I lost faith in you. I was wrong. All that business with the protest, I doubted you and whether we were suited. I let my own stupid worries and hang-ups convince me it wasn't going to work.' I stare at him confused; I wasn't expecting this. But before I can reply he continues, 'My mother poured doubts into my ears and I guess she hit a nerve. The business is so important to the family.'

'I know. In any case I'm sorry about the march, I truly am. I'm not sorry for sticking up for what I believe in though, I'm always going to do that,' I say firmly.

'I wouldn't want it any other way.' He smiles. 'I know you didn't mean to get mixed up in the fire engine business. You got swept along. I just didn't want to believe it. It was easier to hide my head in the sand. It's what I've always done, bury myself away from problems rather like an ostrich.'

Probably due to nervous tension, I have the urge to giggle at the thought of Darcy comparing himself with an ostrich, but I manage to control myself.

'You might think it's easy for me,' he continues. 'I know what people say, rich guy, with all the perks, I know I don't have the financial worries, but sometimes the pressure, the need to succeed is unbearable.'

We've reached the large wrought-iron gates of the walled garden. The snow people have worked their magic here too, a light dusting of snow rests on the wall, the metalwork and within the garden, the fruit trees and winter vegetables. Everything is transformed into a sparkling winter wonderland. Darcy unlatches the gate and opens it for me to go in.

'I always think this is like a secret garden,' I remark. 'Mysterious but in a good way.'

'Still a born romantic then.' Darcy smiles at me.

'Maybe. I think perhaps romances are safer than thrillers in any case.'

'Have you gone off those already?'

'Let's just say maybe reading too many is not a good thing.'

He laughs and takes my hand in his. 'Although it turns out that real life did mimic art. This whole business with Jessica and Daniel. Now we've found them, I feel I can move on. I owe you and Chloe a great deal, as well as the Baroness.'

'Why didn't you tell me about her? Who she was?' I say, a wave of unresolved hurt making me release Darcy's hand and I wander towards the gate at the back of the garden.

'I couldn't. I'm sorry, I really wanted to. What if you had given her away inadvertently? It was a dangerous business and at that time I had no idea the General was involved. He's a nasty piece of work. Better you didn't know about it.'

'What will happen to them?' I ask, carefully examining the delicate frosting on the gate.

'They've all been arrested but are released on bail. The General is in for a hard time though as he was already involved in more minor shady dealings and the police are happy to throw the book at him. Also Jessica and Daniel have a record of setting up illegal gambling through the dating agency and embezzling funds. I'm hoping they'll get what they deserve.' He looks grim.

'I'm sorry about the General. Not that I liked him but for Ellie and... Henry.'

'I hear you stayed with them,' Darcy says quietly. 'That was nice?'

'Nice?' I say with a smile. 'Yes, it was. Ellie and I get on really well and we rode most days.' For some reason I don't mention my outings with Henry. 'And I enjoyed being in the countryside, it was beautiful. Not that I liked the General's company.'

Darcy absently readjusts his necktie. 'And Henry?'

'He's a lovely guy. A good friend.'

Darcy clears his throat. 'And?'

'And what?'

'Anything more?'

'I don't know what you mean.' I search his face. 'Henry and I are just friends.'

'Not that I mind,' he says.

I look up at him. 'No. Why should you?'

'Because...' He steps forward until he is towering above me. I can feel the warmth of his fit, taut body through his shirt and jacket. 'I still love you, Sophie Johnson,' he says, bending his head to kiss me. Automatically my body responds to his touch, it doesn't care what's happened the past few months, as far as it's concerned, he's a necessary part of my life. He kisses me insistently and I respond passionately, all the frustration of lost hopes crammed into that kiss.

We are disturbed by a clang of the gate and spring apart instinctively. Oddly there's no one there, although the gate is still moving and I could have sworn I saw the edge of a long green jacket vanishing round the corner.

The mood is broken however. 'I think we'd better go back,' I say reluctantly to Darcy. He takes my hand and we walk side by side towards the house, sort of together but not together.

'Sophie, I'd like us to start again, go to Paris, forget my

mother and everything else.' He leans and kisses me once more on the forehead. 'Start over.'

'What about Tara?' I ask, the question leaving my mouth before I can stop it.

'Tara?' He pushes his hands through his tousled hair. 'What about her?'

'Well if we're being honest, she did show up a lot.'

'She's an old family friend,' he says awkwardly. 'I don't feel anything for her.'

'But your mother obviously wants you to,' I point out.

'Maybe, but I can't feel something for someone I don't, just because my mother wants me to. We're not living in one of your novels, Soph.'

'Sophie! Look who's here!' I'm stopped by Mel's shout and as soon as I see who it is, I drop Darcy's hand and start running towards the great house.

'Oh my God, Chloe!' I shriek, because Chloe is there, large as life, standing with a big smile on her face on the lawn in front of the house, dressed in a long Regency gown and cloak. 'What are you doing here?' We hug and squeal and jump around, causing the wedding guests to stop and stare, although most of them smile.

'It's like old times, isn't it?' Chloe says. 'Couldn't resist hopping on a plane. Anyway, how could I miss Maria and Charles's wedding?'

'You couldn't but I thought you weren't able to get back. It's so good to see you.' It is as well; I can't believe how much I've missed her. I don't think I've ever been apart from Chloe for so long. 'You look so tanned and healthy!' I laugh.

'I know.' She grins. 'It's not very Regency, is it, but who cares?'

'Not me,' says Nick, who's right next to her. He gives me a kiss and he and Darcy clap each other on the back.

'So,' Chloe eyes me up and down, 'what's all the goss. Are you and Darcy back together or what?'

'That's the thing...' We walk towards the house together arm in arm, but suddenly the relief of recent events and my quandary about what to do becomes too much. All my emotions are fighting each other. 'To be honest,' I half sob. 'It's all going horribly wrong, I just don't know how I feel anymore.'

§.

You know those romantic films we all love watching, the ones where the hero and heroine become intimate at a wedding? Total fantasy. They really can't happen or they don't in my case, because the afternoon rushes past and I manage to speak to practically every guest at the wedding except Darcy or Henry.

I nearly reach Henry on a couple of occasions, but there's always someone to chat to or discuss things politely with so I merely see him in the distance. Chloe managed to give me a quick pep talk in the ladies, just to dab my face, reassure me that it's fine to be confused sometimes and that it will all come out in the wash.

'Do you love Darcy?' she asked outright.

'I think I do, it's just... I mean I did...' I falter unromantically.

'Look, Soph, you either do or you don't. All those other doubts about Tara or his mother or any of the other things that happened and you're worrying about don't matter. You might have all those but the reality is that you have to love him in spite of anything else. If not, then it's not real and you have to move on. Take it from someone who's already been married, there are always parts of someone you might not like, but the love has to be strong enough to make you want to overcome those things.'

'I guess.' I sniff.

'It's like any kind of match. There are deal-breakers, of

course, but other than those, if you really love someone the rest is something you have to compromise over.'

'So I just have to work out my deal-breakers.'

'That's the one. And by the sound of it you need to work out how you really feel about Henry.'

'Henry? He's a friend and probably no longer that after all my mistakes.' I have finally confessed everything to Chloe. It's a good job the toilets are actually quiet otherwise the whole world would know the sorry tale.

'You need to talk to him. And it's good to have friends.' She had looked at me, her head on one side. 'It's just, Soph, you're giving me the totally smitten vibes, I think you really like this guy. And you need to be sure how you feel. Henry or Darcy? Which is it to be?'

CHAPTER 36

I feel as though much of the rest of the day, I am on autopilot. I smile and laugh; I'm the life and soul of the party. But underneath I'm a mass of uncertainty.

'Sophie, this is a gorgeous wedding,' says Ellie, appearing from nowhere, her cheeks flushed from champagne. 'And I hope to introduce you to someone very special to me this evening, other than Izzy of course.'

Izzy and Matthew at that moment walk past and Izzy blows Ellie a kiss. 'I have such great friends, I'm so glad I joined the agency,' Ellie says.

'They're a good bunch,' I agree. 'But who is this special guest? Might it be someone I may have seen you with before in the walled garden?'

'You saw me that night then!' Ellie exclaims. 'I wondered if there was someone out walking in the evening, but I didn't know it was you until Henry mentioned it.'

'I didn't mean to be stalking you; I was only following to check you were okay. Then when I saw you were with someone, I tried to sneak off without you noticing.'

'Henry saw you; he knew you wouldn't say anything. I was

meeting Chris.' She smiles shyly. 'I met him a couple of years ago at uni. He's the love of my life but my father wouldn't accept him because he's not a lord. Father banned us from seeing each other, so we had to resort to meeting in secret. But thank God it's all over. Izzy and Henry rescued me and now my father's ridiculous get-rich schemes are all out in the open. Besides he's going to be lucky to escape prison so I can finally do as I like!'

'Henry's an amazing brother, you're lucky to have him.'

'He is and I am.' She grins. 'I guess we didn't have anyone else while growing up. But he's generally a lovely guy.' She looks at me speculatively, 'Speaking of which, I was wondering, by the way, if you might pass him this note for me?' She looks at me with pleading eyes. 'I need to go and wait for Chris. We're meeting in the walled garden before we join the dancing. I haven't seen him since that day so thought it might be a romantic spot.'

'Very, it's a gorgeous place. I'll give Henry the note. Although I think he may be avoiding me,' I say anxiously. 'I haven't had a chance to apologise, for my behaviour when I was staying.'

'What for? I can't imagine you did anything wrong, I'm just sorry I didn't tell you my plans. But we knew how tough my father can be and thought the least you knew the better. Henry enjoyed being with you. He told me so.' She goes quiet and then repeats. 'Just try, will you? I really want him to pass the note to Chris.'

Reluctantly I take the folded notepaper from Ellie. 'Okay and I'm glad by the way, not about your dad, but how things have worked out other than that.' She gives me a hug and I steal away to look for Henry. This task is easier said than done. I can't find him anywhere.

'Sophie! There you are. Are you ready for the wedding dance?' Emma calls.

'Of course.' I tuck the note down into my purse. Maybe Henry will appear for the dancing.

In the marquee, all the wedding guests are grouped in circles of eight, apart from the group Emma and I join, which has six.

'Please welcome the bride and groom,' Emma declares, and we all clap as Maria and Charles arrive and take their places in our circle. 'The wedding dance is called Lady Nelson's Waltz Cotillion,' Emma continues. 'I believe we all know the steps but if you don't please just try not to tread on your partner's toes!' We all laugh especially as Emma gives Rob Bright, who is already prancing on the spot, like an overfed thoroughbred ready for the off, a particularly meaningful look.

The music starts and we all dance in a circle. Next the men stand still and Emma, Chloe, Maria and I all dance in between them. Then it's their turn. Apart from one slight mistake where Chloe forgets what she's doing and tries to go the wrong way, which makes us all laugh, it works pretty well.

'For heaven's sake, Mr Bright, any more treading on my toes and you will be banished to another group,' Lady C booms loudly.

'Hear hear!' concedes her partner Sir Henry Greaves. I can't believe it, yet another thing these two actually agree on.

I glance around all the dancers. Henry Baxter isn't here. The only place left is the garden. Darcy is due to dance the next with Mel as she's had to put up with the rather incongruously exuberant Lord Bamford for this one as he has become momentarily separated from Gene, so I manage to sneak out whilst no one is looking.

I put my hand in my purse and pull out the note. I wonder why she asked me to give it to her brother when she could have done so. Then I stare at it again. I hadn't noticed before, but the note is addressed to Miss Sophie Johnson.

Dear Sophie,

I have been desperate to talk to you. Just briefly, I know you are otherwise engaged. But I would be really grateful if you would meet me at the field gate? Yours ever, Henry

I hold the note to me for a moment. Yours, Henry? What does that mean?

My heart begins to skip a beat as I consider the meaning of his words. It's still light and the path through the ancient trees towards the open fields at the end of the wooded area is peaceful and I enjoy the air as I lift my skirts and make my way to the gate. There leaning on a post is Henry. He's surveying the fields thoughtfully and I stand back, not wanting to intrude, but he turns and notices me.

'You got my note?' he asks.

'Yes, thank you. I wanted to see you too.' His face brightens. 'Just to say I'm sorry, about thinking those awful things about your father.'

'Why? You were right. You have no reason to say you're sorry. I should be apologising to you. You might have been over-exaggerating his murderous tendencies but as far as his criminal activities you were spot on.'

'Not really. I had no idea what the General was doing, it wasn't my business, but I didn't trust him, that's all.'

'And you were totally right. I knew he was involved in gambling, but I thought it was all legitimate, frustrating though that was. I also knew he was trying to regain some of his losses through marrying us all off to people with money. I couldn't bear his behaviour towards Ellie, it was unforgivable.'

'But you did the right thing; you smuggled her away to Izzy and now she's happy with Christopher.'

'Yes, I'm so pleased for her. He's a sensible chap and will look after her all right. Although she can pretty much look after herself.'

'Of course she can.' I smile. 'Most of us women can, you know. We are more than capable.'

'Don't I know it,' he says, looking more cheerful. 'Would you like to walk a while down to the meadow, like old times?'

'I don't know,' I glance reluctantly back towards the house, 'I guess I should get back to the party.'

'Of course,' he says. 'But we can walk together? I've missed our chats.'

'Me too. And our outings on horseback.'

'Perhaps you could come and ride someday next week, although maybe Darcy wouldn't like it?'

'Darcy?' I say.

'I assumed you were back together,' Henry says diffidently.

'Not exactly. I mean, I guess we are.'

'Oh.'

There's an uncharacteristic silence between us. Tactfully he changes the subject. 'Been reading any more thrillers?'

'No,' I say with feeling. 'I figured maybe I should give them up permanently.'

'I don't know about that.' He laughs. 'Have you read *Jamaica Inn* yet?'

'No, although it's on my evergrowing TBR list!'

'I can recommend it, very thrilling.'

'I think maybe I should stick to romance, although I'm not sure I truly believe in happy ever afters anymore.'

'I'm surprised to hear you say that.' He turns towards me, with his characteristic grin, and gently touches my cheek with his hand. 'Keep your romantic imaginings, Sophie, they're one of the many things I love about you.'

By now we are standing together, just outside the door to the Great House.

'There you are, Sophie,' Emma says brightly, appearing from the marquee. 'We've all been looking for you.'

❦

The rest of the wedding day passes in a blur and by the time I walk up to my bedroom I'm exhausted. I've got that horrible feeling you get after taking off uncomfortably high heels that have been welded to your feet all day, as though your feet belong to someone else or are constructed from two blocks of wood and you're no longer able to use them properly.

Mel is already sound asleep in her room, snoring lightly, her clothes strewn haphazardly all around the floor.

Oddly my door is shut. I'm sure I didn't leave it like that. I hear a scrabbling noise from within and as I carefully open it I am floored by a small brown and white bombshell with a wildly wagging tail. 'Widget!' I exclaim. 'How on earth did you get here?'

As I sit on the bed and fuss the little dog, I discover a small note attached to her neck. I'm amazed she hasn't chewed it, if it were the horrible Roland, it would have been a soggy and ink-splodged mess on the floor.

With shaking hands I unfold the note.

Sophie,

I know you probably don't want to hear this, now you've made up with Darcy, and I understand that, or at least I shall try to in time.

But I can't let all this happen without at least trying to tell you how I feel. Normally I'm good with words, but for some reason I'm struggling. What I'm trying to tell you is that I've come to see you as such a good friend, a true friend, and I guess more than that. I really miss you. It hasn't felt the same since you left Dreyfus and I guess I hoped you might miss me too. Every time I think of you, my heart beats louder and whenever something happens I want to tell you about it, to discuss it with you. The truth is, I miss you Sophie, the way you push your hair out of your face, the way you frown when you're thinking something, your smile which lights up your whole face.

I'll try to understand if you don't feel the same way, sometimes these things are simply not meant to be. And as a thank you for everything, I have sent you a little someone who has also pined for your company since the day you left. You're irreplaceable, Sophie Johnson. Just make sure you spend your life with someone who really appreciates that.

I love you.

Your Henry x

And for once, make-up on and all, I crawl into bed, snuggling Widget into my blanket and cry myself to sleep.

CHAPTER 37

The next day I am woken by a wet snorting in my ear. Widget turns out to be a perfect hot water bottle but rather like a truffling pig first thing in the morning.

Mel bursts in. 'Who's this?' she exclaims as Widget gives her the most triumphant welcome involving a manically wagging tail and lots of kisses.

'She was here when I came back last night.' I raise an eyebrow at her. 'Anything to do with you?'

'Perhaps.' She smiles. 'Henry did ask if he could leave someone in your room. I guess we should be grateful it wasn't him.'

'Mel!' I give her a mock shocked look. 'Honestly, I'm meant to be back with Darcy anyway.'

'Meant to be? Either you are or you aren't. Are you with Darcy or not?'

'Do you know what? I don't think I gave him an answer!' I reply. 'But I just don't know anymore. Anyway, I've got to make a decision about Modiste – all these life choices and I'm hopeless at making them.'

'Just do eenie meenie miney mo,' suggests Mel helpfully. I

throw a sock at her as she leaves the room. She sticks her head back round the door. 'Yesterday was amazing by the way. Everyone was saying it was the most beautiful wedding they've ever been to and Maria and Charles were ecstatic.'

'Yeah it was amazing, wasn't it? I think we all make a pretty good team, you know.'

'Yep I think we do. And Emma's finalised the get-together at Christmas – The Jane Austen Dating Agency Christmas.'

'Can't wait for it, we're all going to sit in Regency dress in the Great Hall,' I say dreamily. 'Log fires, a huge turkey and charades – sounds perfect.'

'Hmm, not sure about the charades,' remarks Mel, ever pragmatic.

I enjoy wandering around the grounds with Widget, who is the best walking companion ever. As I stop and look at a view, she's perfectly happy to snuffle in the remains of scrunched autumn leaves. Then I return to the house for there is a grim job to be done.

I dial Miffy's number.

'Sophie?' she answers, 'how are you? I thought you'd gone abroad or something.'

'No.' I laugh awkwardly. 'We just had a Regency wedding to arrange and you know...'

'I heard you and Darcy are an item again.'

'Wow the jungle drums are pretty efficient.'

'You bet they are. So, have you considered our offer?'

'I have.' I clear my throat. 'I have, and it's been one of the toughest decisions of my life. I've always wanted to work in editorial, this is the chance of a lifetime.'

'You bet it is. When are you starting then, next week?'

'That's the thing, I'm not.' I quickly babble on before she can react. 'I'm so sorry, and I'm extremely grateful for this amazing opportunity, but I can't leave the agency. I love my job and it's not just me, we're a team. The Jane Austen Dating Agency, we're like one big family.'

Miffy's silent for a moment. 'I can understand that. I'm not going to say I'm not sorry though because you have so much talent and I totally want you on our team darling.'

'I know, but this is the decision I have to make.'

'In that case, how about you become our guest editor? That means you put forward articles most months and you'll be on a smaller salary, but you can still be part of the agency?'

'That would be amazing, Miffy, I'd love it!' I jump up and do a couple of victory moves. Thank goodness we're not on FaceTime or she might reconsider her offer.

'That's settled then. And your first commission can be covering the Regency wedding.'

'Absolutely, you're on. Thanks so much, Miffy.'

'Oh and I believe you'll soon have a feature to write on a joint venture between Vivienne and Mel. The collaboration of a top designer with the new kid on the block.'

'Mel never said. That's fantastic, I'm so pleased for her.'

'If Vivienne believes she is talented, then she really has something. I'll need you to make it controversial though.'

'Maybe not too controversial,' I add with a smile.

Miffy laughs. 'Possibly just a tiny bit.'

I can't believe it. Perhaps things do work out for the best after all. To be a regular contributor on the Editorial Team at Modiste as well as managing The Jane Austen Dating Agency. I cut myself a piece of wedding cake left over from yesterday and sit down to enjoy it. Perhaps you can have your cake and eat it after all.

'Sophie.' It's Mel. 'Eating cake at this time in the morning?'

'So, it's delicious and why not?'

'Fair point.'

'I can't believe you're working with Vivienne – on a new collection. Why didn't you tell me?'

'I only found out yesterday and it was Maria and Charles's day. I didn't want to take any attention from them. Besides, that's what Vivienne wanted to talk to me about.' Mel sits and strokes Widget's long soft ears. 'So did you decide about Modiste?'

'I did. I turned it down.'

She stares at me. 'But, Soph, you've wanted to work in Editorial ever since I can remember.'

'I know, but sometimes maybe the thing you've been dreaming of for a long time isn't actually what you think it is.'

'Bit like Darcy?'

'Maybe. But I couldn't leave the agency, it's my life and I love it.'

'I'm so glad to hear it,' says Emma walking in and giving me a hug. 'Can't do without you.'

'I know I'm indispensable.' I laugh. 'But we're like a sisterhood, a team. And in any case, I've been asked to be Guest Editor for Modiste, so I can write for them in my spare time.'

Mel and Emma exchange looks and laugh. My phone bings the arrival of a text and I exclaim, 'Oh you're never going to guess who else has just asked me to write for them?'

'Who?' Emma and Mel reply, peering over my shoulder.

'Vegan Life Magazine,' I reply, laughing.

'But you're not even bloody vegan!' Mel protests.

'Then I'd better get practising. After Christmas that is.' I shoot a look at Emma who's already ordered the turkey. 'It's nearly Veganuary.'

CHAPTER 38

'Sophie? Where are you?' Mel shouts up the stairs later that day.

'In my room, jotting some notes for the editorial.'

She appears in the doorway. 'What are all those books doing in the hall, I nearly broke my neck tripping over them?'

'My psychological thrillers; I've decided to give them to the charity shop. Why?'

'I thought you couldn't get enough of them?'

'No, I figured it was time for me to move on.'

'So it's back to romance then?' She laughs.

'Maybe.'

'In that case,' she says with a smile, 'Emma wants us to do an impromptu photo shoot for marketing for the agency. So can you just put on your blue and white dress?'

'What? Now? It's a bit annoying, I wanted to get started on the rest of the blurb,' I protest.

'It won't take long.'

'But why wouldn't I wear my bridesmaid's dress?' I ask.

'Because... you've already had photos of that yesterday,' she says, but there's a rummy sort of sheepishness about her.

'Oh okay then, if I must.'

I rummage in my wardrobe and put on my blue bodiced Regency dress with a tiny floral pattern on the skirt. Mel reappears. 'Don't forget your cream cape over it.' She looks at my puzzled face. 'It's quite cold out and we want to take the photos outside.'

Soon, I am in my most comfortable Regency dress with the cape drawn over. I've got my hair down, but Mel hadn't said anything about that. 'You need to look romantic,' she says sticking her head round the door again for a quick glance. 'Yes, perfect.'

I hardly have time to adjust my outfit, before she is calling me downstairs. She's nowhere to be seen and neither is Emma. I wander around the building calling, followed closely by the ever-loyal Widget. It suddenly strikes me that this is some kind of wind-up.

They really aren't anywhere, the rotten lot. I walk through the arched doorway to the great house and look out towards the church. Everything is beautifully snowy still; the company hasn't yet arrived to clear up so the scene is picturesque. I squint at the bottom of the gate. Someone is coming on a dapple grey horse, a rider who trots briskly up through the drive and upon reaching the lawn breaks into a canter.

'Sophie, this is your moment,' Mel calls from upstairs. 'I'll look after Widget for you.'

'I don't understand,' I burble.

'Just go, Sophie. That is if you're still looking for that romantic happy ever after?'

I give Mel what I hope is a withering look, but then I laugh. Of course it's what I really have always dreamt of. Who am I trying to kid? Of course I want romance, a hero on a fine horse, dressed in riding britches and leather boots, stunningly handsome, with a kind heart. Count me in.

In a dream, I walk out onto the lawn and it's Henry Baxter, of course it is, who approaches at a canter on his gorgeous dapple grey horse.

'Miss Johnson,' he calls as he comes to a skidding halt and dismounts rapidly. His white shirt is ruffled, his neckerchief loose and I can see a tantalising glimpse of his firmly muscled chest. 'I've missed you so much I can't exist without you.'

He smiles ruefully. 'Since you've been gone, the white rose bushes have died of grief. Are you still full of romantic dreams, Miss Johnson, or have you decided to keep it real? I hope somehow I might have some chance of winning you, make you see how much you mean to me?'

I walk towards him and he takes me in his arms, pressing me hard against his body, his tight britches, the feel of his hands in their leather gloves on my skin, the horse whickering at his shoulder, and instinctively his mouth meets mine and we kiss, gently at first, tantalisingly slowly, then more insistently until my heart is racing and I feel as though my feet might give way beneath me.

'Shall I take that as a yes?' Henry grins, and I laugh back at him.

'Are we running away?'

'Of course. It's what you wanted, isn't it?'

'Oh yes.' I smile and he lifts me up onto his horse, as though I were as light as a feather pillow, long dress, cloak and all.

He mounts behind me and together we gallop away, his arms firmly around my waist, holding me against him, beneath us the thundering hoof beats of the horse ring out and we ride off into the distance, through the beautiful fields and towards the woods and streams beyond with not a care in the world.

THE END

ACKNOWLEDGEMENTS

After completing my debut novel, *The Jane Austen Dating Agency*, I felt strangely bereft. Whilst writing the book, Sophie and the whole cast of characters had become close friends and I realised I simply wasn't done with them yet. Also, my number one fan, aka my mum, and many wonderful readers (thank you so much) were asking for more about Sophie and The Jane Austen Dating Agency.

So here it is. Sophie Johnson's back. I hope you enjoy her latest escapades and that this light-hearted story helps you escape from the very difficult times we are currently experiencing, into the reassuring make believe world of Regency love and romance, even if it's just for a while.

Of course, I couldn't have written this book without the help of a whole team of amazing hard working people. So I need to thank Betsy Reavley and Fred Freeman of Bloodhound Books, as well as my editor Morgen Bailey, and Tara Lyons for keeping it all together and my proofreader, Shirley Khan, as well as Maria Slocombe for publicity.

Thanks so much to my lovely agent, Amanda Preston at LBA for all your fantastic support and advice.

Of course as always, thanks go to my mum and dad for their love, encouragement and tireless support throughout as well as for inspiring me with such a love of books and Jane Austen in the first place. You wanted to know what happened next, Mum, so I really hope you approve. Thanks, Dad, for reading the first book and saying you enjoyed it, when it's really not your cup of tea. It means a lot to me.

Thank you to my supportive, incredible girls, Marianne, Grace, Madeleine and Francesca. I know it's been tough on so many levels, but I couldn't write my books without all your help. Francesca I hope you enjoy the sequel – I know you loved the first one, especially on audiobook on long journeys! Marianne, thank you for understanding that sometimes I just need to shut myself away and write.

Thanks especially to Madeleine for all the help around the house so I don't get too bogged down in dirty dishes and cleaning.

Special thank you to Grace for as always being my number one beta reader and for giving honest feedback, encouragement and support with my writing.

Big thanks to my husband Keith who has finally nearly finished reading my first book! I do really appreciate the effort, as I know it's definitely not your thing. Also for all your love, support and encouragement along the way.

And last but not least, a huge thank you to all of you, my lovely readers, for following Sophie's story and for helping to keep Regency love and romance alive. You are the reason I write.

A NOTE FROM THE PUBLISHER

Thank you for reading this book. If you enjoyed it please do consider leaving a review on Amazon to help others find it too.

We hate typos. All of our books have been rigorously edited and proofread, but sometimes mistakes do slip through. If you have spotted a typo, please do let us know and we can get it amended within hours.

info@bloodhoundbooks.com

Lightning Source UK Ltd.
Milton Keynes UK
UKHW010005270721
387802UK00002B/130